IN THE CANYONS OF SHADOW AND LIGHT

BY EMILY DONOHO

Gypsum Moon Publishing

In the Canyons of Shadow and Light

First paperback edition, May 2015
Revised paperback edition, published by Gypsum Moon Publishing, May 2020

Cover design © 2020 by Emily Donoho

ISBN 978-1-8380357-0-9 (paperback
ISBN 978-1-8380357-1-6 (ebook)

For more information, address:
e.donoho1993@gmail.com.

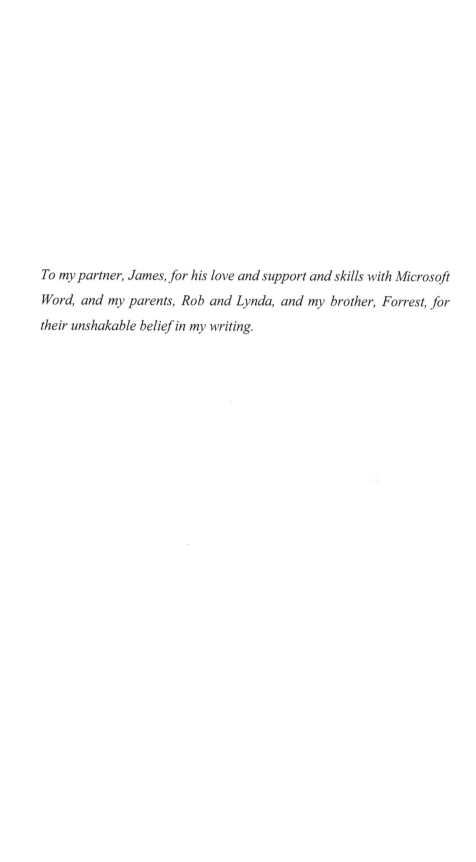

To my partner, James, for his love and support and skills with Microsoft Word, and my parents, Rob and Lynda, and my brother, Forrest, for their unshakable belief in my writing.

Tell me, sweet lord, what is 't that takes from thee
Thy stomach, pleasure, and thy golden sleep?
Why dost thou bend thine eyes upon the earth
And start so often when thou sit'st alone?
Why hast thou lost the fresh blood in thy cheeks
And given my treasures and my rights of thee
To thick-eyed musing and curst melancholy? [...]

Thy spirit within thee hath been so at war,
And thus hath so bestirred thee in thy sleep,
That beads of sweat have stood upon thy brow
Like bubbles in a late-disturbèd stream,
And in thy face strange motions have appeared,
Such as we see when men restrain their breath
On some great sudden hest. O, what portents are these?
Some heavy business hath my lord in hand,
And I must know it, else he loves me not.

--William Shakespeare, *Henry IV, Part 1*

CONTENTS

Prologue
  Part 1: 0800 hours   6
  Part 2: 1200 hours   23
  Part 3: 2000 hours   45
Chapter One   61
Chapter Two   69
Chapter Three   80
Chapter Four   96
Chapter Five   110
Chapter Six   125
Chapter Seven   138
Chapter Eight   157
Chapter Nine   171
Chapter Ten   182
Chapter Eleven   192
Chapter Twelve   198
Chapter Thirteen   212
Chapter Fourteen   216
Chapter Fifteen   228
Chapter Sixteen   242
Chapter Seventeen   254
Chapter Eighteen   261
Chapter Nineteen   271
Chapter Twenty   278
Chapter Twenty-One   295
Chapter Twenty-Two   305
Chapter Twenty-Three 314
Chapter Twenty-Four 324
Chapter Twenty-Five 330
Chapter Twenty-Six   343
Chapter Twenty-Seven 357
Chapter Twenty-Eight 373
Chapter Twenty-Nine 391
Chapter Thirty   405
Chapter Thirty-One   413
Chapter Thirty-Two   425
Chapter Thirty-Three 433

Prologue

Part 1: 0800 hours

The sentencing hearing started at 0800 hours sharp. Since 0630, reporters from every media outlet in the country had crowded the entrance of 100 Centre Street, the Criminal Courts Building. They were jostling for the best position with the international networks, which had sent teams hours earlier. On the other side of the square, a restless group of noisy anti-capital punishment protesters spilled into the street. A line of uniformed police officers in riot gear and two mounted officers kept a wary eye on the sign-toting throng of people.

Even the protest seemed subdued by the heat simmering off the pavement. The cops watching it looked bored and wilted, and their horses were weary and uninterested. The animals' ears flopped to the side, sweat darkening their coats as they stood, stamping and swishing their tails at the odd fly. The city stared past the heat, steaming in fumes of garbage and exhaust amidst the racket of trucks and taxis on Canal Street and Chambers Street.

Detective Alex Boswell and Detective Ray Espinosa approached the gauntlet of police, reporters, and protesters. Though dressed similarly in dark suits, plain ties, and pale shirts, in physical appearance they could hardly have differed more. Alex hailed from a Lower East Side Jewish family. Now in his mid-forties, he was 5'8, broad-shouldered, broad-chested, with a low center of gravity and a paunchy gut that his wide-shouldered frame carried without appearing overly encumbered. Creases furrowed into the skin above his brows and knotted into bags below his eyes, a look of being permanently startled or worried that sometimes worked to his advantage in interrogation rooms. Ray was 6'1, mid-thirties, athletic and cat-quick, a man who started his day with at least a five-to-ten mile run. He had a copper complexion from his Puerto Rican heritage, with high cheekbones and dark, piercing eyes inviting little nonsense.

Advancing between the oblong sentinels guarding the steps of the Art Deco courthouse, Alex kept his eyes fixed on his feet, hoping to avoid recognition. They were simply two detectives, going into the Criminal Courts Building on normal business, and it wasn't like he'd been the primary investigator on the biggest case in New York since the Central Park Five. The case was *People of New York v. David LaValle,* and it was the first time in Manhattan, since 1963, where the prosecutors were seeking the death penalty. Governor Pataki had reinstated it in the mid-1990s, but until now, the only other New York City borough that had used it was Queens County in 1997.

David LaValle's crime had been monstrously heinous – shooting two police officers who had pulled him over for jumping a red light on the streets of Morningside Heights. One of the victims, Patrol Sergeant Zach Alonzo, had been a thirty-year veteran on the cusp of retirement, while his partner in the radio car that day, Officer Cathy Sheridan, was a young cop at the start of her career and more heartbreakingly, four months pregnant. Alex did not doubt that the defendant was a coldblooded psychopath.

It looked like the ideal test case for a DA who wanted the support of the NYPD and the 'law-and-order' voters, proof that he wasn't too squeamish for New York's death penalty statute, even if he was a Democrat. After a month-long trial, the jury had convicted LaValle of two counts of first-degree murder and one count of possessing an illegal firearm. Now the lead Assistant DA trying the case, Simon McNally, had to persuade those twelve men and women that the state of New York should execute him.

It should be straightforward. The defendant had murdered two police officers on a routine traffic stop, and for years, he had ruthlessly presided over a drug corner in Brooklyn. And had not Brooklyn North Homicide detectives told Alex that they liked him for a drug-related killing from 1998 but could never prove it? Still, the idea of executing him was not sitting well with Alex. One of the protester's signs had read 'an eye for an eye makes everyone blind,' and that trite slogan stuck to his mind like flypaper. He had arrested people for revenge killings. Cops called it a 'public service murder' if the vic was particularly unsavory, but the perp still got charged. Revenge was a motive, not a justification. Yet it was now kosher when the state did it? As they entered the courthouse, Alex remained unsettled. He wasn't sure if the state should be killing people at all, and even less sure that he wanted to have anything to do with it when it did. He didn't want to feel responsible for another person's premeditated death. Being a homicide detective made this problematic, as all capital cases were first and foremost murders.

Ray, on the other hand, would shoot the bastard himself, if he could. He had the view that if you took a life – especially a police officer's life – in cold blood, all bets were off, and you deserved what you had coming. That was why he and Alex had so little to say to one another today. Mutely, they sat in the second row of the gallery, packed in like sweaty chickens in a factory farm. Then the prosecution put on a parade of witnesses to testify about aggravating circumstances.

There were the families of the murdered cops; there was a former girlfriend of the defendant, who had regularly filed domestic violence charges against him; there was a former probation officer who had tried to get him to reform his ways but failed; there was the precinct detective, the first investigator on the scene. The precinct detective, whose name was McDonough, wept as he testified, describing the call: shots fired, reported from neighboring buildings, officers down.

While the detective testified, Alex anxiously chewed off his nails, one finger at a time. McNally would call him next. The crowded courtroom was unbearably hot. His shirt clung to his chest and back, the sweat oozing along his skin. A sliver of blood trickled from his ring finger, and he balled his hand into a fist, driving it into his thigh.

Then McNally said, "For their next witness, the People call Detective Alex Boswell to the stand."

Alex shut his eyes for a second and then, without looking at Ray, who muttered, "Good luck, Lex," he got up, walked through the gallery past the rows of blue uniforms and black suits, dozens of cops who wanted this guy very dead, and he stepped into the witness box. The bailiff came up to the stand, Bible in hand, and Alex wrestled his racing thoughts. His spirit felt sick. He needed to settle his mind on what McNally had prepped him to say last week. Never mind what would happen when and if the jury wholeheartedly swallowed his testimony about aggravating circumstances.

"Do you swear to tell the truth, the whole truth, and nothing but the truth, so help you God?" The bailiff had the rhythmic monotone of someone who has spoken that sentence thousands of times and doesn't care anymore.

"I do," Alex said automatically. Whatever he thought, he would dutifully answer McNally's questions with the practice and efficacy of an old cop who had been in court too many times to count. He rattled through his name, rank, grade, squad, like he did in every court appearance. Detective, Second Grade, Manhattan North Homicide.

McNally said, "Detective Boswell, I am sure the jury remembers you from the trial, but it was a long trial and they heard a lot of witnesses. Can you please remind the jury what your role in the case was?"

"I was the primary detective from Manhattan North Homicide," Alex answered. He fixed his gaze on a point in the back of the courtroom, floating in space between McNally and the jury box. McNally had grey eyes and bushy grey hair, and he was strong, fierce and resolute. His second chair, Zoë Sheehan, sat meekly at the prosecution table, playing with the top of a clicky pen, giving off an air of unhappiness and shrinking into the notes and files piled in front of her.

"Please tell us about the crime scene, what you saw when you and your partner first arrived," McNally said.

Though it had been two years ago, how vividly he remembered the chaos around the crime scene: every squad car on the West Side parked on that street with its lights flashing, the manhunt through the streets of Harlem for the suspect, the cops from the Two-Six flooding the neighborhood, distraught, horrified, and angry. It had shattered what Alex now thought of as a lull, after the turmoil of the '80s and early '90s, the crack 'epidemic' hitting the streets hard and fast, birthing high drug use, high crime, high homelessness, high murder rates, high everything. Enough carnage to keep a Manhattan homicide detective working more overtime than he ever thought possible.

In the late-90s, after a decade of mayhem, the city's murder rate astoundingly plummeted. Then came September 11th, the relative affability of New York smashed, the city wounded, and Alex learned about a different kind of fear. Suddenly, every bridge, tunnel, subway, train station, and passing airplane looked like a threat; you never knew what would come next, and you could not stop it. This is what it must be like, living in Belgrade or Tel Aviv.

He dragged his roving mind back to the hearing. The crime scene – a glorious, cool early May morning in 2000, a fresh breeze blowing away the reek of garbage and exhaust, the sun glittering off asphalt, the old stonework gleaming, the trees along the streets and in the parks hinting at new leaves, the city alive and effervescent. Taking leafy Broadway to the office, you would not think anything terrible could ever happen. But at West 115th and Eighth, the bright and calm morning was fractured for the 26th Precinct and for the generally agreeable neighborhood around Columbia University. Alex picked up the phone just as he arrived at the office, a frantic call reporting a cop shooting in Morningside Heights, and with his partner in those days, James Hurley, dashing to the scene as fast as they could drive from West 133rd.

"When we arrived on the scene," he said to the jury, "Patrol Sergeant Alonzo was dead on the street with two bullet holes in his chest, and his partner, Officer Sheridan, was still in the radio car, dead with a gunshot wound to the head."

"Had either of the officers drawn their weapons?"

"No. I don't think they had the chance. Alonzo's weapon was still in its holster. Sheridan's was out, but she obviously didn't even have the chance to get outta the car before she was shot. The car door was partially opened, and she was found half in, half out of the car, so she had presumably tried, but the shooter had moved too fast."

"Had her gun been fired?"

Sadly, Alex shook his head. "Definitely not. It had a full clip."

"We heard earlier from Detective McDonough that the officers had radioed into Central, saying they were doing a traffic stop on a vehicle that had jumped a red light. So, with that in mind, can you explain what you surmised after you examined the crime scene?"

Alex made eye contact with the jury, falling into the comfortable routine of a direct examination. "You're trained that if you're stopping a vehicle, you wanna see the driver's hands, and if you're at all concerned, you get the driver outta the car and have him put his hands on the car and frisk him for weapons. You'll have your firearm out if you're really worried. If you see him reach for anything suspicious, your first and foremost job is to keep yourself safe, so you draw your weapon. On seeing that neither officer had their weapon out, we concluded that the shooter must've ambushed the two victims, shooting before they'd even approached his car or had a chance to draw their firearms."

"Was there any other evidence that supported this?"

"The ballistics reports, as you heard at the trial, suggested that the defendant must've been at least six or seven feet away from Sergeant Alonzo when he shot him. He fired as Alonzo approached the vehicle. The officer hadn't yet done anything, or even spoken to him. At this point, we think the defendant then got out of his car and went to the radio car, where he shot Officer Sheridan. We think it all happened within seconds, as Sheridan did not have the chance to fire any shots, or even leave her car to save her partner."

"Did Alonzo or Sheridan make radio calls or have any further communication with Central after the one where the officers reported that they were stopping the defendant's vehicle?"

"No, none." Alex ran his fingernail against his lower lip.

"What did you conclude from that?"

"They had no chance to call in a ten-thirteen."

Simon's face was grave. "Can you explain to the jury what a ten-thirteen is?"

"Police officer in distress. Gets back-up to the scene forthwith. Anyone who hears someone calling that code will go immediately to that location."

"You're saying they were dead, it was over, before they could get to their radio?"

 "We thought so."

His gaze darted to the defendant, who was sinking into his chair, the look on his face blank, glassy, as if Alex and Simon were talking about someone else. Any cop who could stagger to his or her radio and with their dying breath, make a ten-thirteen call, would do so. The perp had shot Alonzo and Sheridan before they knew what hit them – no time to defend themselves or call for help.

"What else could you determine from the crime scene?"

"Ballistics and the ME reported that the gunshot wound on Sergeant Sheridan was from about two or three feet away. Really close. I mean, we could see that as well, the shot had taken half her skull off. For a gun of that size to cause that kinda damage, it has to be within a few feet of the victim."

"Why is that important?"

"The police car was parked behind the defendant's car, probably ten or twelve feet away. We assumed that the defendant, after shooting Sergeant Alonzo, got out of the car, ran straight over to the police car, and shot Officer Sheridan. He could not have inflicted those wounds if he'd shot from his car. And if he had, there woulda probably been damage to the vehicles, and there wasn't any."

Everyone who had worked the case had felt a chill in their bones as they reconstructed it. Everyone has probably done a traffic stop at some point in their careers. You can't let yourself start thinking that a person in the car will, without any warning, start firing away at you, but that was what this son of a bitch had done. As he testified, Alex wondered if LaValle indeed deserved the needle in his arm. The cops in the Two-Six thought so; Ray thought so; McNally thought so. He wished he shared their certainty. It would be easier.

"We know from your trial testimony how you and Detective Hurley identified LaValle as a suspect. But can you tell us what happened next?"

The car's license plate had been called in by Alonzo and Sheridan, registered to one David LaValle, who lived in Bedford-Stuyvesant. Among the many felonies LaValle had been charged with over the years, one was stealing a gun, a .38 Smith and Wesson used in another homicide, so NCIC had the ballistics in their database, and the bullets found in the dead officers matched it perfectly. The charges against LaValle in that case were dismissed when a judge ruled that Brooklyn Robbery had conducted an unlawful search, but everyone was pretty sure he still had the gun, although it hadn't turned up in aforesaid unlawful search.

Alex gulped down a breath. "I got an arrest warrant drawn up, and then we went to Bed-Stuy, to Halsey Street, with Emergency Services. When we entered his apartment, the defendant made a run for it. Detective Hurley and I chased him out onto the street. A couple radio cars overtook us and blocked off Halsey Street, so he stopped and pointed his gun at me and Detective Hurley."

"What were you thinking in that moment?"

"I was scared. This guy had already shot two cops. What did he have to lose, shooting me?"

"But he didn't."

"No, there was lots of backup. Every cop on the block must've had their gun sighted on him. If he'd fired, he'd be dead. He dropped his weapon, and we arrested him."

"Then what happened?"

"He had asked for a lawyer, so we took him to the nearest precinct, the 79th, and had to wait for defense counsel to arrive before we could speak to him."

"I know the jury heard your testimony about this initial interview at the trial, so I just want you to emphasize here, what was the defendant's attitude when you first questioned him at the 79th Precinct?"

"He was trying to be a gangster, a tough guy. Said he didn't do it." Alex flicked his eyes to the defendant, who didn't look remotely like a tough guy, wearing a better suit than his and cowering beside his lawyer, meek and tremulous, his face perpetually pinched and woebegone. You would not think of him as a sociopath who would brazenly shoot two police officers and threaten a dozen more.

In the Seven-Nine's interrogation room, he had been wearing a hoodie, baggie jeans, a bandana on his head, and what cops called a BFA, a bad fucking attitude. "Fuck the police," he'd spat and then insisted on his innocence.

"He lied to you?"

"He told us that someone must've stolen his car and stuck with that story."

"What else did he say?"

"He called us names that I don't know if I can repeat here."

"If Her Honor will give you permission, can you give us an example?" McNally smiled slightly and looked at Judge Cheryl Grieve, a no-nonsense jurist who had even-handedly presided over the trial.

"Go on, Detective," said Judge Grieve placidly. Like any Criminal Term judge, she had probably heard every swear word you could and couldn't imagine.

Alex adjusted his pelvis in the hard seat. "Well, among other things, I think he told us to go fuck ourselves on multiple occasions and in multiple ways."

"What else did you ask in this interview?"

"We asked why, if he was innocent, did he make a run for it and then threaten myself and Detective Hurley with his gun."

"What were his reasons for that?"

"He said that we were the police, and we were chasing him; he didn't need any more reasons than that."

"And he'd had dealings with the police before?"

"Oh, yes."

McNally picked up a thick pile of papers and said, "The People would like to enter into evidence exhibit 23, the defendant's criminal record."

Judge Grieve allowed McNally to enter the rap sheet as evidence. New information for the jury, since you generally were not allowed to use a defendant's prior convictions during a criminal trial, and LaValle had not fallen under any of the *Molineux* exceptions, though not for lack of trying on McNally's part. However, priors were admissible in a sentencing hearing. And LaValle's rap sheet looked like *War and Peace.*

"Request permission to approach the witness, Your Honor?" queried McNally.

Nodding, Grieve assented in a smooth manner, drawling, "Permission granted, Counselor."

McNally approached Alex and handed him the rap sheet. "Can you tell the jury what this is, Detective?"

"It's the defendant's New York criminal record."

"How far does it date back to?"

Alex looked at the top of the sheet. "1987."

"And, prior to this one, when was his most recent offense?"

"1999."

"Are any of those offenses violent felonies?"

"Yeah, quite a few of them."

"Can you read off some examples?"

Alex shuffled through the sheets of paper. McNally had already highlighted the ones he wanted read, so Alex merely had to find the highlighted lines on the shopping list of bad behavior. He squinted at the tiny typewriter-style writing, thinking these didn't used to be so difficult to see – he ought to get his eyes checked – and then he read aloud.

"First degree assault, 1990. First degree robbery – that's armed robbery – 1992. Second degree assault, 1994. Second degree assault,

1995. First degree assault, 1996. Second degree assault, 1996. Second degree assault, 1997. Second degree criminal possession of a weapon, 1997. Second degree assault, 1999. And numerous charges for possessing and distributing narcotics."

"What did you conclude from that?"

"The defendant has a history of beating people up and threatening them with a gun, and sometimes a knife."

"Thank you, Detective. After you arrested Mr. LaValle, what did you do next?"

"Detective Hurley, Detective Vasquez, and myself went back to his apartment to conduct a search."

"What sort of evidence did you find?"

"We found firearms magazines. Stuff with instructions for making sawed-off shotguns, modifying bullets – that type of thing."

McNally went through the ritual of introducing the magazines into evidence and then showing them to Alex. "Are these the magazines you found?"

"Yes," he said, glancing at the magazines in question, tawdry tabloids, weapon pornography.

"What else did you find?"

"A bunch of old copies of the *New York Post*."

"Was there anything in particular about those newspapers you noticed?"

"Yeah, he'd cut out and saved articles about cop-shootings going back to the '70s. There were quite a few on killings by the Black Liberation Army back in the '70s and '80s. They were stacked on a counter in the kitchen."

"What did you make of that?"

"That he had, uh, an interest in cop-shootings and was sympathetic to a militant group with a history of assassinating police officers." Alex missed a breath and a heartbeat and closed his eyes for a second, hoping no one in the courtroom noticed. Fifteen years ago, he had taken a bullet to his right side, shrapnel from a ricocheted slug. It ripped through his right lung, and the surgeons removed about a third of the lung to save his life. Had it landed a millimeter to the left or right, he would have been as dead as Alonzo and Sheridan. Those perps had claimed association with the BLA.

15

"Now, Detective, did the defendant have any more recent legal problems?"

"Yes." Alex gutturally cleared his throat and drank a sip of water from the glass beside the witness box, urging himself to focus on this hearing, this case.

"What were they?"

"He didn't appear in court when he was due to be arraigned on a minor drug dealing offense in King's County. The judge issued a bench warrant. He was stopped by the Street Crime Unit from the Seven-Nine Precinct as part of their routine stop-and-frisk procedures about a week later. They found a couple ounces of cocaine on him and the bench warrant, so they took him down to the precinct where he was processed on all those charges."

"And after he was let out on bail, where did he stay?"

"With a friend, a guy called Jeremiah Combs, who went by the street name of 'Fish.'"

"And you interviewed Mr. Combs, who, the jury will remember, also testified in the trial."

"Yes."

Combs, or 'Fish,' a lowlife with whom LaValle ran hustles in order to acquire money for their speedball habits, had received a year's probation on a burglary two rap and a promise of a bed in a rehab facility in exchange for his testimony. Last week, Alex had received a handwritten letter in his office mail from Fish, thanking him profusely for eliciting his cooperation in the case, as if it had been an act of Alex's own charity, closing a homicide merely an afterthought, because it had given him the kick in the ass he needed to get clean, and now, two years later, he was still off drugs, working as an addiction counselor. This was a strange job, sometimes.

"Did Mr. Combs tell you about the defendant, what he said after his arrest?"

Alex had to clear his throat again. It felt parched and abraded, and the water didn't help. "He said the defendant had been really, uh, upset about being stopped-and-frisked and spent about a week ranting to him about wanting to kill a cop."

"Objection, hearsay," droned the defense lawyer, William Scott. His voice was tired, and his objection sounded like an attempt to remind everyone that he was still there.

McNally stiffened his spine and grew an inch. "It's a statement against penal interest, Your Honor, and goes to aggravating circumstances."

"Objection is overruled."

Pleased, McNally turned his attention back to Alex. "Detective, what did you conclude from all of this evidence, then?"

"That he had a beef with the NYPD and was planning on causing some kinda trouble. And when he jumped that red light, it was a premeditated attempt to get stopped by and ambush the officers in radio car 9756, or whatever car happened to be there."

"Thank you, Detective. The People have finished with this witness."

Judge Grieve asked the defense attorney if he wanted to cross-examine.

"Yes, Your Honor." Scott rose to his feet, resting heavily against the lectern. He looked worn down, fed up with the whole case but doggedly fighting to the end to save his client from the needle. He studied Alex, sizing him up, the way perps sometimes sized him up when he arrested them, and they were wondering if they could get away with giving him a hard time. "Detective Boswell, what would you say race relations were like – or are like – between the African-American community and the NYPD?"

"Objection, speculation," called McNally.

"The witness is a detective in uptown Manhattan," insisted Scott. "He should not have to speculate on the relationship between his department and the surrounding community."

"Overruled."

Alex briefly met the prosecutor's seething gaze and then replied quietly, "Not great."

That had to be the understatement of the fucking year. 'Broken windows' policing, arresting people for minor misdemeanor offenses, was getting excoriated in the press; Amadou Diallo had been shot 41 times by cops from the Street Crime Unit in the Bronx the previous year; and a couple years before that, four officers had been indicted in federal court for sodomizing Abner Louima while he was in custody. NYPD brass worried federal oversight would saddle the department with a consent decree, like the LAPD.

"Given the difficult relationship, could my client have therefore felt threatened by the officers approaching his car?"

"He had his gun out and the victims didn't."

"Do you think my client, as a black man, had reason to fear or be angry at the police?"

"No." Alex rubbed his tongue against the edges of his back teeth, not sure he believed that himself. Still, he could not very well say yes.

"You don't think, in light of Diallo, that a man such as my client had reason to be afraid of the police, who shot an unarmed black man with no warning?"

"Your client wasn't unarmed."

"Objection, prejudicial," snapped McNally.

"Sustained."

"Would you say that the police, especially since the mid-1990s, have regularly employed humiliating and degrading tactics, racially profiling and targeting men such as my client, under the pretense of dealing with street level drug crime?"

Alex pursed his lips. "No."

"My client was stopped and frisked, wasn't he?"

"Yes."

Stop-and-frisk: a city statute of improbable constitutionality that exempted anyone in a high crime neighborhood from the usual constraints of probable cause. It meant that a police officer could stop and pat down anyone on the street if he or she had 'reasonable suspicion' that the person might be involved in criminal activity. In places like Washington Heights, Brownsville, or Bed-Stuy, that included almost everyone.

"Are you aware that my client was stopped and frisked on at least twenty occasions in the six months prior to his arrest for this homicide?"

"Yes. He *was* selling cocaine on the corner of Halsey and Tompkins Street."

"Allegedly," stated Scott. "Are you aware that cocaine was found in his possession on only *one* of those occasions?"

"It's a known drug corner."

"So, any young black man on that 'known drug corner' is fair game for the police to stop, is that it?"

"If anyone is 'reasonably suspicious,'" Alex countered.

"Objection," barked McNally. "Is stop-and-frisk on trial here?"

"It is important for the jury to understand my client's culture, where he comes from, his mental state," Scott argued.

Grieve inclined her head. "I'll allow it."

Scott's lips moved in a slight smile of relief. "Stop-and-frisk has been said to be humiliating and degrading. Would you say that some of your fellow officers use it to humiliate people, intimidate communities, to harass people on the corners?"

"I don't know. I'm not on patrol. Haven't been since 1981." Alex felt trapped, the lawyer hammering police department policies that had nothing to do with him, and very little to do with the fact that his client had shot two police officers, stop-and-fucking-frisk or not.

"Detective, are you aware that in almost ninety percent of stops, the police do not find drugs or guns or any other contraband?"

"I don't know the statistics."

"Are you aware that more than eighty-eight percent of people stopped are in fact innocent?"

"Your client isn't one of those eighty-eight percent."

"Are you aware that, as a result of 'broken windows' policing and stop-and-frisk, entire communities, entire neighborhoods, feel alienated from and threatened by the police?"

"Objection: this is far outside of the witness' personal knowledge!"

"Sustained."

Scott fidgeted with his paperwork. He looked up at Alex again, his lips compressed into a thin white line. "Detective, you've been in Homicide for a long time, haven't you?"

"Yes," Alex said warily.

"When did you join Manhattan North Homicide?"

"1987."

"So, that's fifteen years as a homicide detective."

"Your math is very good."

"Am I right to assume that you have arrested and charged people with murder, people who killed someone out of revenge?"

"Yeah, I guess."

Fuck, how did Scott know to go there? He must have noticed the doubt in Alex's eyes, or the slight waver in his responses. Was he so easy to read? He had felt confident that his testimony had been trundling along pleasantly enough, his misgivings well hidden.

McNally was crouching on bent knees, but he hesitated for a second.

Scott raced ahead. "You might say it's not right to kill someone because you want revenge, even if they have committed a murder?"

"Objection!" shouted McNally, springing upright, rescuing Alex from that dangerous and uncomfortable corner. "That question is outside of the witness' personal knowledge."

"The witness has been a homicide detective for fifteen years. I think he must have a good idea of what constitutes justifiable homicide, and what gets you done for murder."

"Detective Boswell is here to testify about the circumstances of this case. Not to offer his opinion on ethics or jurisprudence – which he *isn't* an expert in unless he has a PhD in philosophy or a law degree that I don't know about."

"Keep it cool, Mr. McNally," commanded Grieve, her voice languid, but implying a contempt citation could be forthcoming. "Your objection is sustained."

Defeated, Scott looked down, murmuring, "I don't have any further questions for this witness."

"Would the People like to redirect?" asked Grieve.

"Yes, Your Honor." McNally bounded over to the lectern. "Permission to approach the witness, Your Honor?"

"Granted."

McNally advanced to Alex and handed him papers, before scuffling back to the lectern. "Detective, please tell the jury what that is."

Alex looked down at the papers. So that was the game. He must have anticipated Scott's assault on stop-and-frisk and prepared his counterattack. "CompStat reports from 1990 to 2001."

"Objection, relevance?"

"Mr. Scott opened the door with his inquiries about police strategy."

"I'll allow it, but watch yourself, Mr. McNally."

McNally was back on form, commanding the courtroom like a conductor in the New York Philharmonic. He made smiling eye contact with Alex. "Detective, can you please explain what CompStat is?"

"It's a strategy for targeting policing at high crime areas, using mapping and data from precincts to pinpoint places where the most crimes are occurring and tailoring a police response accordingly."

That was the shorthand party line anyway. The reality made police work much more of a numbers game, with enough paperwork to drive you mad.

"According to the data you have there, how many homicides occurred in the 34th Precinct in 1990?"

Alex squinted at the blurry numbers on the report. "One hundred and three."

"How about 1993?"

"Fifty."

"1998?"

"Nine."

"And 2001?"

"Seven."

"Let's talk about Morningside Heights, where this crime occurred. The 26th Precinct. How many homicides in 1990?"

Alex found the CompStat report from the Two-Six. "Fifteen."

"And 2001?"

"One."

"Now, tell me the total number of felonies recorded in the 26th Precinct in 1990?"

"Three thousand three hundred and eighty."

"How about in 2001?"

"Nine hundred forty-five." He kneaded his aching eyes.

"Wow," McNally said theatrically. "Does your experience bear those statistics out?"

"Yeah."

"Can you estimate how many homicides you personally worked – and that's cases from all the precincts north of 59th Street – in 1990 alone?"

Alex wrinkled his brows, taking a punt. "Maybe like thirty or forty." Too damned many, and far more than CompStat related, since it only reflected data when there had been an arrest, thus unsolved murders went unseen.

"How about 2001?" continued McNally.

"Around a dozen."

"This massive reduction in crime, in violent crime, what does that tell you about the NYPD's strategies with regards to policing this city?"

"Uh, it's worked," Alex posited, chewing on the back of his tongue. "The city's a lot safer."

He would not say unequivocally that Rudy Giuliani and his police commissioner, Bill Bratton, could claim that their policing strategies were unilaterally responsible for New York's plummeting crime rate (Giuliani and Bratton, of course, would and did). But no one was going to deny that it had some effect, the city a much safer place, and alongside the shrinking of the crack epidemic, perhaps CompStat, 'broken windows,' and stop-and-frisk had played some role in that. Alex was a homicide detective, not a political strategist or sociologist, so he had no idea. He just knew what he saw on the streets.

"Thank you, Detective. No more questions."

Grieve nodded. "You may stand down, Detective."

Alex withdrew from the witness stand, feeling acid scalding the pit of his stomach. With an air of sad disillusionment, he eased himself into the pew beside his partner. He touched his forehead, dabbing the sweat beading on his brow.

Ray mouthed, *Good job.*

He didn't respond. He lowered his eyelids and saw the crime scene, vivid, graphic, like he was there, not here in a courtroom. Those two cops, senselessly murdered, the bullets tearing through flesh. They had no idea what was coming, no more than Alex did when two guys on the other side of 190th Street fired an automatic rifle at him. One minute, you were on your way to interview a witness, or doing a traffic stop; the next, bullets had annihilated your internal organs, and your blood and tissue had been splattered all over the front seats and the dash of your radio car, or it was congealing into gooey, crimson pools on the street.

The world most certainly would not be worse off if people like David LaValle weren't in it.

The defense team put on a much smaller string of witnesses offering mitigating circumstances. Bad neighborhood, bad childhood, crack-addicted, absent parents, a crack addiction himself, a lost, lonely child sucked into a Bloods set, then a psychologist explaining the defendant's mental health issues, and several character witnesses, including the defendant's now-clean mother, who said he was thoroughly sorry about his crime, and she was thoroughly sorry for abandoning him for crack. LaValle himself took the stand, no longer the mean, angry gangster who Alex and James had collared two years ago. He looked diminished, frightened, and he plead for his life.

The lawyers gave their closing arguments, McNally talking of setting examples, of setting things right for the families, for the police department, and for the city; then Scott imploring that taking another life didn't make those cops any less dead, arguing that a fitter, more humane punishment was letting his client spend the rest of his life in prison thinking about how he got there, and the people of New York should hold themselves to a higher moral standard than blind vengeance. After closing arguments, the jury went out to deliberate.

Part 2: 1200 hours

Alex washed his hands and mused over his reflection in the bathroom mirror. *I look like hell.* He had rich, brown eyes, and the crow's feet underneath them seemed like cracks in the city roads after a harsh winter, while the puffy, dark shadow, a blue-tinged furrow dropping down his cheeks from the corner of each eye, advertised that he hadn't been sleeping well. Sweat shone on his forehead. With some consternation, he studied the middle-aged paunch around his belly. Had he put on weight since this case went to trial a month ago? Sleeping badly and eating crap would do that.

Shaking off his insecurity, he ran the cold tap, splashing water in his face and throwing some onto the back of his neck. He loosened his belt one hole, and he could feel the heat building up, itching, sweat catching uncomfortably between his skin and his pants. It was too hot to be wearing a suit. It was too damned hot and muggy for anything. He rubbed more cold water in his face, letting a few drips strike his chest without sullying his white shirt or his tie, and he envisaged dunking his head into a bucket of it. Then he yanked off his jacket and rolled up his shirtsleeves to his elbows. With the jacket draped over one arm, he slunk out of the bathroom.

Wanting to avoid encounters with the press or anyone he knew, he took a circuitous route through the building that led to the back entrance, and then he crossed Foley Square, heading for the Starbucks on Leonard Street. It was a prosaic square beside the grandiosity of Washington or Union Squares, but it was clean, some care had been taken with lying concrete bricks in geometric patterns and placing benches and flower boxes in tasteful locations, and in the middle sat a modern art statue, an unidentifiable, somewhat phallic-looking shape thrusting to the sky. Unidentifiable to everyone but James Hurley, who once said, "*Of course* they put a statue of a giant cock in the middle of the courthouses. Everyone who comes down here is basically getting fucked. And that includes *us*. I mean, you've had that cross-examination where the defense attorney pretty much sodomized you, not to mention what happens at any meeting in Police Plaza probably warrants an investigation by Special Victims." Squad room chat had never been the same since Hurley left.

A subway entrance for the 4, 5, and 6 trains marked the southern edge of the square, directly across Centre Street from the US District Courthouse and the 60 Centre Street Supreme Court building, the civil courthouse. They were splendiferous buildings, constructed to embody the majesty of the Law. White neoclassical columns the size of redwoods guarded their front entrances, standing sentinel atop flights of wide stairs, and relief carvings and statues of robed women holding scales and Latin inscriptions parading across the white stone.

The Criminal Courts Building, on the other hand, was a monstrosity constructed to reflect the feelings of the people who go into it – tired, pissed, and having just discovered that they're going to be spending the next twenty-five years in one of New York's fine penal institutions. Alex thought the Criminal Courts Building possessed a degree of ugliness only attainable by a special effort of the architects. It had been completed in 1941, Art Deco in style like the Chrysler Building or the Empire State Building or Rockefeller Center, but without their graceful spires or decorative metal cladding. On the outside, it was four conjoined heavy, rectangular high rises with a stepped central tower and the windows and spandrel forming vertiginous bands of limestone and granite rising for seventeen stories, while on the inside, it had seventeen floors of long narrow hallways mottled with dark green or grey paint, wooden benches in front of inauspicious wooden doors leading to offices, judge's chambers, and courtrooms. For this reason, 60 Centre Street was a frequent stand-in for 100 Centre Street in New York crime dramas, film crews preferring the building that looked like an archetypal courthouse rather than the one that looked straight out of the Soviet bloc.

Anyway, the whole Civic Center had strange atmosphere now, watchful, uneasy. Blue and white concrete barriers emblazoned with "NYPD" permanently blockaded the streets near courthouses and government buildings. Military personnel carrying automatic assault rifles prowled around their entrances. The barricades and the military guys had been placed there immediately after 9/11 and now seemed as though they would be permanent fixtures.

Alex glanced at the army guys in their mottled green fatigues cradling their menacing, dark rifles, and he reflected somberly that New York had changed in some profound way. It no longer felt like the New York he knew before last September – it was like the day after 9/11, he had been beamed to some other country, one perennially afraid of civil unrest and violence. A permanent military presence, on display, a chilling reminder of mortal danger. It increased his pulse rate every time he came down here. The New York he knew when he was young had been a violent and sinister place; the neighborhoods that were bohemian and cool now, like the Lower East Side where he had grown up, or West 133rd where the Homicide squad had their offices, you would not have ventured into if you didn't know it nor had your wits about you.

But the terrorist attacks made New Yorkers feel scared and vulnerable in ways 1980s and '90s violence and the crack wars didn't. He didn't know if the military guys standing in front of civilian courthouses and in every train station, bus station, and airport made them any safer from terrorists, but it certainly made his blood run cold when he crossed Foley Square, an intimation that mass destruction and violence could come crashing upon him at any second, with the suddenness and capriciousness that had stunned the city on that clear September morning.

That jury could be out for hours or possibly days, but he opted to stick around Foley Square for a little while out of morbid, prurient curiosity, like bystanders who ogle crime scenes. Besides, it was his day off, and he had nowhere else to be. He bought a *New York Times* at a newsstand on Lafayette, and then settled into the corner of the Starbucks facing the door, the lifelong practice of most people on the job – never having your back to a door. The black coffee and an almond cookie didn't lighten the weight of the world, but everyone else in the Starbucks seemed so unruffled and free, because they hadn't just testified in a hearing that might lead to an execution.

Well, maybe that bit was nothing more than his imagination. You never knew what troubled people. He expelled a great lungful of air and rested his ankle on his knee, opening the *New York Times* to the crossword, hoping he would forget about it for a little while.

Just then, Zoë Sheehan, who must have tailed him as silently as an undercover cop because he had no idea that she was there, popped into the coffee shop and ordered a Frappuccino. Without a word, she invited herself to Alex's small table in the corner.

She stared despondently into her plastic cup of flavored icy sludge, and he wondered why anyone would drink that shit. She didn't look like a lawyer winning a case. Was that why she had followed him here? Had she also caught sight of his doubt in the witness box? Nonetheless, it had little to do with either one of them. They were cogs in the criminal-justice machine.

"You didn't look very happy testifying today," she said awkwardly, gripping her Frappuccino with both hands.

Alex took a bite from the cookie, chewing slowly. Christ, it must have been more obvious than he had thought. "I said what I had to say."

"Yes, I know. I doubt the jury will have noticed anyway."

"I fucking hope not. Everyone else did."

"What do you mean?"

"The defense lawyer's questions…"

"Which ones?"

"Come on, Zoë. The ones about justifiable homicide."

"Oh, he was going to ask you those anyway." She slurped through her straw. "Oh, God, Alex… This is… It's a responsibility I don't want."

He swallowed his cookie and touched his throat. "I don't want it, either, but that's life. If your boss wants to pursue a capital sentence, we just gotta deal and not think about it too much."

"Denial? Is that a solution?"

"It's a solution to a lot of problems."

"I don't think I can turn off my brain like that. You're lucky you can. But even if the jury goes for the death sentence, there will be appeals." She seemed as though she wanted to justify it to herself more than him, tugging worriedly at her long, dark ponytail. "The appellate court could well rule it unconstitutional."

The prospect of interminable appeals potentially overturning the potential death sentence didn't make him feel any better about it. He disliked delving into ethical or political shit in any great detail; he disliked that this case was making him think about it; he also disliked that Zoë seemed to think of him as a sympathetic ear, when he didn't want to talk about it at all.

"I don't feel like Simon understands my objections to this," Zoë bemoaned. "The DA wanted it to be a capital case, the first capital case in Manhattan since they passed the statute in '95, but Simon, he has his ear. He'll listen to him. He could have said forget it, or least tried. But he's just… going after the defendant with everything he has, like he always does."

"I'm sure he understands," Alex said. "He just doesn't give a shit." He looked away from Zoë, his eyes dark orbs gazing out the coffee shop's wall of windows. Outside, the air was so thick it shivered. The whole city had become a steam bath.

"I thought I knew him," she sighed unhappily. "I was shocked when he went along with the boss' decision."

"Why?"

"I thought he might try to discuss it with him, talk him out of it."

"What's the fucking point?"

"Principles?"

Alex shrugged and swallowed a mouthful of cookie.

"I'm surprised you don't want LaValle dead. Every other cop does. I mean, LaValle pulled his firearm on you when you arrested him."

"Yeah, he did." Alex took another long sip of his coffee, paying attention to it sliding down his throat. Then he jotted an answer to the first crossword clue he understood.

"Well, maybe all this stress is for nothing and the jury will sentence him to life anyway. You never know what a jury will do. How long are you going to wait here?"

"Dunno."

27

She studied her Frappuccino on the checkerboard table, stirring ice cubes with her straw. "Well, uh, I have stuff I need to do in the office. If they call us back in today, I guess I'll see you then. If not, well, I'm sure I'll see you around."

"Sure," he said, as Zoë smoothed down her skirt, rising to her feet and, with an importune look over her shoulder at him, resting with his cheek on his hand, the crossword in front of him, she exited the Starbucks.

Yes, he still shuddered at his memories of the arrest. He'd pressed his body against one side of the doorframe, Hurley on the other. In those seconds before Emergency Services busted down the door, the only sound Alex heard was his own heartbeat. The perp's two roommates sprang against the wall, their hands up, frightened, the police charging through the door, the perp legging it, jumping out of the first story window. Alex had glanced out the window at the unforgiving pavement about ten or twelve feet below. A hard landing. Fuck that.

Then he and James ran out the door, through the stairwell and lunged onto the street. They caught sight of LaValle limping at speed half a block ahead. An RMP, blue and red lights whirling, blocked his retreat. He doubled back on himself and saw Alex and James behind him. He drew his gun, glaring down its barrel at the detectives. Alex thought, *Ah, fuck*. He froze mid-stride. The cops in the car responded by drawing their guns, and Alex and James did the same, and there everyone was, a complete fucking stand-off. LaValle had his gun trained on the homicide detectives. If he decided he had nothing to lose, he would shoot one of them.

Alex's heart was galloping, his mind running faster. He wore a bulletproof vest. If he got hit in the chest or stomach, it would hurt but it wouldn't kill him. If he got hit in his unprotected head or throat, it would. He could fire now, but if he didn't disable LaValle enough, he could retaliate and hurt someone. There were a lot of people on the street. You don't want a gunfight on a busy city street. It did not take long, however, for LaValle to realize that there was only one of him and a lot of cops. While he might be a murderous son of a bitch, he wasn't insane, nor did he have a death wish. He dropped his gun. It fell clattering to the pavement. Alex and James tackled and handcuffed him, throwing him on the ground, James reading him his *Miranda* rights as Alex was still trying to get his breath back, wincing at pain in his right lung. That ever-present reminder of 190th Street.

Pinned to the ground, the perp exploded in a volley of swearing.

Through wheezing breaths, Alex had said, "That right to remain silent we told you about… use it!"

Stuffed into the back of the radio car, LaValle snarled, "Fuck off, you motherfuckers. I want a lawyer."

Then he shut up. The case got endlessly tied up in hearings and motions. A 'speedy and public trial' wasn't speedy at all, although it was very public. The press went nuts. It became a racial landmine field, because the defendant was black, because of stop-and-frisk, because of allegations that the NYPD had harassed the defendant. Nonetheless, the wheels of justice ground away like a slow-moving freight train while it seemed as if life stayed in constant flux.

James left Homicide, launched to a post at a Staten Island precinct. Ray, a rising star in the Organized Crime Control Bureau, transferred to MNHS, Alex's new partner. 9/11 happened. In the aftermath of that, there was an outpouring of respect and support for the police that you never in your life would have expected from cynical New Yorkers who had long regarded the NYPD as inept, corrupt, or both.

Alex sighed, pouring the dregs of his coffee down his gullet. He was losing his battle with the crossword, his brain too febrile and unfocused. Hurley had gotten off lucky today, he thought. Simon had decided that he only needed one of them to testify in the sentencing hearing and could not be bothered summoning Hurley from Staten Island a second time. That, and James always came across like an arrogant, mouthy prick in court, with a way of reminding juries why they didn't like cops.

Hurley had always acted indifferently about the death penalty. He probably *was* indifferent. He wasn't the sort of guy who gave any shits about things like that. Like Ray, Alex should feel less sympathy than he had at the moment for a guy who had shot two cops and aimed a gun at his head. Or like James, he should not give a damn one way or the other. There was no doubt then that LaValle deserved it, but Alex felt as though the question of deserving or not was the wrong question to be asking.

Or maybe it wasn't. Did those guys who flew the planes into the World Trade Center deserve it? What about the ones who shot him? Would their executions have made him feel any differently or better than

29

twenty-five-to-life? No, he thought. He preferred to not think about them at all. Revenge was visceral but unsatisfying. Perps he'd collared for revenge killings rarely said that they'd found happiness by evening up the score, blowing away someone else in the tit-for-tat violence of the crack wars. It just branded a target on their back.

In any case, the deliberations only lasted for two hours. Whatever they had decided, the jury obviously had fewer misgivings than Alex. Soon, everyone was back in court for the sentence to be read. The courtroom felt even stickier and muggier, cramped with worry, everyone in it, on both sides of the aisle, sitting on tenterhooks at the edges of the hard pews.

For the two charges of first-degree murder, the defendant was sentenced to lethal injection.

The jury foreman said it haltingly, as though he could not believe the words emerging from his mouth. There was a profound silence. Then several people, including the defendant, burst into sobs. A satisfied ripple of approbation moved through the police officers. McNally turned around, glancing over his shoulder at Alex and Ray. Alex could not read the look on the prosecutor's face, but it wasn't the gloating look of triumph he had when he won a case. There was a tiredness and discontent behind his eyes.

Court was adjourned, and everyone filtered out. Quickly, Alex tried to extricate himself from the overheated, overcrowded gallery. As he battled his way through the shuffling throng, a weepy Detective McDonough and a herd of other cops from the Two-Six blocked his flight.

To Alex's surprise, McDonough, built like a brick shithouse at 6'4, threw his arms around him, crushing his ribs, gushing, "Thank you, Boswell! You did great today. And for the whole investigation. Justice was served today, and we owe so much of it to you and Detective Hurley." He breathed loudly, releasing Alex, and then standing back, wiping his face and his puffy eyes with his sleeve. "The precinct isn't the same without them, but at least their killer has finally gotten what he deserves."

"Yeah, he has," said Alex, with far more sincerity than he felt, though McDonough's sudden embrace touched his heart. Through his thick, muddied confusion and doubt about the whole death penalty thing, he felt a glimmer of satisfaction at the guilty verdict. It would not ease their grief, but it always seemed like some balance had been restored in the world.

Smiling with warmth and shared grief, he squeezed McDonough on the shoulder. "I'm glad it's over." And he was. He was always relieved after a conviction and sentencing, the case done and dusted, the months of investigation and ceaseless trial prep finished, the victims' friends and family freed to get on with their lives, and him with the next case.

"Come out for a drink with us tonight," offered McDonough.

"Sorry, I have a lot to do. Maybe later in the week if I get the chance."

He had no plans for tonight, but while the detective's gratitude alleviated his discomfort a fraction, he still could not face celebrating a potential execution with a night in the pub. Moreover, he hated admitting to people who were only acquaintances that he was a recovering alcoholic. Seven years sober now. It was an awkward thing in the NYPD, with its vast drinking culture, and his way of dealing with it required avoiding nights out with people who didn't know him well and who might want an explanation for why he drank soda all night. And the cop from the Two-Six didn't know him that well.

"You sure?" said McDonough.

"Yeah."

"Maybe I'll phone you up later then."

"Yeah, talk soon."

Then Sheridan's husband, accompanied by the precinct's commanding officer, cornered him by the door. He too gave Alex a great, effusive hug. "Thank you, Detective. We won," he whispered through the tears, repeating those two words like a mantra. "We won, we won. There can be justice for Cathy."

The Two-Six's Deputy Inspector clapped Alex between the shoulder blades so hard it stung, grunting, "Justice was done today. Thanks in part to the boys at Manhattan North Homicide."

Never mind that Alex's lieutenant, the commanding officer of the squad, was a woman. "Yes, we did." Alex edged out the door, finding it increasingly difficult to breathe, but he gave an empathetic touch to Sheridan's husband. The whole case was a cop's spouse's worst nightmare; well, anyone's, really.

Outside the courtroom, reporters clamored for attention, closing their ranks on the detectives and ADAs, shrieking for a comment like a thousand seagulls. Alex, never confident with the press, was pinned against a wall in the narrow corridor, microphones in his face, the questions coming at him like bullets.

"Detective Boswell, are you pleased with the verdict?"

"Do you think Mr. LaValle would have been given the death penalty if he was white?"

"Do you agree with stop-and-frisk?"

"Do you think a significant proportion of the population live in fear of the people who are supposed to protect and serve?"

"I did my job, the jury did theirs," he responded, feeling panicky, the tangy smell of his own sweat tickling his nostrils. Most of the people he arrested for murder had killed someone in those deprived neighborhoods, and the vics were rarely people who interested the media.

Still, the thing they teach you in 'managing the press' training courses is to disengage when they come at you like hyenas. The sound of his heartbeat drummed in his ears. He twisted his body sideways, putting his shoulder into the mob of reporters and forcing an escape route. Freed from the frenzy, he trotted through the corridors, taking a maze-like route that brought him to the door in the underground parking garage. The reporters, in any event, were scrambling off to the press conference in Foley Square, where New York County DA Ken Eisenmann, who loved the press, would be speaking, answering all their questions about the big win today.

Soaked in sweat, Alex huffed out of the garage and walked around the vertiginous towers to the square. The sun blazed with fiery intensity off the concrete, and he felt himself melting and out of breath, his right side painful and itchy. The DA's press conference was gathering near the federal courthouse, and the protest was now marching and chanting along Lafayette Street, the police barricades steering it away from the presser. And Simon and Zoë were sitting dolefully on the bottom steps of the civil courthouse at 60 Centre Street, out of the way of the protest and the press conference. As soon as Alex crossed Centre Street, he slowed, feeling a skippy airiness in the gut, the sensation of gate-crashing a lover's spat.

Zoë sat hunched over on the steps, her knees drawn up to her chin, her expression having taken on a struck, stricken aspect, not meeting Simon's gaze, while Simon had her forearm in one hand, a cigarette in the other, and his grey eyes simmered in a feverish disarray of emotion.

"You sure you don't want to see Eisenmann's presser?" Alex heard Simon asking as he came within earshot.

"I'm sure." Zoë's demeanor was cold, withdrawn and distant, pulling back from him.

"Well, if it would make you feel better, you could always join them." Simon gestured with his cigarette towards about two-dozen protesters who had split off from the main group marching down Lafayette, now staging a die-in in the middle of Centre Street at the southern tip of the square. They lay on the sweltering asphalt, sprawling, writhing, and anyone leaving or entering the City Hall subway station had to thread their way around the massacre while traffic, unable to pass the bodies, snarled up on both sides of Centre Street.

Alex hung back, crossing his arms over his chest. The tension between Simon and Zoë prickled his skin like fine needles. He turned his shoulder and side to them, his eyes locked on Centre Street, pretending to be engrossed in watching the die-in near the subway station.

About a dozen police officers were now attempting to remove protesters from the road. A small flock of reporters had gathered around the die-in, cameras flashing.

He heard Zoë's hissing sigh. "I'm going to the office. I've got shit to do on a few cases."

"Lunch? Fiorello's?" Simon's voice was now more conciliatory.

"I've got to finish those briefs," Zoë answered tonelessly.

With a sidelong glance at Alex, she stood, brushing at her skirt, and then she stalked towards One Hogan Place. Simon met Alex's eyes. The shadow Alex had seen in the courtroom had not yet left his pale face.

Before they could speak, Ray, who had vanished into the crowd when court was adjourned, emerged from the herds milling around Foley Square. "Oh, there you are. I thought you'd be at the presser. Congratulations, Counselor."

Alex wondered what Hurley would have said. Blankly, he watched two uniformed cops carrying a 'body' from the middle of the road, an act which prompted more protesters to rush into Centre Street and throw themselves onto the asphalt. The press, excited by the prospect of a violent encounter between protesters and police, were now swarming in greater numbers. The cops backed off, redirecting traffic, turning vehicles around and sending them on alternate routes.

"Thanks, Detective," said Simon blandly, his elbows on his knees, his eyes flickering in the direction Zoë had gone. He fumbled about in his trouser pockets until he found his packet of cigarettes, and he lit up a fresh one, rolling the lighter between his fingers, always, always, looking towards the DA's office, as if through sheer willpower alone, he could make Zoë reappear. Alex had never seen the feisty prosecutor so on edge after winning a high-profile case. A courtroom victory usually took the edge off Simon.

"I'm going back uptown. Gonna pop into the office and finish those 'fives," announced Ray. "You wanna come, Lex?"

Alex felt weary of the whole criminal justice business; weary of cops, lawyers, courtrooms, protests. The city was oppressive, the humidity suffocating. His suit had become a damp straightjacket. The paperwork wasn't going anywhere. "Nah, I'm going home. It's meant to be my RDO, and I'm taking it."

"I can give you a lift if you want," offered Ray. Alex lived on West 87th, more or less on the way to the office.

"It's okay. I'll walk for a while."

He didn't want to sit in a hot car, stuck in traffic. Even though it was a wretched day for being outside, he needed to walk, to breathe, to clear his lungs and his head, to stretch the aching muscles over his ribs. After a few desultory words, the detectives went in different directions, Ray to the garage under 100 Centre Street, Alex cutting across the square for the corner of Worth and Lafayette, leaving Simon alone at the courthouse, holding his cigarette. It was best to stay out of other people's relationship drama anyway.

Alex walked up Lafayette Street until it met West Houston Street, and the uncompromising, angular skyscrapers of the Civic Center and the towers of the Financial District fell behind him. On the outskirts of Greenwich Village and SoHo, the buildings were smaller, red bricks, weathered stone, wizened by years of wind, rain, and snow, the neighborhood softer, friendlier. Trees and flower boxes lined the streets and colored the medians, the natural colors and greenery softening the hard edges of the city. Small shops, boutiques selling overpriced shit you didn't need – though Alex had a soft spot for the one on West 4th selling world cheeses – cafés, and coffee houses occupied the streets underneath apartments that twenty or thirty years ago would have been the refuges of students and artists living on the fringes of society, but there was a deeper change than just inflation, the Village going upscale, not like it was when Alex was young, walking a beat in the Sixth Precinct, pretending he did not know about his friends living in squats near Bleeker Street.

On Seventh Avenue, he wandered into the heart of the West Village. He navigated Sheridan Square, past the jazz clubs, the folk bars, the greengrocers, the small hole-in-the-wall bookshops, the cafés with outdoor seating. 10th, 11th, 12th, striding past the weathered storefronts, flower boxes, New York University buildings with university banners hanging limply in the still, muggy air. The students passed him on their way to their courses or sat outside the cafés arguing. Seeing them reminded him that he had meant to call his daughter, Sarah, last week, or the week before. She was twenty-three, living near Prospect Park in Brooklyn (that was another change – young people couldn't afford to live in Manhattan anymore), but worked as a nurse in Roosevelt Hospital. He wondered if she had any time off today and if she would meet him for lunch.

15th, 16th, 17th, hiking uptown, and then he rested under a tree at the corner of West 23rd and Seventh. He felt short of breath, the sweat tickling his back and stomach. The old gunshot scars on his right side were hurting him, a raw and tickling pain, and he touched it, wincing, his shirt soaking. It was far too hot to be wearing a dark suit outside.

Then he phoned Sarah on his cell, taking a chance, like the guy in the outfield who never catches the ball. She had a break, and to his surprise, actually wanted to see him. Well, she did drift in and out of phases of reconciliation. They agreed to meet at the 59th Street subway station, which wasn't far from her hospital. They could find relief in the greenery of Central Park, respite from the heat radiating in silver mirages on the concrete. The freshest air you could find without leaving the city.

Succumbing to the heat like an insect trapped under a glass, Alex gave up on his trek, turning west on 23rd, heading for the A and C subway station at 23rd and Eighth. The station was an oven, but then he reveled in those ten or twelve minutes of cooling air-conditioned relief on the train. At the Central Park entrance of the subway station, he lounged against the railings, watching the flow of passerby in and out of the station.

Sarah appeared, striding down 59th, wearing grey trousers and a cream top, the long Jewish curls she got from her mother, or his, bouncing along. Alex felt a fierce pang of guilt. They lived in the same city, and he had not contacted her in several months. His older daughter, Elana, had moved abroad to Australia, but they emailed, and he saw her when she made the occasional visit to New York. He should see the one who was still in the country, yet somehow, he never did. Prospect Park might be on the other side of the East River, but not the other side of the world.

The problem, however, was not geography. He'd never gotten past Sarah's inescapable resentment and their longstanding tempestuous relationship. When Elana came home from Australia, he felt as though they had a passable father-daughter relationship, but with Sarah, it had never been like that. There was always tension, sometimes conflagrating in arguments, sometimes smoldering just below the surface.

She disappeared behind clump of tourists admiring the bronze memorial statue dedicated to the *USS Maine* at the park entrance. A second later, she reappeared, jogging across the road.

When she got to him, she said by way of a greeting, "I saw you on TV this morning, Dad," and then gave him a hug and a light kiss on the cheek.

"Great," he snorted. "Definitely gotta start putting that bag over my head whenever I see cameras."

"How did the hearing go?"

"For the defendant, pretty shit."

"I take it he got the death penalty then."

"Yeah.

"I'm not sure how I feel about that," Sarah admitted.

"Me neither."

That seemed to surprise her. "He shot two cops. There but for the grace of God and all."

Alex rubbed at the side of his throat, looking up at the grand old buildings constructed of grey and white masonry and pinnacled roofs and balustrades lining Central Park West, a grandiose façade left over from the Gilded Age flaunting wealth and class. Across the street from the park, on the other side of Columbus Circle, reared Donald Trump's tower, a monstrosity of blackened glass, sticking out amongst the old stonework like a hideously modern wart, flaunting wealth but no class.

"I must be getting less bloodthirsty in my old age," he said.

They bought sandwiches from a nearby deli, his pastrami and mustard, hers a Mediterranean chicken wrap, and then they ambled into the park, making small talk: the weather, the construction on their commutes, Mayor Bloomberg, and how Elana was getting along in Australia, where the weather was surely better than here and kangaroos ate the vegetables in her garden. In New York City, the only wildlife you saw were pigeons, rats, cockroaches, and the locals. They followed a path wending into the center of the park and curving around the pond. Joggers and cyclists in tight lycra nipped past them.

A group of kids kicked a soccer ball in an open meadow beside the path. The ball bounced across their track, a couple kids dashing after it, unfazed by the heat and humidity. Oaks and cypress trees leaned overhead, shading the path, and insects buzzed amidst the leaves and branches. A few wooden boats floated across the water, creeping sluggishly along the glassy surface, their rowers pulling heavily at the oars.

Alex spoke anxiously, trying to fill space, even though the conversation felt as immovable as those boats. "Are you still dating that guy? The one I didn't like?"

"You don't like anybody I date," retorted Sarah, her eyes flashing, defensive.

Before he could get a hold of his tongue, Alex let slip, "If you didn't date assholes, I might start liking them."

She mantled, her hackles rising. "God, always with some smartass remark, huh, Daddy? The one thing I could always fucking count on from you. It wasn't like we ever got much else – certainly not a role model for a good partner."

There it was, his sordid past, rising like a serpent out of the steaming city air to bite him, his own Goddamned fault because of his big mouth. If he had restricted the conversation to safe subjects like the weather, Elana's Aussie fiancé (who they could agree they didn't like, as his priorities seemed to be surfing, barbequing, and beer, in that order), or city politics, he might have staved off the freefalling descent into embittered arguments, the reinfection of old injuries. When Sarah was less than two, Ellie a little over three, his relationship with their mother imploded; she filed for divorce and he begged the department for a transfer out of the Tenth Precinct in Hell's Kitchen to any post in an outer borough detective squad that had space for him. Then years of throwing himself into work when he was on-duty, the bottle when he wasn't, hiding, fleeing from a melancholy that crept after him, a gelatinous sludge that would smother him should it ever catch up and cover his heart, and, undeniably, dogged by his chronic failing at getting his act together and becoming a part of his daughters' lives. He never was, not enough, forever facing the real indictment, the cutting truth that he didn't quit the drink for them.

He quit because seven years ago, his health failed: an acute attack of alcoholic hepatitis and a bleeding stomach ulcer, a nasogastric tube shoved up his nose and down his throat, liters of blood pumped from his stomach, being scared witless by a doctor telling him that he would be dead of liver failure or a gastric bleed if he continued drinking. Lying in a hospital, his organs giving up on him, reminding him of his own mortality – that was why he detoxed. Sarah had never forgiven him for his absence or his alcoholism.

The guilt and the memories mutated into galling anger. Yes, he had cheated on their mother and turned his back on them, and he had to live with that, just like he had to live with forever unrequited cravings for booze, ulcers that might flare up, and his fucked up liver, but for God's sake, she was twenty-three years old; she wasn't fated to endlessly repeat the bad relationship choices of her parents.

He snapped, "Yeah, at least you should know what *not* to touch with a bargepole –"

"Bryan, his name's Bryan," Sarah whispered hoarsely.

"Bryan," Alex echoed.

"Well, I'm not dating him anymore. I broke up with him two weeks ago. If you could be bothered keeping up with my life, you would know that."

The freefall was accelerating. It never could end well. "You have a phone. There are no armies standing between you and calling me."

"You never call me," she said.

"I called you today."

"Because you're stressed out about that guy getting the death penalty."

"No." What bullshit, he thought. Would he have called her had it been a normal day? A normal hearing or trial? He doubted it. "I'm your father. I like seeing you sometimes. Crazy idea, I know."

"Yeah, it is crazy."

"What the hell does that mean?" He breathed deeply, as if he could somehow drive the pain out of his body with the power of his lungs.

"I don't know," she replied, her voice weakening.

"As much as you'd like to, you can't hold me responsible for everything, for every loser you date, or whatever. You're an adult; you can make your own decisions."

"Now you're just being patronizing." She looked wounded.

"I don't mean to be. I'm just saying…" He paused, looking for the right words but there didn't seem to be any. There never did.

"What are you saying?" Sarah bridled.

"What do you want me to say?" It was like she was still fourteen, angry and petulant, and him still on the sauce, guilt-ridden and incapable of explaining it to anyone. "Every time I see you, it's like 'Hi Dad, thanks for screwing up my life.' I know, I fucked up but good. Short of inventing a time machine, what the fuck do you expect me to do? How come I can talk to your sister without getting into fights?"

"Ellie's always been more forgiving," said Sarah coldly. "And she lives ten thousand miles away."

They crossed a little bridge that arched over the stream feeding into the pond. Alex stopped in the middle of the bridge and leaned over the railing, staring into the water burbling, swirling in white foam around the rocks. He felt Sarah's anger scouring holes into his back, the acrimony that festered for years, simmering until something he said, perhaps his offhand remark about the now-ex boyfriend, caused it to erupt. He wondered what possessed him to call her. It was always this way. One wrong step or mistimed sarcasm, and she would lash out.

"I don't know what to tell you, Sarah. You wonder why I don't call you that often."

They stood on the little bridge, engulfed in an excruciating silence.

Her voice quivering, Sarah blurted, "Yeah, why can't you just…I don't know…Be more supportive? Act like you give a shit. Bryan was a really good guy, and all I get from you is that you think he's an asshole. Like… You're such a fucking stereotype. The alcoholic police detective with family issues. That asshole is on every crime show ever made. I mean, I know you spend your day looking at dead bodies and all, and you have to do all that *CSI* stuff, and maybe my stupid little breakups don't mean shit to you, and your whole sense of reality has been screwed up by working in the police. Maybe that's why it's a stereotype. That stuff fucks you up."

"What, is that your mother's theory?" he fired back. His ex had never missed an opportunity to tell the girls what a jerk their father was, another thing that had made it impossible to repair any damage.

"My mother's theory?" She shot him a disgusted look. "You always think it's like Mom has this conspiracy to undermine you or whatever, but she's so totally moved on from you. It's obvious, isn't it? I have a friend at work who's married to a cop, and she says it makes him not give a damn about stuff that's important to *her*, but you know, isn't starving, beaten children with a crack-addict mom in a basement in some shitty Brooklyn rowhouse. But you know, if you at least *acted* like you cared. Instead of always firing off the wiseass one-liners like, I dunno, you see the detectives doing on *Law and Order* or whatever, you know, at crime scenes. Do you really *do* that? I'm not a crime scene, Dad, and you just come across like you don't care –"

"I do care," Alex interrupted hoarsely, the fall attaining dizzying speeds, the ground rushing towards him.

The look in his eyes cut off her rant, as though the realization that she had genuinely upset him derailed her attack. Deflated, she grabbed a branch off a nearby tree and distractedly snapped off the twigs.

"Tell me, what's this shit –" he gestured as if he could capture her anger with his hands, "gonna accomplish?"

"I don't know. I wish I could be more like my sister."

"Yeah, I don't know, either."

She glanced down at her watch. "My break is nearly over."

"I'm sorry it's always like this."

"Yeah, me too."

They didn't know what else to say to one another. It had been 'like this' for so long that neither one of them knew how to change it. Stuck like lost tourists, going in circles, not a street sign in sight that showed prospects of leading them out.

"I really did think it would be different after 9/11," Sarah muttered.

"The city is different." But he knew what she meant.

"No, I mean things between us."

"Yeah."

On that day, she had come to him, walking almost the length of Manhattan from the NYU hospital, where she had been a student nurse, to the MNHS offices on West 133rd and Broadway because they had evacuated all of downtown, unbelievably, and closed down all the subways, tunnels, and bridges, making it impossible to get home to Brooklyn. He was working like every cop in the city was working. Even though they could not get to Ground Zero, it had been 'all hands on deck' uptown to keep order and figure out what the fuck was going on amidst the confusion, the panic, the new terrorist threats coming from every which way. Most of the detectives from the Manhattan North and Manhattan South Homicide squads had been co-opted into frantically investigating and chasing down rumors as threats of more attacks flew across the airwaves and media.

Dusty and sweaty, Sarah had run into the office that evening, after spending all day in the hospital treating victims of the attack. She was frazzled, scared, tearful, weeping to the officer manning the Wheel desk, "My father's Detective Boswell. Where is he?" She could not phone him since cell phone lines had buckled. He could have gone to Ground Zero – a lot of cops did – and he could have been in the Towers as they fell, trying to get people out. There were a lot of police officers missing. He wasn't downtown but he was out, so the Wheel officer, the only person in the office at that moment, had given her a cup of coffee, and then she waited at Alex's desk in the squad room.

He remembered telling her, "I'm sorry, I can't leave just yet," before giving her the key to his apartment and talking a couple guys in a radio car into giving her a lift to West 87th because it was impossible to get a taxi.

"It's okay, I can walk. I walked here," she had insisted. "I don't want to inconvenience anyone."

"No fucking way," he replied. "You're not walking through Harlem, all the way to my apartment, alone in the dark. These guys are headed downtown anyway." Harlem was a lot better than it used to be, but it was still Harlem.

He'd met her there the next day, as soon as work sent him home for a few hours of rest. Caught up in the middle of events bigger and infinitely more terrible than their own tiny, insignificant dramas, they hadn't – for what seemed to be the first time in memory – fallen into their old habits of sniping arguments. They sat on the sofa watching the television, looking hopelessly for insight in the space-filling repetition of 24-hour news and platitudes from Rudy Giuliani and George Bush. The endlessly repeated footage of the planes appearing out of the icy blue sky and the towers collapsing shocked them so many times they felt numb.

Then Elana finally got through on Alex's landline, blubbering, "What the fuck is happening there? Are you all right? Where is Mom? I've been watching the news, and I can't get a hold of anyone in the city!" She had managed to get through to MNHS shortly after Alex had left the office, who confirmed that he was okay.

It was amazing she had, as the police were struggling to locate their own personnel. Alex and others in the squad had spent three days frenetically searching for Detective Bill Ryan, his old friend, a veteran homicide detective who had been at One Police Plaza that morning for a meeting. No one could contact Bill. Then, the worst news: someone in 1PP saying they'd seen Bill running into the Towers immediately after the first plane hit. They knew it then. Bill was a smart, experienced, resourceful detective. If he'd come out, he would have found a way to get in touch with someone, even in the absence of every single phone and subway line in the city. The cop in One Police Plaza who saw him take off his jacket and his tie before running into the World Trade Center was the last person who ever saw him.

The attacks brought unfathomable grief and shock to the whole city, but for Alex, the loss of Bill Ryan made the pain all too grievous. In those days and weeks that followed, the city had a wounded, surreal feel to it, and so did the job, since most of the detective squads in the city were sent on details to the Fresh Kills landfill on Staten Island, the biggest crime scene anyone had ever seen, where all the rubble and debris from the World Trade Center was being removed. They had to wear white biohazard suits, goggles, and masks, and sift through the debris for remains of victims, who would be individually identified with whatever relics detectives could find. It was macabre, harrowing work, and everyone was exhausted, emotionally, physically, and every cop was close to someone who didn't make it. To keep yourself sane, you had morbid, dark conversations with your colleagues scavenging alongside you. They entertained one another with their grisliest tales. Because you had to keep some tenuous connections to your old reality while you came to terms with this dystopian new one, fighting with seagulls for remains and looking at the columns of smoke rising from Lower Manhattan.

But within a couple months, the city went back to business as usual. The work on Staten Island at last reached a point where there was no more rubble and no more victims. Work in MNHS picked up its pace. The solidarity born out of 9/11 did not seem to last very long, and people went back to killing one another for the mundane reasons they usually killed one another. The closeness Alex had felt with Sarah also retreated, and he felt bitterly disappointed and depressed now that they'd resuscitated their old arguments.

"Sorry, Dad," she said, drawing him out of his reverie. "I've upset you. I'm sorry. I'm sorry I called you a stereotype. I'm a terrible daughter, I know."

"Well, I'm a terrible father. And I'm probably a fucking stereotype. I don't know. Look, you'd better not be late for work. We'll talk later."

She touched his shoulder, as though she could find some intimation of reassurance in that moment of contact. Her eyes had a glassy sheen. Swiftly, she spun on her heel and walked back towards the West Side.

Aimless, he wandered through the park until he found himself standing beside the Jackie Kennedy Reservoir, that surprisingly immense expanse of water with its fountain in the middle, spraying water in a fifty-foot high arc. The concrete banks dropped steeply into the water, and the path bustled with walkers, joggers, and cyclists. The castellated towers of the San Remo and Eldorado on the Upper West Side and Billionaire's Row on the East Side soared out of the canopy of trees on the boundaries of the park, the illusion that the buildings lined the shores of the lake, like a seaside resort.

Alex bought himself an ice cream bar from one of the little vans scattered through the park – so much for his promise to eat healthier this week. Licking his ice cream, he rested his elbows on the fence, gazing miserably into the murky grey and brown water lapping at the foot of the concrete ramps.

Really, he only had himself to blame. After divorcing Sarah and Elana's mother, he'd gone off the rails, with the drink and everything else, and wounded and angry, he'd gotten that transfer out of the Tenth to the One-Oh-Three Precinct detective squad in Jamaica. It was a wild precinct. Jamaica was a tough neighborhood, and the guys he'd worked with in that precinct were pretty bonkers as well. He moved into a slum of an apartment in Ridgewood, shared with a couple other cops. It had low rent, a good thing given how much of his detective third grade's salary was going to child support, but it had been a roach-infested hole. It also gained notoriety as the unofficial One-Oh-Three Precinct party apartment, the epicenter of boozing and mayhem. He'd more or less cut himself off from his kids' lives.

Moving back to Manhattan and joining the Manhattan North Homicide squad, one of the most coveted assignments in the Detective Bureau, may have boosted his career, but it didn't salvage his connection with his kids, nor did he save himself from his worst impulses. He still drank too much. He still wrecked relationships. The most spectacular train crash involved a girl named Charlotte Anderson who lived in Greenwich Village. Two years, his longest relationship since his ex-wife, and he'd deluded himself into believing it was working out. But his fatal pattern had been set. She had suddenly bolted from New York after he accidentally knocked her up. It was his last committed relationship amidst a series of casual girlfriends and lonely, meaningless sex.

That darkened his mood even further. His own brain mocked him, taking him on a subway ride down a line where each stop was another clusterfuck. He finished his ice cream and flung the stick into a nearby trashcan. Was it any wonder that Sarah still hated him?

A buzz at his hip snapped at his attention like a barking dog. He snatched his cell phone and flipped it open. Simon McNally.

Seeing the lawyer's name reminded him of the hearing, so he sounded annoyed when he said, "Yeah, what is it?"

"Hey, why aren't you out tonight?" shouted McNally. Alex heard a racket of voices and music in the background. He was in a bar.

"What?"

"The Blackthorn. Celebratory drinks. Why aren't you here?"

So many reasons, but he said, "You didn't tell me." Detective McDonough had, but never mind.

"What?" yelled McNally over the noise. He sounded wasted.

"You didn't tell me," repeated Alex, louder.

"Oh. I'm telling you now. Everyone's gone home except for a few guys, but you should come. I thought I said… But there was all that bullshit with Zoë, and I must've spaced it. I was wondering why you weren't here. The primary detective should be here."

"Who's there? Cops?"

"Nah. Well, some detectives and some patrol officers from the Two-Six were, but they left fucking hours ago. It's just me and a few other ADAs."

Alex's heart sped up. Earlier in the day, he hadn't felt like it was appropriate to celebrate the death sentence in a bar. And AA might have a view on going into a pub when feeling this upset. On the other hand, he had spent seven years on the proverbial wagon, and it hadn't made a damned bit of difference. He found himself not particularly caring or even remotely interested in whether or not he remained sober.

"Are you coming?" McNally drunkenly shouted.

"Fine, yeah," he said and pressed 'end' on his phone.

Part 3: 2000 hours

He spun away from the reservoir and strode towards the Upper East Side. The sky darkened, from the pallid hues cast by the sun setting behind New Jersey, to the dark, bluish grey of the light-polluted, starless night sky, and the humidity grew thicker and heavier.

And then, as if the clouds themselves had enough, they burst, pelting the city in a torrent, and the cold, blind rain doused Alex's self-pity. Head down, he trudged along Fifth Avenue. Rain soaked through to his back and shoulders and fell in his eyes. His sodden trousers clung to his thighs, and water squelched in his shoes. Plodding along the sidewalk, he tried to keep his mind blank: don't think about the previous twelve hours; don't think about the contempt in Sarah's eyes; don't think about the look in David LaValle's eyes when the jury announces the death sentence because of what you said on the witness stand; don't think it has anything to do with what you said; don't think about everything you did to deserve Sarah's enmity; don't think about self-loathing; don't think.

He passed below the triple arching neogothic facades of the Metropolitan Museum. A few soggy tourists wandered up and down the stairs. Passerby hurried along the street, wrestling with unruly umbrellas. He maneuvered around groups of worried Upper East Side women, wearing improbably short skirts and even more improbably high heeled boots, leaning anxiously into the road, peering through the gloom for a passing taxi with its light on. As was the way, any cab that zoomed along Fifth had its light off.

Into Midtown East now, where old men huddled in doorways, a paper at their legs and a cardboard box at their heads. Water raced down the gutters in raging rivers and passing cars kicked it up in wild arcs of spray. On East 51st Street, near Grand Central Station, he sheltered under the awning of the pub. The Blackthorn Tavern. He was trembling. Yet he wasn't cold, even though his clothes were dripping wet, and his soaking shirt and trousers stuck to his skin.

He looked at the door of the pub, the lights glowing welcomingly through the frosted window, beckoning. Hesitantly, he pushed open the door, crossing the threshold, but then he paused. His eyes adjusted to the dim lights. It was loud, the Who playing on the PA, the din of conversation foaming from the after-work crowd and the escaping-the-rain crowd. Immediately, he spotted some detectives from the Midtown North precinct in the far corner. They didn't see him, and he wanted to keep it that way.

Then he saw Simon propping up the bar, conversing boisterously with two men and two women. Simon had changed out of his courtroom uniform of suit and tie. He was wearing faded jeans and a tatty blue t-shirt with the words 'It takes balls to climb with nuts' written across the back, and the image of a stick-figure climber dangling from a cliff on the chest.

No sign of Zoë. So that had gone well. Alex minced to the bar, squeezing into the empty space next to the prosecutor, saying, "Hi,

Simon. Hi, Marie." He knew one of the women, Marie Adams, another ADA in the Trial Bureau. She wasn't in a power suit, either, but jeans and a red t-shirt with 'Smith College' imprinted on the chest, and her blonde hair pulled into a loose ponytail, the stray strands whisking in front of her face.

Holding up a pint of rust-colored ale, Marie nodded her head. "Alex."

McNally almost jumped out of his seat. "Detective Boswell!" He jerked his head towards his companions. "This is one of the best homicide detectives in New York! Primary investigator on the LaValle case. *Lots* of murderers would walk free if it wasn't for this guy!"

Alex felt blood coloring his cheeks. The prosecutor was clearly hammered.

"Alex, this is George, who's an ADA in the Rackets Bureau, and Nick, you've surely met Nick, he's in Sex Crimes. You know Marie, of course. And, sorry…your name?" He squinted at the other woman.

Alex thought she looked familiar, but not someone he knew from the DA's office. A striking redhead, her face lightly freckled, her blue eyes smoldering, intense.

"Lauren Collucci." She introduced herself like he should already know that.

The name rang a bell in his mind, but he could not place it.

The Sex Crimes ADA, Nick, threw a shit-eating grin at him and bubbled, "Lauren's an actor. She's in a new show. One about the DA's office –"

"*Law and Order*?" suggested Alex dubiously. That show had been around for years.

"No, no, it's a new one, about a corrupt ADA having a crisis of conscience. Anyway, she's been following me around, seeing how we really do things in the office." Nick laughed. "You know, seeing what the job's really like."

"We're still filming the pilot," the actor explained. "But I've been in a *Law and Order* episode. I played the sister of a victim. Got to be interviewed by Jerry Orbach and Jesse L. Martin." She smiled amiably at Alex. "Detectives Briscoe and Green. Homicide detectives. Simon's told me you're the finest detective in New York. Better than Briscoe. You should be the star of a TV show."

47

Alex eyefucked Simon, a man better known for floridly castigating you over your loose interpretation of 'plain sight' or 'reasonable suspicion' than for anything resembling a commendation. When sober anyway. "I think in his state, he'd say the homeless guy sitting on the street out there is the finest detective in New York."

Proving the point, Simon slurred, "It's not all courtroom drama all the time. But it was this morning. You want a drink, Alex?"

Alex was tongue-tied. He should ask for a soft drink, but that wasn't what he wanted to drink. Seeing McNally staggeringly wasted brought back a glimmer of sense, and he thought he should escape now. Coming in here in his downhearted mood had been one of his worst ideas, impulsive and stupid. "I'd better not."

McNally would have none of it. "Oh, come on. Just one night. It's not time to go home yet. Far too early. The night is young. Come on, you really want a drink."

"Yeah, that's the trouble," Alex said softly as his seven years of resolve wavered.

"Why's that? Don't let it trouble you," said Simon, too far gone to remember why Alex, for the last seven years, never was.

Alex didn't want to openly admit that he was alcoholic, recovering or otherwise, in front of Simon's work colleagues. He felt his willpower emaciating, and the voice in his head, the last holdout of sound judgement, screaming at him to leave the bar, battling with the part of him that had decided he didn't give a shit anymore.

Addiction won over indecisiveness. He heard himself saying, "All right, Counselor," and he was looking at the beer pumps along the bar and the rows of spirits in shining bottles on the wall behind it. "Doesn't fucking matter anyway. I'll have a Budweiser. It's on tap?"

When the pint appeared, Simon toasted him, saying, "To not fucking mattering!"

He hadn't touched a beer in seven years. It was sharp and cold and refreshing, the antidote to the oppressive humidity and the weight he had been carrying around all day. He sucked the beer down quickly, a man lost in a desert finding water.

"That's the way, Lex," Simon said exuberantly. He never called Alex that. It was a police street name he'd picked up on his beat in the Village long ago. "This is fucking amazing. Out in the pub, with your pals. I'm going out for a smoke." He climbed unsteadily off the bar stool and lurched to the door.

Alex glanced towards the Midtown North detectives who he didn't think recognized him. He shouldn't be here. What was he doing? The booze had nearly taken his life. His eyes darted guiltily to Marie, wondering if she knew, but she seemed oblivious to the subtext that wasn't there anyway, laughing at Nick telling a story about a defendant arrested for having sex with a park bench in Washington Square.

Well, you can work with people, only discussing the legalities of criminal justice, and they don't know you beyond your job. A sharp, acidic burn in his stomach got his attention, the beer sloshing against a half-healed ulcer he'd been fighting ever since the LaValle case went to trial. *Fuck you,* he thought at it, painfully reminded that his body shouldn't tolerate alcohol anymore, and he reached into his jacket pocket, his fingertips brushing pill packets of antacids.

"Boswell, helluva job on the LaValle case," said George, the Rackets ADA. "I'm glad we got that cop-killing son of a bitch. Good guys won."

Alex grunted and poured the beer down his throat. His old gunshot injury twinged, and he felt a blunted ache under his breastbone.

"You must be happy it's over. That's a hell of a redball. First capital case in Manhattan and all that. And a pregnant cop. Ugh."

"Yeah, it's taken ten years off my life," Alex responded.

"I hear that."

Alex finished his beer and ordered another. His mouth was desert dry, and he sucked the pint down, worriedly noticing the beer level in the glass rapidly reducing. He should pace himself. The ADAs were laughing about a case of Marie's where the defendant, on the witness stand, had flashed everyone in the courtroom, and Lauren Collucci smiling, taking it in, this underbelly of New York.

"Detective Boswell?" she said, suddenly aiming her sycophantic attention at him.

"Uh, yeah?" he responded uncertainly.

"Or do you prefer Alex?"

"Whatever."

She daintily lifted her glass of wine to her lips. "You know, I've had this thing in mind, a script, about a detective whose partner gets killed in the line of duty, and there's a legal problem, the exclusionary rule, so evidence gets suppressed and the guy who kills this cop can't be prosecuted. Instead of letting the murderer go free, the detective quits his job, so he's no longer bound to the rules of the NYPD, and then he goes after this guy as just, like, a civilian, and eventually kills him. What do you think?"

"I think that's the plot of *Die Hard*," sniggered George.

"It's, uh, illegal," Alex offered guardedly. He pushed his tongue into his teeth. Killing someone yourself out of revenge or waiting a decade for some prison official to shoot poison into a prisoner's veins for the same damned reason. Was there a difference? Due process, supposedly. He scratched at his scalp, pissed at himself for circling back to the case, and then he guzzled that beer.

"You shoot stick, Alex?" inquired Nick, saving him from the movie pitch. "I hear rumor you're pretty good. And my ass is getting numb, sitting on these damned stools."

"Huh," said Alex.

Altogether steaming, Simon barreled onto his stool, drunkenly clapping Alex on the shoulder. "Think I need more whisky. It's good to see you here, Detective. Good to see you. It was good to see you in court today. It's always good to see you in court. We fucking nailed him, didn't we?"

"I don't think you need any more whisky," said Alex.

"No, no, I do. Definitely need more whisky. I'll have another dram of Bruichladdich," he said to the bartender, his tongue rolling easily through the Gaelic traffic jam of consonants. "The best whisky comes from Islay, Lex."

"I used to drink whatever got me drunk. Didn't care where it was from." *Used to?* His fucked up past, his present, all these shadows he thought he had put in a sealed bottle and locked in the basement, but he only christened a ship with it, and it had come back to the harbor.

Simon buried his fingers in the bone and muscle on Alex's shoulder. "You're still soaking wet. 'Cause it is still soaking wet. It's still fucking raining. There's rivers, right in the middle of the roads. You ever seen a road turn into a river? Like the Hudson, flowing down the middle of Madison. That's what it's like out there. You know how hard it is to light a cigarette when everything is soaking wet? Fucking impossible."

"It's been a wet summer," said Nick. "It's been shit, actually. We've hardly gotten any climbing done, have we, Simon?"

"It's global warming," Simon observed. "They're always talking about global warming, and you know, it's definitely warm. At least today. Very warm. They always say on the news, it's the warmest or wettest or driest summer in history. But if every year, the weather is the warmest, or wettest, or whatever, then there's no such thing as normal, right? So how can it be wetter than normal, if they don't even know what normal is...Like last year, it was hotter and drier than 'normal.' You know, they say that if global warming happens, the oceans will rise and that's Lower Manhattan, under fucking water. Can you believe it?"

Then the prosecutor pitched to his feet and staggered off in the general direction of the bathrooms. After he had been away for some time, Marie said to the three men, "You might want to check that he hasn't passed out in the john."

Alex eased himself off the barstool, not very steady either. The one positive here was that at the rate McNally was hitting the booze, he wouldn't remember a thing about any of it in the morning. Carefully, Alex nudged open the men's room door and peered in, scanning the urinals, the sinks, the stalls. No one there. At least Simon wasn't yet at the passing out in the bathroom stage.

He found Simon on his way back to the bar, and the lawyer crashed into him, grabbing his elbow, saying, "Christ, Alex, I'm fucked."

"You're all right," said Alex, guiding him to his seat, where he sagged against the bar, his eyes starry and glazed.

"Hey, Simon, you hanging in there, buddy?" asked Nick, giggling, slapping Simon on the shoulder. "I asked Alex to play a game of pool. Whaddaya think?"

"Terrible idea," slurred Simon. "No one can beat him."

That only encouraged Nick, who was moving in the direction of the pool table.

Alex followed him, and he sensed the other four drifting after them. *Seven years out of the habit of playing with a few drinks in me*, he thought. He wondered whether he could still play a respectable game in this state. Nick was racking the balls, methodically, as if he had to think about the order of the numbers.

"Want to break?" said Nick, as he lifted the rack off the neat little triangle of balls.

"I'll see how it goes," Alex answered, working chalk into the ratty end of his cue. Then he leaned over the table, sliding the cue between his thumb and forefinger, and, with a powerful stroke, whacked the cue ball. The racked balls exploded across the table, two striped balls rolling into pockets. Not too bad. Perhaps he hadn't lost his intoxicated game after all. "I guess I'm stripes," he commented.

The ADAs and the actress said nothing, only watching with amazement as he executed a smooth series of shots, pocketing four striped balls in about two minutes. Then he went for an ambitious bank shot and missed, the cue ball gliding past its intended target. Dammit. Shrugging, he rested his back against the wall, sipping his beer.

Marie finished her beer and placed the empty glass on a table. "Well, I think I'll skip the rest of the carnage. I know how this ends. Emma will be missing me." She was tugging on her coat, checking to be sure she had her cell phone and purse, before waving at everyone, pushing her way into the crowd between the pool table and the door.

"Who's Emma?" asked Lauren. "Her kid?"

"Her dog," Alex supplied. Marie might not know about his alcohol problems, but he knew that she had a German shepherd called Emma.

Nick's first shot deposited a ball into a pocket, but on his second, the cue ball weakly bumped into the four ball, rolling it only a couple inches. Effortlessly, Alex dispatched the remaining striped balls, before making short work of the eight ball. Then Simon claimed he was too drunk to play, which was undoubtedly the case, given that he could barely stand, while Lauren primly said that she didn't play. Alex's next victim was George, who didn't let him break this time. A solid ball rolled into a pocket on the break, and then George chased another into a pocket, but missed on his third shot. He slouched against the wall, having only prolonged his inevitable defeat, and Alex pocketed four balls in quick succession but then found himself snookered with an impossible shot, forcing him to concede. That gave George another chance. He pocketed one ball and missed his second.

While Alex scanned the table for a promising line, Simon staggered to his feet, staring blearily at his cell phone. "Fuck her!"

"Fuck who?" asked Nick.

"Never mind." Simon reached for his red Gore-Tex jacket, bunching it under his armpit, stumbling away from the pool table.

"Where are you going?" asked Alex.

"Home," said Simon.

"Want me to go with you?" Alex felt like the one responsible person there. He'd always been a lucid drunk, the reason he got away with so many years thinking he didn't have an alcohol problem, because even when doing stupid things, he usually acted rational.

"S'okay."

"As long as you can remember where you live. And there's no dignity in passing out or vomiting in a cab."

Simon gave him a lopsided smile. "East Village. East 6th. See. I think I can manage, Detective."

Lauren stood and touched Simon's arm. Dumbfounded, he stared at her, his bloodshot grey eyes dazzled.

"I live near there, East 12th and First. We can share a cab," she offered.

"Yeah, sure, that's great," mumbled Simon. The actress was guiding him with a suggestive hand on his back, Simon reeling drunkenly out of the bar, bumping into the doorframe.

Alex exchanged a look with Nick and George, all three raising their eyebrows.

"I won't tell Zoë if you guys don't," said Nick.

Had Simon wanted Alex's help, Alex might have saved himself, but with his last escape route falling into a cab, he felt flattened, beaten. He let his illness take him. The compulsion was stronger than any person. How arrogant, thinking you can whip it back with willpower. Most of the people in his AA meeting had relapsed, many more than once. He ordered a shot of Jameson. As he studied the golden liquid in the glass, he had second thoughts. Had he lost his mind? But he'd rocketed onto his alcoholic trajectory and felt powerless. Too late to apply the brakes now.

He drank the whiskey, blenching as it rasped at his throat and stomach. Then the harsh burning faded to a warm glow, oozing through his body, his limbs tingling. Each sip of whiskey felt like a sudden punch to the gut, and the fuzzy sensation spreading as his heart pumped alcohol to his extremities and his organs. Nick and George were lounging on their cues, discussing the probability of Simon sleeping with Lauren. Simon's ethics and Zoë not a factor, apparently, or less of one than Simon's intoxication and Lauren's attractiveness, and how likely one was to affect the other. With Marie away, the two ADAs could agree out loud that Lauren was a stunning woman – you could not say those things around Marie without being called a misogynist.

Lost in his own world, Alex ignored the lawyers, easily firing a series of solid balls into pockets, one after the other, a bank shot here, knocking it in with another ball there, and then one more, a straight line to the pocket. He fished the pills out of his jacket, two for reducing acid and two for lining the stomach, and he shoved them down with a mouthful of whiskey. Oh, he wished he wasn't here, his heart shriveling, too depressed to bullshit with the ADAs. He cocked an ear towards them. At no point in his life had he ever cared about Simon's sex life

His nostrils flared as he exhaled a protracted breath, and he rested his hip against the table, searching for his next line. He found one, and the pool cue shook unsteadily, but he eased it between his fingers, lightly nudging the cue ball. The eleven ball rolled into the pocket.

"Hi," said Zoë.

Shocked, Alex snapped his eyes away from the table.

Her hair was wet and bedraggled, strands escaping from the ponytail, and her eyes were puffed-up and reddened, as if she had been upset.

Nick and George both became engrossed in chalking the tops of their cues.

"Hi, Zoë," Nick responded, looking guilty as hell.

Alex latched his gaze onto the pool table in a careful study of his next shot. If she didn't already suspect that her boyfriend was up to something, she would now.

"Simon called me. Where is he?" she asked, her voice hard. "He's not answering his cell."

"Simon's headed back to the East Village," Alex answered.

She folded her arms across her chest and gave him a withering glare. "Alex. You've been drinking."

"Only a little." He shrugged apologetically. Then he stretched across the table, neatly depositing the seven ball into a pocket.

"I doubt that," she said coldly. "You shouldn't be drinking."

"I shouldn't be doing a lot of things." He tried to ignore the way Nick and George were looking at him with guilt in their glassy, drunk eyes.

"You shouldn't be drinking?" Nick echoed.

"Well, no, but it was only a matter of time before I fucked it." Alex's voice was raspy and bitter. The truth comes out some day. He fired the cue ball hard, two balls exploding with a sharp crack, flying into pockets, *thunk, thunk.*

"You're an alcoholic?"

"So they tell me." He sprawled across the table, heartsick at the blunt reminder, and bounced the cue ball of the side, into the four, which disappeared into a pocket.

"How long you been on the wagon?" George spoke quietly, embarrassed.

"Seven years," Alex said tonelessly without looking at him.

"Jesus, man. I didn't know."

"How could you? Fuck it."

"When did Simon leave?" Zoë demanded.

"Dunno," Nick said, begging Alex with his eyes to screw up a shot so he could be busy with something. Not standing here like a douchebag, covering up for his friend.

"He phoned me, said he was trashed, said he was here, and he wanted a lift." She sounded infuriated. "Thinks I'm at his beck and call and then takes off anyway. You don't know how long ago he left?"

"Twenty, thirty minutes?" suggested George.

"What the fuck. He leave alone?"

"Yes," Nick replied, just a little too quick.

"Who else was here?"

"Marie Adams was here for a little bit," said Nick. "But she left a while ago." No mention of the actress. A glance skated amongst the three men, Alex hoping Zoë didn't notice.

"He just fucking left? Like that?" Her tear-stained eyes gleamed in the dim lights.

"He's probably unconscious in a cab somewhere," Alex guessed helpfully, rubbing more chalk into his cue.

"He'd deserve it. Was he that drunk?"

"He was pretty hammered."

"Hammered enough to pass out in a taxi?"

He shrugged. "Coulda been."

"Fucking hell." Then, her tone softer, she added, "Alex, why don't I take you home. It's the Upper West Side, isn't it? It's on my way to Riverdale."

"You wanna stay for a drink first?" he offered. "You look like you could use one."

Her glare could have frozen the entire East River. "No, come on, you've had enough."

"Hey, don't I get an offer of a lift?" teased George.

"Fuck you, George. You're not on my way home. Alex, let's go."

"Let me finish this," he said in a soft voice, indicating the pool table. Only four even-numbered balls remained. He could clear them in a minute.

"Fine, if it won't take all night," grumbled Zoë irritably.

"It won't." Alex finished off his whiskey and then steadied himself against a wave of nausea as it disagreed with his system. Fuck, he had become a lightweight. He used to have more of a stomach for this. But it settled, and he felt quite a bit drunker.

He glanced at Zoë, standing off to one side, her shoulders stiff, arms across her chest, glowering at him like he had robbed a bank. The look in her eyes, steel and stone, reminded him of the way Sarah had looked at him that afternoon, or the way her mother or other ex-girlfriends used to look at him when he staggered home after a long night on the sauce. That chilling combination of contempt, vitriol, and immense disappointment.

Breathing into his lower lungs, he narrowed his eyes on the two ball, slinging it into a pocket. In rapid succession, the rest of the striped balls and the eight ball followed it, rolling into pockets in a series of thunks, one, two, three, four, five! That was the last. And thank God, because the whole room was listing sideways.

Even Zoë seemed impressed. "If that's what you can do drunk, you must be a hell of a player sober."

"Well, spend a lot of your life in bars..."

"You're not spending any longer in this one. Get your jacket." Without dithering for a second longer, she took him resolutely by the elbow and steered him towards the door. Too drunk and tired to resist her determined energy, he let her lead him to her car. The rain had eased off into a steady drizzle.

"So.... What happened today?" Zoë said, starting the car and pulling out of the parking space.

"What?"

"Why were you getting drunk with Simon and those two assholes?"

"Simon called me," Alex replied dully as the world rocked back and forth like a carnival ride.

The car splashed through puddles concealing the potholes in the road. Zoë took an emotional breath. Her voice trembled. "A bunch of them went out right after the presser. There were some cops. Quite a few, actually. And half the Trial Bureau. I guess all those people left after a couple drinks. I didn't go, and I guess Simon decided to stay out all night and get wrecked because he was pissed at me. But you know you shouldn't do that."

"Are you my AA sponsor?" he spat, irritated at the flak. Like his kids. Like his exes.

"No, Alex," she said, her voice softening, shying away from his intemperance. "It's just... I don't know... Everyone says it's a damned good thing you got on the wagon..."

"Because sometimes, you fall off the wagon," he whispered, as though it would make sense to someone who had never been where he'd been. She fell silent as the car – and his stomach – bucked and shuddered through more potholes and deep puddles. Alex was grateful for the silence. His eyes kept unwittingly falling closed, and when they did, his head spun around until he forced them open.

After a while, she said, "Have you ever decided that you'd had enough?"

"Drink?" He wrinkled his brows together. "Well, not until I black out. That's the damn problem."

"No, not that. Criminal justice."

"Every morning," he quipped.

"Be serious."

He didn't really follow. It was not the sort of conversation one should have while drunk, or sober for that matter. "What else would I do?"

"What keeps you going?"

"Dunno. The prospect of unemployment." Still hiding under the wiseass, he realized.

"There are other jobs."

"For you. You're smart, you're young, you're pretty, you're a lawyer. There are a million jobs for anyone with a law degree. You can do whatever you want."

"That's not the point. What's the law *doing*, Alex? What are we doing? Are we somehow standing between good and evil? Is that it? Is David LaValle evil? Are we for executing him?"

"I don't know." He bit into his lower lip; it was peeling and cracked, bleeding a little. He tasted the salty blood and scrubbed it off with the back of his hand. Pain thumped obstinately against his forehead. The alcohol had dehydrated him.

"I'm tired of the violence. It's just relentless. Every day, I look at my pile of cases... All the horrible, stomach-turning things people have done to each other. Things you don't want to ever think about. Pictures I'll never unsee. But I have to think about it every day. And now the state is the perpetrator of violence too."

"You could ask your boss to transfer you to Rackets or Cybercrime."

Oblivious to his sensible suggestion, she asked, "You don't wonder...how can people behave with such malevolence and cruelty towards one another? You must think about it."

"I really try not to. I'm a voice for the dead. That's how I think about it. They can't tell us how they ended up that way, so I gotta figure it out."

Water shot across the windshield when they splashed through the river caused by an overflowing storm gutter. The car wiggled its rear end as the wheels momentarily lost contact with the asphalt.

"I wish I could see it that way," she said sadly. "That's a nice way to look at it."

The inside of the car swirled around as his body absorbed that last swig of whiskey. Oh, shit, he used to handle his drink better than this. He shut his eyes, trying to slow the spinning, but that made it whirl faster. If he puked in the ADA's car, he would never live it down.

"I think I need out of it," Zoë said shakily.

"If that's what you feel you need to do..."

"I haven't told Simon I applied for a job litigating for the ACLU. I don't know how he'd take it. I don't know what he thinks." She frowned at the wet road. "You know the stories. Maybe I'm nothing more than his latest conquest in a long list of fresh-out-of-law-school ADAs."

"I think only you would really know if he gives a shit or not." He was fighting against gravity itself, tumbling down a tunnel. If Zoë wasn't insisting on this conversation, he would gladly let himself slide into that hole. Not an unpleasant place to be until you woke up with a killer hangover the next morning.

"He hasn't said anything to you?"

"Guys don't have that kind of conversation with each other. I mean, Simon doesn't with me." He thought about Simon leaving the bar with that actress. *Don't say anything.* Maybe the wrong thing, but ignorance is bliss, and sometimes, sharing a cab really is just sharing a cab. No, no sense in upsetting her further or impugning Simon when he had no evidence anyway that the man was guilty.

"I wish he had that conversation with me sometimes," she said wistfully. "He used to make me feel wanted, like we had something special. And that I wasn't just another drone in this big city. The usual crap people say, I guess. Now I'm not so sure. Maybe he doesn't give a shit about me, outside of how good I am in bed."

"You think?"

"I don't know," she repeated, her voice husky. "He says all the right things, but I don't know."

"I think he was upset when you stormed off after the hearing this morning."

"Why do you say that?"

"He spent half the day in that bar, didn't he? He was wasted out of his fucking mind by the time I showed up. I've never seen him that plastered, and I've been to a lotta bars with him. We probably ended up in a bar after every trial win – well, if it was my case – since he joined the Homicide Division. That was like '89. It's a lotta fucking bars."

"Oh," she said.

"That's the way *I* always used to deal with things when I was upset." Or the way he dealt with things now, because he wasn't a recovering alcoholic, merely an alcoholic who could not handle anything in his life without turning to drink.

"You were upset by today?"

"I guess so." His freshly inflamed ulcer burned like someone stubbed out a cigarette inside his stomach, and he rested his shoulder against the door, curling around himself in alcoholic nausea.

"By the hearing?"

"It wasn't a great start to the day."

Zoë downshifted as they approached an intersection. "What else happened?"

Chapter One

Alex sunk his teeth into a peeling tag of skin on his lip and looked skeptically across the table at Theresa Gillard. His mind flew through a million things that would be less unpleasant than a conversation with a psychiatrist about his thoughts and feelings. Prostate exams. Catheters. Depositions. The DMV. Internal Affairs. Passover with his mother. Ideally, this wouldn't take long, and it would be painless, but he wasn't convinced on any of those counts, and the meeting seemed onerous and inevitable. The last few weeks had been like a rickety, dangerous rollercoaster, the last time he felt really well in himself was, admittedly, a while ago, and after last night, his entire body twinged and ached like half a dozen guys had kicked the shit out of him.

The MNHS interview room seemed more confined, more intimate, the lights dimmer and the walls closer, than it had ever been when he used it for meetings or for naps when he stayed long past the end of a four-by-twelve. It was a sparsely functional room, walls painted with that semi-gloss municipal beige, a stained, slate grey carpet on the floor, and the ceiling fluorescents illuminating everything under a sallow, yellow glow. A bedraggled sofa with olive colored upholstery squatted along the wall under the window, while a flimsy folding table and three chipped plastic chairs occupied the center of the room.

Outside didn't enliven him, either. The sky looked bleak and monochrome, threatening snow. Grey clouds, grey buildings, grey pavement. What snow remained from the last big snowfall had become dirty slush, melting into grotesque shapes where the snowplows had piled it into banks along the sides of the roads. New York winters could make anyone gloomy.

His impatient irritability made no more of an impression on Theresa Gillard than the ominous clouds hovering darkly over the Harlem tenements. She was an imperturbable woman in her mid-fifties, her brown hair distinguished with streaks of grey, and her green eyes self-possessed and clear. Under normal circumstances, Alex knew her as a forensic psychiatrist, evaluating any hapless soul the police or District Attorney sent her way for their ability, or lack thereof, to appreciate and understand the nature and consequences of their actions, and she also ran her own small private practice on the Upper East Side. No manifestation of the fucked up psyche surprised her. Thus, she treated everyone, no matter how mad they were or what they had done, with unassailable serenity. Though professionally zen-like, she never acted cold nor clinical, embracing even the most distressed patients with empathy and compassion that seemed limitless.

Unfortunately, he was the subject of it, not an unstable witness or a bonkers perp. Because he had those orders, he'd come into work today at 0800 hours with a painful knot in his stomach. He'd signed into the command log at the Wheel desk and dodged the Wheel officer's questions about his hand, and then he spent the morning at his desk looking at a property log, writing up a DD-5, and reading a supplemental report Ray had written. His left hand was swaddled in a bloodstained ace bandage, frayed at the edges, wrapped around his palm, and then running in a lumpy, amateurish binding halfway up his forearm. It hurt like hell. He almost cried in agony when he tried typing with it, so he gave up, resting the arm limply on the desk while he wrote up the 'five and operated the computer with his right hand. One-handed typing frustrated him, a simple task like a 'five vexingly tedious, sluggish, awkward, taking twice as long as it should. Fed up, he took a breather, went for his third coffee, and his boss intercepted him at the coffee machine.

"She's here," Lieutenant Jo Gibson had said. "Interview room one. What did you do to your hand?" The lieutenant was a short, stocky black woman from the South Bronx. She kept her hair in tight, short curls and wore drab business suits, which she spiced up with colorful scarves and gaudy earrings. At once, she took no shit from anyone, and she could be hard and scrappy, but she had a warm spirit and was fiercely protective of her personnel.

"Cut it slicing a stale bagel, ma'am. You really think I need this?"

She had not said anything – she'd given him that look which rendered words unnecessary: *you know it and I know it*. His C/O had ordered him to see a shrink, so he had to see the shrink, and while it did not bear thinking about, in his heart he knew that she was saving his ass. She knew him too well.

Alex stood and paced about uneasily. "I can't be here all fucking day. I've got a lot to do." But he suspected, given the events of the last two or so weeks, that Gibson would be putting him on limited duty, chaining him to his computer for a while.

"We'll be here for as long as we need," Gillard replied and then said nothing.

There was a pause so long it felt like alcohol poured on a wound. Alex slowed his pacing, and then sighing deeply, he sank down again at the table and bit off the corner of his right thumbnail, as though anxiety squeezing his heart could be loosened if his teeth cut close enough to the sensitive part of the nail to hurt. A terrible habit he'd suffered his whole life. He wondered if Gillard noticed. Probably. After all, he would notice tics like that in an interrogation.

"All right," he grumbled. "Let's get this over with."

"I see you've hurt your hand. When did you do that?"

"Last night." The hand throbbed, threatening to detonate into excruciating pain if he tried doing anything, like typing, as he had discovered. But she was here to investigate what had gone wrong in his head – what the hell did his injured hand have to do with that? Everything.

"How did you injure it?"

At first, he didn't answer. He didn't remember, like he'd suffered a blackout. If he hadn't known for sure that he'd been stone cold sober, he would think he'd gotten wasted and done something stupid. But telling her that he didn't remember would make him look crazy, and he wanted to downplay that.

"I cut it slicing a stale bagel," he said with exaggerated conviction. "The knife slipped."

"You cut it slicing a bagel?" Gillard repeated.

"Yes," he insisted. "It's not hard to do."

Oh, fuck, she didn't believe him. Thousands of times, he had given a suspect or a witness the same look: that of utter disbelief. He had spent a lifetime becoming an expert in culling the truth from bullshit. Psychiatrists must do the same.

"Okay," said Gillard emotionlessly.

Alex swallowed and forced his features into a queer, numb smile. "Yeah." A dull kitchen knife had slipped on a bagel so hard you could have played hockey with it, a common enough injury. He could convince himself of that truth. That was why his bathroom had looked like a crime scene this morning. He'd cleansed his wounds there.

But another image flashed through his mind: the stained-glass panel on the bathroom door, shattered into jagged pieces, strewn across the tiles. This morning, he had made a half-assed attempt to sweep up the broken glass, but his hand hurt, his body was sore, restless sleep had exhausted him, and he didn't know how it got there in the first place. Slammed the door too hard? The apartment was one of those old New York City tenements, built in the second half of the nineteenth century and receiving the legal minimum of maintenance and modernization for much of its life. That ancient glass finally meeting its end was surely only a matter of time.

"What is it?" Gillard asked, noticing the faraway look in his eyes.

"Nothing."

She arched an eyebrow. "Are you sure?"

"My apartment's old, falling apart. Just thinking about what I need to fix."

"Mmmm. One could be very psychoanalytic about that," she suggested wryly.

"What?" And then he thought about it for a second. "The state of my apartment's hardly a metaphor for what's wrong with my fucking head." *Was it not?* Worn out and falling apart? "Part of the bathroom door fell off this morning. That's it."

She nodded, but with her head tilted to the side, and Alex wanted to run, her face was so unbearably kind. A wayward strand of silver hair fell in front of her eyes, and she pushed it behind her ear. Then she slid a piece of paper across the table, saying in an amicable tone, "Okay, Alex, have a look at this, all right? Just something we have to do to start with. It won't take you more than a couple minutes."

It was a multiple-choice questionnaire, which he found bleakly funny. "Like a *Miranda* waiver," he cracked. He sat in front of the questionnaire, a pen in his hand, worrying at it for a long while, each question confronting him with the monstrous pain he'd been fighting for weeks, an ache like a fracture in his heart, a tiredness so vast, the Kafkaesque sensation of losing his grip on reality itself. *Little interest or pleasure in doing things. Feeling down, depressed, hopeless. Having trouble falling or staying asleep.* Yes, yes, yes. Rate it on a one-to-five scale. The pen quivering in his hand, he circled fours.

He finished it, ten questions, and handed it back to Gillard, who turned it over, regarding the answers with an expression he couldn't read, and then slipping it into her briefcase.

"You were in a car accident two years ago," she said. "One where a young assistant district attorney died. Is that right?"

"Yeah." Blindsided, Alex defensively folded his arms over his chest. Where the fuck did that question come from? He felt his blood pressure rising.

"Can you talk about it?"

Once again, he stood up and walked over to the window, distracting himself by watching the ceaseless flow of cars and people on Broadway. Everyone in Harlem, going about their business like a normal day, and he was imprisoned in here. The day she'd asked him about hadn't been normal, either, and he never wanted to talk about it again. The capital sentencing hearing in the morning, arguing with his daughter in the afternoon, and then meeting those ADAs in the Blackthorn that evening. After that, a blacked-out space, and his memory returned while he lay strapped to a backboard in an ambulance, wondering how he got there.

Then came the dreadful, destructive thought: was it not his fault that Zoë was dead? A pointless question, and you would think a twenty-year veteran of the Homicide squad would know better than to ask it, but he'd never chased it from his mind.

"I was drunk," he snapped. "Zoë Sheehan was driving me home. Next thing I know, I'm in a bus, and EMS is asking me if I know who and where I am and what hurts."

"Is that all?"

He shot her an irascible glare. What information could she want that wasn't in the police reports from the accident scene? Nothing he could tell her.

Her expression remained unperturbable, but she scribbled on her notepad, as if his inability to remember the car crash had some significance beyond that of a mere alcoholic blackout.

She asked reflectively, "You don't seem very happy talking to me. Would you agree with that?"

She was a keen observer of people, as keen as any police officer. Caught out, he stared intently at the tenements and traffic. "No, I guess I'm not."

"Any reason?"

Because you'll make me see things I don't want to see, the shit I don't know how to talk about with anyone, and God forbid any cop beyond this squad finds out I'm talking to a shrink. But he couldn't articulate that. He caught his tongue between his back teeth.

"It's not an easy thing. But your friends and colleagues are concerned about you."

"I know," he admitted.

"Why might they be concerned?"

He returned to the table and studied his hands, the left swollen with motionless fingers under the bandage, the right strong, hardened and rough from years on the street. "What did Gibson say to you?"

"That your behavior has been concerning. Why might she say that?"

"I don't know," he breathed unhappily. "I've been a bit depressed. That's all. Is that more concerning than usual?"

"Your Lieutenant thinks it is. Do you?"

"I've had better weeks," he responded evasively. "But what are you gonna do?"

"Figure out why you've been feeling the way you're feeling and find a way for you to feel better."

His throat hurt like he'd swallowed steel wool. "I'm depressed because it's the fucking holidays. Always reminds me of how shit my relationship with my kids is. Gibson's never made me talk to a shrink before."

"There's more to it than that, isn't there?"

He knew that the answer was yes, but he was afraid, and he didn't answer.

She glanced down at her notes. "Tell me about the cases you had. Starting with the last week of October."

"We were working one involving the death of an autistic boy at a place called the Elm Tree Care Home in Washington Heights," he said, his shoulders sagging. Gibson had ordered him to be here, and Gillard had

66

light and power in her. His emotions were scattered, frail, damaged, and the pain in his hand wore him down so much he marveled that he had written up half a DD-5. "Then there was that armed robbery in Harlem, which we worked without a break. Then the next day, we had a Brooklyn assistant district attorney DOA in his apartment."

"Two new cases in twenty-four hours," she mused.

"I guess that was unusual. At least now. It was what we did all the time until about the mid-90s, but you shoulda seen what a shithole this place was then. And I was a lot younger."

"Ray said you stopped being quite yourself after that," she commented.

As if he could not rest his eyes anywhere, he looked at his bandaged hand, and then the window, and then the door, the squad room, life, on the other side. She had talked to Ray. He wondered what his partner had said about him. Between bouts of disapproval over aspects of Alex's life, like being a recovering alcoholic, a divorcee, a very lapsed, non-practicing Jew, Ray could be a good friend. Really, he was a good partner, a good cop, loyal and honest, with a perspicacious, analytic mind suited to detective work.

No, you couldn't fault Ray, as a partner or as a detective. But he wasn't James Hurley. With James, Alex had the telepathic connection that sometimes gets forged between police partners, where you know exactly what your partner is thinking and what he will do, maybe even before he does. There were still things about Ray that Alex didn't understand. You didn't always know what side of Ray you were going to get; the moralistic, God-fearing proselytizing Catholic evangelist, or the incisive gentle, and funny friend. How could Ray's faith be so absolute when he did this job? Alex thought that religion was primarily the delusion of having control over your fate, or the bigger delusion that bad shit happened for a reason, when the one thing you learned working homicide cases was that people didn't, and the universe was heartless, capricious and arbitrary.

"We were up all night working that robbery-homicide case," he explained. "A cop was killed. That fucks with your head." The stress of the conversation compressed his lungs like a beam fallen across his chest.

"We'll get to that. Let's start with this case – the autistic victim. You went to New Jersey for it. To interview some potential witnesses?"

Those three months could have been three years. Three months ago, he'd still been right enough in himself. In the intervening weeks, he had tried to get back there but couldn't, and he was homesick, not for a geographical location, but for a feeling of wellness, of wholeness, of normality, that he had lost. He felt as though he had traveled a long and weary way and now only wanted to return home, but it seemed as if an endless, dark sea lay between here and there, and he didn't know how to cross it.

Chapter Two

October 26th

An ambulance had been called to the Elm Tree Home, a private residential care facility for disabled children in Washington Heights. The subject of the call, one of the young residents, was DOA when EMS arrived. Consequently, detectives from the 34th Precinct squad showed up to investigate, and they brought in Manhattan North Homicide. The first thing Alex, Ray, and the Three-Four detectives did was antagonize the staff at the care home by treating it like a crime scene: securing it and removing everyone from the immediate premises. The staff resisted, insisting that the residents would be disturbed by the chaos of cops everywhere and half the building cordoned off by crime scene tape. And the boy had just died. That was it. It wasn't a crime scene.

At the time, as he coolly explained the finer points of death investigation procedures to the agitated manager, Alex got a funny feeling in his gut about the place, and his gut was rarely wrong. It wasn't wrong this time, either, because the assistant Medical Examiner determined that the boy, Peter Kazparek, a seventeen-year old black male from Trenton, New Jersey, had died of a cardiac arrest, but she also found contusions covering his body. She listed the case as pending, which meant not committing the state of New York to a manner of death, leaving the door open for the detectives to continue their investigation.

Alex and Ray hauled the manager and several staff members into the interview room at the Three-Four and presented them with this evidence. They explained that Peter was severely autistic, with a habit of self-harming, throwing himself against walls and so on. Alex and Ray ran this theory past the assistant ME who had done the autopsy, Dr. Miriam Shapiro, and she had scowled, calling that theory utter crap. You cannot get the sort of injuries that boy had from self-harming alone. Impossible.

With it looking increasingly suspicious, Alex and Ray got a warrant for the care home's CCTV tapes and accessed Peter's medical records. The CCTV from around the time of death showed Peter sprawled across gym mats, flailing about in a fit of awkward, uncoordinated violence, four attendants grabbing him, pinning him down while he convulsed, and they held him there for several minutes until he stopped struggling. He apparently stopped breathing as well, because that was when the staff panicked and phoned 911.

A smoking gun – except it wasn't. The care home had an explanation for that too. They told the detectives that the technique the staff used to subdue Peter was called "therapeutic crisis intervention," supposedly a safe way of restraining someone who might otherwise harm themselves or others. And Peter, prone to fits of violence, occasionally required such restraint.

The medical records also revealed that Peter had a cardiac condition and a sordid history of what the staff euphemistically called "challenging behavior." He had come to the Manhattan care home, apparently known for its willingness to take on "difficult" cases, after a stint at a place in Trenton, closer to his parents. The cardiac condition suggested his death may have been bad luck and criminal charges were not warranted. But the "therapeutic crisis intervention" seemed less than therapeutic and had resulted in physical injuries, which suggested they were. Gibson told her detectives to take a trip to Jersey for a chat with the people who had worked in Peter's previous care facility.

And that was how they ended up in Trenton. They walked into the home, a squat single-story building, square and bland, with a courtyard in the middle and handrails level with their hips attached to every wall. There were some inoffensive landscape paintings of bucolic fields. In the reception office, they held out their shields, Alex saying to the secretary, "I'm Detective Alex Boswell. This is Detective Ray Espinosa. We're from the NYPD. Is there a manager, or someone in charge, we could speak with?"

The secretary rolled a pen between her fingers. "What's it in regards to?"

"An ongoing investigation," explained Ray.

That didn't reassure the secretary, but she muttered, "I'll call him"

"Thanks," said Ray.

The manager's name was Raul Mondragón, and he took the detectives to his office further along the hall, saying, "NYPD? I'm guessing this has something to do with Peter Kazparek."

"Yeah, what do you know about that?" asked Alex, opening his memo book.

Mondragón shrugged. "Just the blurb I read in the *Times*. Such a shame. He could be a nice boy. What is it I can help you with?"

"'Could be?' We're just wanting to know what he was like when he was here, why he left, if he was any trouble."

"Um, you see, Peter had severe learning disabilities and was mostly nonverbal, although he had a few words and could communicate a little bit. When he got frustrated, he tended to lash out and would attempt to injure himself and others. We are not equipped and our staff generally doesn't have the training to deal with an individual with needs as serious as Peter's. He needed 24/7 care and supervision, which we don't provide. We are just a day center. Have you spoken to his parents?"

"Yeah," said Alex. "They said that it wasn't safe anymore for him to stay at home and needed a place with 24/7 care."

"It's a hard thing, to send your son away. I think they hoped that he would be okay being here with us during the day and home at night."

"As I understand things," Alex said, "He wasn't."

"No," Mondragón agreed.

"Is that why he left?" Ray asked.

"His parents were struggling to work with him. He was a six-foot six boy with profound LDs who would get extremely frustrated when he could not communicate. We had recommended to his parents and Social Services that they seek out a residential facility with more extensive resources than ours that would do a more effective job meeting his needs."

Alex turned his memo book to a new page. "Were you aware of any medical conditions?"

"Many of our service users have them," explained Mondragón.

"But did Peter?"

Mondragón flicked his eyes to the side. "Sorry, I can't really discuss a service user's medical issues."

"Well," said Ray. "We were told that he had some kind of heart condition. Can you confirm or deny that?"

71

"I guess I can confirm that," Mondragón answered uncomfortably.

"Do you know what, if any treatment he had for it?"

"I am afraid you will have to ask his parents."

"We did," said Ray. The parents had been treating the condition and had asserted that the care home in the Heights had been aware of it. "He was."

"Well, you know as much as I do. I imagine his parents were forthcoming with you."

"They were, but they've been understandably distraught."

"Of course."

Switching subjects, Alex queried, "Did you ever have to physically restrain Peter?"

"Oh, no. We don't do that here."

"Not even if someone is violent, huh?"

"We train our staff to remove themselves from any potentially violent situation. But it's not really an issue anyway. Our service users generally aren't violent or dangerous."

"Generally? Was Peter violent or dangerous?"

"As I said, he lashed out when he got frustrated. But we tried to use other ways to keep him from damaging anyone or anything. No restraint."

"Do you think he might have ever required it?'

Mondragón twitched his head. "Every service has its own way of managing problems. I could see how that might be one way of working with an individual such as Peter, and under some circumstances, perhaps it was necessary. He could be very challenging."

More waffle than you would find at an IHOP. Twirling the pen in his fingers, Alex met Ray's gaze in a tiredly eye-rolling way. Then he said, "What do you know about something called 'therapeutic crisis intervention?'"

Mondragón shrugged blankly.

"It's a technique for restraining people," explained Ray. "Are you aware of it?"

"I am aware that it exists but it's not something we train our staff to do. As I said, we are a day center, and we usually do not work with people who have more difficult needs."

"Is it safe?"

72

"It is generally regarded as safe, yes."

"Can you tell us what it is?" Alex was losing hope that they would get any more out this guy beyond unenlightening management-speak.

"Not really. As I said, Detective, our philosophy here is not to use any kind of restraint, but in facilities where they take individuals who may occasional require more direct intervention, it is an accepted practice. Look, I have a meeting at two. If you have any further questions, I'd be happy to help, but I have to be at this meeting."

Alex and Ray said they would be in touch and let him go, before asking staff they saw around the facility if they had known Peter. Several did, but they didn't proffer any new information. Then they cornered a female carer at the coffee machine.

"I didn't know him well," she said. "I mean, I've been here for a while but didn't work with him."

"Any reason why not?" asked Ray.

"Only men were allowed to work with him," she replied.

Alex threw his fishing line into the water. "Because he was violent?"

The woman looked uncomfortable and stirred sugar into her coffee. "Well, that was generally believed to be the reason. It was never really stated outright. At least not to us."

"So maybe holding the guy down for however long was legit," pondered Alex, thinking aloud as they left the care home.

"And the bruises?" Ray asked.

"Probably not legit," he sighed. "If they were caused by what we saw on the CCTV."

"ME says they couldn't be the result of self-harm. And some of them were old. That could mean a pattern of abuse. Could you call it assault two?"

"I dunno. I think we'd better see what the DA wants to call it. If you assault someone and they die of a pre-existing medical condition as a result of your assault, what do you think that is?"

"Manslaughter? Criminal negligence? Do you know about the medical condition?"

It was like Penal Law jeopardy. "Yeah. You know about it."

"So, are you liable?"

"Dunno… Did you intend to cause injury?" Alex chewed on the inside of his lip.

"Probably not. It was reckless, maybe. Man two?"

"Should you have perceived a 'substantial and unjustifiable risk' that a reasonable person would have known? Anyway, I'm hungry." The whole justice system was predicated on what a 'reasonable person' should have known, done, or understood. The trouble was, Alex thought, most people weren't that reasonable. The archetypal 'reasonable man' in all the statutes, CPL, and case law was someone who didn't exist.

On their route back to the interstate, they stopped at a 7-11 in a service station on Route 9, picking up a snack. Ray bought an apple, while Alex bought a bag of potato chips and a Snickers bar, and they ate standing outside the car in front of the shop, breathing in the Jersey smell of smoky factories and chemicals. Part of the job. Grabbing what you could on the run. Ray, an exercise and health fanatic, always found fruit and wholesome sandwiches while Alex, a hedonist when it came to food, would nab whatever he saw. He promised himself he would compensate with a swim or a long walk.

"I think we gotta talk to more people who deal with guys like Peter," he commented between potato chips. "See if this sort of 'restraint' is standard practice in these places. He was big a guy. If someone like that starts throwing punches, what are you gonna do?"

"Has anyone looked for other complaints against the home in the Heights?" Ray said as he kept looking askance at Alex's lunch. "Jesus, Alex, a candy bar and potato chips. You must have a cast iron stomach."

"It's two out of five food groups. That makes it healthy." Alex laughed, because his stomach was anything but cast iron, its walls eroded by his years on the drink, and he kept antacids to hand. Cast iron! How he wished.

"Whatever you say, man. I feel ill looking at it."

"Potato chips are like a vegetable," Alex said.

"Yeah, in the same way French fries are."

Alex sneezed mid-eye-roll, the Jersey fumes crawling up his nasal passages. "They are. Anyways, me and Wheeler have been looking for complaints—"

"To the police?"

He shook his head and blew air through his nostrils. "I fucking wish. No one's complained about the place to the police."

"Social Services? ACS?"

"If they have, they're not saying."

"If these things happen, I imagine they try to keep them on the quiet side."

Alex washed down the potato chips with a diet coke. "What, you think the Elm Tree Home is regularly beating the crap outta the residents, and they're covering it up?"

"*You* were at the autopsy," Ray pointed out. "You saw the bruises on the kid. What do you think?"

Licking chocolate off his fingers, Alex replied, "Yeah, and Shapiro said his heart was likely to crap out anyway. I don't know what I think."

"Kid was definitely held down," contemplated Ray as he finished his sandwich. "Be nice if someone would give us a straight answer about how often it happened and what this 'therapeutic crisis intervention' shit actually means."

"Why would anyone give us a straight answer?" Alex said derisively. "No one's gonna say shit that makes them look culpable in a homicide."

"Or liable in a lawsuit."

"That too." He threw the plastic bag into the trashcan and then returned to the driver's seat. This trip fed his uncertainty. He drummed his fingers against the steering wheel. The cynical part of him wished that Shapiro hadn't pended the case, which would have effectively shitcanned the file. Then he would not be in New Jersey, driving himself crazy trying to figure out where bad luck ended and criminally negligent homicide began.

Somewhere around the exit for the Newark Airport, traffic slowed, forty miles per hour but moving. However, by the time they reached the I-78 exit, movement ceased. Red taillights flashed across four lanes of highway. Cars on the tunnel exit weren't budging, while ones on the Turnpike crept forward. It would be a slow drive to the George Washington Bridge. Ray fiddled with the radio, looking for a traffic report, but then a jam on the New Jersey Turnpike was a daily occurrence, not news. Finding nothing, he flicked it to classical, a slow modernist piece that would cure Alex's pernicious insomnia.

"Jesus," Alex sighed and took control of the radio and changed the channel again, finding 1970s rock, the Clash, 'London Calling.' Far more acceptable.

Ray grinned, "Reliving your misspent youth?"

75

"The '70s and '80s were the height of rock music. It's all been downhill since."

On their left, the flat, dirty industrial wasteland of Newark inched past. Factories, refineries, warehouses, the occasional tatty-looking strip mall and greasy diner, and rows of sand-blasted, decrepit apartments, while on their right were the docklands: industrial structures rising out of polluted swamp and mudflats. Container ships were berthed near grotty warehouses, and huge cranes hung their spidery metal arms over the brown and grey water. When the Turnpike rose in an overpass, they caught a glimpse of Manhattan's skyscrapers peeking out across the water from Bayonne. Then the Turnpike crossed the long causeway, flanked by marshes of long reeds, the occasional clump of trees, grey water, and hulking tower blocks across the inlet.

The road split in two after the airport, the 'local' lane on one side of a concrete barrier, with exits to places like Secaucus and Harrison veering off the sides, and the 'express' lane on the other side, where there would not be any exits until just before the George Washington Bridge, except for ones connecting the road to I-78 and the Holland Tunnel and I-80 a few miles north of that.

Brake, accelerate, brake. Alex's foot jerked over the gas but driving like an asshole would not get you there any faster. He let his unmarked silver Ford creep along.

His train of thought rolled away from the traffic. There must be paperwork if an incident occurred – same as with the police. If someone got violent, you had to write up a detailed report, especially if they or you were injured in the process. If there had been a pattern of incidents, there could be a trail of paperwork, unless they were covering it up.

Further north, they left the smoky industry behind. These were the more upscale suburbs of New York City. Large trees and office buildings flanked the interstate, but here, the towns were concealed by the trees and hedges planted alongside the Turnpike. Glimpses of office parks, houses, and strip malls flashed through the foliage. After a complicated junction with I-80 – apparently constructed by someone who had thrown a plate of spaghetti on the floor and declared it to be the design for a connection between two major interstates – the road slung around in an arc, angling east towards Manhattan. As it cut through Leonia, a few miles before the George Washington Bridge, the local and express lanes merged. The traffic came to a standstill. Cars jostled one another in slow motion as the two creeping columns of traffic blended together.

The mass of cars ahead of Alex lumbered forward like a huge, somnolent metal serpent. He tapped the accelerator. Every light on the Crown Victoria's dashboard lit up. The accelerator sunk to the floor, and the engine didn't utter a sound. Suddenly, the car rolled backwards, a sickening lurch towards the tractor-trailer truck behind them.

"Fuck," Alex hissed. His heart stopped with the car. In a panic, he slammed on the hazards, and then he yanked up on the emergency brake and thrust the gear shifter into park.

"What the hell," Ray said. "What are you doing?"

"I don't know. Engine's just cut out. It's not going." Stating the obvious. It clearly wasn't going. He swore at department cars.

The truck at their back blasted them with his horn. Another tractor-trailer truck merging from the other lane brushed so close they could see every hose in its rusty undercarriage. It also sounded its horn. The traffic that had been moving all too slowly a second ago was now moving far too quickly. The glacier of vehicles would crush them as it squeezed their stricken car on all sides.

Ray grabbed the police radio, speaking to Central, explaining that the car seemed to have died, announcing their car number and position.

Alex turned the ignition off, his go-to response for when his computer froze, and it usually fixed it. He didn't think a restart would work with a car, but anything seemed worth trying. He turned the key. The engine grumbled to life, shuddering. The dashboard lights flicked on and off. He gingerly pressed his foot against the gas, and the engine rumbled, the rev counter shooting up. He shifted the car into "drive." It jumped forward.

"It's going, it's working. Tell Central we're all right."

Fear tightened around his innards like a rubber band. He did his New-Yorker-aggressive-driving best, darting and weaving across the three lanes merging into their lane, forcing open gaps between vehicles, until he edged into the new outside lane, beneath a green sign warning drivers that this was the last exit before the toll on the George Washington Bridge. Then he swerved off the interstate, towards Leonia and Palisades Park.

Ray was saying, "Maybe we should just get back to the office as soon as possible," but Alex ignored him, driving through a leafy neighborhood in Leonia where he found a restaurant and several shops with a big parking lot.

Here, he stopped and then slumped back against the driver's seat. He breathed deeply for a minute or two. The rubber band around his diaphragm slackened. His hands had a slight tremor. The potato chips churned uncomfortably around in his stomach, and he wished he hadn't eaten the entire bag. Yet nothing that serious had happened. The car had almost broken down in the middle of the New Jersey Turnpike. That was all.

"Are you all right?" Ray looked perplexed.

"Yeah," Alex said unconvincingly. "I just wanna check the engine." Heading off any further questions, he popped the hood and went outside to look. Standing there, he stared at the engine and the innards of the car, the inexplicable mass of pipes and hoses, reminded that he didn't possess any useful knowledge whatsoever about automotive mechanics. He didn't even own a fucking car. "What do you know about cars, Ray?"

"Not a lot. I pay a guy to fix mine. Well, we should check the water levels."

"It didn't overheat," observed Alex, but Ray was screwing the cap off the expansion tank and peering inside. It was full. Overheating hadn't been their problem. Having not found any absolution by gazing at the engine, they slammed the hood shut.

"You know what Ford's an acronym for, right?" said Alex.

"No, what?"

"Found On Road Dead."

Ray smiled. "Want me to drive?"

Alex tossed him the keys. "If it starts."

It did. Alex pushed an antacid out of the pill packet in his coat pocket while Ray drove through the side streets and followed the signs directing them to the interstate. They merged onto the Turnpike through the EZ-Pass lane, and then traversed the George Washington Bridge, its great iron trestles and skeletal towers filling their vision, the high rises and walk-up apartments of upper Manhattan ahead of them.

Ray's cell phone rang as they bounced and rattled through potholes. "You'd better get that, Lex."

Alex flipped open the phone. "Boswell."

"Oh, hi, Alex." Jo Gibson's drawling South Bronx voice, crackly and hard to hear. "Where the hell are you guys?"

"We're on the GW Bridge. Nearly back."

"It's taken you a whiie."

"Traffic's horrible. And we had a bit of, uh, trouble with the car. But it seems okay now."

"Right. How'd that interview go?"

"Inconclusive. Look, we'll brief you when we get back."

He couldn't brief her now. His head started hurting, and he had lost the capacity to cogently think about the case, much less update his boss. One moment, he had a clear idea of what their next step should be; the next, he didn't. And every time they passed a truck, his heart beat faster, and he flinched a little.

Chapter Three

October 28th

Alex lay on his side dozing, ensnared in a dream that blurred into reality, fuzzily aware of the light outside and the soft, cozy flannel sheets warming his skin. The piercing cry of his cell phone shocked him into consciousness. His eyes flew open, and he felt groggy, disoriented. Where was the phone? Why was the wall in the wrong place? Then he knew; he wasn't at home. He was downtown, at Becky's apartment.

It woke Becky, who said grumpily, "Aren't you going to get that?"

"It'll be Ray," he murmured, groping for the phone. Only Ray or his lieutenant would be calling at 0600. The words "Ray - cell" flashed on the screen. He flipped open the phone and said in a phlegmatic tone, "Hi, Ray."

"I know it's early, but Night Watch detectives called the L-T. She wants us forthwith at a homicide on West 123rd and Malcolm X," announced Ray gruffly.

"Ah, damn," Alex breathed.

"It was an armed robbery of a bodega," said Ray. "One person killed."

"A stick-up job in Harlem couldn't keep for two hours? What the fuck is the point of Night Watch?"

"The vic's a cop, Lex."

"Oh, fuck." He sat up. A cop. His stomach collapsed inwards, the sadness cutting his bowels like a knife. There but for the grace of God. In fairness, he was due to catch a fatal police shooting. His last one had been LaValle, four years ago, hellish enough to give him the karma to not catch any more for a while. His karma was up. "I'll be there as soon as I can. I'm in TriBeCa."

"TriBeCa?" Ray sounded momentarily confused. "Oh, you're really not—"

"I'll be there in the hour." Alex cut Ray off before he heard any more about it. His relations with Becky Schreiber had never fit into Ray's paradigm of acceptable relationships. Becky worked for an environmental NGO somewhat attached to the UN, and they had an on-again-off-again, at times not-a-relationship, because she was technically married, albeit separated from her husband, and he was wary of anything resembling real commitment. Ray thought of marriage, no matter how rocky, as a categorical prohibition against sleeping with anyone else.

But what the hell did Ray know? He didn't know that Becky had taken Alex to a place where he was not chained to his past, to disappointment, catastrophe, and more baggage than JFK. His last fling, with a *New York Times* reporter, had started in February '02 and disintegrated by April '02, brought to its knees by his personality flaws and the requirements of the job. Too many planned weekends away unraveling because he had to suddenly work, too much unexpected overtime when a case demanded it, and his melancholy temperament too much for her to deal with.

He'd stayed the hell away relationships after that. But at the start of his affair with Becky several months ago, each day they spent together had brought him new sight and wonder at a city whose dark secrets he knew only too intimately. She showed him the city in a way he had never seen it. The skyline of shining glass and light rearing out of the East River as you followed the pedestrian pathway on the Brooklyn Bridge with the herds of wide-eyed tourists. All his life here, he'd never walked across the bridge, just driven, swearing at other drivers. Or the way the silver Art Deco arches of the Chrysler Building reflected every nuance of daylight, from burning with red hues in the sunset, to glittering with a rainbow of colors in the sunshine or silvery grey in the rain. Or the early morning walks with the steam rising from the manhole covers, the smoky light of dawn slanting amongst the buildings, casting a rosy glow on the stone. Or a fresh cup of coffee from a Greenwich Village café, shared with laughter and affection, tasting better than any coffee he had before.

After his break-up in 1992 with Charlotte Anderson, he had disbelieved that he could experience the breathtaking high you get from an intense relationship ever again. Surely, he'd become too cynical, his heart too hardened. But he had. He'd discovered that he was not used up, cast aside, collecting rust like the derelict subway lines.

"What's going on?" grumbled Becky from the other side of the bed when Alex dropped the phone on the floor.

"Work," he said, lying back down for a second, just to get his head together. A cop-shooting. It would be messy and terribly sad and hopefully it would not reawaken the trauma from his own. Then his mind pivoted back to Becky. Had the sun only shone for a moment? The wonder he had felt three months ago had lost its luster. She'd been acting prickly and distant for the last couple weeks. His two days off had been reduced to one, and there had been an all-night stakeout to apprehend a perp, so when he'd seen Becky on his RDO, he had been exhausted and somewhat cantankerous.

He had resolved to act less self-centered, more committed, and make coffee and breakfast before his eight-by-four started. On his next RDO, he might use the extra money he made doing all that overtime to take her to a Broadway show or a nice restaurant. That would make up for everything, for not being there when he said he would and for being an asshole because he'd been tired. But now he had to throw on clothes and run. No time to discuss going to a show.

"A murder?" She stayed on the far side of the bed. A month ago, she would lie on his chest or shoulder, capturing every second together. She said she liked listening to his heart.

"Yeah. Some kinda stick-up job in Harlem."

"What's a stick-up job?"

"Oh, an armed robbery." He refrained from identifying the vic's job. It might freak her out. Then he heaved himself out of bed and kicked around in the bottom of Becky's closet for the spare suit he sometimes kept here. It was heaped in the back of the closet, looking no better than the one he had worn yesterday. If he'd been at home, he would cram in a high-speed shower, but as he was at the opposite end of town and the hot water in Becky's shower didn't work, he had to live without one. He doused himself in deodorant. As he got dressed, he felt her eyes on him, reproachful, anxious.

"What is it?" he asked.

"Nothing."

Nothing. The most inappropriately used word in the English language. He knew that when his ex-wife or various girlfriends said 'nothing,' it almost always meant something quite important that he had to figure out for himself, because they weren't going to tell him. He sighed heavily. There didn't seem to be anything to say, yet in the pregnant silence that followed as he buttoned up his shirt, there was far more than nothing to it. The air in the tiny bedroom felt stuffy and stale, the air limpid, the walls pressing inwards.

"I'm sorry I have to run off like this," he said.

"Oh, don't be," she replied. "That's the job, isn't it?"

"I can make you coffee before I go," he offered.

"No, don't worry about it. You have to go all the way uptown."

He sat on the small wooden chair in the corner of the bedroom tying his shoes. Oh, there was so much he was desperate to say to her, but not now, not when he needed to fly uptown with a clear head, and perhaps not ever, because, as his ex-wife and her psychiatrist would happily attest, he had never been any good at talking about his innermost thoughts, feelings, and fears.

He risked saying, "Next week sometime?"

A moment's hesitation. She burrowed further into the duvet. "Well, I'm away next week."

That buffeted him with surprise and disappointment. "Ah, right. You hadn't said."

"I'm visiting my parents."

He remembered that her parents lived upstate, in one of those comically misnamed towns on the frozen plains of upstate New York, like Geneva, Rome, or Liverpool.

"I'm sorry," she said unconvincingly, as if she really wasn't. "I should have mentioned that."

"It's not a big deal. Maybe the weekend then?"

"Yes, maybe."

He wasn't reassured. The chill in the room seemed colder than those frozen plains upstate. God knows, he'd been through enough to read the signs. Given how he had spent the last few months refusing label it as a *relationship,* he was surprised by how sick he felt at the prospect of it ending. But he had to be sanguine about it. He bit his lip, tying his tie around his neck. A blizzard always followed clear skies, the way of the world, or the way of his world. With a chesty breath, he flung on his coat. "Have a good time with your folks."

He joined a line in front of a street van on West Broadway and Reade Street with a cold cluster of other hunched over coffee addicts, their caffeine deprived, grey faces skewed in sleepy discomfort, like forgotten extras from a zombie movie. The Pakistani guys in the van understood New York efficiency, swiftly moving through the line. Alex ordered a black coffee and a bagel, and then he trotted to the subway, eating as he went.

Had he ever known where he stood with Becky? She had her own baggage, an ailing mother upstate, a kid in college, and the not-ex-husband, some IT guy working for JP Morgan earning a considerably higher salary than a cop. Had she not tried ending it last month, but then changed her mind? Was that where the excitement resided: in the uncertainty, in the constant threat of implosion that shadowed them, in their histories of relationship dysfunction? It was like riding the rollercoaster at Coney Island, the one that twists and rolls upside down. Only he wished his heart didn't flap whenever he saw her name on his cell phone. There was a lot to be said for being single and not giving a shit.

0615 on a Saturday, and the Chambers Street subway station seemed reposed, bereft of its anthill of frantic commuters. Signs on the walls warned that due to weekend work on the tracks, 1 and 3 trains would only be running every half an hour, the 2 suspended, and after 14th Street, the trains would only be making express stops. The MTA had gone out of its way to fuck with Alex's plan: transferring to the A or C at 59th and taking it to 125th.

He gulped down the lump of stress in his throat. Anyone experienced in the art of New York City subways knows how to alter their route on the spur of the moment, when the trains don't go when and where they are supposed to. He would take the 1 to 72nd, and then walk the two blocks to the A and C line station at 72nd and Central Park West. Then, to his dismay, his Metrocard bitched that it had run out of money. Losing patience, he had the customary argument with the bad-tempered machine, imploring it accept his crumpled twenty-dollar bill.

A scruffy, bearded homeless guy wearing a threadbare green coat and baggy grey trousers was busking in the tunnel, mangling guitar chords, singing 'Born in the USA' off key. *You're sure as fuck not Springsteen,* Alex thought testily. The jangling, out-of-tune guitar echoed hollowly, driving nails into his nervous system. The busker was abysmal, failing to eke a single in-tune note out of his voice or the guitar. Alex released a weighty sigh. A cop-killing, tensions with Becky, weekend track works screwing with his subway line, Metrocards, and now atrocious subway station buskers. Yeah, he must be stressed out and irritable. It had been a long year, and the coming of November and December always depressed him.

He rested his back against one of the pillars, waiting for the 1. But he did not see the two bright lights shining down the subway tunnel or the silver train screeching and rattling beside the platform. Rain mingled with blood on a wet, dark road. The lights of emergency services vehicles flashed across his vision. Then the train's brakes hissed. His mouth hung open, and he gasped for air.

What the hell was that? Long after his shooting in 1987, he'd heard gunshots that weren't there, or saw visions of his partner bleeding on the ground. But this wasn't that. Whatever – he tried shaking it off as he boarded and found an empty seat in the corner, where he folded his arms over his belly and closed his eyes.

A thudding pain rapped against the back of his eye sockets. Static buzzed in his head. Like a radio stuck between frequencies, it overran the roaring wheels, the shuffling commuters, the white tiles flashing along the walls and station names through the windows. Canal Street. Houston Street. Christopher Street-Sheridan Square. It sounded distant and strange, the geography of some foreign and remote country. Nothing felt familiar. It wasn't his city. It didn't feel like his city.

Alex didn't know what to make of it, but he felt frazzled and uneasy. Had Becky upset him this much? Or the cop-shooting? The steel and iron guts of the subway station solidified in his vision as the train decelerated, and the conductor announced the next stop, 168th Street, Washington Heights.

168th! Fuck! He'd forgotten – and not noticed – that the 1 wasn't making the local stops. It had shot from 96th to 168th, rising above the city on the elevated tracks and then plunging underground again, and him oblivious to the appearance and disappearance of daylight through the windows. The train screeched into the 168th Street station.

Alex realized that not only had he failed to get off at 72nd, he hadn't finished his coffee, either. He'd clutched the warm paper cup for the ride, nearly the entire length of Manhattan.

Not in a good state of mind for working a cop-shooting, he ran off the train, traversing through the narrow tunnels and fetid air until he got to the A and C platform, where he downed his coffee in one gulp, enduring the gnawing pain below his ribs. At least the A line cooperated, a train appearing, its headlights throwing a golden light down the black tunnel. Holding his gut, he boarded and took the train to 125th Street, this time keeping his eyes fixed on the window.

Ten minutes after he climbed out of the subway station, he arrived at the crime scene, a block of shops on the corner of West 123rd and Malcolm X Boulevard. Over a dozen blue and white police cars were parked like a dealer's lot: in the middle of the road, pulled on the curb, double-parked. They'd set up a staging area between 123rd and 124th, and Alex signed himself into the scene. People he knew nodded at him, grunting, "Hey, Lex," or "Hey, Boswell," depending on how well they knew him. Their faces were dour and grey. Police tape cordoned off a bodega called Armando's, and gawking passerby hovered beyond the staging area.

Alex found Ray beside the victim, a thirty-something white male wearing a leather jacket and jeans, prone on his back, his arms flung to the side, and two bloody bullet holes in his chest. Blood stained his plaid shirt and oozed into tacky pools on the sidewalk. A detective? A plainclothes unit like AntiCrime? An off-duty officer? No one Alex knew, thank God.

"Whaddaya got?" he asked.

"Took you a while," grumbled Ray.

"It's Saturday," Alex replied, tetchy. "Trains are fucked."

Ray nodded his understanding of weekend tribulations with the MTA and handed Alex the vic's shield. "His name is Officer John Irvine. Works at the Five-Two in the Bronx, in a plainclothes AntiCrime unit. He was off-duty. Had just finished his tour."

"Did he try to stop the robbery?"

"Must have." Ray gestured towards the victim's gun lying next to him, already tagged by CSU. "CSU's found a couple bullets, 9mm

Parabellum, possibly from an NYPD service weapon. They're across the street. His gun is missing five rounds."

Good for him, thought Alex, although not quite good enough, as the robber had left the scene and this guy was dead. Alex handed the shield back to Ray, and then bent over the body, examining the bullet holes, one a few inches below the throat, the other on the left side of the chest, near the heart.

"Can we move him?" he asked Ray.

"Yeah, we're good," Ray replied.

With the help of the assistant ME, they tipped the body sideways, searching for exit wounds. Irvine's back was soaked with blood. Breathing through his clenched teeth, Alex prodded around, but the blood and the shredded flesh and leather jacket concealed bullet holes, so, with great care, Alex removed the jacket. Then he easily located the exit wounds, one in the middle of the back, one on the right side. Two bloodied .45 caliber bullets lay tagged, several feet from the policeman's body.

Pain shot through his knees as he got to his feet. Flexing his legs to shake off the stiffness, he scanned the sidewalk, the street, the gutters around the vic, wondering where other slugs might have landed. He sketched the crime scene in his memo book, a stickman for the victim, square boxes with labels like 'bodega' for shops and apartments, rectangular boxes with wheels for cars, 'x's where slugs had already been found, a gun-shaped squiggle for the dead policeman's firearm.

As Alex drew his crime scene, a uniformed officer from the Two-Eight Precinct approached them, asking if they wanted to speak with the young man who worked in the bodega. The guy's name was Tyler Walker, black, twenty-something, and he sat in the back of an ambulance, a blanket draped over his shoulders, shakily clutching a cup of tea with both hands.

"Can you tell us what happened?" asked Alex after he and Ray had introduced themselves. The poor guy looked like he'd suffered the biggest shock of his life, going into work at his dull, mundane job, like every other day, and then staring down the barrel of a gun.

"I had just gone into the shop and was putting stuff on the shelves," he explained. "The doors were open. We'd just gotten a delivery, you know. Delivery truck left and these two guys, they came into the shop. Wearing ski masks over their faces. They both had guns. They told me to empty out the till. I says, we don't got nothing in the till. Person who closes the store at night puts everything in a safe. Then they says, 'Then empty the safe.' I says, I don't gotta key. They stick a gun in my face and say, 'You sure 'bout that?'"

"Did you have a key?" Ray asked.

"Yeah, we all know where the key is. How else we supposed to put money in the safe at night? I did. I open it. I didn't know what else to do. Gave them everything that was in it…"

"How much do you think that was?" asked Ray.

"I dunno… like a thousand bucks. Maybe a bit less. Maybe a bit more."

"You don't know?" echoed Alex, his eyebrows rising doubtfully.

"Naw, man. The night person tallies that up. I wasn't on night shift last night."

"Who would?" The store, if staying in the ballpark of legit business, would record their takings somewhere.

"The night shift dude," repeated Tyler, "They woulda written it on a notebook that we keep under the till."

Send someone to look for that, Alex told himself, catching Ray's eye. Then he asked the witness, "Can you describe them, the robbers, at all?"

"They had ski masks and gloves on. But they was both white. One was short, the other taller."

"If they had masks on, how do you know they were white?" asked Ray.

Tyler rolled his eyes, as if only an idiot would ask that question. "Man, they *sounded* white."

"Do you remember what else they were wearing?" Alex insisted. 'They sounded white' was a weak-as-shit identification in court, although it made perfect sense on the streets.

"Not really. I was just looking at the gun."

"Then what happened?"

"They left the shop. I tried to phone the police, but that's when I heard the shooting. I hid behind the counter. Kept my head down until the shooting stopped and heard the ambulances and police car sirens."

"You didn't see who was shooting?" asked Ray.

"No. No way. I was lying flat on the floor."

"Any idea how many shots were fired?"

Tyler pursed his lips in a fearful frown. "Lots."

"Thanks, Tyler," Alex said, smiling dourly. "You'll be taken to the 28th Precinct to give that statement to a detective in writing, all right?" On first glance, the witness appeared too traumatized to be a suspect, but they had to rule him out, or in. He would be searched for a gun or money, his hands swabbed for GSR, his name run through assorted databases, and in the meantime, Alex would continue his dialogue with the crime scene.

"Yo, Boswell."

Alex whipped his head around, seeing two uniforms attached to a paunchy black guy, whose hands were cuffed behind his back, but he carried himself as though being arrested was part of his daily routine.

One of the uniforms said, "These are homicide detectives, Jamal. You need to tell them what you told us."

The wit made nervous, sporadic eye contact with the detectives.

"What?" said Alex impatiently.

"Uh, see that green Dodge parked there..." stammered the witness.

Alex glanced at the car, a beat-up green Dodge Intrepid, jacked up on three wheels so it tilted at a precarious angle, and one wheel removed, lying flat on the road beside it. An NYPD Traffic Unit tow truck waited behind the Dodge.

"I was uh... takin' that wheel off –"

"Why were you taking the wheel off?" asked Ray. "You gotta flat?"

"Ummm," wavered the witness.

"He was stealing the tires. Big business 'round here," explained one of the uniforms.

"I figured." Alex rolled his eyes, thinking in some ways, Harlem had changed profoundly from the '80s and '90s, and in other ways, it hadn't changed at all. "Don't stop now. You were helping yourself to a wheel. Then what?"

"These two guys, white guys wearing ski masks, rush out of that grocery store with a bag and wavin' guns around. They come up to me and say, 'That's our car,' then start wavin' their guns in my face. I wasn't gonna take that shit, man, so I pull out my gun. Don't want to be getting involved in no violence, but you do what you gotta do."

Alex wondered if he had a permit for a gun. Unlikely. He asked, "Did you shoot at them?"

"They run off. But they'd robbed the store, you know."

There was a kind of moral hierarchy to criminality, reflected Alex. A guy who steals tires can be horrified by a couple guys who hold up a store. "Yeah, but did you fire your weapon?"

"One of them turned 'round, fired off a round at me. So yeah, I shot at them. Two rounds. Didn't hit anyone. They fired another round at me but missed. Then, outta nowhere, this guy, this white guy, he's shoutin', wavin' a badge, sayin' he's a cop. He's gotta gun too. One of the guys, he say something like he don't wanna go back to jail. They just turn around shot at him, and I saw him fall. I guess they hit him. Then they run into the middle of the street, stopped the first car that came, jumped into it, and drove off."

"Do you know which one shot the cop? Could you describe what he was wearing?"

"Nah, when the dude said he was a cop, I turn and leg it, 'cause I don't wanna go back to jail, neither. That cop coulda picked me up for dischargin' a firearm too." He gave a resigned shrug.

"Then what did you do? You came back to this car."

"Yeah. I figured, they wasn't gonna come back or call the police after all that, so I thought I'd get another wheel off before the police came to the store." He glanced at the two cops who had arrested him. "But they came pretty quick."

"He was loosening the nuts on the other front wheel when we arrived," one of the uniforms added.

"You have his gun?" Alex asked. The cop dutifully handed him the weapon, a Beretta M9, which he cursorily examined before slipping it into an evidence baggie and then logging the chain-of-custody on the baggie and in his memo book.

"What's gonna happen to my gun?"

Once we record its ballistics data, melted down, like the thousands of other illegal guns the NYPD collects, thought Alex. He said, "As you said, you fired, the victim fired, the robbers fired. That's a lot of bullets flying around. We gotta match them to the right guns – standard procedure. And if yours don't match the bullets in the victim, no one thinks it was you who shot him."

"It wasn't me."

"Then the ballistics will prove that, won't they."

"Did you get a look at the car they jacked?" asked Ray.

"Sorta. A van. A white one. It had writing on it."

"Could you see the writing?"

"Kinda. Think it was some kind of florist. Maybe."

"A florist?" repeated Alex.

"Yeah, I'm sure that's what it said."

Alex wrote in his memo book, *florist van,* adding several question marks after the word. Two squad detectives from the Two-Eight joined them, a portly black detective called Duncan Finnane and his skinny Italian partner, Luca Gribaldi. Alex took them aside, leaving Ray asking Jamal more questions, and he advised, "You'll wanna take this guy back to the station house and get a full statement, recorded, the whole nine yards." He grimaced skeptically. "Forthwith. Says he and the robbers fired off a few rounds at each other when they caught him stealing tires off their getaway car. For all I know, he coulda shot Irvine."

Finnane and Gribaldi nodded.

"We got a stack of wits Night Watch sent to the station house," Finnane said.

"Move him to the front of the line." Alex's two decades in Homicide meant precinct detectives often did what he told them to do, unquestioningly, which sometimes surprised him. They returned to Ray and the tire thief, the precinct detectives taking over from the uniforms, herding the cuffed man into their car.

The tire thief protested, "I'm gonna get some kind of deal for telling you what I seen, right?"

"As long as you keep telling us, pal," Alex heard Finnane say as they secured him in the back seat.

Dozens of Crime Scene Unit officers, uniforms, and detectives scoured the streets, the rooftops, and the gutters, searching for guns or slugs or other evidence, while teams from the Two-Eight and MNHS canvassed the area for more witnesses. There were too few witnesses, and at the same time, too many. People were reluctant to get entangled with police and courts and told the cops they hadn't seen a thing because they got the hell away when they heard gunfire. Or the cops heard conflicting stories – the robbers were white, no, they were black; they ran up the street, no, they jumped in a car, a van, a taxi, a black one, a blue one. No one offered any useful descriptions of the robbers, but Finnane interviewed a witness who had hidden behind parked cars when the shooting started. She corroborated part of the tire thief's story, describing a van with the livery of something on it, and the robbers dashing out in front of it, stopping it, leaping inside. Then she had seen the van racing away towards the West Side Highway.

"If you're gonna jack a vehicle, at least a delivery van gives you a ready-made space to stow the driver," Alex cracked to Ray, who responded with a disgusted scowl.

The detectives walked into Armando's. It was a densely packed bodega: claustrophobic aisles of canned and fried food, an aisle of fresh vegetables, an aisle of booze, a small freezer stuffed with pizzas, ice cream, and frozen meals. They retraced the robbers' alleged steps, from the front door, to the till, to the storage room in the back – where CSU was dissecting the safe – then back to the door, searching for evidence, something the perps might have dropped or disturbed, but they didn't see anything.

One of the CSU cops, Detective Cardoza, touched Alex's shoulder. "Boswell, I think we've located most of the shells from our shootout. Wanna have a look?"

"Okay," Alex said.

"In addition to the two bullets that hit the officer, we found three around him," Cardoza explained. "Thus far. So, our perps got off at least five rounds. These went through Irvine, God rest his soul." The .45 slugs sat adjacent to the chalk outline, evidence cones beside them.

"I know," said Alex, who had taken note of the bullets earlier. "*Could* they have come from our tire thief? He had a nine, but he coulda had another weapon on him that he got rid of before he was collared."

"Could have," said Cardoza. "But looking at it, I reckon they came from over there." He pointed to a spot on the opposite block, where a couple of his guys were searching the sidewalk.

"Ray said that the cop got off a few rounds."

"Yeah."

Alex marked the locations with 'x's' on the crime scene sketch, resting an elbow on one knee. "You find any others?"

"No. We're looking. Could have gone into the gutter."

Alex tilted his head to the side, narrowing his eyes at the offending storm drain. Slugs liked finding their way into storm drains. "City sewers must be filled with fucking bullets."

Fiddling with the zipper on his windbreaker, Cardoza led him across the street, pointing to more evidence cones and bullets. "Can't say for sure 'till the lab looks at 'em, but I'd say these came from an NYPD service pistol. A Glock 17, like most of us, including Officer Irvine, carry. And look here. Shell casings. From a .45. So, someone was standing here firing one. Probably not your tire thief unless he phoned up the *Starship Enterprise* and was beamed in seconds from where the Dodge is parked to here."

"We'll try that one with a judge."

A homicide investigation was like writing a novel backwards, stringing disparate fragments together until you had a coherent story you could tell an ADA, a judge, a jury, each stage and turn of the investigation like a long editing process. You would find something new, or something you thought was a fact wasn't, or a witness changed or forgot their story or disappeared entirely, and you had to revise, rewrite, rearrange your evidence into a different narrative.

Alex studied the policeman's bullets that had missed the perps, scattered amongst a slag heap of black trash bags piled on the curb. Instinctively putting his forearm over his nose, blocking the sour, pungent odor of fresh garbage, he crouched down for a closer look. He also carried a Glock 17. These bullets probably came from a gun just like it. He knew the bullets on the ground would be matched to Irvine's gun, or not, which would rule that narrative out, or strengthen it. Closing his eyes, he imagined Irvine walking along this block, tired after a midnight tour in the Bronx, returning home. Perhaps he'd seen the two perps hold up the bodega; perhaps he'd only just caught the altercation between the robbers and the tire thief, but instead of reporting "shots fired," Irvine, his blood up, joined the fray. Did he think everyone would surrender once he identified himself as a police officer? Did he imagine that the perps, who figured they had nothing to lose, would shoot him instead of risking an arrest?

Alex tried imagining other narratives because often, you have to think like a defense lawyer rather than a cop. Perhaps Jamal had thought Irvine was involved in the robbery and, in spite of Cardoza's assertions about the *Enterprise*, had fired at him. Perhaps Jamal was in cahoots with the robbers, the whole 'stealing tires off the getaway vehicle' story a giant ruse to deflect attention from their escape. Perhaps there was another person out there with a gun – this was Harlem after all – who had fired his weapon when the shooting started, and he'd hit the officer. But you have to follow your gut and trace the most plausible story in front of you, even as you check and rule out other stories. Finnane had found that eyewitness who corroborated the tire thief. That was the narrative they would track at this second.

Alex and Ray left the remainder of the canvassing to the patrol officers and precinct detectives, bombing down Broadway to their office, anxious to hunt down the alleged van before the robbers got far in it.

Gibson caught them in the hallway, falling into step with them. "DA's office called, wanting an update. I said you were the person to talk to, since you'd done the crime scene."

"Which DA?" asked Alex.

"McNally."

He laughed. "I shoulda fucking guessed."

Gibson rolled her eyes shrewdly, McNally never wasting an opportunity to get his hands on a high-profile, combustible case. He liked his adrenaline sports. "Well, call him and update him. First, update me."

They briefed her on what they knew, and she flipped through their memo books.

"They've run the license plates of the allegedly intended getaway car," she explained. "It's a stolen vehicle."

"There's a surprise," said Alex. "Who's it stolen from?" He wondered if the tire thief knew or suspected that the Dodge was stolen. Why else choose it, of all the cars parked on the street? People involved in those rackets had a sixth sense. Someone in possession of a stolen vehicle would be unlikely to report the missing tires to the police, as it would, of course, become apparent that the vehicle wasn't theirs in the first place.

"Who knows? Marcus and Liz are working on it. Once the people at the vehicle impound get the VIN number of the car to us, I'll get them to trace it."

"We gotta contact Robbery, see if there are any pattern reports matching this MO—" Alex said

"Marcus and Liz are on that too," Gibson assured him. "This one's all hands on deck. Your priority is finding the robbers and the van."

Ray started phoning florists and any other business that might employ someone to drive a white van, starting with ones in Harlem, but the search would expand. Alex dialed the District Attorney's office and McNally's extension.

"Can you meet now?" asked the prosecutor in his irascible way.

"You seen the news? We're up to our eyeballs."

"Yes, yes, I'm sure you are, but it's a cop-shooting, and I need to know what's happening. My boss is going nuts, and he's got the mayor, the Commissioner, and a couple senators on his ass."

"Yeah," moaned Alex breathily, reminded of how much he hated redballs. He didn't share the prosecutor's love of adrenaline sports.

"Come down here, give me something I can brief him on, and then I can keep everyone off your back," insisted the lawyer.

Ray, who had already found four places who weren't missing white vans, interrupted, "Does he want to meet with you?"

"Yes."

"We'll probably need to be downtown at some point anyway. Why don't you just go? Keep him on side."

"He wants a briefing on Irvine," said Alex. "Shit's gonna hit the fan."

"It usually does."

Chapter Four

Forty-five minutes later, Alex parked the car underneath 100 Centre Street and met Simon in front of the DA's office. Everything downtown seemed bizarrely calm after the mayhem uptown, but Alex felt adrenaline desiccating his mouth as they ambled along a path in Columbus Park, the small green patch across Baxter Street from the DA's office. It had been a cold fall, and the grass had died, stomped into a muddy soup.

Meetings with Simon were recurrently outside, as he viewed it as an opportunity for a long cigarette break. The lawyer exhaled smoke, watching a black lab leap after some pigeons, the owner shouting histrionically.

"What's happening?" McNally asked. "I talked to your boss, but she said you'd have more information as you handled the crime scene."

Speaking breathlessly, Alex explained, "Off-duty police officer from a Bronx precinct – the Five-Two – tried to stop a robbery of a bodega on West 123rd. He lives in the neighborhood and was on his way home. He didn't stop it and was killed by the robbers, who've fled the scene, and we're trying to figure out where the fuck they've gone. He was killed with a .45. No sign of that so far, but the Two-Eight squad and CSU have got a search of the area under way."

"Great. Sounds like a clusterfuck."

"It gets worse. They're tracing a stolen car and trying to find another hijacked one."

"What?" said Simon. "Is the stolen car the same—?"

"No, the perps couldn't use what we think was their intended getaway car, which was stolen, so they hijacked another one."

"What? Why couldn't they use it?"

Alex forced a beleaguered grin. If you didn't laugh when you could, this job would send you careening into a breakdown. "Some mope was stealing the tires and had one wheel off when they ran outta the store. Mazel tov. A fucking hero. We got two eyewits who saw them jack a white van."

Simon took a long draw from his cigarette. "Is that it?"

"As far as I know." Alex glanced at his cell phone. No word from Ray, his other MNHS colleagues, or anyone at the Two-Eight.

"You think they're still in town?"

"I fucking hope so. I don't think they drove outta town. All the anti-terrorism squads were watching the bridges and tunnels for the van, almost as soon as the shooting was called in. And we've alerted Highway Patrol for New York, New Jersey, and Connecticut, just in case they got outta the city. We're working on the basis that they abandoned the van 'cause it's too damn obvious, but they could hop a train or a bus without getting noticed."

Simon lit a fresh cigarette and glanced at his watch. "I guess you need to get back to it. And there's a parole board hearing I gotta get to, for someone who definitely should stay in prison."

"Yeah."

"But one more thing… I talked to Phil McLean today. Do you know Phil?"

"No."

"Oh, he's one of the ADAs in the Appellate Bureau. He's been handling the *LaValle* appeal. He hasn't gotten in contact with you?"

Alex sucked in a slow, audible breath. "No." He'd heard something from Gibson a few weeks ago about LaValle soon having a hearing at the New York Court of Appeals and then blocked it from his mind. He'd never untangled LaValle's sentencing hearing from the way everything else that day had gone to hell. At least the NY County DA, now that he wasn't staring an election in the eye, or because the shadow of 9/11 was three years distant, seemed a little less bloodthirsty, and he hadn't pursued the death penalty on any case since.

The prosecutor must have noticed his reaction, saying with uncharacteristic gentleness, "It wasn't your fault, Alex."

"I just don't wanna think about it."

"It was my fault."

"Yeah, now's a shitty time to get into that. I gotta keep my head clear."

"Do you not want me to tell you about the appeal?"

He heaved out a churlish exhalation. "You've got me in suspense. But I thought the conviction was upheld." Although he hankered to get back to his investigation, hearing about LaValle's appeal was like a highway pile-up he could not help but rubberneck.

"It was affirmed by the Appellate Division of the Supreme Court. This is the New York Court of Appeals. The next level up."

"Right. Gotcha—"

Simon was in law professor mode. "Then, the next level after that would be the US Supreme Court, but I don't see them granting *cert* for this case since I don't believe the issues being raised by the defense are of national significance—"

"I know how it works," Alex said irritably. "I didn't go to law school, but I'm not an idiot."

Simon tilted a greying eyebrow at him.

"What are they saying to the Court of Appeals? Give me the cliff notes." He braced himself for an earful of legalese, as Simon liked nothing better than to expound on the technical details of the law with the passion most people reserved for talking about the Yankees.

"Phil showed me the brief. The defense team is saying that the statute is unconstitutional for quite a number of reasons. They're throwing everything at the court, hoping something will stick; pretty much what people do in most appeals since you never know what argument is going to catch the attention of the justices. The main thing is that it violates due process because it places undue coercion on the jurors. They're also saying that it provides an inadequate description of what terms like 'serial murder' mean and therefore allows for too much prosecutorial discretion. Also, it penalizes defendants who opt for a trial instead of pleading guilty, because a death-eligible defendant can plead out to life imprisonment, *and* that it violates equal protection due to the uneven way it is applied across all the different jurisdictions in the state, and, of course, that old equal protection chestnut, that black defendants are more likely to be sentenced to death than white defendants."

"At least they're not saying we fucked up," Alex commented, relieved. His ass wasn't on the line.

Simon smiled. "No, they're saying the legislature fucked up."

"So, what happens?"

"Oral arguments in front of the Court of Appeals are today." Simon glanced at his watch. "Probably around now. I'm just giving you a heads up that the sentence or conviction could be reversed."

"What, you think it's likely?" Alex did not think he would care very much if the sentence got reversed, but the conviction? Retrying that case would be an unplanned visit to the ninth circle of hell for all parties.

"Conviction, probably not. You remember… we had an airtight case. Not even the defense team is challenging anything in or before the trial. But the sentence, I don't know. Odds are the Court of Appeals is leaning that way. There has been another case, one from Suffolk County in 2003, where they vacated the death sentence and remanded it for new sentencing proceedings, stating that they were deferring on any concerns about the constitutionality of the capital provisions themselves until they had reviewed them on other cases that they knew were in the pipeline – ours and one from Queens County."

Alex translated the legalese in his head. The Court of Appeals had already heard a death penalty case, passed the buck back to the trial court, putting off making any decision about whether or not the death penalty statute was kosher until they heard LaValle's case and this other one from Queens. "Why not decide on it then?" he asked. "Why wait a year for this one?"

"They didn't invalidate the statute then. It was a much narrower decision, which invalidated several provisions on the grounds that they violated the Fifth and Sixth Amendments but left the statute, for the most part, intact. The defendant in that case only argued that those particular issues – being offered a plea bargain at a certain stage in the proceedings, after the DA had applied for notice to seek the death penalty – impugned his right to a jury trial, whereas the scope in our case is much larger and the court will be in a position where it will pretty much have to uphold the statute or not, rather than whittling away at bits of it."

That did not answer any questions. "Right," said Alex, wishing he hadn't asked. He was fretting about the cop-shooting, and his curiosity about New York Court of Appeals reasoning was limited under the best of circumstances.

"We'll see what the Court does," said Simon.

Alex removed his cell phone from his pocket, flicking it open. "I gotta get back to chasing these shitbirds uptown."

"Yes. Another fucking cop-killing. Go figure it would be the same day as oral arguments for *LaValle.*" Simon blew a puff of smoke out of his nostrils.

Alex arched a laconic eyebrow and grimly pursed his lips. It had occurred to him too.

While Simon threw his cigarette butt into a trash can and waved goodbye, with a gesture indicating 'call me,' Alex was on his cell to MNHS, praying that Ray had made headway with his phone calls to florists or anyone missing a delivery van. To his surprise, he got Gibson on the line, who told him that Ray had gone to a florist on 116th and Lenox with Marcus Wheeler and Liz Greenwood, not long after Alex had left the office. The florist had reported a missing driver. There was a BOLO out on the van.

"What about the stolen Dodge? The original getaway car?"

"We think it came from New Jersey. We're asking the police there if they have any reports of a stolen vehicle matching that description." She didn't sound optimistic. In terms of figuring out where the robbers were at this moment, it was a dead lead anyway.

As soon as he snapped the phone shut, it protested with a loud ring. "Ray," said Alex. "Whaddaya got?"

"You're downtown," said Ray, sounding out of breath. "Go to Chelsea. West 24th between Tenth and Eleventh. Van could be there."

"You found out which van? And where it is?"

"Yeah, it's a florist in East Harlem. They deliver flowers for weddings, funerals, wakes, *quinceaneras,* whatever. Guess our tire thief has better eyes than you thought. They told me one of their customers called and bitched the driver hadn't shown up. Office called the driver, whose name is Tariq Khalid, no answer. They told me that this guy has worked for them for years, was totally reliable, not even a sick day. It's a white Mercedes Sprinter van. They also gave us the plate numbers. We put a BOLO out on the van."

"Why the fuck do you think it's in Chelsea?"

"Gibson, Wheeler, Greenwood, and I thought they wouldn't wanna go far in a stolen van with the name of a shop written on it. It's like saying, 'Police, find me!' We thought they'd dump it quickly. And with teams at all the bridges and tunnels, it wouldn't be that easy for them leave unnoticed. Anyway, a couple cops radioed in, saying they'd ticketed a white Sprinter van with 'Lenox Flowers' on the side for violating alternate-side-of-the-street parking regs."

Alex smiled to himself, bemused. Alternate-side-of-the-street parking, one of the most stroke-inducing aggravations for New York City drivers, had helpfully broken their case. "I'll see you there."

Once out of the parking garage, he wheeled south to City Hall and then nudged his way into the procession of cars and trucks crawling along the narrow corridor of Chambers Street. Skyscrapers leaned overhead, casting the street in shadow. He followed a line of taxis and a lumbering oil tanker truck onto the highway underneath a footbridge linking two glass-plated skyscrapers, and then, with four lanes of highway freeing the traffic from the congestion of Lower Manhattan, he slammed his foot down, sweeping around the truck, flying uptown to Eleventh Avenue.

Up in Chelsea, he veered onto West 24th. Police had already encircled the van, a white Sprinter with 'Lenox Flowers' and a Manhattan phone number in green and yellow lettering on the sides. Alex parked at a cockeyed angle between two RMPs and leapt out of his car. In the front seat of the van, two CSU guys were dusting for prints and plucking potential evidence out of the fabric. When Alex caught their eyes, they gave him a look that meant they hadn't found shit yet. Certainly no bodies, dead or alive, in the back of the van. That would be too much to hope for. Bunches of flowers were piled towards the cabin, CSU trying to not disturb them, evidence, but no obvious evidence of hiding a body or hostage.

Several more CSU techs were dusting the door handles for prints, although the witnesses reported that the perps had worn gloves. The rear doors were splayed open, and three CSU cops in blue windbreakers crouched in the cargo area of the van, dusting, swabbing, and shining UV lights on every surface, from the white bulkheads to the plywood boards on the floor. Alex peered inside, breathing in the pungent aroma of flowers, the scent reminding him of taking an ex-girlfriend to the Botanics. He sneezed, feeling inflammation in his airways and sinuses, so he stepped back, holding his face in his hands.

Someone asked, "You all right there, Boswell?"

"Yeah," he answered, blowing his nose. "Just got a lightweight respiratory system."

"Lived in this city too long."

"The city smog I can handle."

Ray, Liz Greenwood, and Marcus Wheeler arrived on the scene in a Crown Vic as Alex was questioning the cops who had ticketed the van. Alternate-side-of-the-street regulations required vehicles to be on the other side of West 24th Street between 0800 and 1100 hours. The cops had written the ticket at 0915 and told him that when the BOLO came out, they recognized the van as a dead match for the one they'd ticketed earlier that morning.

The three MNHS detectives gathered around Alex and the traffic cop. Ray's two companions had joined MNHS last year, Wheeler fairly savvy, but relatively young and somewhat lazy – Alex thought – from the Four-One Precinct, and Greenwood an introspective, experienced death investigator, transferred from the Brooklyn North Homicide squad.

"What needs doing?" asked Greenwood unceremoniously.

"A canvass of everything. Start with a ten-block radius," Alex replied. "Two white guys and the driver."

"We've got a photo of the driver," she said. "Wife's beside herself. Says he never goes missing. Never even comes home late. You got anything else on the 'white guys?'"

He laughed bitterly. "Nope. You gotta ask if anyone was acting weird."

"In New York?" Greenwood said misanthropically. "That's everyone."

Showing his teeth in a sarky grimace, he held out both hands, palms up, and then slapped them on his thighs. He had nothing.

Without any further complaints, Wheeler and Greenwood organized a canvass of the apartments, the attended parking lots, and the art galleries on both sides of the street.

Meanwhile, Alex poked around the van and the art gallery. Years ago, these places were all warehouses and factories, and every street on the western edges of the Tenth stank of garbage, fish markets, butcher shops, and gasoline, half of it run by the Mob, the other half the Irish gangs. He'd been a young precinct detective working these streets in the early '80s, canvassing or looking for evidence, the neighborhood destitute and dreary, filled with gangsters and ghosts, and on a dark night his heart would be pounding, every sense on alert, aware of the violence lurking in the wilderness of abandoned warehouses, bucket-of-blood bars, decaying factories. Now, it had metamorphosized into a wilderness of bohemian cafés, modern art galleries, TV studios, open air parking lots, and eye-wateringly expensive apartments.

And CCTV. His eye cottoned onto a camera attached to the art gallery, a panopticon watching the streets. Had the Mob still run these streets, that camera would have been smashed to bits.

Leaving the memories behind, the detectives entered the art gallery and flashed tin at the man working the front desk, a thin and effeminate white guy, dressed in a suit and tie with a sheen like fish scales. On the far side of the lobby, a fountain monopolized the exhibition space, spitting water in bubbling jets while a mattress floated in the middle and goldfish swam around the mattress. Art? Alex almost missed the gangsters.

"I'm Detective Boswell, this is Detective Espinosa," he said. "The van parked in front of your building was used in a robbery earlier this morning."

The witness' eyes widened in horror, and he gasped, "You mean, those guys were *criminals?*"

"You talked to them?" No, it wasn't like the '80s anymore.

"Yes."

"What did they look like?"

"They were white. I'm not good with faces. I always said, I hope I never have to be a witness to a crime, 'cause I'm terrible at faces." His face flushed, embarrassed, and he had a nervy, anxious grin.

"What *can* you remember?" Alex scratched his throat, abraded from shouting at people all morning.

"One was short, the other was tall. The tall one was injured. He had his arm in a sling, well, not a real sling, more like a makeshift sling. A bandana, I think it was bandana, around his neck."

Alex wondered if one of Officer Irvine's bullets had found home after all.

Ray asked, "What did you talk to them about?"

"They were leaving the van there at... I don't know... seven am? I came into work early. Told them that the alternate-side-of-the-street parking comes into effect at eight. You know, I was just being helpful. It was a florist's van. I thought they must be nice. You know, how can florists not be nice? The one guy said he was taking his friend to Grand Central and would not be long. They looked a bit frantic. I don't know why you would park here to go to Grand Central. Maybe to take a subway?"

Alex and Ray sent a uniform off to radio the MTA police and put them on the alert for anyone who fit that description in Grand Central Station, Penn Station, and the Port Authority. Those skels could be well on their way to Boston or Washington DC or anywhere in five hours. Had the robbery really been five hours ago? Where the fuck had the time gone? Alex glanced at his watch, gulping down his aggravation with the ponderous speed of the investigation, the robbers indisputably in the wind.

"You have CCTV cameras out front," he said bluntly. "You got access to those tapes?"

"*I* don't, Detective," said the man. "Our security personnel do."

"Well, can we get them?" snapped Alex.

The wit contacted security, and the guard, a white-haired ex-cop, materialized with a box stuffed with tapes. The guard handed the detectives the tapes, rambling about his time with the NYPD: how the department wasn't the same anymore, the young cops had no respect for veterans, there was too much bureaucracy, the city was less crime-ridden, sure, but being a cop wasn't the same anymore. Alex sucked a deep breath into his belly, counting the seconds, a technique his AA sponsor advocated for alleviating stress. He had no time for this. He had to consciously preserve his focus. Getting stressed out and discombobulated would be counterproductive. He exhaled harshly and smiled humorlessly, thanking the ex-cop for the tapes.

Marcus, Liz, and the Two-Eight squad continued with the canvass, while Alex and Ray raced to One Police Plaza. 1PP was a fourteen-story red brick cube at the base of the Brooklyn Bridge, with the Financial District's skyscrapers on one side, Chinatown's pagodas and crammed streets on the other, and City Hall and the courthouses at its back. It faced a square overlooked by a sculpture of interlocking red discs the size of pickup trucks that James Hurley, with his vivid imagination, claimed looked like a huge ass. Once it had stood in the shadow of the World

Trade Center but now, coming here always reminded Alex of its absence. As they parked in the cavernous garage underneath the building, he cringed at the twinge of Bill Ryan's death, like his old wound, and the sickening memories of the debris at Fresh Kills.

Without ceremony, they bolted for the forensic video lab on the eighth floor. By the time they burst into the lab after a ride on the slowest elevator in the world, the video guys were hurriedly prepping the equipment. They plugged the tape into the machine and watched the pixelated black and white footage. Cars and people on West 24th.

"This is like 72 hours of CCTV footage," complained Derek, the lab guy. "What time should we be looking for?"

"About five or six hours ago," Alex answered. The perps had been stupid enough to park obliviously in front of a CCTV camera, potentially a break for him. But only if the damned camera was working, and they had walked in front of it.

Derek fast-forwarded through the tapes, images blurring past on the screen. "What am I looking for again?"

"A white Merc Sprinter with yellow and green writing on it. Two guys in it," said Ray.

"Well, you can't really see colors on this," said Derek. "I can look for a white van, though."

"Could you read the writing?"

"I might. Oh, there's a white van. That's a Sprinter."

Tense, they watched the blurry footage of a white Sprinter van rolling down the road. The van stopped, two black guys climbing out.

"That's not it," Alex moaned. "Our guys are white."

The footage plodded along languidly. Alex chewed at his fingernails until they hurt. He glanced at Ray, who was playing with his cell phone.

Another white van cruised under the camera's eye. Transfixed, Alex stared at the screen, nails still in his mouth. Ray stopped playing Tetris or whatever he was doing. Two white males climbed out of it. The passenger had one arm tied up in a bandana.

"That's it, Derek," Ray said. "Focus it in on those guys."

Derek's hands flew across his keyboard. The footage hovered over the two men, and he zoomed in on their faces. Nobody looked particularly recognizable on CCTV.

Ever the optimist, Ray asked, "Can you get a better shot?"

On the screen, the guys hobbled along the street towards Tenth Avenue, and the injured one paused, peering over his shoulder, and the camera caught his face. Derek stopped the footage. Then he found another image of the shorter, uninjured perp, not facing the camera so it could be anyone, but he couldn't do better.

"Print those," Alex ordered. "We need to send it out as a BOLO. It's gotta go to every train station, bus station, and precinct in the city. And to PDs in Boston, New Haven... Anywhere he could get a train to in a few hours."

For another minute or so, they watched the perps disappear from the camera's view.

"Now what?" Ray asked as they jogged out of 1PP.

Hope someone identifies the suspects from those images or Greenwood's canvass gets lucky, Alex thought. "We'll take a couple of those print-outs to Grand Central," he panted. "They told that guy in the gallery they were going there. If they did, maybe someone saw them." Chances were slim to none, but he couldn't cope with sitting on his ass. Besides, someone had to chase every useless lead.

They announced their location over the radio and cut across to the Bowery, and then they sped uptown with lights and sirens going full tilt. At Grand Central, they met uniforms, a Two-Eight detective, and MTA police, and they gave everyone copies of the images. There were trains everywhere, leaving every few minutes. And with the little automatic ticket machines in every corner of the station, no one to track who bought what and where. Everyone spread out, trying to look inconspicuous as they did not want to alarm any civilians. These days, a big, obvious police manhunt in Grand Central might freak people out.

Train stations had their own rhythm, trains arriving, leaving, the disembodied voice over the PA serenely announcing, "The train at Platform 1 is departing for New Haven at six 'o' five." The LED signs on the wall flashed destinations and times, places in Westchester, upstate, and Connecticut. People scurried, eyes down, holding newspapers and laptops, worrying about where they were going or where they were coming from, or whether or not they would make their train, or who waited at the end of their journey. Had the perps caught one of those trains? They could be anywhere, at any one of those dozens of stations from here to New Haven or Poughkeepsie or Port Jervis.

Alex advanced to the information desk underneath the famous Grand Central clock, while Ray did the rounds of the shops and coffee bars. He flashed his shield at the waiting commuters, jumping to the front of the line. Smiling politely, he rested his elbows on the desk, saying, "I'm Detective Boswell from the NYPD. Has anyone here seen these two guys?" He slid the photographs across the desk. "One of them would probably have his arm in kind of a sling."

The clerk peered at the photographs and then passed them around to her colleagues at the desk. There were uneasy mumblings. Someone said in a hushed, panicked tone, "They're not terrorists, are they?"

"No, not terrorists," Alex assured them.

"Don't recall seeing anyone who looks like that, sorry."

He left the information desk, climbing the spiral stairs to the upper concourse, searching for Ray. The perps might not have gone to the information desk, especially not if they could anonymously buy tickets from the little machines, but they might have nabbed a coffee or alcohol. Ray was in the ritzy wine bar near the top of the stairs, showing the photos to the bartender and the impeccably dressed wait staff.

He saw Alex near the entrance and walked over to him. "Lex, I've been round everywhere. No one remembers seeing these guys."

Alex breathed out and pressed his belly against the railing. Hazy light shone through the terminal, the sun refracting through the arched, cathedral windows. He looked up at the vaulted green ceiling with the constellations gleaming across it. The giant American flag, another post-9/11 addition, dangled precipitously from the Big Dipper, a red, white, and blue eyesore amidst the gothic arches. Alex found it as out of place and jarring as the army guys with their rifles, a reminder of war rather than a memorial to the dead.

The PA placidly announced, "The next train to depart from platform three is the six-twenty-one train to Brewster. Calling at Harlem-125th Street, Tremont, Fordham, Williams Bridge, Woodlawn—"

Gibson's voice crackled over the portable radio: "Detectives Boswell and Espinosa, go to Penn Station. Now."

"Penn?" Alex said.

"I've just got a call from the police there. They have your guy. Go."

"One guy?" said Ray.

"One," she answered shortly. "Go!"

"Ten-Four, Lou," acknowledged Ray.

They sprinted out of Grand Central and cleaved through the Midtown traffic on Park. Then they turned crosstown on 34th, shoving aside the barriers of yellow taxis blocking the intersections. At Penn, they parked amidst marked police cars and an armored Emergency Services van, and they legged it into the station, dark and dingy, with weak, flickering fluorescent lights, and grotty, stained carpet underfoot. You had to forgive New York for Penn Station.

Half a dozen MTA cops met them near the entrance.

"Where is he?" Alex asked, puffing for air.

"Beth Israel Hospital," one of the cops answered.

"What?"

"He collapsed in the middle of the concourse just outside Starbucks. Passerby reported it to us. When we attended him, we recognized his picture from the BOLO you sent out and radioed it in. But he was a ten-fifty-four. EMS were here before you. Said he was in a bad way and shoveled him into a bus. It's not like he was in a state where he could go anywhere quickly. He had a wound on his arm and EMS said there was shrapnel in his chest."

"He did well for having shrapnel in his chest. He's certainly led us on a wild goose chase," commented Alex caustically.

"Here, we took this off him," the cop said helpfully. He handed the detectives the man's wallet and a threadbare black backpack.

They donned rubber gloves and rummaged. The wallet contained a Costco card, an expired Visa credit card which stated that his name was Harold Kitchener, and an Amtrak ticket to Washington DC. From the backpack, they fished out a brick of cash, wadded up in plastic sandwich bags, and a Smith and Wesson Model 64. A .38 special. It wasn't the gun used to kill Officer Irvine. Alex released a slow, discouraged breath. It would be far too much like good luck for the murder weapon to still be on the murder suspect.

"What about his accomplice?" asked Ray. "Any reports of someone matching that description?"

"Not here," said the MTA cop. "This guy was definitely on his own."

"Are you sure?" said Ray. "If he collapsed, his accomplice could have left him and run off to catch the nearest train."

"He came in alone. We looked at our CCTV," insisted the cop.

"What about the wit who saw him collapse?" asked Ray. "What happened there?"

"Some tourists from Michigan said that they saw him limping along, and as they passed him, he just fell over. He wasn't very responsive when they spoke to him, so they got our attention, and we called the paramedics."

"Are the witnesses here?"

"They were on their way to catch a train to Newark Airport. I doubt it."

"You didn't keep them?" Ray looked annoyed.

"We didn't think it was important," said the MTA cop, glancing sheepishly at the floor.

"What were they gonna tell us, Ray?" Alex grumbled. "Sometimes, it's all right to just let people catch their plane."

He flipped open his cell and phoned the criminal information division at 1PP, relating the perp's name. They ran him through the acronym soup, DCJS, NCIC, CARS, WOLF, and SAFEnet, searching for a record and for outstanding warrants. The detective on the other end of the phone read off a litany of felonies and misdemeanors, ranging from possession, to criminal mischief, to aggravated second-degree assault and, of course, first-degree robbery, which was what the New York penal code called armed robbery.

Chapter Five

October 28th

While Harold Kitchener underwent surgery in Beth Israel Hospital, Alex and Ray took the backpack and its contents to the property clerk, where they catalogued said contents with the order that everything be sent to the lab forthwith. They uploaded the serial number on the gun to NCIC. Then they joined Wheeler and a team in Chelsea, hunting for the missing van driver. Already, the police had alerted every hospital in the city to be on the lookout for anyone who fit his description. Greenwood and Finnane visited his wife, his church, his favorite bars, interviewed his friends and acquaintances. Alex and Ray combed through every obvious spot they could think of near West 24th where one might stow a hostage or hide a body, but they came up empty handed.

Uptown, Gribaldi showed Jamal a photo array, and he failed to single out Kitchener's mugshot from a six-pack. Then they discovered that the original getaway car had been reported stolen in Hoboken, and the perp who had lifted it currently serving time in New Jersey State Prison on something else. The detectives couldn't connect him to Kitchener. Downtown, the pictures from the CCTV had made the neighborhood rounds, but no one remembered seeing anything suspicious.

By midnight, they were beat but with no leads, and the cops guarding Kitchener radioed to report that he was alive, conscious, and out of surgery. Alex and Ray hurried back to the hospital, where they met Gibson. A cop-killing brought the lieutenant herself out on overtime, interrogating suspects.

"He's not quite lucid," said a late-shift nurse, and she made them wait in the corridor outside Kitchener's operating room for half an hour.

The three of them slumped wearily in the plastic chairs placed in the hallway. Passing hospital staff squeezed carts filled with tubes and machinery past them. Ray and Gibson talked quietly about the tribulations of raising teenagers. Ray's oldest was thirteen, and Gibson had a fifteen-year old and a seventeen-year old and warned him it would get worse before it got better. Alex rocked his head back, spacing out, the memories creeping up on him. His lower back and right side burned with a nagging ache, like they always did after a long day. Old injuries, flaring up. His last visit to an ER as a patient had been the car accident. Lying in the ward with an IV dripping into a vein, being treated for shock, and scared his back was broken because it hurt a lot and he had a tingling, numb feeling in his legs.

There had been CT scans and x-rays of his chest, spine, and pelvis, and eventually ER staff concluding that none of his injuries were life-threatening. He'd fractured three ribs and injured soft tissue his back, but not broken it. They gave him enough benzos to assuage the worst of the pain, but otherwise left him to be dealt with in the morning. Alone in the ward, he'd shut his eyes, trying to lose himself in the Diazepam but he had no peace. Then Gibson, of all people, showed up. The traffic cops on the scene had needed to contact *someone* and, on seeing that he was MNHS, they'd phoned her. Her detectives were like family, so she'd ditched her actual family in the middle of the night and caned it to Mount Sinai.

When she arrived on the ward, he'd been dozing, high but somewhat conscious and wishing he wasn't. What the fuck had happened? A car wreck? That was what he had asked EMS while they monitored his vitals in the back of the bumping, lurching ambulance. Yes, they said, we pulled you out of a car wreck. Gibson had looked horrified when she saw him. He supposed that he must look dreadful, as it wasn't like Gibson to look anything other than calm and in control.

She'd told him that Zoë had been DOA. God, what had he done? Fucked up, fallen off the wagon, and Zoë was dead. He'd broken down then. His C/O had to sit quietly with him while he cried. Should she call his family, his daughter who she knew lived in Brooklyn? Wildly, he had begged her not to do that. It upset him even more. Call Ray, call Marty Vasquez, call Hurley, call anyone. But please, don't call Sarah. Don't let her see him like this.

Gibson and Ray cut into his reminiscence, discussing interrogation strategies. Yawning, he stood and stretched, as if he could clear those cobwebs from his mind. A sharp twinge of pain shot through his spine.

111

Then a sudden noise from the OR diverted his attention from his sore back, and the door swung open, the surgeon emerging from the operating room, giving the three of them a put-upon glare.

"He's conscious," he said. "But he's still coming out from the anesthetic."

Gibson firmly took charge in her South Bronx projects no-nonsense way. "We've already been here half an hour. There's a man out there who could be dead or dying, and he's the only one who knows where he is."

The surgeon looked unhappy. "Well, make it brief."

As they stepped through the door, the surgeon wearily added, "One thing… According to our bloods, he has traces of heroin in his system."

"Thanks," said Gibson.

No surprises there, thought Alex.

Machines beeped and hummed. That awful hospital smell, antiseptic and sickness, corroded Alex's nostrils. Kitchener gazed at them, addled from opiates and anesthetic. Blearily, he cast his eyes across the room to a nurse, who was fiddling with machinery.

"Are these cops?" he slurred, his voice hoarse and breathy from the intubation.

Gibson began the interview. "I'm Lieutenant Jo Gibson. This is Detective Alex Boswell and Detective Ray Espinosa. We're trying to figure out what happened to you uptown today and why you got a bullet in you, and a police officer is dead. Is this your shit? If it ain't, why do you want to make it yours? Think about it. We'll be back to talk some more."

With that, the three of them stepped out of the OR and eyed their watches for ten minutes, not speaking to one another. Fighting through his spacey tiredness, Alex reminded himself of the facts because you don't interrogate flailing around in the dark. Gibson and Ray were probably doing the same. Then they went back into the room.

"I was walkin' down 123rd, people got crazy and started shooting," explained Kitchener.

"Come on, don't feed us that bullshit," said Alex. Already, off to a promising start. The suspect just admitted that he had been at the crime scene. Often, they tell you that they were nowhere near it. "A convicted armed robber, carrying a gun which he probably doesn't have a permit for, minding his own damn business, happens to be caught in the crossfire of, wait, an armed robbery."

"Just minding my own business," Kitchener repeated.

"Sure," Alex said. "Please, tell us how you just happened to walk into the middle of an armed robbery." You give the suspect a chance to tell you a story, lock him into it, and then you attack any inconsistencies or statements that you know are lies. You get him to explain those inconsistencies until he is so hopelessly entangled in a quagmire of deception that he doesn't know which way is up anymore and has lost out on any chance of keeping his story straight. This can take hours. But they didn't have hours. They would have to escalate the pressure quickly.

Kitchener mumbled, "My apartment, it's on 120th. I was walkin' along, going to the subway station 'cause I had to get down to Penn Station. 'Cause I was gonna go see a friend in DC. I walked past the bodega, and there was two guys, and they was firing at each other, like across the street. I think one of the guys was stealin' tires off a car. Maybe the other guy was its owner…. I dunno. I just tried to run, just get out of the way, felt something in my arm and kept running."

"Where did you run?" Alex said. "To the van you jacked?"

"I didn't jack no van."

"Why are there pictures on the CCTV of you getting out of a Mercedes Sprinter on West 24th Street with your short pal?"

"I-I… phoned him—"

"What's his name?" interrupted Alex.

"Crazy Eight."

"Crazy Eight?"

"Street name. I dunno know his real name."

"Okay, you phoned your pal. Then what happened?"

"I says I hurt my arm. Got shot. He says he had a car and would pick me up and take me to the station. Picked me up at 121st and Broadway."

"Where did he get the van?"

"No idea. He just showed up in the van."

"You told that guy who worked in the art gallery that you were going to Grand Central," observed Ray.

"Got confused."

113

"Really?" said Alex. "Have trains ever gone outta Grand Central to DC?"

"I was in a lot of pain."

"Then why didn't you go to the hospital?"

"It was just a bullet in the arm. Not a big deal."

It probably wasn't to someone in Kitchener's circles, thought Alex. He asked, "You didn't notice the alternate-side-of-the-street parking signs where you left the van? Not even after the guy who worked in that art gallery told you?"

"Figured Crazy Eight was gonna move the van after he left me at the train station."

"Or you'd killed the driver and stolen the van, so you figured if it was ticketed or towed, it wouldn't be your fucking problem."

"No, we wasn't gonna be parked there long. If Crazy Eight left the van there—"

"Someone left the van there. It got a ticket after nine 'o' clock. I looked at it after eleven."

"-it wasn't my problem."

"Right. Who is this friend in DC?" The antiseptic and chemicals permeating the stuffy, overheated hospital room kindled a headache. He felt sweat accreting under his armpits.

"Gordy."

"Gordy got another name?"

"Dunno."

"You have an address?"

"No."

"You were going to DC to meet someone, but you had no idea where in DC you were going?" Alex chewed on the top of his pen.

"He was gonna meet me at the train station."

"And why were you going all the way to DC to meet this guy?"

"He's a pal. You ever gone out of this city to meet your pals?"

"How do you know him?" Alex pushed.

"Around," grunted Kitchener.

"Around where?"

"Just around. The streets."

"He's a dealer," suggested Alex.

"He's just a guy I used to hang with. Moved to DC."

"And 'Crazy Eight?' Where'd he go?"

"I dunno. He walked me to the train station and then left." Kitchener looked nervously around the room.

"Did he go somewhere to dispose of the van driver? Is that it? Did he kill or tie up the van driver, and after dropping you off at Penn, he went to clean it up?" Alex offered the 'out,' an explanation or justification for the perp's actions, and he shifted the responsibility to the accomplice.

"Don't know about no van driver. Crazy Eight just picked me up in that van. Said he had borrowed it from a friend."

"Why'd you leave it on West 24th? That's ten blocks to Penn."

"Parking around Penn sucks. We don't mind walking."

"With a bullet in your arm?"

Kitchener wriggled his shoulders in an approximation of a shrug.

"Let me get this straight," said Alex. "You were walking down 123rd, minding your own business, and you went straight into the middle of a shoot-out, got caught in the crossfire, and then, instead of going to the ER, you called your friend 'Crazy Eight' to pick you up and take you to Penn Station in a vehicle that was identified by witnesses at the shooting as jacked by *two* people."

"I don't know where the van came from," insisted Kitchener.

"Where did you call 'Crazy Eight' from? You gotta burner phone?" A cell phone call could be pinged from the towers.

"A payphone."

"How old school. Which payphone?" Alex straightened his achy spine and folded his arms across his stomach. "We'll get LUDS from all the payphones on 123rd and find out what calls were made that day. There aren't many payphones now that everyone has a cell. It won't be difficult."

"I can't remember."

"Why don't you explain why you have over nine hundred bucks in the backpack we found on you?" interjected Ray.

"I won it on the ponies."

"Oh, yeah? Which track?" pressed Alex. "Which race? Which horse?"

"I don't remember."

"Give me a break, pal. If you win that kinda money on a race, you damn well remember which horse it was. Hell, you probably remember the clothes you were wearing, whether the guy next to you at the OTB smelled of cigarette smoke or aftershave, and what you had for lunch that day."

"I only won a little. Rest of it was for a job I did for someone."

The guy changed his story faster than a presidential candidate in the upcoming election. "Like holding up a bodega? Witnesses described a tall white guy. How many tall white guys with guns and robbery one convictions do you think are hanging around West 123rd?"

"I dunno… It wasn't me."

"Who held up the bodega then?"

"I dunno. One of the guys who was shooting?"

"He was a fat black guy. Witnesses in the bodega said they were held up by two white guys."

"Wasn't me."

"It was *your* car that this guy was stealing tires off, wasn't it?" Alex averred. "You were pissed, threatened him with a gun, he shoots at you, off-duty cop jumps in and gets caught up in the cross-fire." Another story, another out.

"Wasn't my car. I didn't shoot at anybody."

"Ah, come on. I'd be pissed if someone was stealing my tires."

"Yeah, well, it wasn't my car."

"Technically not," agreed Alex. "It was stolen. But it was a car you were about to drive away in, and you couldn't, 'cause some schmuck had taken a wheel off."

"No, don't know nothing about that car. I don't have no car. I use my girlfriend's when I need one."

"Was it your pal's car?"

"Don't know nothing about the car," repeated Kitchener. "Thought it belonged to the guy who was shooting at the guy stealing the tires."

"He was shooting at you," growled Ray.

"It don't have nothing to do with me."

"You owe money to your dealer?" asked Alex, swinging around, attacking from a different angle. "That why you robbed the store?"

"I don't know what you're talking about."

"Doc said you been shooting dope," Alex informed him.

"So? I gotta problem. I'm workin' on it," Kitchener said in a smarmy tone.

"You gotta pay for it somehow."

"Yeah, but ain't robbed no store."

"Did your pal say he didn't wanna go back to prison after the cop identified himself? Or did you? We know you got a long rap sheet."

"I didn't know the guy who got shot was a cop," stated Kitchener. "And I didn't shoot him."

Gibson stepped in. "Witnesses said they heard him identify himself as a police officer."

"I was runnin' away. I didn't hear nothing like that."

"You gonna tell us who you were working for and what this well-paid job was. And tell us how we can contact that person?"

Kitchener considered all three of them. "What do you want?"

"We want to know where the driver of that van you stole is," said Gibson.

"Come on, Harold," Alex said. "We've all been in this game for a long time. We've seen your rap sheet. You know that we know that you're feeding us a line of bullshit. It'll be easier on all of us if you tell us the truth now."

"I didn't kill no one. I don't know where Crazy Eight got the van."

"You'll want us to find the driver before he dies," said Ray. "They found his blood in the back of the van." There had been no blood in the back of the van.

"That bullet they dug out of you, it's from a Glock 17. It matches the bullets from the gun of the police officer you shot and killed," said Alex, ramping up the pressure. They had no idea whether it did or not. It had only just been sent to the ballistics lab, and Alex feared that shrapnel battered from ricocheting off buildings and cars would be unidentifiable. But you say what you have to say.

Kitchener's eyes shifted. "I think I want a lawyer."

"You *think* you want a lawyer?" Alex's breath caught before it left his lungs, and a needle of adrenaline stabbed his heart. "Once you have a lawyer, we can't help you. Then the DA can charge you with whatever they want. Murder one. You better think about that hard."

"No, no, I want a lawyer."

That brought the interview to a skidding halt. Maybe they had put too much pressure on too fast, scared the perp into lawyering up. Dammit. Normally, Alex would tap dance with a suspect for hours, but the van driver might be out there, still alive but injured, dying. They left the OR,

117

and Alex chewed into sensitive part of his thumbnail. Should have played the 'fuck-with-the-guy's-head' game for a bit longer, before switching tactics to 'lying-about-evidence-you-don't-have.' Time was running away. But they put in a call to Legal Aid's night attorney, a holdover from the days of night arraignments.

Alex nursed a cup of coffee in the waiting room, aiming for his caffeine overdose. He contemplated lying across the chairs, capturing a minute or two of rest. They were plastic, cold and rigid, but now that he was sitting around, doing nothing, he realized how much he stank of exhaustion.

Meanwhile, the pageant of late-night medical catastrophes filed through the waiting room: someone who had cut off his little finger. An EDP who faded in and out of consciousness, thrashing and writhing like a wild animal while two nurses tried to get a needle into him. A teenager who had been cut in the hand by one his buddies because they'd been horsing around with knives. A frail old man with skin the color of the walls and clouded eyes passing out, and medical staff rushing him out on a stretcher.

It had been an hour since they had phoned Legal Aid's emergency number, and they promised they were sending somebody. From where, thought Alex. Fucking Vermont?

Ray was phoning his wife. "Yeah, we're still waiting on that lawyer, honey. No, I don't know when I'll be home. I'll phone you. I love you." He hung up with a sigh but didn't say anything. Unlike a lot of cops, he never kvetched about his wife.

And Gibson was calling Wheeler, the stony look on her face telling Alex that Marcus didn't have good news. With a glum expression, she put her phone into her purse. "Wheeler just told me that some New Jersey cops went to the prison for a chat with the guy who originally stole that car. Said he sold it to someone, a pal of his. Apparently, the recipient of the stolen vehicle was found dead about six months ago, after a drug-related shooting in Newark. Trail goes cold there."

"Who shot him?" asked Alex. "Maybe they took his car."

Gibson shrugged effetely. "No one knows. Newark PD never found the perp."

Just then, the door of the waiting room swung open and Chris Leonard, the long-awaited defense attorney, appeared. He was a small, pale-faced man with scrunched, beady eyes, a thick mass of wavy hair, and convex rows of buck teeth.

"Glad you're here," drawled Gibson.

"I had to come from Queens," the lawyer said with annoyed sibilance. "Which room is my client in?"

They led him down the hallway to the ward where the docs had stowed Kitchener, and he went in to consult with his client while they loitered outside. Alex swayed into the wall but didn't think his body could digest any more coffee. His heart was flapping in wacky arrythmias after his previous cup.

At last, the lawyer emerged and motioned Alex, Ray, and Gibson into the room.

"My client might be able to tell you what you want to know," announced Leonard. "But first, we will need to speak with a DA."

Gibson said, "Now?" She looked at her watch. It was pushing 0100.

"You want to find that driver?" croaked Kitchener.

"You'd better fucking hope we do, pal," said Ray. "This is a death penalty case, and you're gonna be first in line for the needle."

Maybe, Alex thought, sharply reminded of his chat with McNally, LaValle's appeal, a conversation that felt like it had been a lifetime ago even though it had been less than twenty-four hours.

"If that's your attitude, Detective—" started Leonard, his pockmarked face reddening.

Gibson was giving Ray one of her 'cool it' looks, and Alex admired her deep wells of patience. No one makes lieutenant in the NYPD without some patience for bullshit. He indulged in his fantasy of violently ripping the morphine drip right out of the perp's arm.

"If your client cooperates, the DA will consider it –" Gibson began.

"Jesus. I'm not naïve," the defense lawyer snapped. "I know *that* police game. My client says nothing until there is an *actual* agreement in place with an ADA."

"We'll phone the DA," said Gibson and herded her detectives out of the room.

The on-call ADA in the Trial Bureau tonight was Marie Adams, whose idea of being on-call did not include being called down to Beth Israel Hospital after 0100 hours. "Who the hell does the motherfucking defense

119

lawyer think he is?" she spat at Alex. "What do you think I'm going to do?"

He imagined that Marie was in her apartment, eating Ben and Jerry's ice cream, watching *The West Wing* reruns, while he was in this hospital, his feet and side and back in agony, and she had the temerity to bitch at him? "How the hell am I supposed to know? But we're busting our fucking balls trying to save someone's life. Just come down here and see what you can shake loose from this asshole."

She growled that she would, like she was doing him a favor, but they both knew that she didn't have a choice. *The West Wing* had to wait.

When Marie strode into the hospital in grey slacks and a navy blue blouse, gripping a shiny, black leather briefcase, you wouldn't think she had rolled out of bed at 0100. The heels she wore clicked against the hospital floor. And she was tall without heels, around 5'11, standing over a lot of men and well over Alex, who made around 5'8 on a good day. Square-shouldered, blue eyes flashing, she exuded an air of exasperated authority and slick professionalism.

All of a sudden, Alex felt slovenly, sweaty, bruised shadows bulging under his eyes, his tie loose, his shirt rumpled. He probably smelled. Weary of repeating the story – by this stage, they had told the defense lawyer, NYPD brass, a *New York Times* reporter – they briefed her on the situation, urgently emphasizing the plight of Khalid. She nodded, her lips pursed, her brows gnarled, and then the four of them joined Kitchener and his lawyer on the ward.

"My client is prepared to tell you what you want to know," Leonard announced. He had the haggard look of a lawyer stuck with a nuts client. "But a deal needs to be in place. If you sign this, he will cooperate with your investigation." He handed Marie a piece of lined notebook paper with rough handwriting scrawled across it. "This was his idea," the lawyer added hastily.

Reading it aloud, Marie said, "This is an agreement between Harold Kitchener and the New York County District Attorney's Office. If the driver of the van in question is found alive, Mr. Kitchener will be sentenced to no more than ten years in prison on second-degree manslaughter, and if he is found dead, Mr. Kitchener will be sentenced to no more than fifteen years in prison on first-degree manslaughter."

"Who the hell writes a plea bargain on some scrap paper," exclaimed Gibson. "What kind of bullshit is he trying?"

"Want it in writing," Kitchener slurred.

Alex started laughing in muffled spasms, giddy from lack of sleep, holding his face in his hands, his eyes smarting, far beyond words or an appropriate response. He desperately wanted to find the driver, dead or alive but most likely dead, and then sleep. And here was this bum, trying to wrangle ten years out of them. Unbelievable.

Before the detectives could lob abuse, Marie said to Leonard, "This isn't my case. I'm just the poor soul in the Trial Bureau stuck with the office cell phone tonight. What makes you think I'm even authorized to make a deal on it?"

The defense lawyer frowned petulantly, his lower lip jutting out. "My client will not say anything incriminating unless he knows that there will be something in it for him."

"If he wants a deal, Chris, you know it is between you and the riding ADA, who isn't me."

"It isn't anyone," said Leonard, his cheeks glowing with cranberry red elation at putting law enforcement in a difficult corner. "And you know it won't be until my client is arraigned, and it goes through ECAB. So, if you want him to incriminate himself by giving you this information, he needs a deal in place now."

"It definitely won't be me after he's arraigned, either," answered Marie irritably. "Cop-killing and felony murder rolled into one? McNally will probably assign it to himself."

"DA's office politics can't impugn my client's Fifth Amendment rights," disputed Leonard. "He's not going to say anything until he has an agreement with your office."

"We'll talk about it outside," Marie said to the fuming cops.

They retreated to waiting room and sat in two rows of chairs attached at the back, so Alex and Ray had to crouch on their knees, facing Marie and Gibson.

Stiffly, Alex crossed his arms. He suppressed a yawn, and then said, "Kitchener's been lying like a fucking rug from the moment we started talking to him. I doubt he's all of a sudden had an attack of honesty now." The edges of the chair dug painfully into his knees.

"I agree with Alex," said Ray.

"Of course you do," sighed Marie, who had done this long enough to know when police partners backed one another, there was no shifting either one. "What do you think, Lieutenant?" She looked at Gibson, hopeful she had a cooler head than the detectives.

"I'm thinking Alex is right, and he's probably dead," Gibson replied in a calculating tone, "But if it turns out he's alive, and here we are, sitting on our butts, and we could have him now, it ain't gonna look good."

"Well, remind me of the evidence," Marie said.

"So far, shrapnel from what might be a nine in his arm and chest, a backpack with about nine hundred fifty bucks and a Smith and Wesson in it, and CCTV pictures of him getting out of the van," replied Gibson.

" 'Might be' a nine?"

"We're hoping ballistics can match it to Irvine's weapon, but it's pretty fragmented." Gibson wasn't sugar-coating this. Alex would have tried. "I wouldn't hold my breath, to be honest."

"Great. How much did he take from the grocery store?"

"A little over a thousand," said Ray. "We think he used some of the money for an Amtrak ticket to DC. Those are around a hundred bucks. Maybe a hundred fifty."

"That could be from some kind of cash-in-hand job, couldn't it?" She tilted her chin and pressed her lips together with composure that made Alex feel even more schvitzik. "Do you have evidence that this van is the car he used as a getaway vehicle at the robbery?"

"We have a description of them jacking a similar vehicle," explained Ray. "A white van."

"Come on, guys. There are thousands of white vans in the city. How do you know it was this one?"

Alex ground his fingers into his shrivelling eyes.

"Eyewitness said it was a florist's van," Ray said, seeming unsure. "And this one is."

"An eyewitness!" The prosecutor expelled a sharp breath, her nostrils flaring. "They saw the van for what, less than thirty seconds? While hiding from a shoot-out. Could they reliably read the writing on the side? You don't have any proof beyond a reasonable doubt that it was *this* van."

"His wife and Lenox Flowers have reported him missing, and these guys definitely left his van in Chelsea," said Alex.

"Yeah. Chelsea. How do you know they were in Harlem?"

"He placed himself at the scene. He told us he was on 123rd at the time of the shooting."

"Did you read him his rights?" asked Marie.

"No, he wasn't in custody."

"Three detectives interrogating him while he's strapped to a hospital bed in the middle of the night. How *isn't* that custody? You should have read him *Miranda* before you talked to him. Anything he said to you there could be inadmissible."

"He knew his rights," volleyed Alex, sniffing in consternation. "He asked for a damned lawyer before we got anywhere."

"Yeah, you know perfectly well that doesn't matter, Alex," Marie replied.

"And *you* know it's a fuzzy line," he growled. He knew that the legal test was 'what a reasonable man, innocent of any crime, would have thought if he had been in the defendant's position.' Like most legal precedents in that absurd world of law and language inhabited by lawyers and judges, it was open to every manner of interpretation.

Gibson calmly countered, "It wasn't much of an incriminating statement, anyway. He blamed his friend for stealing the van. Said he didn't know anything about it."

Marie nodded. "Maybe he stole the van off the street downtown somewhere, and the driver has gone to visit his other girlfriend and obviously not told his wife where he is."

"That's a load of bullshit," sighed Alex morosely. "Kitchener has a rap sheet as long as Broadway."

"That's the sort of stuff a defense attorney is going to say. And give me a break, you know his priors won't be admissible in court. Can you put him at the scene of the robbery at all? I mean, in the absence of his statement. Like beyond a reasonable doubt."

No one answered.

"What about the Smith and Wesson?"

"Unfortunately, Officer Irvine was shot with a .45 and that's a .38 special," said Gibson.

"Right. You don't have the weapon."

"It's probably in the river," said Ray in a disgruntled voice. "Along with the van driver."

"He doesn't have a permit for that firearm," commented Alex wryly. "You could charge him with criminal possession of a weapon."

"Yeah, a D felony. Great. Look, going by what you're saying, right now, we don't have enough evidence to charge him with murder. It's a moot point anyway because *I* certainly can't authorize a plea bargain with him, not on my own back in the middle of the night. I won't be the riding ADA on this case, and I'd have to run any plea by a Bureau Chief anyway."

"What do you want to do?" asked Gibson.

"We keep looking," argued Ray. "Fuck the plea. He's probably lying to us anyway."

At last displaying her own tiredness and frustration, the lawyer twirled her fingers through several strands of wayward hair. "Well, no one in the DA's office is going to make a deal with this guy at two in the morning. No one. Leonard is nuts to think anyone would."

"Maybe he misses the lobster shifts," suggested Alex. He shut his dried-out eyes for moment, reliving the feeling of being dead on his feet, like he was now, of the atmosphere in arraignment court after 0100, all at once bewildering, somber, comic, and chaotic, the best Off-Broadway show in the city.

"Yeah, well, I don't miss them. Thank God the courts keep sensible hours now. He's not making a deal at this time of night. I'll bring this to McNally or whatever Bureau Chief is first in the door in the morning. If we're lucky, you'll find the van driver between now and then, and this will be a non-issue."

Chapter Six

October 29th

Music burbled out of bars and clubs. People cascaded onto First Avenue, strolling down the sidewalk, laughing, stumbling along in drunken revelry. Herds of yellow taxis and other traffic surged uptown on First, that giant artery pumping cars through the city. The energized, partying atmosphere of the East Village seemed at odds with their mood and their miserable, bogged down murder investigation.

As Alex bent over to climb into the driver's seat, a shot of pain exploded at the base of his spine. He fell into the car in a graceless heap, breathing out, "Oh, fuck me!" His right side joined in with a galling ache, but he was accustomed to that.

Ray looked at him, worry and weariness enshrouding his face. "Is it your back?" he asked.

Through gritted teeth, he panted, "Yes. Give me a minute." He slumped over the steering wheel, swearing. The car accident had left him with these back spasms and no real diagnosis or cure, beyond painkillers, waiting it out, icing it, or soaking in a hot bath.

"Is there anything I can do?" inquired Ray, who had put up with this for the past two years. "Find some ice or something?"

"How the fuck are you gonna do that?" Alex said, finding biting sarcasm through the pain irradiating his head. "Flash tin to people at these bars and demand a pack of frozen peas?"

Ray smiled at him. His first of the night. "That's exactly what I'm gonna do."

While his partner searched for something frozen, Alex swallowed three ibuprofens and screwed his eyes shut. Molten tongs were plunging into his lower back. He felt a little depressed, missing the time in his life before the accident, when he didn't suffer this incapacitating back pain. It did not seem as if it would get any better. How long had it been since he had no chronic pain at all? Over seventeen years, before the shooting that had left him with permanent injuries to his lung and ribs. He was tormented, wasting away like he had leprosy, one disintegrating body part at a time.

The flashing lights of an NYPD radio car from the Ninth Precinct danced inside the Crown Vic. They would be wondering why the silver Ford was parked illegally on First, but they would radio Central and run the plates, learning that the car belonged to MNHS. And then they would, he hoped, leave him alone. Indeed, the radio car sped up, vanishing.

Ray reappeared looking like a junkie who'd scored, carrying something tucked tightly under his left arm. He opened the passenger side door. Then he showed Alex his acquisition, a bag of frozen peas. "I was going to get ice, but that would melt, and you and the seat would be soaking wet. I know you were being smartass about the peas, but it seemed like a better idea."

Alex forced a smile, imagining Ray, as serious-looking a detective as anyone could fathom, with his dark, Latino eyes, olive complexion, angular face and muscled, athletic form, flashing tin to some guy in a café or bar, demanding frozen peas. When the police requisition frozen peas, you damn well give up your peas. He shoved the peas underneath his shirt, the cold slicing through the skin, painful at first, but then it defused the indefatigable heat, and after a few minutes of icing, the sensation of a knife driving into his back faded to blunt force injury, the level of pain he could tolerate.

"Thanks, Ray," he said gratefully. "You must've felt ridiculous."

"The guy in the bar was sure confused. Is it feeling better now?"

"Yeah. A bit."

"I guess I'd better phone Anna and tell her I'm not gonna be home tonight." Ray frowned sorrowfully at his phone.

"Tell her it's overtime, and you'll take her out to dinner. Forty-eight bucks an hour. Who's gonna complain?"

His back, for a start, but he could think straight again. He had to think straight about the case. Where should they even begin searching for the van driver, when every search so far had failed?

Unhappily, Ray put the cell in his pocket. "She's pissed. But we gotta *try* to find this guy. What now?"

"Kitchener's apartment?" offered Alex. No one had searched there yet, but they had his address from his DCJS record. He flipped through his memo book. East 120th. Near First Avenue. Alex knew the area. One of those blocks in East Harlem still plagued by drugs, violence, and crime, where gentrification had not yet supplanted the crackhouses and prostitutes.

"We don't have a warrant," Ray said.

"Doesn't matter. It's an emergency, a hostage situation."

"Even though we think the hostage isn't a hostage, but is a DOA?"

Alex gently squished his fingers into the bags under his eyelids. "*We think that, but if Gibson and the DA agreed with us, I'd be in my fucking bed. On those grounds, he's a live hostage who could be in need of immediate medical attention.*"

Ray nodded and palmed his forehead, yawning. "If there's any evidence in plain view, that'd be nice. Think there's much of a chance of that, Lex?"

"No," said Alex pessimistically.

After wedging the frozen peas between the seat and his spine, he started the car and gunned it up First Avenue. The skyscrapers formed canyons of light, and the sidewalks were crammed with people spilling out of late parties at Midtown venues and making drunken kamikaze dashes across the road. Then they flew through the deserted streets of the Upper East Side. Only a handful of pedestrians strode warily along the empty sidewalks. The traffic vanished, Alex racing unhindered past apartments that cost more to rent in one month than he made in a year.

Past East 98th, the neighborhood changed again, now into dark streets, boarded-up buildings that looked like they'd been bombed out during a blitz, the three-dimensional work of graffiti artists leaping out of plywood boards and railway pylons, and garbage strewn along the gutter like no one cared anymore.

Ray radioed through to Operations and got a number from NYCHA for the super of Kitchener's building. And for the fun of it, warrant checks and NITRO checks, but he came back clean. They phoned him. Yes, it was nearly three in the morning. But it was urgent. And they were the police. The super hadn't been pleased, but he cooperated and agreed to meet them at the apartment. They cruised slowly along 120th, Ray peering through the gloomy street lighting for the building number. The street was deserted. Not even the dope fiends were out searching for that last hit of the night.

"Here," said Ray.

"You sure?" said Alex, stopping the car and squinting at the building, a dilapidated Harlem brownstone with flaking stonework and peeling, cracked window frames. He couldn't make out the number at all.

Ray grinned at him. "It's your eyes, Lex."

They left the car double-parked in front of the building. Alex crawled out of the car, mindful of his back. His spine ticked with tremors of pain as he stood up. Kneading his lower back, he limped wearily after Ray, who had rang the buzzer.

The superintendent, a black guy wearing a blue bathrobe and matching furry flip-flops, shuffled grudgingly down the creaking iron fire escape stairs. "This really couldn't wait?"

"No," said Alex. "Open the door."

"I knew that guy was trouble."

"What do you mean?"

"He just seemed sketchy, man."

"Any reason in particular?"

"Nah, he was just a sketchy motherfucker."

"You seen him recently?"

"No."

"When was the last time you saw him?"

"Dunno... A month ago?"

"You know if he's slinging?"

The super gave a disaffected shrug. "Probably, but not here. I ain't never seen him at it.

He fiddled with a key ring that would befit a prison guard, and then he gave the warped door a shove. The detectives flicked on the light, revealing a messy, odiferous apartment, permeated by mold and dust. Alex breathed through his mouth but doubled over with a sneezing fit.

They could only look around the apartment and only search places big enough to hold a hostage. In minutes, they'd cleared the place, stepping around piles of rotting cardboard boxes and junk on the floor, broken bits of furniture, moth-eaten clothes and dirty dishes piled here and there, and a disgusting, battered microwave on the floor, guarding the entrance to the kitchen. Roaches, but no hostages.

"You saw him a month ago?" Alex asked the super. "Here?"

"Yeah, when he last paid the rent."

"Just him?"

"Yeah."

"Has he not paid for this month?" asked Ray.

"He kept saying it was coming. He'd get the money soon. Blah, blah, blah."

"But you said you hadn't seen him for a month."

"Email, Detective," said the super dryly. "It's the 21st century."

"Is there a computer here?" Ray fancied himself as kind of an amateur hacker.

"We'd need a warrant for that, Ray," Alex said tiredly.

At the same time, the super rolled his eyes. "Does it *look* like he gets the internet? He hasn't paid his phone bill in months. I think he goes to the library. What'd he do?"

"Robbed a store," answered Alex evasively.

"I guess he was getting the money."

The coffee Alex had been chugging all night had gone through him, and he felt desperate for a piss, at the stage where he thought, *it's either here or the street.* He risked the malodorous bathroom. The smell was like the sewage treatment plants on Staten Island. He breathed through the gaps in his teeth. This place housed enough mold to keep a biologist entertained for weeks, probably new species of it.

A cockroach, surprised by the light, scuttled across the floor. For the hell of it, Alex scanned the shower again, although they'd cleared this room like all the others. Two large spiders looked at him eerily. A shiver ran down his spine.

When he emerged, Ray asked, "I guess you double checked the can?"

"Yeah, found a roach and a couple spiders so big you could put a saddle on and ride 'em in the Belmont."

"There's a pile of unopened mail at the door," said Ray. "I think it's mostly junk."

To search anywhere else or open his mail, they would need a warrant and Tyvek suits. They swiftly vacated the noxious apartment, and the super trundled up the fire escape, muttering, "When you catch him, tell him he owes me the rent."

Alex said, "Trust me, that will be the least of his problems."

The detectives looked at one another. Alex had nothing to offer. His eyes stung from the effort of keeping them open. His lower back complained in loud twinges, and he pressed his fingers into the soft, gently pulsing indentations in his temples on both sides of his head.

Ray was flipping through his memo book, re-reading his notes. "If we can get a hold of information from his last robbery arrest…"

"How the hell are we gonna do that?" Alex asked, his voice heavy. "Break into the DA's office at three in the morning? We've already pulled OLBS sheets."

"The file might have more info."

"Yeah, but we're not gonna get it until after 0800." Case files were stored in the DA's office on their records floor, and then after five or so years, moved off-site.

"OLBS said that he was collared by a Detective Fred Symington –"

"Fred Symington?" blurted Alex, astonished.

"Yeah, you know him?"

"We were partners at the One-Oh-Three together. Fuck. Really? Haven't seen him in years."

At the end of their tours in Jamaica, Alex and Fred would go to the pub together to play pool, solve the world's problems, and drink to their own. But they had hardly seen one another since Alex moved back to Manhattan in '87. Only once, when Fred visited Alex in the hospital while he was recovering from the shooting, but afterwards they drifted apart and then fell out over priorities and department politics.

"I guess he works for Manhattan Robbery now."

"Jesus, really? He was desperate to get into Major Case, last I heard. But that was a long time ago. I didn't know he'd moved to Robbery."

"Well, if we got a hold of him, he might know something about our perp. Presumably he did some kind of investigation before he collared him. If he's an old pal of yours, you have a way to get a hold of him?"

"Not easily. His number won't be on my cell."

Torpidity and cold clogged his brain. How could he contact Fred? Would Fred want to speak with him? Feeling his asthenic back, he wiggled into the driver's seat. During their last phone conversation, Fred had sniped at Alex about abandoning his family, and then Alex heard from a mutual friend that Fred had been cultivating a grudge for three years, pissed that Alex got a transfer to an elite squad while Fred's career ground to a halt, a detective third grade in the One-Oh-Three, no promotion in sight. But that was 1990. Fourteen years could heal wounds and bring promotions.

Ray said, "I have a friend in Robbery. You'll remember Detective Sylvia Napolitano."

"No shit, you tried to hook me up with her like a year ago." Sylvia had been half-Italian, half-Caribbean, dark-skinned but with Italian features, intelligent and witty and far too together to see much hope with him. They'd gone on a couple dates, but there had been no chemistry. "Nice lady. I think she figured she could do better than me."

"Oh, come on, Alex. It wasn't like that."

"A recovering alcoholic forty-six year old detective?"

Ray blew out a perturbed breath. "If that's how you see yourself... Never mind. I'll phone her and see if she has a number for Detective Symington."

He put the phone to his ear, and after apologizing for calling at the ludicrous hour, he related an abstract of the case and wrote a number down on his notepad, which he handed to Alex. Then he had a desultory conversation with Detective Napolitano – his kids were all right, his wife was all right, Alex was all right – before hanging up the phone.

The number had a 917 area code. Alex dialed it, identifying himself only with his first name, and his guts queasily snarled. Had he fucked it up or had Fred fucked it up, or did their friendship never stand a chance? It had a niche, one time, one place, but couldn't survive any other.

"Alex?" Fred said groggily, and then, working out who it was, he switched to Alex's affectionate street name. "Lex? What the hell? What's going on? Oh, God. You're not drunk, are you?"

"Unfortunately not," said Alex. Of course, Fred's first assumption, a drunk dial. Did Fred even know he'd been in rehab? He must, through the wire. Whatever. As succinctly as he could, Alex explained their predicament.

"Oh. Right. Christ, man, I don't hear from you in years, then you got some case you're chasing. I kinda remember that shitbag. I'm sure there's some details in my memo book. You *really* need to see it now?"

"Yeah, now," pleaded Alex. "This guy's life is on the line." Fred had a strong sense of duty. Whatever he thought of Alex, he was still a good cop, first and foremost.

131

"Celia's gonna kill me, going to do work stuff at this time. Fuckin' three am. I told her I wouldn't – well, can we meet in Lower Manhattan? I live in Bay Ridge now. If we meet by 100 Centre Street, I can be in and out quickly. Is that okay? I want to help you, Lex, but I'm just trying to keep the peace here."

He agreed to meet Fred at Foley Square, the other end of Manhattan. Driving took more concentration than it usually did, but even so, he relished the novelty of cruising along FDR at an easy 70 and not feeling like the traffic was raising his blood pressure, rare indeed for a New Yorker. On their arrival at Foley Square, he parallel parked inconspicuously on the street.

The Civic Center was quiet, completely deserted, and Alex found that unsettling. Up until April of last year, the Criminal Courts were busy even now, with the infamous 'lobster shifts,' all-night arraignments instituted in the early '80s because there weren't enough hours in the day to process all the criminals pouring into the court system. You would step through the wooden doors of AR-1 to find yourself in a surreal world, police officers, lawyers, defendants and their families, clerks, and judges, everyone struggling to keep their eyes open in the commotion and confusion of arraignment court in those lingering hours of darkness. In recent years, crime rates had fallen so low that the DA, fed up with paying a prosecutor to litigate lobster shift arraignments, had argued that there was no need for it anymore, and state court officials had finally ended it. No one missed it. Nonetheless, Alex found it disconcerting, the eerie silence of 100 Centre Street after twenty-one years of lobster shifts.

Pacing a circle to stay warm, Alex breathed into his hands. The frigid air sliced into his lungs. Then Fred arrived, driving an old Chevy Impala, and the three detectives huddled on a bench on the edge of the square, their backs to the federal courthouse. Anyone who saw them would have wondered what they were doing there, if they were doing a drug deal.

Fred shook his head and pulled his woolly hat tighter against his ears. "Alex, I don't see you for however many years, and you got me out at four in the morning. You haven't changed at all."

"I'm sober," said Alex.

"Yeah, I heard that. But you're still you."

Alex wondered what he meant. But he had no time to revisit the past or rehash their final narky argument. "We just need a name, a lead,

132

something about this guy," he begged. "'Cause right now, we got nothing. And by the time we get search warrants or pull the file from the DA's office, this vic could be fucked."

"You always had a good reason." Fred smiled slightly.

"Sometimes. If it was on the job, I probably did, or thought I did. If it wasn't, it was just 'cause I was off my head. But what've you got?"

Fred had half a dozen memo books balanced on his knee. His hands quivered with the cold as he flipped through them, reading by the golden light of the streetlamp shining above their bench. As Fred scanned his books, Alex folded his arms tightly over his stomach, holding in what little warmth he could.

"Manhattan Robbery?" he asked. "When did that happen?"

"A couple years ago. When I made first grade."

"First grade?"

Fred smiled rapturously at him. His cheeks looked fuller than Alex remembered. He'd put on weight. "Yeah. I left the One-Oh-Three in 1993. I made second while doing a stint in Bronx Narcotics. Then they sent me to Robbery, and I busted up a major racket related to the Russians."

"That's great," said Alex, his voice solemn with weariness. Fred had got those coveted promotions after all, and he made more money and had more juice than Alex.

"Oh, here... Kitchener? Is that your perp's name?"

"Yes," said Ray, speaking brusquely. "What have you got?"

Fred squinted, reading through the sepulchral lighting. "Collared 2/13/03. He'd robbed a bodega on East 129th with an accomplice called Johnny Bailey four days before."

"With a gun?" asked Alex. An accomplice? His respiration quickened.

"Nah, a knife. A big, hunting knife. You don't get to use it as a pattern. Uniforms on the scene got some of the street players to identify him. He's known around. Looks like I did a line-up, and he was positively ID'd by a witness. He has – or had – a Puerto Rican girlfriend who lives at 157th and St Nicholas. Her name is Analisa Santos. I collared him near her place. That's about all I got on him here. Sorry, Lex. Hope that gives you something. He didn't talk to me in the precinct. Lawyered right up."

He scribbled the girlfriend's address on a post-it note and handed it to Alex, who folded it up, placing it in his wallet. It was a hell of lot more information than they had an hour ago.

"You get a motive, anything?" Alex asked, losing the sentence in a yawn.

"A couple jonesing dope fiends, what do you think the motive is?" Fred replied, smiling.

"Was he charged?"

"Yeah, but it got dropped. Witnesses forgot and one died, and we had no case. Same old shit. But they arrested Bailey for trespassing not too long after. He was slinging dope in the lobby of a building. That stuck."

"Do you know if Bailey's out?"

"Probably. He got probation for that."

"What about the 'street players?'" queried Ray. "Maybe he's still hanging out with the same low lifes."

Reflective, Fred considered the pages of his memo books for a moment, the handwritten lines bringing his mind back to names, faces, crimes. "He won't be. Four guys identified him. Three are in jail and one's dead. It's that kind of crowd." As he shut the books and stuffed them into his bag, he said to Alex, "I can't believe you're sober now. Wow. Good for you."

"Well," said Alex, "I couldn't go on doing what I was doing."

"And I heard through the wire that you'd made second grade as well."

"Yeah, like six years ago."

"Really? Christ, man, you've been in Homicide for more than fifteen years," said Fred, sounding flabbergasted. "Seems like Jamaica wasn't *that* long ago."

"No, it doesn't," Alex concurred, still feeling troubled. So much had happened between then and now.

"You look good, better. You've lost weight."

"You think?" Alex said, doubting it. "Last time you saw me, I was hooked up to IVs and ECGs and could barely fucking walk."

"Yes, I know. But I mean, before. When we worked together. It's no surprise, with you being off the drink." Playfully, he swatted Alex's stomach with the back of his hand. "You've always had a bit of a gut on you, but you do look healthier."

Self-consciously, Alex hung his head, so his gaze fell to the paunch around his middle. "I got pretty ill. That's why I had to quit."

"Surprised that didn't happen to more of us."

"My doctor said only like thirty percent of heavy drinkers get serious health problems. Lucky me, one of that thirty."

"Huh, well, I'm really sorry. Sounds like you had kind of a shit time. I'm sorry I didn't stay in touch. Life got crazy and busy."

An apology? It wasn't an admission of guilt for being a douchebag, but he'd uttered the word 'sorry' and he looked contrite.

"Lex, we really gotta move," interjected Ray, his steely gaze catching Alex's eye, pulling him back into the present, the cold night, the empty courthouses, and the hopeless search for a victim.

"We should get a coffee or something sometime," said Fred, standing and stretching. "Catch up properly. You still in that place on the Upper West?"

"Yeah." Alex felt himself breathing rhythmically, his skin turning hot. During his last conversation with Fred in 1990, he'd begged Fred to come to his newly-bought apartment for a party, and Fred accused Alex of being immature and irresponsible. He had been both but hearing the charges against him had hurt more.

"Never thought you would end up there."

"Hey, don't knock it. It's a nice neighborhood." He managed a weary, wry grin. "I spend my days dealing with the bottom of fucking society. I thought, well, if I was gonna buy an apartment, it shouldn't be in some shithole. It would be just like work."

"Beats a rented hovel."

"Yeah, and I always seemed to find the worst ones. Remember the homeless guy who lived in the entryway of the place in Ridgewood? And everything else about it!"

"Well, like I said, you look pretty good, Lex."

Alex snorted sardonically. "For four in the morning!"

"At least we're not mixing the Nesquick and whisky this time. Jesus, that was awful."

"It seemed like a good idea at the time." A phrase that justified or at least explained a lot of the decisions he'd made over the years.

135

"Most things do when you're drunk out of your mind," giggled Fred. To Ray, he said, "Your partner, he was a *legend* back in the One-Oh-Three."

"That's one way to look at it," said Alex.

"Well, hope that was helpful," said Fred sincerely. "I'll see you 'round, Lex. Take care of yourself. You have my current number now. Call me sometime."

He stood up and jauntily strode off in his bouncing gait towards his car. Alex watched him go, lost in recollections of smoky pubs and drunken parties in Queens. The sky was beginning to show that pale, early morning hue, a bluish tinge creeping over the sparkling skyscrapers and fading, twinkling lights of planes flying into LaGuardia, JFK, or Newark.

"Guess we should find the girlfriend," said Ray.

Alex unlocked the car. Acid sloshed against the walls of his empty stomach, and it growled at him unhappily.

"You all right?" asked Ray.

"Yeah, but I think we should get something to eat." An hour off his feet, more coffee, and some food might revive him. He considered the possibility that the perps had dumped the hostage with the girlfriend or near her place, but he needed something to cool the pain in his stomach and to wake up.

Ray agreed. "We're gonna fall on our faces if we don't. We'll find a twenty-four hour diner or something like that in the Village."

They found a diner with 1960s-style booths and chrome trim on the tables and chairs on Mercer Street, populated by the motley late-night crowd of students, cops, nurses, shift workers, and the under-employed. Relieved to be eating, they watched the dawn lighten the sky while attacking a bottomless pot of coffee, Alex working through a stack of fat, fluffy pancakes and maple syrup, and Ray, at a loss for healthy options in this joint, tolerating an egg on an English muffin.

Disgustedly inquisitive, Ray asked Alex about the shithole apartment in Queens. The place where the main door didn't lock, the shower didn't work (they used the precinct showers), Alex had a pizza box replacing a bedroom window at one point, and they were perpetually chasing roaches with cans of Raid. Their slum landlord had refused to do anything about any of it, and they were young enough to find it funny.

Then Ray queried, "What was that about him seeing you hooked up to IVs?"

"Oh." Alex pushed a pancake around his plate. "He came to the hospital to see me after the 190th Street shooting. I was pretty fucked. Then life got in the way, and I haven't seen him since."

"That was '87, right?"

"Yeah."

He swallowed a mouthful of pancake that didn't want to go down, suppressing a croaking gasp of raw, unraveled emotions. Here he was, worried about trivialities like food and not sleeping and distant quarrels, while Tariq Khalid was out in the cold somewhere, tied up, wounded, dead, who knows? Another triviality wormed into his mind. He glanced surreptitiously at his phone. The screen showed nothing. No missed calls or texts unrelated to work. The insanity and intensity of the day had consigned the whole mess with Becky to a locked corner of his brain. On seeing she hadn't tried phoning him, he drove it back there and chided himself. The case. The only damned thing that should be on his mind. Talk to the girlfriend; find out if Wheeler's continued canvass in Chelsea turned up anything; then what?

They rushed through their meal, and then at 0530, they paid up and ran for their car. The city was stirring with a different kind of life, the last of the late-night revelers tripping home and the first of the early morning commuters emerging onto the streets. With daylight, Alex hoped for a second wind, his body tricked into forgetting he had been up for twenty-four hours, but he felt dazed, like he'd run headfirst into wall. At least he had a belly full of pancakes and coffee.

He threw the car keys at Ray. "Your turn to drive."

Chapter Seven

October 29th

Just after 0600, an hour or so ahead of the morning rush hour, the detectives parked on the street and then plodded up a stoop to the apartment on Fred's post-it note. A female Latina voice answered the buzzer. They announced that they were the police and asked for Analisa Santos. A second's hesitation, and then the buzzer released the locks, and they were greeted at the door of the second-floor apartment by a petite, doubtful-looking Puerto Rican woman. The Puerto Rican community and the NYPD did not always have the best of relations. Ray spoke to her in Spanish, which put her more at ease, and she let them in, still speaking Spanish with Ray as she led them through a cramped hallway to the kitchen, a shallow bay with some late-90s appliances.

"You're wanting to know about Harold?" she said, switching to English for Alex's benefit. "He's in trouble again?"

"Yeah, like I said, he's tried to rob a bodega," said Ray.

She cursed in Spanish. "I thought he was reforming his ways, getting out of the whole criminal thing. Or that's what he told me. I really did think after the last time he was getting his act together, becoming, you know, a normal, useful part of society. He was even helping with Miguel's – that's my son – soccer team. He said he didn't want to go back to prison."

"Committing armed robbery is a lousy way to stay outta prison," said Alex, and his eyes roved the living room. It had a sofa, a rocking chair, an old television, and a cadre of statues of the Virgin Mary and various saints holding vigil over the furniture. No hostages.

"I should have known," she continued, sounding vexed. "He was hanging out with the people he hangs out with. I didn't like them. There was something… Told Harold none of those people could come into the house. I didn't want to have anything to do with them. I didn't want them near my son. Why couldn't he find some nice, normal friends, people with jobs and families?"

"Do you know the names of these people?"

"The one he was with the most was called Bailey."

Alex's heart skipped several beats. The name from Fred's memo books. "Does the name 'Crazy Eight' ring a bell?"

She shook her head again, her long hair swishing like a horse's tail. "That's like a gangster name. Should it?"

Alex squeezed his lips together noncommittally and shrugged.

Ray asked, "What did Bailey look like?"

"Short. Mean. I didn't see him much. Tried not to. I knew that he was someone Harold had been friends with years ago, which wasn't a good thing."

"Would you recognize him if you saw him?"

"I don't know."

They showed her the picture from the CCTV. "Is this Bailey?" Alex asked.

She put her hand to her mouth, considering the picture, and then said, "It's a short gringo. Bailey is a short gringo. I don't know."

Alex jotted down in his memo pad that she may have ID'd the second suspect, but he wouldn't describe it as a positive ID. The city was full of 'short gringos,' including himself. But his gut told him she probably did know. Rule one of any investigation – everyone lies to the police. "We've been in Harold's apartment. Doesn't look like he goes there much."

"That apartment," she snarled. "It's awful. I won't go there. He was staying here. Unless I get sick of him. Then I kick him out. Maybe he goes to the apartment. Maybe he goes and stays with a friend."

"What friends?" queried Alex.

"Who knows. More druggies. Don't want people like that near my son."

"If he's not here, and not at his apartment, where might he go?"

She grumbled, "Under a bridge? I don't know."

"When was the last time you saw Harold?" asked Ray.

She hesitated and started drying a glass on the counter. "Uh, last week."

Alex and Ray looked at one another, both detectives' internal polygraphs hitting red.

"You sure about that?" said Ray.

"Analisa," Alex said, his voice grave and sober. "You said you wanna raise your son right. You don't wanna get in trouble by lying to the police. We can canvass this block, talk to all your neighbors, and if anyone saw Harold some time that *wasn't* last week –"

"Okay, he came by yesterday morning," she confessed, still grasping the glass. "He was injured. Hurt in his arm. Said he'd been in a fight that night in some sleazy bar he goes to. I don't know, I don't ask."

"You gotta name for this bar?"

"I don't know. When he gets drunk, he can do stupid things, like get into fights. Said he needed to borrow my car to move some soccer equipment. As I said, he's been helping with Miguel's team."

"What soccer equipment?"

"A couple goals. A bag of soccer balls."

"Did you let him borrow the car?" asked Alex.

"Yes," she answered, her face flushing with strain, and she kept on drying the glass.

"For how long?"

"I told him he had to bring it back in twenty minutes. I had to drop my son at school and go to work. I work for a caterer. He did."

"Was he alone?"

"Yes."

"You sure?"

"I didn't see no one else."

"After he borrowed your car, what happened?"

Worried and restless, she wrapped the dishtowel around her hand and vigorously dried a plate. "I don't know. I went to work. I was in Westchester at some rich lady's house for most of the day. Didn't hear from him. Didn't know what he was up to, 'till you guys just came here now and told me. I can't believe it."

Alex's suspicions were redlining. *Soccer equipment, my ass,* he thought, clearing his throat. "Sorry, can I use your bathroom?"

She pointed him towards a door in the hallway, near the entrance. He turned and walked towards it, hearing Ray switching back into Spanish in his absence. This was not a bullshit ruse; he had to pee again, the disadvantage of those limitless coffee refills. But he took the opportunity to survey the hall, and then, after he'd pissed, he conducted a fastidious plain sight search of the bathroom. He scowled at his reflection – fuck, he looked pallid and sleep-deprived, and exhaustion puffed up the furrows below his eyes. Anyway, the toilet bowl and the bathtub were sparkling, the floor squeaky underfoot and slippery, as if she had cleaned it not long before. You could lick the place.

An immaculate bathroom was evidence of nothing, as far as the courts were concerned, but Alex found it fishy as hell. On his return to the kitchen, he opened a new page in his memo book. "What's the name of the catering company?" When Wheeler and Greenwood started their tour at 0800 hours, he would ask them to verify that the catering company was a real catering company, that Analisa really worked for them, and that she was where she said she was.

"Five Boroughs Catering," she replied.

"Can we see the car?" asked Ray.

She wrapped herself in a jacket and scarf, and then led them down the stairs to the street just outside, unlocking an orb-shaped grey late-90s Ford Aspire with a dent in the rear bumper and rusted wheel arches. They ran their eyes over the car, peering closely at the seats, the footwells, the insides of the doors, searching for traces of blood or anything unusual. They asked her to open the trunk, and she obliged. Nothing leapt out as suspicious or incriminating. It would take some ambition and creativity to squeeze a body into the tiny car, but if Kitchener had done so, there might be DNA or microscopic evidence: fibers, hair, blood.

But to search the car, they would need a warrant. Alex exchanged a significant look with Ray, those two unspoken words, *search warrant.* Ray bobbed his head, agreeing with him. They smiled emotionlessly and thanked her for her cooperation. For all they knew, she had helped the perps move the vic, so the last thing they wanted was her attacking the inside of the car with a bottle of bleach (Alex thought she had already done so with the bathroom).

If someone had moved Khalid with this vehicle, he might be within ten or fifteen minutes of 157th Street. Anything that narrowed their search parameters promised respite and hope. And maybe, after three years, he and Ray were finally getting in tune with one another.

141

"See, there's nothing in the car," said Analisa, blushing furiously as if she had expected there to be something and was embarrassed that there wasn't. "Can I go now? I have to get my son ready for school."

"Yeah, no problem," Alex said. He fished a card out of his inside coat pocket, next to antacids and a pen. "If you think of anything else Harold might've done or said, call or email me."

Covering her mouth, she stared at the card. "You're Homicide? Unbelievable. He's got homicide cops looking for him now. That's like...like...something that happens on TV. How do you get homicide cops in real life?"

"You kill someone," said Alex.

She spun on her heel and stormily stomped up the stoop. "If that bastard ever gets out of prison, we're done."

We have to get him into prison first, Alex thought.

They circled the block on foot, searching for evidence of someone moving a body or a bleeding hostage.

"Think she's telling us everything, Lex?" Ray asked.

"No."

"What do you think we should do?"

Alex shrugged as he leaned over a rusty iron balustrade, peering into a trash-filled window well, breathing through his mouth as the pungent reek of rotting garbage prickled his nostrils. "Nothing. Until we have some idea of what she isn't telling us. She say anything to you when I went off for a piss?"

"Nah, we talked about Puerto Rico. I was just trying to soften her up a bit. She's from San Juan, the opposite end of town from where my parents live. And she has no idea where Kitchener's bucket-of-blood-bar is. Could be in Jersey, for all she knew. Or so she says. I guess you had a look 'round?"

"She's cleaned the fuck out of the bathroom." Alex scratched at his eyes with his sleeve. They felt as though they were drying and shrinking into his head. "But who knows? Maybe she's one of those people who can't stand a gross bathroom."

Dump spots were plentiful – boarded-up buildings, the Hudson, Highbridge Park, Riverside Park, Trinity Church Cemetery if the perps had any sense of irony. They canvassed the neighborhood for at least three hours, and Alex struggled to keep track of how many streets they walked, how many parks and bushes they scuffled through, how many people they interviewed. People shied away from them or eyefucked them or looked inconvenienced when questioned. Some things hadn't changed. Washington Heights was no longer a madhouse, the drug-saturated corner of chaos, violence, and lawlessness that had besieged the Three-Four Precinct in the early '90s drug wars, the kind of place where, at one point, the NYPD quartermaster refused to make routine deliveries of stationary to the station house. But parts of it remained pretty rough, and many of its residents still preferred avoiding the police.

At 0815, Alex phoned the office and got Wheeler and Greenwood checking out Analisa's story and running background checks on her. Next, he contacted the Three-Three and Three-Four detective squads, asking them to check their databases and lists of Washington Heights street names. Had they ever come across a white junkie called 'Crazy Eight' or Johnny Bailey who matched the description of their second robber?

Then Alex called in on an old informant, who told them that he hadn't seen nor heard of anything like that. And he assured them that he would. He usually knew where trouble was in the Heights. *Yeah,* thought Alex, *that's because you're usually in it.* But while he was fairly mad and smoked a lot of crack, he'd been a reliable CI over the years. Utterly discouraged, they persisted with their hopeless canvass, Alex thinking that if Tariq Khalid wasn't dead eight hours ago, he would be now, and increasingly convinced that this may have been a superfluous exercise from its outset, that Kitchener had dumped the body in the river, and six months from now, he would wash up on a beach in New Jersey.

His phone rang. Marcus Wheeler. Alex flipped it open, saying tiredly, "Heya."

"Hi, Lex," said Marcus. "We did what you asked. Looks like Five Boroughs Catering is indeed a legit business, at least according to the NY Department of Taxation and the Corporation Division. If they are a front for laundering drug money, they're doing a good job as no one knows about it yet." Alex imagined Marcus' weird, bucktoothed grin as he said that. "I talked to them, and they confirmed that Analisa Santos works for them, and she was at a wedding reception in Mount Kisco from about noon yesterday and has a job at a Bar Mitzvah in Riverdale today."

"Right," coughed Alex. He slapped his palm over his mouth, stifling a yawn. "Do you have numbers for the people who had the Bar Mitzvah or whatever? Call them, just to corroborate."

"Ten-four," said Marcus. "You all right?"

"Unh," Alex grunted.

"That good, eh?"

"Yep," Alex sighed.

"Oh, and I got a call from Detective Indelicata at the Three-Four. He was looking for you—"

"Indelicata's handling this?" Alex interrupted, annoyed. Everyone knew Vito Indelicata was an asshole, but they also thought he was a genius. Alex also knew Indelicata was an asshole, but he must be the only person in the NYPD who didn't see him as a genius; in part because he'd seen, first-hand, Indelicata's slimy, dishonest methods, and in part because they'd fallen out in the early '90s, a chasmic and insoluble disagreement over those methods.

"A redball that could get his name in the news?" Marcus responded. "Obviously he is. He said I could pass on a message. Apparently 'Crazy Eight' is a popular street name – who woulda thought? But not a lot of white guys around there. The one they found matching your description is indeed called Johnny Bailey. Thirty-two years old. They've collared him for assault a couple of times and some narc charges. Is that helpful?"

"Yeah." Alex sucked in a whistling breath through his teeth and told himself to stay clear-headed and professional. He had a tidbit, a lead. Who cares if Indelicata was sticking his overblown narcissistic toe into the investigation? "It confirms what we've heard about Kitchener's accomplice. Does Indelicata have an address for him? Maybe worth checking it out, though I doubt he's anywhere near it now."

"Ten-four," said Wheeler, adding, "Gibson's downtown. Getting her balls busted by the Chief of D's—uh, well, you know, if she had balls, that is, they would be getting busted—"

"Gotcha, Marcus," cut in Alex. "We're busting ours, and we've got fucking bupkes. No one's seen this guy. It's the Heights. Everyone's blind or has fucking amnesia, as usual."

As soon as he hung up with Marcus, the phone screeched again. He envisioned the satisfaction of throwing it into the river. The number had the Manhattan DA's prefix, and he could not keep the weariness and impatience out of his voice.

Marie said, "I take it you haven't found him."

"No."

"Any leads?"

"Working on it."

"I've talked to McNally. He says he'll negotiate a deal with Chris Leonard if you don't find this guy by midday. He's met with the Chief of D's and the PC."

"If we don't find him by midday, it'll be even more likely he's dead. What the fuck is McNally thinking?" Alex exploded.

"I don't know, Alex. You sound beat. He's probably thinking it'll look really bad for everyone if the vic is being held hostage somewhere, and we can't find him. And he's not been awake all night. But that's it. Keep looking for now." She hung up before he gave her more flak.

Fuck, he felt beat. His mind was woollier than ever, his back and his right side inflamed, throbbing painfully, and blisters scoured his feet. He reiterated Marie's news, and Ray growled, "What's with these lawyers? How are they even thinking they can give this asshole man one for killing a cop and felony murder?"

"We find Khalid, they won't."

About half an hour later, Marcus got back to them with an address in the Heights for Johnny Bailey. Not far from where they were – 155th, a run-down building with plywood boards nailed over half the windows and graffiti tags sprayed on the walls. They pounded on the flaking, splintered door, disturbing the neighbors. A Latina woman with two kids in tow emerged from her apartment next door, shouting angrily at them in Spanish. Ray answered. The woman told Ray that no one had been in that apartment in weeks.

When Ray pressed her for a description of the person who lived there, she told him that she didn't know. He didn't believe it, but they couldn't do anything about that. Alex and Ray quietly discussed whether or not they could legally bust down the door. They could, given that it was a hostage situation, and with Indelicata's identification of Bailey, and Analisa's statement that Kitchener had been hanging out with him, they had reasonable cause to believe Bailey had been involved.

145

Good enough. Guns drawn, they put their shoulders against the door, officers from the Three-Three behind them, counted to three, and then kicked open the door, shouting, "Police!"

Covering one another's backs, they crashed into a darkened studio apartment. They conducted a quick search, clearing the apartment, which took seconds as it was tiny and empty. A few scared roaches scuttled under a bed with a broken, stained mattress and a three-legged kitchen table at opposite corners. Alex slid his gun into his holster and breathed in the damp, stale musty scent of a building that rarely saw life or warmth.

Sneezes rocked his body as congestion prickled his sinuses. A cloudy feeling was building in his chest. He palmed his sternum. This place must be bitterly cold in the winter and unbearably hot in the summer. On the floor they found old needles, syringes, and discarded bottle caps. If you were high enough, you wouldn't care about the heat or cold. Whoever had stayed here used it as a shooting gallery, but Alex surmised that they hadn't for some time. They nosed around the apartment, but neither detective believed that Khalid would be stowed here.

When they left the place, defeated, the neighbor was standing on the stoop, and she said to Ray in Spanish, "I told you so."

By 1130, their tempers had unraveled, and they were snapping at one another, giving in to gloomy, tattered exhaustion. The vic had vanished. Most likely in the river, although there was always Marie's defense lawyer theory; that he'd taken it upon himself to go missing, which people did sometimes, and the carjacking episode was nothing more than coincidence. But even in the chaotic bafflement and disaster of people's lives that Alex investigated every day, coincidence was something he usually treated with skepticism. Chains of coincidences were evidence.

Gibson called Ray's cell. "I think we should keep looking," said Ray. "It's daytime. If we could get a search warrant for this apartment, we could have a better look at it."

Gibson said something, and Ray responded glumly, "No, I don't know. I'm not sure, Lou." He met Alex's eyes. "Lex, Gibson's at the DA's office with McNally. She wants us down there."

"I could do with a break. And we're not finding shit. We've fucked up something." Alex felt like molasses had replaced the blood in his head.

"Or he's in the damned river," Ray asserted.

"We've got orders to go, so we'd better go."

The analogue clock on the wall of Simon's office displayed twelve-fifteen when the detectives arrived. Simon explained that Marie had briefed him on last night's interview, and he was now inclined to take Kitchener's deal. Faced with a cop-killer getting a manslaughter charge, Alex changed his mind about giving up. What if they acquired search warrants? Kitchener was on Probation from his last robbery charge. What if they contacted his probation officer?

"We know, broadly, where in the city he might be, who he talked to, where he went," Ray insisted.

"I've been briefed by Greenwood, Wheeler, and the Two-Eight squad this morning," said Gibson. "They got nothing and have interviewed a load of witnesses in the Tenth and been all over downtown and all over the Two-Eight. We got Robbery and Auto-Crime on it as well, but they haven't got anything either. Our perps got records, but they're opportunists. They'll rob whoever, whenever, with whatever. No real MOs, other than stealing money for dope."

"It's twelve-fifteen," said McNally. "That's enough. *You've* had enough. You've been up all night looking and you haven't found him. I'm going to accept the deal."

Alex had the sensation of his body tipping sideways, and he flexed his shoulders and core muscles, staying upright. That last spark of energy and fight fizzled out, leaving him bedraggled, tired, and stinking. Sweat, city grime, body odor. He yearned for a shower, and he felt too dazed to be upset.

"You're gonna give a cop-killer ten years in jail," Ray reminded Simon.

"Maybe save the life of the van driver." McNally shrugged in an 'I'm-only-doing-the-best-I-can' sort of manner.

"Is this the message you want to send?" Ray pressed, his voice hitting a strident note. "We're prepared to negotiate with cop killers? Who's *making* these decisions?"

"The DA. The Chief of Detectives. Commissioner Kelly," said Simon. "It's a plea bargain," he added acidly. "We make them all the time."

"Have the DA and Chief of Detectives thought about how this is going to look to the boys – and girls – in blue?" Ray shot back.

147

"The powers-that-be feel that out of all the bad options available to us at the moment, this is the best, as we still have a chance of saving this man's life," replied Simon icily. "I've spent the whole morning in meetings with the top brass of this office and the police."

"Almost as much fun as canvassing vacant lots in the Heights," quipped Alex sleepily. "Except less needles."

Simultaneously, Ray snapped, "No, it isn't. I'd be shocked if Khalid's still alive—"

"Cool it, Ray," drawled Gibson, throwing him a tight-lipped glare. "This is the decision we've made."

Following orders, Ray shut up, but he remained surly and bitter, and when the meeting ended, he snarled under his breath to Alex, "How would you have felt if the guys who shot you only got attempted man one? This is an affront to everyone."

Alex held his clammy forehead and felt faint. The last thing he wanted to think about was his shooting. The prison sentence hadn't felt like retribution. He hadn't felt vindicated or gratified when those perps were convicted and sentenced, just numb and sad, and he'd gotten very drunk straightaway after the trial. No, guilty verdicts and prison couldn't repair the damage to his psyche nor his body, nor could it weld his partner's severed spinal cord and let him walk again. In a way, it didn't matter. His right side still hurt, and it always would.

But he didn't have words for that. Ray wouldn't understand anyway. "I'd be pissed," he agreed softly, because agreeing was better than talking about it.

An hour later, Simon, the detectives, and Chris Leonard crowded into an examination room in the hospital. Kitchener, now recovering in a communal ward, was wheeled into the examination room. Otherwise every patient on his ward would overhear criminal justice not working.

After the nurse parked the defendant's wheelchair, Simon read the statement and then complained, "What the hell, Chris? This isn't enough. If I'm going to agree to this deal, I need a fuller statement. Names. Places. Details. He needs to say exactly what he did and who he did it with."

He handed the paper back to Leonard, his fierce grey eyes flashing. Alex glanced at Ray, who wasn't concealing his fury. The thing that stopped Alex from sharing in Ray's boiling indignation, other than sheer exhaustion, was the look on McNally's face as he demanded more details from the perp. He'd known McNally for years; the wily prosecutor had an agenda, a plan, secretive and clever – he felt it in his gut.

Leonard squirmed. "My client has admitted to committing the crime. Isn't that enough?"

"He gets nothing except for a couple of murder one charges unless I get a complete statement."

The defense lawyer wilted, conceding to McNally's terms. While Leonard wrote, Kitchener dictated that he and his pal 'Crazy Eight,' a.k.a. Johnny Bailey, entered the bodega through an open door, when new stock was being delivered at five-thirty am. At gunpoint, the kid in the shop unlocked the safe and handed over the cash. Then they busted ass to their getaway car, the green Dodge Intrepid, only to find it on three wheels, the tire thief busy at work. A shoot-out ensued between them and the tire thief, and when the cop joined in, Bailey flipped out, afraid of another arrest. As he was currently on parole, this would land him back in prison without anything in the way of due process. He fired his weapon at the cop. Here, Kitchener hastened to explain that he'd told Bailey not to, but Bailey did it anyway. After the cop fell, they panicked, grabbing the first car they saw on Malcolm X, the white Merc, forcing the driver at gunpoint to drive them downtown, where they tied him up in a building, and then they abandoned the van in front of the art gallery.

"Where is Khalid?" asked Alex.

Ray demanded, "Where's the gun you used to kill the cop?"

"Crazy Eight tossed it in the Hudson, man," said Kitchener fuzzily. "You'd think he'd hang on to a gun he'd just shot a cop with?"

"My client says the van driver is in a boarded-up warehouse on 12th Avenue and West 50th," Leonard stated. "And this isn't an interrogation."

"Why did you go back uptown to borrow your girlfriend's car then?" Alex queried, ignoring the defense lawyer.

"Had to help her move some sports equipment."

"After committing a robbery and a murder?" Ray asked skeptically.

"My client has told you what you want to know," Leonard said. "No more questions. Harold, don't say anything else."

Hell's Kitchen. Nowhere near where they had been unearthing every damned stone in Harlem and Washington Heights. In fact, nearly at the opposite end of town, but within fifteen or twenty minutes of where Kitchener and Bailey had ditched the van. They had used the van to dump the driver, their first theory. Then what the fuck was he doing uptown, borrowing his girlfriend's car? Alex felt stretched too thin, and he couldn't unravel the tangled yarn of clusterfucks. He could only grasp his sore ribs and back, annoyed with himself for not expanding the search operation he'd hastily organized from the van's location hours ago. He had initially ordered a search within a twenty-block radius. Should have been thirty. You would think someone would have taken the initiative to expand it while Alex, who could not be everywhere at once, had been interrogating the perp and chasing other leads. Clearly, no one had.

"Is he alive?" asked Simon.

"He was when I last saw him," Kitchener said. "He'd seen our faces, so we tied him up, left him in the building. I didn't wanna kill no one. I just needed the money. Things just got outta hand when we caught that asshole stealin' tires off the car, and he started shooting at us."

Bullshit. Alex caught Kitchener's eyes shifting guiltily towards the ceiling.

"I'd say things got out of hand when you went into the bodega," growled Ray.

"Didn't expect no one to steal the tires, not in daylight!"

"Where is Bailey?" asked Alex.

"My client has told you what is needed, as per the agreement," Leonard insisted, scooting towards Alex and inserting his body between Alex and his client.

Alex urged, "What happened to Bailey?"

"Dunno," Kitchener murmured. "After we left the van on West 24th, we went separate ways."

"Where would he have gone?"

"Dunno." Kitchener rocked back in his wheelchair, fluttering his eyelids.

"This is *enough*," Leonard said cholerically. "My client is injured and tired." He took the handles at the back of the wheelchair and started to turn it towards the door in the jerky, uncoordinated manner of someone unused to pushing a wheelchair.

Simon gave Alex and Ray a simmering glare. *Shut it.* He cleared his throat and said, "Go. To West 50th. Now."

They went. Sirens and lights ablaze, they crossed the city on 14th Street, Ray at the wheel, driving the police car flat-out as traffic parted ahead. Accompanied by two radio cars from the Tenth Precinct, an ambulance, and Simon, they screeched up on the sidewalk next to the building, which had to be accessed from the alleyway intersecting with West 50th. It was a shell-shocked relic of the old days in Hell's Kitchen, burnt out and falling down, like the war was over and the other side had won. And indeed, it had, because there were signs on the building from a construction firm, advertising that the warehouse was due to be demolished, the lot transformed into expensive West Side apartments.

Simon frowned at the signs, breathing out a lungful of smoke. "This used to be some kind of factory, and now it's going to be more luxury apartments. Just what the West Side needs. You'd start to wonder if there isn't a conspiracy to drive the working class out of Manhattan."

"The city's been doing well," Ray said. "It's a by-product of capitalism, real estate going up. People make their choices."

"I don't think it's always about choice, Ray," Simon answered in a splenetic tone. "I mean, no one makes the choice to be poor. Could you or your family afford what they're gonna build here?"

"Probably not, but I made the choice to be a cop."

Alex checked out the boarded-up windows, knowing better than to discuss politics with either Simon or Ray, and both at once, God, you would want to be in Brooklyn. Or further, he thought, his ears catching Simon reminding Ray that he too was part of a union, and Alex edging out of earshot along the side of the warehouse. He glanced at the discarded beer cans, coke cans, cigarettes, wrappers, condoms, the odd needle and vial on the ground. He could see where people had pried off boards.

The door was still locked and barred – anyone breaking into the old warehouse had gone through the windows. Several police officers busied themselves ripping the shit out of the door, as they didn't intend on crawling through a grotty hole in a plywood window. Once the door had been removed, Alex, Ray, and four other cops entered the warehouse, their flashlights in one hand, their guns in the other. The ADA, on the other hand, well out of his comfort zone, nervously hung back near the street with EMS, nursing a cigarette.

Gun raised, Alex shone his flashlight into the airless murk, covering Ray's back, the uniforms covering his. His heart was cantering. Rats scurried out of their flashlight beams. Thin slivers of sun pierced through the holes torn in the plywood, illuminating tiny splashes on the dusty floors and rotted wood and concrete.

Alex coughed, holding his chest, his eyes watering. No sign of life. Only the astringent smell of death stinging his nostrils and throat. Unmistakable. Something had died here. Khalid? Some hapless homeless person? Maybe the rats or a raccoon. He aimed his flashlight into dark corners, revealing debris, syringes, rags, discarded bottles of cheap vodka and tequila, piles of wood, ashes where people had lit fires to warm themselves. The old warehouse had been a shelter for someone, although it seemed vacant. But he kept the gun out of its holster.

"Lex! Alex!" called Ray. "Over here!"

He trotted over to where Ray crouched down in the shadows underneath a support beam, shining his flashlight down at his feet. In the dark, he couldn't see Ray's face, but he sensed the heavy foreboding in his partner, and he knew. As he approached, the putrid stench of a DOA seared his nostrils, sinuses, and lungs.

His stride slowed for a second. Even as he had been cynically arguing that Kitchener and his accomplice had killed the vic, he'd clung onto a thin thread of hope. But there had never been any hope. Had he not known with all the certainty born out of his years on these streets that Kitchener was stringing them along with unashamed bullshit?

A caustic taste of betrayal washed through in his mouth – by the DAs; by luck or fate or whatever; by his own judgment which had plainly deserted him. That shitbird got off with man one for felony murder, for murdering a cop. Alex drew in a forceful, dust-filled breath, hacking at his sore lung.

"I can tell you now, he's been dead for the better part of a day," he hissed hoarsely. "At least. He sure as hell doesn't smell like someone who only died a few hours ago."

Then he removed the mini flight bottle of aftershave that he kept in his inside coat pocket, spraying it onto his sleeve. An old detective's trick.

You can put your forearm over your mouth and nose and breathe, a short respite from the stomach-turning reek of decay. Some detectives liked Vic's Vap-o-Rub. Others preferred cigars. Alex swapped between aftershave and Vic's.

"No fucking shit," Ray agreed. "Can I have some of that stuff?"

Alex holstered his firearm and squatted down beside the body with Cardoza from Crime Scene and Miriam Shapiro, one of the assistant MEs. The vic had a massive bloodied head wound, a blunt force injury, and blood had saturated his clothes and his face. It shone dully in the beams of their flashlights. Yet the concrete beneath him didn't look like a crime scene, with only one small puddle of blood. He had not been killed nor bled out here. Clenching his jaw, Alex reached for one of the DOA's hands. The skin had been grazed off the knuckles. Defensive wounds. Khalid had put up a fight. And in Alex's hand, the arm and the fingers were icy cold, but limp and supple.

"He's not in rigor," Alex stated to Ray and anyone else in earshot. "He's definitely been dead for the better part of a day."

With decomp setting in and *rigor mortis* long gone, there were no doubts in Alex's mind that time of death had been at least twenty-four hours ago. *Fuck,* he spat into the dust. Pissed that they'd been played by the perp.

"I suspect that's your cause of death," said the ME, shining her light on the vic's head.

"Butt of a gun, you think?" asked Ray.

"Possibly."

"You don't cause that much damage to someone and think they're gonna be all right, do you?" Alex sarcastically asked no one in particular. He stood up, his thighs aching, and pain chewed at his lumbar vertebrae. Then he circled the perimeter of lights CSU was setting up, stretching his muscles.

"Well, we'll have to get him to the office to fully assess the extent of the damage," replied Shapiro. "But I imagine not. Did you see the marks on his hands?"

"Yeah," Alex answered. "Looks like he threw a punch at someone."

Simon stood nearby, approaching in that wary, scuffling manner of someone who hasn't seen many dead bodies.

"So, he's dead," said the lawyer.

153

"No shit. Can't you smell it?" Alex retorted.

"He's been dead for a while," Ray said, incandescent.

"We don't have time of death yet," replied Simon.

"It wasn't an hour ago, I can tell you that," said Alex, putting his forearm over his nose, taking a whiff of the aftershave. "It was at least twenty-four hours ago."

Shapiro bobbed her head in agreement. "It's hard to see much until we get him downtown, but PML indicates someone moved him."

"Kitchener was bullshitting you when he said Khalid was alive," Ray bitched. "He was dead when they brought him here, and Kitchener knew that."

"I know." Simon stared down at the body, now bathed grotesquely in a glaring, white light.

While the assistant ME continued to examine the body and prep it for removal to the office, Alex and Ray explored the warehouse, trying to understand how the perps moved a body into the warehouse without using the door or any of the accessible windows, where the holes seemed far too small. You could wriggle in yourself but stuffing a dead body through was a different matter. They found a pile of debris, stacked concrete blocks leading to a window higher up, perhaps fifteen or twenty feet, and the sun throwing a thick yellow splash of light through a gap in the plywood. It looked like someone had demolished a non-structural wall (hopefully) but didn't clear the remains.

Alex's flashlight caught something. He squatted beside the blocks. Blood pooled on the concrete at his feet and dribbled down the blocks like viscous candle wax. His ears pricked forward. He pushed at the bricks. They seemed solid. Then he untied his tie, handing it and his flashlight to Ray, saying, "That's blood. Give me some light, Ray. I'm gonna check out that window."

"What? Are you sure this is a good idea? I mean, with your back—"

"Jesus, I'll be fine. Just keep the light on me. Anyway, if it collapses or I fall off, there's a bus already here." Alex clambered onto the blocks. He felt a twinge in his side and a slight ache in his back. As he climbed, he tested each block before he put his weight on it. They wiggled, loose debris threatening to topple off onto Ray.

Ray called, "You alright, Lex?"

"Yeah, fine," he shouted.

154

Steadily, he climbed upwards, following the bloody trail, forgetting to test the blocks and for a sickening moment, losing his balance as one abruptly shifted underneath him. He inhaled sharply, clutching at a handhold, scrabbling with his feet, the smooth soles of his shoes giving him no grip, and using his knee and his upper body strength to thrutch himself up onto a ledge near the window. The plywood boards had been removed, every one of them. Alex rested on his knees beside it, breathing dust-free air into his lungs. A dumpster in the alley led to the window from the outside. He had a clear view of the studio on the other side of the alley. The edge of the window was covered with blood, like some intoxicated graffiti artist had tried painting it but had given up part-way through. The dumpster, however, looked clean, at least from this vantage point.

Several uniforms appeared near the dumpster and were waddling about, searching for evidence. Had Khalid been alive when they brought him here? Had they coerced him at gunpoint into climbing the dumpster? And then, he finally refused to go in – most sane people would – and there was a scuffle, the robbers hitting him with a rock or the butt of a gun. While Khalid bled out more or less where Alex now crouched, the robbers tried to figure out what to do, and then they manhandled and hauled him down the ruined wall. It played.

Warily, Alex downclimbed, looking over his shoulder for the next foothold and lowering himself onto the blocks. He sensed Ray's nervous gaze at his back. His mouth was dry. Sweat trickled from his armpits, down his sides. Descending was harder than ascending. A block rocked as he put his foot on it. Falling would hurt. He gripped the edge of the one he was holding, shredding his fingers on its rough surface but regaining balance.

This must have been a hell of a job, he thought, climbing down, towing an unconscious or dead body. Ray's relief was palpable when he finally touched solid ground. He felt his heart decelerating.

"I can't believe you just did that," said Ray, passing him his tie and flashlight. "That looks really unstable."

"Neither can I," Alex replied, catching his breath and realizing his blue shirt and dark grey suit had clouded with powdery dust, mixing with sweat. "But I reckon it was worth the adrenaline rush."

"What did you find?"

"Window's covered in blood. I think they killed him up there, then dragged him down that."

"Can you get to it from the other side?"

"Yeah, there's a dumpster you can climb on."

"Why do you think they killed him up there?" Ray squinted up at the window.

"There's a lot of blood on the window and the blocks. I couldn't see any outside. Dunno…" Alex folded his arms over his chest, considering the window and the rubble. "It's like they got him as far as the window alive, and then hit him with something up there."

"You think you could drag a body down this?"

"Me personally?" Alex said with flagging sarcasm. "Not a fucking chance. But if there were two of you and you were desperate… Yeah, probably."

Cardoza, the CSU detective, scowled at the slag heap of debris with deep apprehension. "You mean we gotta climb up that?"

"Well, I just did," said Alex, brushing dust off his right knee and thigh, and then he draped the tie around his neck but didn't bother tying it. "If I can do it, I'm sure your guys will manage."

Chapter Eight

October 29th

Back in his cubicle, Alex squinted at his computer screen, his eyes declining to bring words into focus. Soon, he would need to get reading glasses. He had been promising himself this for the last two or three years. He was forty-seven after all, and he had spent most of his life reading tiny print in poorly lit precincts and offices.

Facing the more banal aspects of the job, he stuttered and coughed along on two cylinders. If he put his head down, he would fall asleep, right there in the middle of the squad room. In the adjacent cubicle, Ray, distorting his arms in a yoga pose, looked no better. Yawning until his jaw popped, Alex opened a search warrant affidavit for Analisa's car, writing his name and command, and then running out of gas. He saw Ray grab a case binder, Kazparek, and riffle through its contents. Someone had left a post-it note on the top of the file: a lawyer had phoned the office snooping for information. Peter's parents were suing the care home. This was America. Of course they were.

Probable cause, Alex said to himself, the suspect going wildly out of his way to borrow his girlfriend's car immediately after committing robbery and murder, but for what? Not for moving Khalid's body, since no one without a helicopter could travel from the Heights to Hell's Kitchen and then back in twenty minutes. No judge will grant you a search warrant if you don't specify what you expect to find. The vic was nowhere near Analisa's place, and the proceeds of the robbery stayed with Kitchener. At a loss, Alex stopped typing and removed his shoes and pulled the sock off his left foot, resting it on his thigh and examining the blister bubbling out of the big toe. Popping it would hurt more than leaving it alone, so he gently wiggled his sock back on, wincing.

"I still don't know if they want to pursue charges on this," Ray was saying, referring to Kazparek. "Last I heard, DA didn't think there was enough for even an arrest warrant. And who are we gonna arrest anyway? The manager? The carers? Fuck knows… I can't even figure out who's responsible for what in that place. These civil lawyers are gonna have their work cut out for them. You look wrecked, Lex."

"I'll be fine." Alex had a transitory vision of liquefying coffee grounds in a bottle cap, and then plunging it into a vein in his arm with a syringe. You would get the hit immediately. Smiling humorously at the thought, he limped into the kitchen, a walk-in closet that housed a microwave, a sink, the coffee machine, and a mini-fridge. MNHS kept enough coffee stacked in the cupboard to supply them through the apocalypse. He slid the pot into the machine, rammed the filter into the top compartment, which always required a sharp whack with a fist, and then he flopped against the sink, zoning out, eyes blanking while coffee dribbled into the pot.

When he returned to his cubicle, he found Ray talking to a tearful plainclothes cop. Twenty-something. African-American. He looked like he hadn't slept for two weeks, and his young face was drawn and creased with grief and pain.

Ray cocked his head towards Alex and said, "This is my partner, Detective Boswell. He's the primary on the case."

Alex's eyes hopped from the cop to Ray. This should be making sense. Ray was looking at him like he should know what the hell was happening.

"Alex, this is PO Simmonds. He is—" Ray did that thing, stumbling over tenses, "-was Irvine's partner."

Ah, shit.

Alex sunk onto his chair and furtively hid his mug behind some files because it felt inappropriate to drink coffee out of a mug that said, *Homicide unit: our day starts when your day ends,* in front of a vic's grieving partner. Then he clasped both hands over his belly, saying, "I really am very sorry."

There was no way to express his shared pain or say anything consoling. Losing your partner was like losing a family member, a spouse, a part of yourself. Most cops would say their partners knew them better than their spouses did. Someone who was more than a colleague, a friend, who knew you better than you might know yourself. They knew all your flaws, saw you under life-threatening pressure and the crazy stress of the job, and they still liked you. Intensity and danger forged an impermeable bond of loyalty, respect, brotherly or sisterly love. Cops who had lost their partners never got over it. Alex knew. When he'd taken that bullet to his lower chest, his first partner in MNHS, Eddie Trenemen, came far closer to death, spending weeks in the ICU fighting for his life.

"You've got the guy?" Simmonds' voice shook, and he addressed the floor, as if he could not bear to make eye contact.

"Yeah. Yeah, we've got him," Alex reassured him.

"The news said it was a robbery. He tried to stop it?"

"He died a hero," Ray said. "Trying to stop those guys."

Alex rested a hand on his hip, the thought jumping into his head, *Yeah, a hero or fucking stupid,* and he flinched. You're not supposed to think that when a fellow officer is killed or injured. But people do, of course: "I would never make any decision that bad" ameliorating the fear of "there but for the grace of God go I" that you feel when you investigate the murder of a cop.

Besides, Irvine, off-duty, all on his own with no backup in sight, had used deadly force to forestall the robbers. Had Irvine not been a cop, had he been an ordinary civilian who got himself shot turning West 123rd Street into a Sam Pekinpah western, the detectives would have stood over his corpse trash talking him: how he had it coming, charging into the middle of that shit when he could have called the police and stayed alive.

Ray was saying, "If it hadn't been for your partner, we might not have caught the robbers. He shot and wounded one of them."

"He was a good cop, selfless," Simmonds wept. "It was always like him, to go into a situation, no matter what. He went into the Towers, the South Tower, trying to evacuate people just after the plane hit it. Just barely got out before it collapsed."

Alex could not stop himself from looking at what used to be Bill Ryan's cubicle, now belonging to a detective from the A team called Angel Ramirez, and he shuddered.

"I can't believe it, I can't believe he's gone," Simmonds whimpered. "Do you know, do you even know, what it's like, to get a phone call from your C/O, saying something has happened to your partner?"

"Yes," Ray said. "I mean, it's not the same, because he wasn't dead, but there were a few minutes where I didn't know that and thought he could be, and I felt sick."

"You know how nuts the Five-Two can be? I thought if anything was gonna happen, it'd be on the job, you know? And I'd have his back, but look, look at this. No one was there for him. What am I gonna do?"

"Maybe talk to your C/O about some compassionate leave," suggested Ray. "Your head ain't gonna be on the job at the moment."

"You'll get the guy, right? Is the evidence good? You have to get him."

"Yes, we will,' said Alex, feigning confidence. *Ten years.* A lava-like wave of acid rolled through his gut. When the plea bargain came to its final disposition hearing, how would he ever have the heart to tell this guy that Kitchener would only do ten-to-fifteen for killing his partner? The sentence mattered. The charge certainly did.

Simmonds wobbled to his feet. "You'll keep me posted, right?"

"Of course we will."

After he'd gone, Alex recovered his coffee and asked, "What were you talking about, Ray? Who did you think was dead?"

"You," said Ray.

"Me?"

"The car wreck with Zoë."

Alex stared at the DD-5 on the desk, his face contorting with stress. He saw the sallowly lit hospital room, heard machines beeping and hissing in a droning rhythm, and Ray appearing at about 0400. Ray's face had broken up, close to tears. Alex had never seen him like that. But he himself had been crying a lot so he hadn't thought much of it. "You thought I'd been killed?"

"For about five minutes. I got a call from Highway saying there'd been a car accident, fatalities, and you were in the hospital. I thought the worst, was pretty freaked out, to be honest, until I talked to Gibson and learned you weren't dead or on life support."

"You never told me that."

Ray turned on his computer. "You had enough to deal with."

Then the phone rang.

Alex and Ray both wavered and glowered at the offensive machine. Alex's intuition warned him he would not like it. He swigged a mouthful

160

of coffee and reluctantly picked it up. "Detective Boswell, Manhattan North Homicide."

A detective from the 20th Precinct. "We've got a DOA in an Upper West Side apartment."

Tetchy, Alex snarled, "Is it suspicious? I hope you're not calling Homicide because some poor old bat died of heart attack."

"Of course it's fucking suspicious," grumbled the detective. "The vic has a bullet in his head."

They needed another case like Broadway needed more potholes, but they'd caught it. The B team was still catching today. Greenwood was out with Finnane, the unenviable task of giving the death notice to Tariq Khalid's wife. Both Greenwood and Finnane had developed a rapport with her, so they'd volunteered to do it. Wheeler was somewhere else, hiding from the phone.

The cop said, "The apartment's right over Lincoln Center, off West 66th and Amsterdam." He rattled off the address and hung up.

After Alex had recapped the conversation, Ray exclaimed, "Lincoln Center? West 60s! That's a *nice* neighborhood. What were you saying to your pal last night about the bottom of society?"

Weak with shuddery exhaustion, Alex shrugged on his jacket, and when he stood, a torrid round of pain stabbed through his back and his side. His face bleached, but he felt flushed and hot. He doubled the recommended dose of ibuprofen, and Ray shot him a look of acetous disapproval.

"That's terrible for your stomach."

"My stomach's already fucked."

"All the more reason for you to be more careful. That stuff will make your ulcers worse."

"It's fine. I take it with antacids." Damn Ray and his sententious health lectures – sometimes, he thought he was getting better at living with it. Sometimes, he realized that he wasn't. "Anyway, when has social class *ever* been a barrier to people being venial?"

"You just don't expect it… in that area."

"You know having money doesn't stop people from getting up to really weird shit."

They were both sick of being in the car, neither wanting to drive, so they tossed a coin, and Alex lost. He scribbled a semblance of his name

161

on the logbook to sign out a Crown Vic. Then he fought like battle-fatigued soldier through snarled trenches of Broadway to Lincoln Square, only to find the semi-circle drive in front of the building chockered with half a dozen RMPs. More police vehicles blocked the spaces on West 66th. After practicing that longstanding New York ritual of looking for an elusive parking space, he decided, *fuck it,* double-parking next to a radio car a block away from the apartment building. It was a high rise of smoky, black glass, rearing above the classical architecture and European-style square between the Metropolitan Opera and the Juilliard School.

To his annoyance, the square was amassed with people listening to a jazz band playing dissonant tunes in front of the Juilliard School. The music disconcerted him. He sped up his pace, limping hurriedly through the crowd, which suddenly, maliciously, trapped him in Lincoln Square.

A fountain of adrenaline spurted through his bloodstream. He couldn't breathe. Both lungs deflated. Sirens screamed in his head. His heart thudded against his breastbone like it would shatter it. Lincoln Center disintegrated. He didn't hear the Coltrane tunes. He stood in the middle of a lonely street, the rain pouring down, and those sirens howled in his ears. He heard nothing else.

"Alex?"

Ray's voice sounded distant, as if shouting across a deep canyon.

"Alex!" Ray repeated more forcefully, grabbing Alex's shoulder.

Alex whirled around, Ray's fingers digging into his shoulder bringing reality back to him in a dizzying rush. "What?" He looked into Ray's severe, chiseled features, now etched with concern.

"You okay?" Ray asked.

Alex shook his head and blew out a lungful of air. "I'm fine. Just tired. Yesterday was an exhausting shitshow. Like I said, my back's bothering me."

Ray looked doubtful but he didn't say anything else until they reached the building. As they squeezed through the barricade of radio cars and flashed tin at the cops stationed at the entrance, Ray observed that it would be sweet, living in an apartment right over Lincoln Center, if you could afford it and liked the opera.

Alex had no reply, not even a tasteless joke. His throat and mouth were agonizingly parched, and he couldn't swallow. There was a bitter taste on his tongue. He dug his shaky hands into his belt. Walking through the revolving door, he tried to go through the mental checklist he always had before processing a death scene, but he could not keep his thoughts aligned, or think at all. He'd slammed into a stone wall, the fatigue of being awake for more than twenty-four hours, his emotions rising dangerously close to the surface.

Uniforms from the Two-Oh patrolled the lobby. The detectives nodded towards the cops and flashed tin at the doorman, before taking his details. The doorman knew the DOA's name, Sean Ferrin, and added that he was a lawyer of some sort.

Alex steadied himself, but he would sell a limb for water. "Has anyone who doesn't live in the building come in during your shift?"

"Nope," said the doorman.

"No guests, anything?"

"No."

"How long is your shift?"

"Eight hours. I'm just about to sign off. If I can get outta here."

"You'll have to go to the precinct house and give a statement to the detectives."

The doorman sighed, hassled.

Then Alex and Ray rode the nippy elevator up to the 52nd floor. Even the elevator in this place had a mirror and a red carpet with gilded Persian artwork. *This is how the other half lives,* Alex thought. He made the mistake of looking at himself in the mirror. His complexion was pale, the brown eyes watery, pupils wildly dilated. Sweat shone at his hairline.

"A lawyer, eh? That makes half of this city into fucking suspects," he cracked.

The comment bounced off Ray like a basketball on a blacktop. "That doorman says no one's been in the building."

"Wonder what a NITRO check on this building would tell you. Old Jews complaining about the paint job, the criminally ugly carpet, the Juilliard student parties." Alex forced the joke with a tight smile. If he could fake the wiseass, he could cover up whatever happened in Lincoln Square. "That's what my mother would be doing."

"Well, it has CCTV. I saw the cameras. We can check them too."

A female uniform, the rookie charged with the unenviable task of sitting on the DOA, met them near the elevator.

"Whaddaya got?" asked Alex.

She looked relieved. "The DOA is a white male, probably in his fifties," she reported eagerly. "Looks like he's got a gunshot wound to the head. He's in that apartment at the end of the hall. My partner's with him. The cleaning lady came in and found him."

"Where's the cleaning lady?"

"She's in the apartment with the precinct detectives."

"Has anyone else disturbed the scene?"

"Just EMS, sir."

The detectives signed in and ducked under the crime scene tape zigzagging across the hallway. On the deceased's door, Alex noted four locks, jotting it down in his memo pad. You could grade New Yorkers' paranoia. Two locks were normal. Three meant they were a little neurotic but still within reason (Alex had three). Four meant they thought they were living in Bed-Stuy or East New York, even when they were on the Upper West Side, or they really did live in the projects, in which case it was sensible. More than four meant that they were either nuts, or someone was genuinely out to get them. The latter most likely had a rap sheet of their very own.

Alex ran his gloved hands along the door, touching the locks. His skin heated up under the latex. The locks looked and felt undamaged. At his back, he heard CSU shuffling along the hall, rustling in their Tyvek suits. He tugged booties over his shoes, nudged the door open, and stepped into the apartment, his feet feeling soft and awkward.

A moon-faced rookie cop slouched on a white leather sofa, the TV on, but he wasn't watching it. Two bored paramedics stood over a middle-aged white male, dressed in a Saks Fifth Avenue black suit and tie, like he had been out for an evening at the opera across the road. The man wasn't giving EMS much to do. He lay crumpled on his left side, and had a gunshot wound in his temple. Blood had soaked into the pale beige carpet and spattered on the white wall like a lame imitation of a Jackson Pollock painting.

This was real, and the weird stuff in his head wasn't. A DOA, who needed him to find answers. *Thank fuck,* he said to no one but himself. He had a routine, the things he did at every callout. First, he burned some coffee grounds on the stove, masking the putrid smell of death permeating the apartment.

Then the homicide detectives went through the standard litany of questions to the first officers, the EMS crew, and the cleaning lady. When did you find him? About two hours ago. Do you know him? Cleaned his apartment once per week. He was usually at work. Where was work? Brooklyn. Do you *really* know him? No, he just leaves the check. Who else was staying in this apartment? No one. You sure? No. Has anybody found a weapon? Not yet. They were looking. The standard litany of answers was, for the most part, unhelpful.

Someone from 1PP radioed in, relating that the city of New York believed that the apartment was owned by Sean Ferrin, and there were no outstanding warrants nor complaints associated with the place.

Holding his breath, Alex knelt on his right knee beside the DOA, eyeballing one of the man's hands, then the other, hunting for defensive wounds. Not a mark. Nothing on his face or neck, either. His clothes were unblemished – if you discounted the blood spatter – his pearly white shirt buttoned all the way to the throat, and his tie more neatly tied than Alex's at this moment. Lightly, Alex prodded the body. The poor bastard was as stiff as a two-by-four, *rigor mortis,* dead for at least eight hours, but not more than eighteen hours.

Then Alex checked him for lividity, gently unbuttoning the shirt so he could see the flesh. A dark blue-purple tinge greeted him, discoloring along the ribs and the upper arm, except for where his weight pressed into the floor, the shoulder, the curve of the ribs, the hip cast in a ghostly white. He'd died here, where he fell.

Next, he inspected the gunshot wound, taking note of the halo of powder burns around the edges. The shot had been fired at close range, and he made some rough calculations about the angle and trajectory of the shot, inferring from the wound and from the blood spatter on the wall that the vic had probably been sitting on the floor, the gun level with his head. Possibly, of course. Until you, the ME, or CSU take actual measurements, you never write your initial crime scene observations in concrete, committing language that can bite you in the ass on cross-examination.

A precinct detective stood behind him, watching him work the body, transfixed. Finally, he said, "Boswell, my partner and I have talked to some of the neighbors. Mostly, no one knows anything. But we took a statement from one who says he might've heard a gunshot at one or two in the morning."

"He report it to the police?" Alex inquired, still on his knee, waving at Andre Brown, the assistant ME, who hustled through the door and dropped to a crouch beside the DOA.

"Alex, what do you think?"

"He's got a gunshot to his head, he's in rigor, and I checked lividity. No one's moved him." Alex stiffly rose to his feet and twisted his hips from one side to the other, stretching his spine.

The precinct detective stated, "No, the witness thought it was a car backfiring."

"A car backfiring *in* the building?" Alex raised a cynical eyebrow.

"This ain't Washington Heights. The people in this building, they're not gonna know what gunfire sounds like."

Fair, thought Alex.

"Is that witness still here?" asked Ray.

"No, he said he had to go to work. We took a brief statement."

"We'll have a look at that later," said Ray. "Maybe bring that witness back into the precinct."

"How well do they know the DOA?" asked Alex.

"This is New York," the precinct detective said dismissively. "You think people actually know their neighbors?"

"You never know," retorted Alex. "Maybe they saw him bringing prostitutes into the apartment every night or something, or heard the wild parties, or the domestics, or the gambling ring."

"Yeah... Or an opera singer," sighed the detective.

"Hey, he could be running a prostitution ring with opera singers," said the other Two-Oh detective. "Or Juilliard students. Think of what you could do with a violin bow."

"Don't discount the mishegoss theories," Alex said, and he set off on an exploration of the apartment.

While Alex was nosing around the kitchen, a cop found a wallet, stowed in a drawer, and he got Alex's attention, handing him the wallet.

The first item Alex pulled out was an American Bar Association membership card with the DOA's face in the left-hand corner. "Sean Ferrin, J.D.," he said, reading the card. The next card was a New York driver's license. Same name, same face, this address.

166

Ray removed another card. Alex heard him take a gulp. "Oh, shit. He was an ADA in King's County."

"In that case, there could only be like two million people who would want him dead," Alex quipped, but his voice scraped in his throat. "Take a fucking number." That explained the excessive locks.

"This must be an expensive apartment," Ray speculated. "It's not like he's earning a bazillion dollars working in the KCDA's office, not like he would in private practice."

"Fuck knows,' Alex replied, unwilling to speculate.

"How much does an ADA make? Enough to have a place like this? Expensive West Side neighborhood? You could spit and hit the opera. With a doorman?"

Ray was getting ahead of himself. Scratching at the corner of his left eye, Alex swiveled away and opened several drawers, uncovering a monochromatic collection of white shirts, white socks, black y-front underwear, plain solid-colored ties. This guy didn't even vary the color of his underwear.

Unexpectedly, Alex's brain leapt to a case from 2001. One of the co-defendants, a cop Alex had vaguely known from their days in Queens, had been found guilty of taking bribes and conspiring to commit murder. The son of a bitch had tried to weasel out of the charges, deflecting attention by accusing Alex of accepting payoffs when he'd worked at the wild One-Oh-Three in the '80s. Alex's transgressions most certainly included drinking far too much and sleeping around, but most certainly did not include skimming money off drug busts. Ray, only recently assigned to MNHS, had almost believed the fuckwit. So had IAB, but they cleared him, although he'd sweated it and almost started drinking again. Still, Alex had been wounded. The IA stuff he could blow off, but Ray, his partner, should have trusted him. Just because he wasn't the paragon of abstemious behavior and virtue didn't mean he was capable of sinking to other – and far worse – lows. There was being a whistleblower when you had evidence of malfeasance, and then there was just being a prick when you didn't.

"Do you just assume everybody's getting some payoff now?" Alex snapped, over-sensitive.

"I'm not," said Ray, surprised by the rebuke. "I'm just saying, it's a luxurious apartment."

"Who are you? Serpico? You can't assume everybody's corrupt."

"What the hell are you talking about? I didn't assume anything. I was just thinking aloud…" Ray folded his arms over his chest and gave Alex a strange look. "I'm sure there's a rational explanation anyway. Why does he only own black underwear and white socks? Is that weird?"

Alex spread his fingers across his forehead. "Yeah, there probably is. Never mind. Doesn't matter. And yeah, it's fucking weird." Sleep deprivation, the headache, pain searing holes in his spine and ribs – it conflagrated and left him reactive and histrionic. He'd flashbacked to that unsettling case from three years ago but given Ray's baffled expression and wiseass remarks about the DOA's wardrobe, he guessed that it had not been on the younger detective's mind at all. Why had it suddenly been on his? Because he'd run himself aground. Oh, he desperately needed to finish this tour and then sleep for about forty-eight hours.

"Boswell! Espinosa!"

They jerked their heads towards the detective who'd called out. The precinct detective and the assistant ME had rolled the body and found a gun.

Alex and Ray sprinted across the apartment and examined the weapon, a Smith and Wesson M&P .22. It did not look like it was used much, lacking the scuff marks of a gun regularly slid in and out of a holster. Alex removed the magazine. Nine rounds, but the gun would take ten. He guessed that the tenth was in the vic's head. Then he light-checked the bore using the reflection of his thumbnail. Not much wear. He tied a tag to it and located the serial number. Next, he phoned the ATF's National Tracing Center in West Virginia, describing the firearm and reading off the serial number to the wearied agent on the other end of the line. He was probably one of about a thousand cops phoning the Tracing Center today, and he knew that the agents would be excavating thousands of microfilms and a rat's nest of an antiquated library catalogue, hunting for records, because federal law insanely prevented the ATF from computerizing any data relating to firearms sales.

Once he'd set that in motion, he bagged the weapon, prepped it to go to the ballistics lab for testing, and then he squatted on his haunches near the ME. "Exit wound?"

"Can't see one," Brown answered.

Alex re-examined the entry wound on the side of the forehead, a bloody hole, flecked with shards of bone and grey matter. "Then it's probably still in there."

The ME nodded as he slipped plastic bags over the DOA's hands. Alex stood, swearing at his pain, and he continued to inventory the apartment.

A survey of the ADA's paperwork, filed alphabetically on a shelf in his office, revealed that he lived alone, but he had an ex-wife and a kid in Westchester. He had worked in private practice at a prestigious criminal defense firm before embarking on the life of public service in the Brooklyn DA's office. He was on the committee of the Lincoln Square Synagogue. Receipts and credit card statements showed he'd shopped at the Whole Foods at West 97th and Columbus, and he had recently donated three hundred bucks to Senator Chuck Schumer's election campaign.

Alex hunted for evidence of vices: gambling, drugs, women, men, anything. Instead, he found two copies of the Torah and a wide-ranging selection of history books, everything from Napoleon to post-9/11 US intervention in the Middle East. There was no booze in the apartment, and he didn't keep much food. Soymilk, whole wheat bread, spinach curry in the fridge, a small collection of vegan cookbooks. The kitchen was so clean you could do surgery.

Even Ray observed, "Man, this guy is like an OCD neat freak."

Alex arched his eyebrows. "Pot and kettle, huh?" he teased. Then he picked up the only decoration in the kitchen, a brass Star of David perched on the windowsill, and he held it up to the light, a guilty reminder of his own Jewish blood and traditions that he paid little attention to most of the time.

They finished processing the scene and rode the elevator back to the ground floor, and then looped around the building towards Lincoln Center. Alex dreaded going anywhere near the square, but if he asked Ray to bring the car to the main doors of the apartment, he would have to explain why. How could he? Just that he had an acidic, sour feeling in the pit of his stomach. He stopped breathing as they navigated the square. But the crowd had dissipated and only a handful of people lingered near the fountain. That frightening disengagement with reality didn't make an appearance, only his splitting headache, queasy stomach, and the cop who they had blocked in, lounging against his car, giving them an icy stare.

Once inside the Crown Vic, he drooped his head and neck over the steering wheel and pushed his palm against his right eye. The veins in his forehead pulsed, dilating and then constricting. Years ago, he could withstand more than twenty-four hours on his feet, but he supposed age and not taking care of himself as well as he should were getting the better of him.

Ray hadn't stopped staring at him with that quizzical countenance. "Are you sure nothing's wrong?"

"I've been awake for more than twenty-four hours. I'm tired, and my head's fucking killing me. We still got aspirin in here? I guess I don't handle twenty-four hour tours as well as I used to."

"Should you be doubling up on your painkillers?"

"Yes. It's fucking aspirin. It's fine."

Lips squeezed into a thin, doubtful line, Ray dug around the car's glove compartment and proffered two aspirin tablets. A bottle of water kicked around the passenger door pockets, and Alex grabbed it, quaffing down the pills with the water.

Chapter Nine

November 1st

At 0800 hours, Alex's cell rang, the unheralded noise shocking his heart. Breathless, he swiped at the bedside table and answered, and the ME's office informed him that his Lincoln Center DOA was next in line for an autopsy. Oh, thank God, he thought, rolling onto his stomach, and then stumbling out of bed. The night had been interminable, waiting for dawn to overtake insomnia, or for his body to give up its fight against sleep and relent with a few hours' rest. His nerves had crackled with energy, he could hear himself breathing, he tossed and turned, but everywhere felt uncomfortable, a painful hyper-awareness of every physical sensation, from the sheets bunched against his skin to the pressure of one leg against another. Then he'd sunk into a somnolent state of waterlogged, lacquered unreality, dreams so vivid he thought he was awake, but everything was misshapen, squalid and corrupted. He woke up looking haggard, an empty shell of a human being.

Anyway, one would think that an ADA would be prioritized, but he wasn't, and there had been a line ahead of him. Like the damned DMV. Get your photo taken, eyes tested, and bowels removed. Besides, nobody had found evidence of foul play, so they hadn't pressured the MEs to rush him. They had rushed Irvine and Khalid, but their autopsies hadn't revealed anything Alex hadn't already worked out, for the most part. Alex knew how they died. And he'd interviewed Khalid's wife and kids, and Irvine's parents and his Five-Two colleagues. Khalid was a devoted family man who sent any extra income to his parents in Syria. Irvine had been the life of the party, an amateur stand-up comic on the New York dive bar circuit when he wasn't on the job.

Yesterday, the perp had been wheeled into the Criminal Courts Building and arraigned. The ADA running AR-1 had charged him with first-degree murder, much to the surprise of Kitchener, his lawyer, and the detectives. Kitchener, who had been about to plead guilty, abruptly changed his plea to not guilty. The arraignment ADA, unaware of the late-night deal, had wondered why everyone acted so baffled. McNally had asked him to charge Kitchener with first-degree murder, which made sense given the facts. That told Alex that the prosecutor had concocted a scheme before he took the plea bargain.

Alex did some stretches his physio said would ease back pain, and then he ate cereal, downed two mugs of coffee, chased it with a couple antacids, and called Ray, leaving a message with his wife, Anna, that he was on his way to the ME's for the autopsy before their tour started at 1600 but Ray didn't have to show his face if he didn't want to. He said it casually, and Anna seemed subdued and uncomfortable with talking about autopsies like you would talk about a meeting with your accountant. Anyhow, Ray probably did not want to go. Unexpected overtime was a sore point between Ray and Anna. Alex added that Ray also didn't need to bother attending another meeting in the late morning, this one with McNally.

"I'll be downtown already, so I'll just go on my own. Tell him I don't need back-up," he jested to Anna.

"Right, I will," she answered, unresponsive to cop humor. Then she added, "Is it an important meeting? If it is, he'll want to go."

"I doubt it."

"Okay."

He rode the subways down to First Avenue and East 26th Street and strode into the Office of the Chief Medical Examiner on the grounds of Bellevue Hospital, a sprawling complex of modern and historic buildings covering three city blocks. The original structure, the center piece, was an eighteenth-century psychiatric hospital, red bricks, Georgian archways with prominent, pointing gables, castellated towers and wrought iron gates. The rest of the hospital had sprung up around it, a mishmash of architectural incoherence, from 1970s cinderblock cubes to angular modern buildings of glistening steel and glass. The morgue and ME's office lived in one of the new buildings, half beige stone, the other half shimmering glass reflecting the sky.

Entering the waiting room on the ground floor, he grunted a greeting at the admin assistant, who said, "Hi, Alex." 36,000 cops in the NYPD, and the admin assistant at the ME's office knew his first name. Behind the admin assistant, the words, 'Science serving justice' stretched across the entire length of the wall. When he pushed through the steel doors, he shivered and rocked at the smell, a putrid concoction of formaldehyde and decomposition.

Assistant MEs seem impervious to the odor and to the presence of bodies, shrouded in white sheets, lying around the exam room like there had been a drunk party here the night before. Andre Brown smiled cheerily at him. "Hi, Alex, you're here for, um..." He looked at his paperwork. "Sean Ferrin."

"Yeah," Alex answered.

The pathologist weighed Ferrin and made note of his physical condition – excellent if you disregarded the bullet in his brain – and then he removed the plastic bags that had been placed on Ferrin's hands at the crime scene, scraping samples from under his fingernails. If he'd fought with someone, their DNA might be there. Once the ME had finished that job, Alex yanked on latex gloves and stepped forward, picking up a lifeless hand, rolling the DOA's fingers in black ink to take his prints, and then he swabbed the hands for GSR. With well-practiced care, he stowed the prints and adhesive swabs in marked baggies, signed and dated.

His hands sweated under the gloves, and he ripped them off and placed his back against the wall. The reek of decomp burned his nostrils and throat, and he felt sick to his stomach, which flustered him. How many autopsies had he observed? He didn't get nauseous anymore, a damned badge of honor. Somewhere across the room, an assistant ME dropped a metal object, and it clanged against the metal floor with a jarring ring. Alex's heart stumbled over a beat.

"You suspect suicide?"

He rapidly fluttered his eyelashes and touched his forehead. Brown was looking at him expectantly.

"Oh. Yeah, well, he was in his apartment in the middle of the night, a .22 was found underneath him, and no evidence of forced entry." They hadn't yet ruled out Ferrin letting someone in, but they had no evidence that he had done so.

The ME examined the skull and measured the gunshot wound. "This was fired at point blank range. Look, you can see the gunpowder burns around the edges of the wound, and the entry angle here, yeah, that was

173

right against his head. He either did it himself or someone got the muzzle right up to him." Then he raised one eye towards Alex. "You all right, man? You look worse than him." He indicated the corpse.

"You know the cop-shooting that happened a few days ago?" Alex said lacklusterly.

"Sure. Miriam did the autopsies. That your case?"

"Unfortunately. I feel like shit. Haven't slept in fucking days. I feel worse than him."

"Well, no question about that. He ain't feeling much."

Ferrin was soon looking a lot worse than Alex, because Brown had sliced open the ribcage and removed the internal organs, weighing them, observing their condition, taking samples of tissues and fluids for toxicology scans as he went. Ferrin wasn't overweight; he wasn't a drinker; and his lungs showed no indication he was a smoker.

"That's a healthy liver. Look at that," Brown marveled as he placed the organ on his scale. "Goes to show, where a conscientious lifestyle gets you."

"Looks better than mine," Alex said caustically. His would bear scar tissue from heavy drinking for the rest of his life.

"Looks better than a lot of people's." The ME removed the liver from the scale and fished out more organs from the abdominal cavity, brightly explaining, "I'll open up the stomach later, see what his last meal was."

"He was a vegan," Alex commented. "It'll be sprouts or something awful."

"Yeah, but you cut open someone who lived on McDonald's and beer, you realize there's something to it."

Alex snorted, a small, derisive laugh.

Next, the ME peeled the face off and used a circular saw to slice open the skull, and Alex dropped his gaze to the floor, sorry he ate breakfast. When he raised his eyes, half the skull had been removed, like opening a soft-boiled egg.

The ME observed, "Look at the lesions in the brain from the bullet zinging around in his head. Way more brain damaged than my ex-wife, no doubt!" Jauntily, Brown removed the brain and probed around the squidgy grey mush while Alex silently conversed with his stomach about behaving. Yes – stress from the Irvine case, and then combining it with coffee, sugar, formaldehyde, and innards.

The pathologist announced, "Gotcha," holding up a small lead lump, pinned in his tweezers. "What do you think?"

".22," Alex said as he snapped on a fresh latex glove and took the small bullet from Dr. Brown, who then placed the brain on the scale. Later, when he dissected it, he would trace the slug's path.

Alex peered at the bullet in his palm: smooshed up, indentations in the lead from ricocheting against the skull, but he had seen far more damaged ones. Ballistics might be able to make something out of it. He slipped it into an evidence baggie, writing his name, command, and shield number on it.

As for Sean Ferrin, that was that. Dr. Brown said he would write up cause of death as gunshot to the head, and they would contact Alex whenever he had results from a tox scan and a stomach contents analysis, and then he whistled the tune to 'La Cucaracha' as he began the process of reassembling the body.

"See you next time," Alex said. "Same place, different body."

He stood on First Avenue, breathing. The morgue stuck in his nostrils. At each breath, he could taste that rancid decay in the back of his throat. He bought a double expresso from a street van and washed the decomp taste out of his mouth.

Then he walked to Centre Street for his meeting with McNally even though it drizzled, that steady rain that feels light on your skin but gets you soaked. He needed the exercise. In recent months, he'd been half-assed about swimming or walking, and he feared that he was putting on the weight. His physio said that extra weight would aggravate his old injuries, and his body had become less magnanimous as he inched closer to fifty. The physio gently implied he should be twenty or thirty pounds lighter. While he was not prepared to take on the full Ray Espinosa regime of yoga, pilates, and running, he urged himself to get serious about swimming again. Next week, perhaps, which was what he'd said last week. But the dreary weather or loneliness or his flabby sleeplessness sapped his energy, and he'd let his pool membership lapse.

Security at the DA's office interrupted his moody introspection, and he fished his shield out of his damp pocket, and the cops on the detail sent him around the metal detectors. He realized his left forefinger was bleeding. Shit, he'd bitten his nails off so inattentively he hadn't noticed. On McNally's floor, he zagged into the bathroom to clean his hand, before he knocked on the prosecutor's door. The lawyer had a large corner office that advertised his importance because it contained a mahogany desk two men could lie across and a plush leather sofa. McNally had decorated the walls with a dozen photos of him climbing mountains. Often, Alex wondered why someone who liked mountains and the outdoors that much lived in New York City, but he'd never asked.

Without any time-wasting small talk, McNally explained to Alex that he'd told his colleague in AR-1 to charge the perp with first-degree murder. He felt confident that he could fight off a motion to dismiss on the grounds that the "contract" he had signed in the hospital was null and void. Contracts made under duress – say with a gun to your head or to someone else's – cannot be enforced. That was the good news.

"Then what's the bad news?" Alex spaced out, his eyes lost on the dreary, grey river, the sheets of drizzle, and the skyscrapers of the Financial District like windswept, standing stones on this sunless, windy day.

"His confession is unlikely to be admissible in court, as he made it thinking he was going to get ten years, and that's no longer the case."

"What? We lie to suspects all the time, saying they might do less time if they cooperate with us. As far as I know, that's still kosher."

"Yes, true," said Simon. "But Alex, *you* don't actually have the power to make any kind of plea bargain with anyone. I do. If *I* tell a defendant and his lawyer that we are making an agreement, for a defendant's cooperation in exchange for a reduced sentence, then that carries more weight than if you say it. I mean, I can, and I will argue that it was a voluntary statement and, as you say, the courts have indeed upheld the right of the police to suggest, as an interrogation technique, that a cooperative defendant can do less time. But it's in a grey area. Very grey, and not in our favor. Leonard will tell the judge that it's unconstitutional as fuck if prosecutors could make plea agreements, and then renege on them but use the evidence obtained as a result of the deal in proceedings against the defendant, and this would be a very bad precedent to set." He smiled humorlessly.

Alex grasped how legal precedents worked. "But it's not a precedent for your usual plea bargain, is it? I'd say the circumstances were pretty fucking exceptional. The perp's a manipulative son of a bitch. There's no way Khalid woulda survived those injuries without going to a hospital, and the ME thought he'd be pretty fucked in a hospital."

"And that is my argument for why we should keep his confession. But I'm just telling you, warning you, there is a good chance that my argument won't hold. We need enough evidence to sustain an indictment, *as if* we didn't have the statement."

"When we were in the hospital, did you know the statement would be excluded if you bailed on the plea?" Alex proposed jadedly.

"I thought it was likely, but I had the Chief of D's, a guy from Bloomberg's office, my boss, all demanding that I do whatever was necessary to find the hostage, and basically saying it would be my ass – and yours, to be honest – on the line if we didn't find him quickly." The ADA flung a foot against the edge of his desk, and he loosened the knot of his tie. "I did what I had to do, given the circumstances. You find more evidence, it will all be fine."

Alex had no trouble reading Simon's underlying message: *I saved your ass, you save mine.*

"I'm taking the case to the grand jury tomorrow," the lawyer stated.

"They'll indict?"

"I have a stonking detailed confession admitting everything, and it hasn't been suppressed yet. They'll fucking indict in about a minute. He's a ham sandwich *holding* the smoking gun."

"Unless we lose the confession. Then he's nothing, not even a shitty cliché," Alex responded dryly and checked his watch and then his cell phone. "I'm on the four-by-twelve today, so I'd better go," he said.

"Fine, fine, I'll see you tomorrow in the grand jury room," said Simon impatiently, snatching his desk phone and shoving it under his jawbone.

Then Simon took the case to the grand jury. New York law requires a grand jury indictment for all felony prosecutions, the easiest court appearance a cop will ever face because it is just you, the ADA, the jurors, and a stenographer. Grand juries don't decide guilt or innocence, but rather, they determine whether or not the government has enough evidence to proceed with their case. The standard of proof is considerably lower than a trial and only the ADA asks questions. The jurors can, but they often don't.

Alex, Ray, the Two-Eight detectives, the ME, and other police officers testified, along with Khalid's wife, Irvine's colleagues, and the kid from the bodega, and without much equivocation, the jurors indicted Kitchener for two counts of first-degree murder, one count of first-degree robbery, two counts of first-degree assault, and one for possession of an illegal firearm. A grounder if no one suppressed the confession, but Alex knew it would unravel in a heartbeat if a judge swung an ax at it.

Afterwards, Alex and Ray re-interviewed Kitchener's girlfriend, searching for more evidence to support the indictment, but she didn't provide any. The indictment didn't change her story. Alex's disquieted gut feeling persisted; he did not find her credible, but he could not articulate why, other than trust in his gut and his two decades of death investigations.

But that wasn't probable cause. Taking a chance anyway, they called a judge and brought him an oral warrant application for her Ford Aspire.

"*What* crime are you saying this car was used for?" Judge Gennaro asked, after he'd read the emailed affidavit and the witness statements supporting it.

"In furtherance of the robbery and two homicides," Alex responded, playing with the computer mouse and holding the phone against his head with his shoulder.

"The proceeds of said robbery were found with Mr. Kitchener at Penn Station, is that right?"

"Yes." Alex inwardly winced.

"And the second homicide victim was found at the opposite end of town from the vehicle in question, correct?"

"Yes. But the suspect used this car immediately after –"

"A couple *hours* after," corrected the judge.

"Well, yes, Your Honor. But we don't believe this witness' story."

"She's got no record. Going out with someone who has a record isn't a criminal act."

"She's not *that* naïve. She's from the Heights. Given the perpetrator went straight to her apartment, it's reasonable to suspect that she might've aided and abetted."

"Being from the Heights sure isn't evidence, Detective," the judge warned. "Do you have any evidence that the witness is lying?"

Creases furrowed into Alex's brows. "Who the—" he coughed, covering up his near miss of, *who the fuck. Don't swear!* "Who moves soccer balls and some goal posts after committing armed robbery and two homicides?"

"I don't know, Detective, but a strange story isn't necessarily a fabricated one, is it?"

Alex ground enamel off his back teeth, balling both his hands into fists so he would not bite his nails. He sometimes tried to mitigate that habit.

He didn't get the search warrant.

If they put a tail on Analisa for a few days, they might discover something yielding more probable cause than a bullshit story and a gut feeling. Alex contacted Finnane, who agreed with him, and they applied for authorization at 1PP.

Where else could he go, he thought. Finnane was doing the ass-covering work, double checking the victims' families and connections in case it hadn't been random, but the detectives were ninety-eight percent certain that it was. They had obtained warrants for the perps' emails and ISPs and established that Kitchener downloaded a lot of porn, but he didn't buy drugs and guns online nor write about buying drugs and guns online. Bailey, on the other hand, frequently railed against the government on Reddit and had bought a gun through a website. Computer Crimes traced the website, and they found the seller, a local shitbird in Newark. But he hadn't sold Bailey a .45. It had been a Glock 19, a 9mm, and it had been six months ago. Moreover, they reported no recent activity on Bailey's accounts. He'd either changed his email and server to something with better encryption, or he wasn't using the internet at all.

What about Fred Symington? He might remember more about his collar now that it wasn't four in the morning. Alex called him, feeling his nerves. A thin layer of sweat warmed up his palms. In the clear light of day, Fred might also remember that he'd spent years nursing a grudge. But Fred sounded overjoyed when he heard Alex's voice. Yes, they could meet up. How about tonight? The Glendale. Fred gushed about the Glendale. Such a great bar. Alex must know it.

"Yeah," Alex said diffidently. An old cop bar on Bleecker Street. It had been one of his haunts when he drank, and he preferred avoiding it. Too many memories. He didn't want to sit in a bar, particularly that one, but Fred could not fathom meeting him anywhere else. The Alex Fred knew would be in stitches at the suggestion of a café. So, Alex resolutely faced the Glendale.

But he had no other leads, and he spent the rest of his eight-by-four retracing Sean Ferrin's steps in the last twenty-four hours of his life. He'd driven to work that morning. He had a classic 1978 Pontiac Firebird he lovingly maintained, and it lived in the attended parking garage underneath his building. The garage security guards reported that Ferrin had driven the car out and in, like he always did, and nothing had aroused suspicion. Then Ferrin ate dinner at a vegan restaurant on West 70th and Columbus. The waiters recollected seeing him and said he'd eaten alone and read a book. Alex finished his tour feeling nowhere, with no evidence that anyone had followed Ferrin or that Ferrin had planned a suicide. But sometimes, people just go about their day normally, and then blow their heads off.

On his way to Greenwich Village, he grabbed a pizza from a take-out joint near West 72nd and ate it sitting on a bench in Sheridan Square. He'd changed into jeans and an NYU hoodie, and he inelegantly nibbled at the pizza while protecting his hoodie from dripping cheese. Fred – and Ray for that matter – would reproachfully argue that being a domesticated, responsible adult didn't encompass eating greasy pizza at 2000 hours on a bench. But Alex had never been any good at that.

Then at the Glendale, he drank diet coke, while Fred knocked back the Coors Light. Thank God none of the cops who frequented the bar now were regulars from the early '90s. Nor were the bartenders. The faces in the bar were insouciant. The detectives sidestepped their difficulties and Alex's alcoholism, Fred's brushy eyebrows wiggling in wonder at Alex's diet coke, but he didn't comment, and they caught up on one another's lives, retelling a few stories from the One-Oh-Three, gossiping about mutual acquaintances, and finally, Alex prodding Fred for anything else that might be percolating in his head about Kitchener and Bailey.

A bit tipsy, Fred threw back his head, laughing, "Yeah, I thought you'd get to that eventually! You know 178th and Wadsworth?" Around 1990, Fred had stopped drinking or going out, but his kids had become adults, and he must be off the lead. Too bad Alex never would be.

"Uh-huh," Alex answered. He wiped at an eye with the back of his hand. "It's a dope corner."

"Yeah, well, that's where your guy's alleged accomplice, Bailey, used to buy his shit."

"What, you think a bunch of dope slingers are gonna talk to us?" Alex stirred the ice around in his coke with the straw. One of the commandments of Heights dealers: thou shalt not cooperate with the police.

Fred slapped Alex's bicep with the broad palm of his hand. "They're not the favorites of the local slingers, Lex. It wasn't just bodegas they'd hold-up. Anything. Anyone. Any caper to get money to score, and they weren't above stealing people's stashes if that failed. I thought of you, you know, that you might be investigating those shitbirds one day. But I thought *they'd* be the DOAs."

"It's nice of you to think of me," Alex said dryly. A pair of white stick-up artists in the Heights wouldn't get much loyalty from the community. People might talk.

"It's a school night," said Fred, standing up. "And the wife won't be happy if I stagger home wasted." He spoke as if Alex had been drinking whisky instead of coke and would be staggering home wasted, which rankled him. "But it's been good to catch up properly."

"Yeah," said Alex, swallowing the last mouthful of diet coke, and he considered telling Fred that he had nearly died of a ruptured ulcer at the Glendale, but he sucked on an ice cube instead, swishing it around his mouth as it melted. Fred didn't need to hear the details of that story.

They paid their tab, and Fred said, "Don't be such a stranger," and he strolled off towards the W line station on Prince Street.

He was a stranger, Alex thought as he turned the opposite way, heading for the 1 line station on Houston Street. Life had thrust them apart. Fred didn't have three kids in the early '80s, and Alex hadn't been shot, and those things change you. The breach in their friendship hadn't mended. It had grown wider, if anything, but there was no more anger or resentment. Just indifference. And a lead on that damn case, which made the discomfiting trip to the Glendale worthwhile.

Chapter Ten

Alex trudged into his apartment, dumping his shoes in the hallway, and then he melted onto the sofa, trashed after a crazy set playing whack-a-mole with his cases. A double homicide, a cop-killing, the one case he did not want to fuck up, but it seemed poised to fuck up. He knew Kitchener was guilty, but he had a confession the ADAs purported might not be legal, and everything else looked preternaturally circumstantial. The lab reports from ballistics, forensics, and the ME had trickled into his inbox today: not a trace of hair, blood, or tissue on the Smith and Wesson from Kitchener's backpack matching Khalid nor any other vic or perp. The forensics techs and ME said that the injuries were consistent with the butt of a gun, but not that one.

Meanwhile, the ME had scraped out DNA samples from under Khalid's fingertips and entered them into the city's database, the New York state database, and CODIS, the federal database. But no one would see those results for weeks. Anyway, the DNA might be too damaged to be viable, but if it wasn't and the profile matched Kitchener, it would be the *coup d'état,* neatly closing the case with a bow on it. Other scenarios incurred an ulcer. If they got a hit on the state or federal databases, it would indicate Khalid had an altercation with someone previously convicted of a violent crime or sex crime. If the profile didn't match Kitchener or find a hit on the databases, it would indicate Khalid had an altercation with someone who hadn't been convicted of those things. Either way, reasonable doubt unless that profile matched Kitchener's accomplice, who's DNA wasn't on the databases.

They had re-interviewed Khalid's boss and several witnesses from West 123rd and Malcolm X: the eyewits apologized for their terrible memories, and Khalid's boss could not place him at *that* intersection, claiming he didn't know what routes his drivers took. Furthermore, only two eyewits had ID'd the hijacked vehicle as a white van with livery, the tire thief and the woman who had hidden behind parked cars. Neither witness warmed Alex's heart. The tire thief had perjury convictions, among other transgressions, which meant he would be useless in court even if he told the truth like a monk. The young woman, Flavia Blanca, had more than half a dozen prostitution convictions under at least three different aliases, and her only address was the homeless shelter on 135th and Lexington. Proving the adage of Murphy's Law, after her cursory interview with Finnane, she had vanished without a trace. People at the shelter remembered her showing up, albeit briefly, but no one knew where she'd gone. Nobody on the street had any information about her.

Finally, the ATF had emailed Alex, writing that they'd traced the .38 special in Kitchener's possession to a gun shop owner in Bayonne, who had sold it to an acquaintance of Kitchener's. The acquaintance told the cops he'd given it to Kitchener in exchange for a couple grams of heroin but tying the firearm to Kitchener or to the junkie in Bayonne didn't achieve much, because they had no evidence of it being used in any crime. And as for the .45 that had killed PO Irvine and possibly killed Khalid, it could have passed into another dimension for all they knew.

During today's four-by-twelve, Alex and Ray had refocused on their other infuriating whodunit, driving to the Elm Tree care home with a warrant for any files related to restraint or "challenging behavior" and wasted an hour arguing with the management over the fine language in the warrant, before being left on their own to sift through dusty boxes of papers in a dank basement.

Alex must have scanned or sped read through hundreds of files. Any that related to a difficult or challenging resident, they transported the office for more careful perusal. Then they had to write a meticulous inventory detailing everything they confiscated, the requirement of the CPL. His eyes ached from hours of reading small print in bad lighting. He had resolved that maybe this week, or this month, he was going to call the DEA about their optometrists. Their medical insurance had been pretty useless, but this was a simple problem in comparison to complicated gunshot wounds or fuzzily diagnosed back pain, frequently recommended in the newsletters that arrived in his mail every month. Maybe they expected detectives to go blind.

Seeing spots, he turned on the lights in the living room and kitchen. His living room was just big enough for the sofa, the TV, and a small coffee table. The bedroom barely fit a double bed and a wardrobe, leaving a squashed corridor of floor space your body almost fit through when it wasn't filled with dirty laundry. The kitchen was smaller than most closets. Most of the space in the apartment was up, ten-foot high ceilings and ornately carved skirting boards, a checkered pattern around the room, flowers in the corners. The place didn't hold heat, and it transformed changing light bulbs into a high-risk activity, but the high ceilings offered an illusion of space when there wasn't any.

Alex didn't collect much tchatchke. A bookshelf with a few trashy novels, some cassette tapes, some vinyl, a couple CDs, photos on the wall of New York City, his daughters, and an Aboriginal painting of a kangaroo from Elana. The coffee table looked like a bomb had exploded at a paper factory, cluttered with bills, bank statements, payslips, medical insurance shit, Detective's Endowment Association newsletters, something about his pension, a letter from the police department reminding him that he was due to be retested at the firing range, and take-out menus. Crap he meant to file away or throw away, but it had taken on a life of its own, a sedimentary rock filing system, where he could locate things in the pile based on when he last saw them. And it had long arrived at the stage where doing anything about it had become too big a project to deal with when he was tired after work.

He checked the voicemails on his landline. No one had called him. And Becky would phone his cell anyway. He hesitated over the phone, the temptation to call her wrapping talons around his heart, squeezing until he nearly relented from the pain and dialed. But he resisted it. He'd already left her two voicemails. He'd lobbed the ball into her fucking court now. He breathed out, as if he could propel the pain out of his chest. He wasn't playing this game. If she wanted to talk to him, she knew where to find him. He'd already come to the conclusion, born from years of torturous experience, that if someone drops off your planet for days or weeks without a word nor a reason, and they are neither dead nor in the hospital (a bit of detective work had established that neither was the case), it is probably over.

Pushing his fingers into his sternum, he glared angrily at the phone, as if it bore responsibility for his troubles. *At least I deserve a fucking call.*

Hurt bathed his insides in hot steam. He released another emotional breath, and then he stalked into the kitchen. If there was a way for something to go wrong in a relationship, he would find it.

Also, he was starving, but he had no food in the apartment – he hadn't bothered with a shopping trip this week. Upon excavating the freezer, he came across a tub of Ben and Jerry's chocolate fudge brownie ice cream. That would do.

Without looking at the use-by date – he didn't want to know – he threw it in the microwave for thirty seconds. The microwave beeped cheerfully, and Alex removed the ice cream tub and padded to the living room, where he ate freezer-burned ice cream straight from the tub and punched the remote on the TV, inattentively watching *Scrubs* reruns. He scoffed half the tub, suffering pangs of guilt, because he should be worried about his weight, his heart, his health, so he reluctantly hit the brakes and stuffed the ice cream back in the freezer. But he was still hungry and too tired to schlep to the 24/7 bodega on Columbus.

He scanned the sparse kitchen and found an overripe banana. Slightly disgusted, he finished off the squidgy banana and then stayed up for another ten or twenty minutes. At 0215, he flicked off the TV and wandered into the bathroom, brushing his teeth, washing his face. He had another four-by-twelve tomorrow. The brutal tours were the swing shifts, when they switched from four-by-twelves to eight-by-fours. 1600 to midnight, and then 0800 to 1600. You work a set for four days: two four-by-twelves, and then two eight-by-fours, and when the shifts swing, you only have seven hours between them. But you get two days off before another set starts. He hit the light in the bathroom, treading barefoot into the bedroom, stripping off his clothes, curling up in bed.

His insomnia and nightmares left him in peace, taking an anomalous and unexpected vacation, and he slept. Until screaming sounds penetrated his consciousness. He opened one eye and looked at the time on the alarm clock beside the bed. 0700. He closed his eyes, rolling over onto his back, resting his hands on his stomach, pissed off at people having a drunken row in his Goddamned stairwell at 0700, the first night he'd slept soundly in months. *What the fuck, people,* he thought. The shouting continued. He heard something crashing, the building shaking. His cop's instinct kicked him awake. There was an edge to it, fear and anger, something beyond your usual drunken argument that made the hairs on the back of his neck stand up.

Grinding his teeth, he tumbled out of bed and groped around on the floor for clothes. He found a pair of sweatpants and an old NYU t-shirt with holes under the armpit and a threadbare collar that Sarah had given him some years ago. Tugging the t-shirt over his belly, he advanced to the door, putting his ear against it. A woman's voice, hysterical and terrified. And a male voice, raised and brimming with rage.

Alex unlocked the door, but his gut rumbled a warning. Heeding it, he hurried back to the bedroom where picked up his firearm, kept in a locked drawer in the bedside table, and he shoved it into the elastic waistband of the sweatpants. He grabbed his shield and his cell phone as well, thinking he didn't look very much like a cop at the moment, just a middle-aged white guy in sweatpants with a bit of a gut on him.

Lightly, silently, he opened the door and slipped into the stairwell. He saw two figures at the bottom of it, male and female. His NYPD brain made an immediate assessment: white, both in their late twenties. The girl he recognized as one of the five or six people who lived in one of the downstairs apartments. She cowered against the wall, hands up, her face blotched with tears, and the male, his face tinted red, standing over her, with the lopsided stance of someone who is very drunk. Alex had never seen him in his life.

As Alex edged down the stairs, the male bellowed, "You fucking lying bitch," striking her hard across the face with his forearm. She shrieked and fell, collapsing into the wall, and he hit her again. Alex picked up his pace. The guy reached for something on his other side and pulled out a gun. The girl sobbed. Alex's heart leapt into his throat.

He drew his gun and bounded down another flight of stairs, getting a line of sight on the perp, shouting at the top of his lungs, "Police! Freeze!" He kept moving down the stairs, the gun fixed on the son of a bitch.

Both looked up at him, shock plastered on their faces. They hadn't heard him until now.

"Drop the gun and get on the floor! On the floor! Now," he yelled.

Most people do. The perp didn't. He stared at Alex, eyes kaleidoscopic and bloodshot.

"Get on the fucking floor!"

186

Still, the perp didn't move, didn't drop the gun. Frozen, he held it in a death grip. Alex felt the adrenaline rocketing. He made some fast calculations. If he fired, the bullets could ricochet and hurt him, or the vic. This asshole was taller than him, but he was a scrawny kid. Alex weighed around one-sixty pounds, and while he carried a little more weight than he would ideally like, some of it was muscle. He had the advantages of weight, strength, surprise, training, and enough adrenaline powering through his body to fight a bear. Now he had to one hundred percent commit. Hesitation or doubt could be fatal.

A couple steps closer to the perp, and then he sprinted forward, hurling himself into a headlong dive, and slamming into the perp broadside. Together, they crashed into the concrete floor of the entryway with a sickening crack of flesh and bone. Alex heard the sound of the gun clattering to the ground and his neighbor's ear-splitting shriek. The jarring impact vibrated through his body, but adrenaline made him oblivious.

He rolled off the perp, scrambling to his feet, retrieving the weapon, a Ruger SP101, a small gun people used for concealed carry. Deftly, he engaged the safety and shoved it into his waistband. He kept his Glock trained on the perp, yelling, "Don't move! Don't you dare fucking move!" The guy wasn't moving. He lay on the floor moaning, badly winded, probably injured. Alex didn't give a shit. For all he cared, he could have broken the perp's back. Gun in his right hand, he freed his cell phone from his pocket with his left and called 911.

When the dispatcher answered, he automatically fell into NYPD radio-speak, "Ten-thirty-four at 124 West 87th. One male suspect down. One female, possible fifty-four. Ten-twelve. K."

"Are you a police officer, sir?" said the dispatcher.

"Oh, yes, my name is Alex Boswell. I'm a detective. Shield number 8652."

"Ten-fifty six," said the dispatcher, asking him to verify if an ambulance was needed.

He shifted his gaze to his neighbor, whose face had blanched. She had bruises on her face, swollen lips, a graze on her cheek. With all the noise he heard, she might have other injuries. "Affirmative," he said.

"Ten-four," said the dispatcher. "We'll get a unit to you right away."

"Copy that," said Alex, hanging up. The perp groaned, wriggling, and Alex barked, "What did I say? Don't fucking move an inch!" He looked at his neighbor and added gently, "I'm sorry, what's your name."

"Jess," she whimpered, her terrified eyes pinned on the Glock, like it was scarier than the boyfriend.

Gesturing with the gun, which made her face go whiter, he asked, "What happened? Who is this guy?"

"My boyfriend," she whispered, but she didn't seem capable of explaining anything else. She trembled like a leaf in a storm.

Hell of a fucking boyfriend. "Has he done anything like this before?" Expressionlessly, she stared at him.

He heard banging on the door, and crab-walking so his weapon didn't leave the perp, he darted over to it and flicked open the Yale lock. Four uniforms piled into the stairwell. Alex knew the sergeant, a Mexican cop called Elias Ortega. The sergeant's eyes widened to the size of manhole covers as he took in the surreal scene: Alex, in sweatpants and a tatty t-shirt, holding a stricken young man down with his gun.

"Boswell? What the *fuck?* I got a ten-twelve and reports of a thirty-four. Didn't know who or what. You off-duty, man?"

"I was," said Alex. "I live upstairs. Heard screaming. Went to check it out and this shitbird was assaulting my neighbor here," he indicated Jess. "And threatening her with a gun."

Ortega looked down at the perp. "Jesus. He don't look good. You shoot him?"

"No, I tackled him."

"Jesus," Ortega said again.

Two officers slapped the bracelets on the perp's wrists and wrenched him to his feet, reciting *Miranda*, but he was in too much pain to not remain silent. They hauled him off to a waiting squad car. With the perp secured, out of his building, and no longer his problem, Alex let go of the breath he'd been holding for the whole incident.

"You got his gun, Lex?" said Ortega.

"Yeah," said Alex, extracting the revolver from his other side. It had four rounds in the cylinder, one in the chamber. A shiver shot down Alex's back; he didn't want to think about what would have happened if the perp had fired. He handed it to Ortega, who slipped it into an evidence baggie. Once Ortega had documented chain-of-custody, they

188

turned their attention to Jess, who had slumped against the wall again, her face the color of the grey floor.

Alex rammed his own gun into his elastic waistband and squatted down beside her, saying, "You all right, Jess?"

She didn't answer, cowering, catatonic.

"That bus coming?" he asked Ortega.

"Yeah, shouldn't be far behind us," answered Ortega.

"You're gonna be fine, Jess," Alex said in a soothing voice. "There's an ambulance on its way. They'll fix you up, and then Sergeant Ortega here is going to talk to you and figure out what happened and try to help you, okay."

She nodded, her eyes full of fear.

"You know you're bleeding, right?" said Elias.

"What? Am I?"

"Your elbow."

He glanced down at his right elbow. He'd scraped off a layer of skin, and it was raw and bloody. Oh, well, he could deal with that later. Sirens wailed outside, and then an EMS crew joined them in the entryway. They asked Alex and Ortega a few questions and surrounded Jess, covering her with blankets and hustling her to the bus outside. They were quick and professional. Elias sent his partner with her. As soon as she was treated and capable of answering questions, they would get a statement from her.

Then, as unexpectedly and rapidly as chaos had erupted in the stairwell, it fell quiet. Like a usual morning. The usual noises. Traffic and people outside. Alex sunk down on the bottom steps, now breathing hard as if he couldn't get enough air to power his staccato heartbeat. He put his right hand over his chest.

"You okay, man?" said Elias, seating himself beside him.

"Yeah, my heart's just going at about a hundred miles an hour."

Elias patted him on the back. "I bet. You get the big balls points of the day. All alone, no backup, throwing yourself onto a guy armed with a loaded gun."

"Well, it was either that or shoot him. I didn't wanna risk a ricochet or the fucking hassle in my life of a year-long investigation."

"Who does? Anyway, you know I'm gonna have to get a statement off you," said Ortega.

"Can we do it upstairs?" asked Alex. "It's fucking freezing here." For the first time since he left his apartment, he noticed the cold. Goosebumps covered his arms, the hairs standing up. Adrenaline ebbed, and he felt the stinging wound in his elbow, and he was a little shaken. He'd lived in this apartment since 1990, and the only trouble in fourteen years had been two of his neighbors having a dispute over one's whining dog, and Alex hadn't made that his problem.

As he led Ortega up the stairs to his apartment, the sergeant said, "I knew you were local to this precinct. Didn't know you lived in this building."

"Been here since '90."

Alex filled the coffee machine but changed his mind. Fuck it, he felt jittery enough without the caffeine hit. He whacked on the faucet, cleaning dirt out of the scrape on his elbow, flinching, the wound stinging, and then he dabbed it with a paper towel. The office had gauze floating around. He would steal some at work later.

They sat on the sofa, Alex shoving some of the crap accumulating on the coffee table to one side, so Ortega had space to write. A few more deep breaths, massaging his eyes, and then putting his hands on his thighs so Ortega would not see how badly they shook, and he calmly related the incident. His heart rate was dropping. God, he hadn't done this street cop shit, like breaking up a domestic, in years.

Elias put his pen in his mouth and contemplated his notes. Then he asked, "Do you know the names of the people downstairs? Or anything about them?"

"No, I just know them on sight. Sometimes I say hi when I see them in the stairwell."

"Huh, well. Guess I'll send a couple guys round to talk to them when they're home. If we need you again, I'll phone you. Do I still have your number?" Answering his own question, he scrolled through his list of contacts. "Oh, yes, I do." Closing his memo book, he stood up, touching Alex's shoulder. "You sure you're all right?"

"Yeah, I'm fine."

"Fuckin' brass balls, man. Well done."

"You do what you have to, don't you?" Alex breathed. He'd never thought of himself as courageous, but sometimes the job demanded it. How many times in his career had he buried fear in a back compartment and faced a thousand dangerous situations? He wouldn't think about fear, just what he had to do.

"I'm gonna head to the station house and see what I can get out of our perp," said Elias. "Then see how my partner's gotten on with the vic."

Alex nodded, licking his cracked lips. After Elias left, he changed into a suit, and then he shrugged on his winter coat and wrapped a scarf around his throat. He felt agitated, restless. If he resumed his routine morning things, he might settle his head. The brisk November air would clear his brain.

The day was grey but clear, the clouds patchy and high, as if they could not decide whether to snow or to let the sun through. His breath steamed out of his nostrils. He shoved his hands into the pockets of his coat and made barely acknowledging New Yorker eye contact with a few familiar faces on the street. At the bakery on Amsterdam, he bought a chocolate croissant and a *Times,* and then he made his way back to his apartment, where he finally brewed that coffee, reckoning he could drink it without giving himself a heart attack.

Sudden noises outside startled him: a clattering garbage truck, a barking dog, a siren on Amsterdam. Each time, he stopped reading the newspaper, his chest tight, his senses on red alert. Blinking, he shook his head like he had something in his eyes and scrubbed his face. Shock from this morning's surreal incident. A gun-fueled domestic in his own building wasn't something he'd ever anticipated. Still, he could be pleased with how he'd handled it. He wasn't badly hurt, although he might be a little sore tomorrow; Jess wasn't more injured than she'd been before he'd intervened, and the perp was apprehended. Poor kid. She could have been his kid, or anyone's. But he wished his brain didn't feel like it was floating around inside his skull, and when he moved his head quickly, it sloshed into his temples.

Then he read the paper inattentively for another forty-five minutes. War and violence in distant places. Acid dissolved his stomach lining. He stood up, joints creaking, and he felt slow and lethargic, like he had gelatin in his blood vessels, but at the same time, he was tense and jumpy, as if more violence here waited for him, silent but ready to detonate. Yet West 87th had resumed its Upper West Side affability, as though nothing had happened.

Chapter Eleven

November 10th

Marcus Wheeler followed Alex into the bathroom and helped him clean the wound on his arm, saying, "NFL tackling a guy with a loaded gun. Fucking ballsy. You didn't think he'd fire at you or his girlfriend first?"

"I didn't let myself think about that," said Alex. "I knew I was heavier, stronger, and faster, and he wasn't Arnold Schwarzenegger. Ouch."

"Sorry, Lex you've taken most of the skin off." Wheeler gripped his arm, holding it still.

"If I didn't think I could take him, I wouldn't have done what I did."

"I'm sure," agreed Marcus with a loopy, bucktoothed grin. "Fucking people, eh? I hope your neighbor's all right. You know your neighbors well?"

"Yeah, me too. She looked pretty shook up when the bus took her. And I don't know them at all. There's like five twenty or thirty-somethings in that place."

"I guess that's how young people afford Manhattan rent nowadays."

"I know. It's fucking nuts. If I sold or rented out my place, I'd be fucking rich."

"And homeless."

"Nah, I could afford a mansion in Poughkeepsie."

Marcus wrapped the bandage around his elbow and secured it with tape. It chafed where his joint moved, and pain leaked into his bones, stiffening the whole arm, right down to his hand. He buttoned up his shirt and retied his tie, before following Marcus out onto the squad room.

Another cup of coffee, and then Alex opened one of the boxes attached to the Kazparek case, his disillusionment rising when he saw the sheer volume of reading staring at him from inside the box. The other side of police work: where you didn't take down armed perps. Coughing from the plumes of dust, he launched into his reading project without enthusiasm. The first case was a resident who was non-verbal and who liked to bite people. He'd apparently nailed a few staff members. But he was also not mobile without a wheelchair, and nowhere in his file did they suggest restraint. Staff just had to get out of his way.

The next was more promising, someone who liked to bang his head violently into walls when he got stressed out. *Who doesn't,* Alex thought wryly. He found notes in the file, written authorization from a doctor and the service user's parents for physically restraining him if he got violent. Alex placed that one into a 'follow-up' pile. They could contact the parents or the physician. The third file described a girl who ripped her clothes off when she was unhappy. Fourth file had a similar MO, except the service user was particularly prone to ripping off their clothes in public.

He rested his forehead in his hands for a minute, thinking this would be easier if he didn't feel like shit. Then he skimmed through file number five. The guy would scratch and hit people when upset, and Alex saw that restraint was authorized. Okay, follow-up. He put it on top of his follow-up pile and then heaved himself to his feet, taking a breather. His attention remained shot to hell.

Ray had arrived and taken his own a stack of files. Names, descriptions, and some idea of the process by which restraint had to be authorized, which involved an evaluation by a manager in the care home, a psychologist, and in some cases, a social worker. Alex identified a psychologist whose name appeared on several files. He typed the name into Google, the computer responding with a phone number and address for the psychologist's practice. It beat squinting at tiny print in the phone book or discovering that there were three dozen doctors named John Smith or whatever in New York City, and then contacting all of them. He called the psychologist, identifying himself as a detective and guardedly asking the man about restraint.

"Detective, it is unfortunate that this child has died, but I don't believe 'therapeutic crisis intervention' is inherently harmful," the psychologist said. "In fact, quite the opposite. It has improved the lives of many people in residential care homes, since components of it include teaching people how to better manage their stress and avoid crises in the first place. The point of TCI is that it *prevents* the use of restraint."

"But not all the time," ventured Alex, wishing he had techniques for managing his stress.

"No," sighed the psychologist. "There are times when it is needed, when the person poses a substantial danger of harm to themselves or others."

"And it includes physical restraint training?" he asked, already knowing that it did.

"Yes," said the psychologist.

"Have you ever known of anyone to get hurt while being restrained?" He gnawed on his pen, wagering with himself over the psychologist lawyering up.

"Usually not if staff are properly trained. But sometimes... All these cases are risk-assessed-"

"If the resident had some kind of cardiac condition, would that be included in a risk assessment?"

"If it was assessed as a risk," replied the psychologist. "You can be trained, but you can't control everything. As a policeman, I am sure you must understand."

"Can you tell me about the training staff received at the Elm Tree Care Home? You've approved of physical restraint for several of their residents."

Silence, the sound of the psychologist balking.

Alex idly turned an ear towards Liz Greenwood, also on the phone, and she was saying, "You mean to say that he penetrated, but didn't ejaculate?"

The psychologist's voice hardened. "I don't know what I'm permitted to say, Detective. I'm sorry. I think I'd better consult with our attorneys before answering any more questions."

Less than five minutes. I must be psychic. "We would appreciate more details. We're just trying to figure out what happened to Peter Kazparek. Can you call us back and arrange a meeting with us, and your lawyer if you like, and we can discuss this further?"

"Okay, Detective," said the psychologist unhappily, and he hung up the phone.

"Lex, did he lawyer up?" asked Ray.

"Yeah. Didn't take long." Alex delicately rubbed his sore elbow.

"I guess if someone is criminally liable for something, then that could make a whole lotta people civilly liable," reflected Ray, placing files in the box. He noticed Alex touching his elbow and added, "Marcus said you got a pretty good scrape there."

"Yeah, it's a little banged-up," Alex said. "Let's get outta here." His head felt airy; he kept blanking out while reading. Working the streets might get the blood pumping with more conviction.

"Where?"

"See if we can find those witnesses Fred told me about in the Heights."

"Seems tenuous," said Ray.

"You got any better ideas?"

Ray didn't, so they drove uptown through Harlem. Both detectives sunk into sour moods. Every cop-shooting transported Alex back to his own – fear and pain and nightmares, an ache in his side. He rested his hand against his floating ribs, acutely aware of his scars and slipping rib cartilage, and they ground to a halt in traffic around the City College campus.

The light changed, but traffic didn't move. The light cycled back to red, and Alex wondered if they'd blown their shot at saving Khalid by not finding the van sooner, chasing it from the scene – more speed, more organization, more manpower. He felt like he'd fucked up, and Khalid had died because he'd been running point on the investigation, and he'd been too slow. Usually, by the time he got involved, the vics were dead or in the hospital. Live hostage situations weren't on his customary beat, and saving lives was rarely his responsibility; just investigating ones snuffed out. True, the ME hypothesized that Khalid died early on the 28th, which meant that realistically, there was very little Alex could have done. But he mulled over every decision and action he'd taken, certain he'd made some poor ones.

Ruminating like this would not do him any favors. A tough case demanded a clear mind, dammit. Since Alex always found some solace in the mantra, 'it-could-be-worse,' he twitched his head, shaking off his worries and checking his rearview mirror. Muscles in his neck bunched and pulled, like he'd hurt it tackling that guy. He fixed his eyes on the campus, preoccupied, remembering. Now *that* was a fluky, fucked up case, the disaster at City College in 1991.

Himself and Hurley had been out doing something else when they got a call on the radio that *all* MNHS personnel were to report *forthwith* to the gym at CCNY. The radio call didn't say why.

They had looked at one another in confusion. Alex had never heard a thing like it in the four years he'd worked there. He radioed Central, asking for confirmation, and Central confirmed.

Then they had jetted to CCNY, listening to their radio. Cops were reporting rumors of shots fired at a rap concert on campus and multiple deaths, multiple injuries. That worst case scenario you train for but hope never happens.

By the time they'd arrived, they couldn't get their car near the gym, as so many emergency vehicles had already piled in. They parked a couple blocks away. As they sprinted across the campus, Alex felt terror like a cold bite and his heart raced – he could be rushing headlong into anything, and for all he knew, active shooters were still out there.

It turned out they weren't. It wasn't a shooting at all. Eventually, they ran into Bill Ryan, Marty Vasquez, and Matt Cohen, MNHS colleagues, who explained that there had been a basketball game in the gym, sponsored by a couple rap artists, and a large number of people had been killed or injured, crushed in a stampede in the stairwell outside the gym.

"It was a what?" Alex asked, baffled. Cohen, a twenty-year veteran, hadn't understood it, either. But he told Alex and James that MNHS' needed to identify the dead, notify next of kin, and interview witnesses in order to figure out what had happened and determine if a criminal offense had been committed.

Cohen, Vasquez, and Ryan warned them that the gym was bad, one of the worst things they had ever seen. And when an experienced homicide detective warns you something is bad, it's going to be horrific. They saw bodies strewn across the gym floor, dead and dying or severely injured. Blood smeared across the floors and walls. Young people clustered into groups, holding one another, crying. Dozens of EMS personnel running around triaging people: who could be saved and who couldn't. Bodies being laid out alongside the bleachers (it would be nine dead and twenty-nine injured, but no one knew that until much later).

"You ever *seen* anything like this, Lex?" James had asked him, looking wobbly. James, who after his years in Street Crime, had been hard to shock. Shocked himself, Alex shook his head. They swallowed their feelings of horror and revulsion and started interviewing witnesses.

Amidst the mayhem, Lieutenant Corcoran arrived and got into an argument with a captain over how best to deploy his detectives, the chain-of-command losing some of its resonance. Corcoran sent Alex and James to Columbia Pres, where they could interview people who had been injured in the thick of things. Those witnesses had explained that the concert had been sold out, thousands of tickets, more than the gym's capacity, but people had kept coming anyway. The campus security tried to keep order but couldn't. A heaving mass of people who hadn't got tickets rushed the door, busting the glass panels, surging into the narrow stairwell, the sole passage into the gym. And there was only one open door between the gym and the stairwell. People were trapped, crushed in the swelling crowd, suffocating.

A hospitalized witness described a man next to him collapsing, knocking him down as he fell, the frenzied crowd trampling both of them. The witness miraculously escaped with a broken leg, but the other guy died. Alex flinched, his stomach in a backflip. He came across some pretty grisly ways to die in this job, but that sounded like one of the worst.

No criminal charges were ever filed, but the college and Sean "Puffy" Combs paid out after a lawsuit in 1998.

Thirteen years later, the college seemed peaceful, only a memorial plaque to the victims serving as a reminder of the tragedy. And the images of bloodied young people writhing in agony on a gym floor that had never left Alex's head. He worked his forefinger into the corner of one eye. Revisiting that case hadn't done his sinking spirits any good.

"You're quiet," observed Ray.

"I'm just tired and sore."

The campus dwindled from view in the rearview mirrors, and Alex breathed deeply, feeling the air moving his chest, and with the hand not on the wheel, he wiggled his memo book out of his pocket and threw it onto Ray's lap. "I took notes after I talked to Fred," he said. "Have a look."

Ray looked and said, "This lead's a weak sister."

"It's the best we got at this second."

Chapter Twelve

November 10th

The detectives parked on 178th and approached the intersection with Wadsworth. The George Washington Bridge conquered the skyline to the west, and the elevated highway soared above Washington Heights, casting the six and seven story walk-ups and a cluster of three red-brick tower blocks under its shadow. The roar of traffic on the interstate sounded like a hurricane, and vehicle fumes stuck to the lungs.

The drug crew who did their business on this corner made them for cops. Two men in suits – who the hell else would they be? Two teens sitting on a news rack muttered something. One kid sprang into a run, disappearing around a corner, while his pal glued himself to the newspaper box, giving the detectives a haughty eyefuck. Lookouts. The market had shrunk from its dazzling heights in the '90s but addicts still needed a fix. Even in the apocalypse, someone would always be keeping the slingers in business.

Surveying the corner, Alex made rough guesses – who was slinging, who wasn't, who was running and buying, and who was living here, working here, or commuting through here. He could read Heights drug corners like a book. Then he shoved his hands into his coat pockets, straightened his shoulders, striding in a blasé, swinging gait towards the teenager slouching on the *Metro* box.

The kid leapt off the box, but Alex broke into a run and caught him by the arm.

"Hey, I got *rights*," the kid protested.

"You acting suspiciously, I got the right to frisk you," said Alex. "I do that, what am I gonna find?" He hauled the kid to the nearest building and shoved him face-first against the wall, keeping his other eye on the street. Ray watched his back, his hand near his firearm.

Two guys on a nearby stoop glowered at them, one a heavyset black guy, his arms covered in a ladder of track marks, and his companion, thin and reedy, with a dreadlocked Afro. Alex held those guys with a glare. *Don't fucking move.*

Out of the corner of his eye, Alex watched track mark's swollen hand drift to the small of his back. Alex's heart bunny-hopped. Ray tensed and moved towards him. But the hand stayed still. Dope fiends, working for the slingers, paying off their debts. The rest of the crew had by now cleared off, the corner quiet but for people who had nothing to do with the narcotics trade walking briskly past.

"What you want?" whined the kid.

"What's your name?" said Alex.

"Blue Dog."

"Blue Dog? That's what your mother calls you? What've you got?"

"I ain't got nothin'."

Alex started patting him down. The kid protested, "Hey, hey, you ain't a narco. What you after?"

Alex paused his frisk. "We're looking for a couple guys who hang around this corner." He motioned to Ray to bring the mugshots of Kitchener and Bailey, which he did, one eye still fixed on the street. "You know these guys?"

"No, ain't never seen 'em," said Blue Dog.

The Washington Heights hymn. Alex didn't believe him, but he fixed a menacing eye on the junkies occupying the stoop. "What about you? You know these guys?"

"What'd they do?" said track marks.

"You know them?"

"Maybe. What you want with my cousin?"

"Your cousin?"

"Yeah, that boy's my cousin."

"Huh," Alex breathed. The teenager had slumped like a rag-doll in his grip.

"These guys, they committed two homicides," snapped Ray, standing rigidly, flaunting his contempt for the drug corners and for the people who frequented them. He had no sympathy for junkies and crackheads. "People make the *choice* to smoke crack," he had once moralized.

But Alex had seen the corners eating people alive on Rivington and Eldridge, the Lower East Side neighborhood where he grew up; he'd seen crack ravage Washington Heights like a wildfire, the 'war on drugs' a terrible public health crisis that no one treated like one; and he himself had barely crawled out of the bottle alive. He'd thought about rejoining with, "You think I made the *choice* to fall out with my kids and fuck up my body," but making it personal seemed like a bad idea. It wasn't a moral choice, he wanted to cry. Whether it was booze or crack or heroin, it was an unfurling shadow, and it might suffocate you. However, he had grunted, "Hmmm," and let it go.

Anyway, track marks had also been thinking about Ray's question. "Who they kill?"

"A cop and a delivery driver," spat Ray. "You read? You read the fucking news? Innocent people, getting killed in armed robberies."

"Look, we're Homicide, so we don't give a shit about slinging," Alex explained, sounding reasonable. "And word on the street is you don't give a shit about these guys. I hear they'll steal a stash, stick guns in people's faces, cause everyone a lot of trouble. But whatever, you don't play ball here, I'm gonna call the Three-Four precinct, and they'll put a couple sector cars here and fuck up business for the rest of the day."

The fiends sized him up. You fill a corner with cops, the dealers and their crews move operations elsewhere, but people would rather the cops left them alone. Still, silence, except for the roaring stream of engines and wheels against asphalt. Alex patted down Blue Dog, and the kid's face blanched when Alex probed the pockets of his saggy jeans and fished out a baggie of weed. Hardly the crime of the century, but it would do. Wordlessly, he raised one eyebrow at the witness and reached around for his cuffs, hooked to his belt near his right hip.

"Ray, put in a call to the precinct." Throwing a glare to the two fiends on the stoop, he said, "See? Don't fuck with us, we don't fuck with you. You seen these two stick-up artists?"

One last chance, or he would collar the kid for possession, drag his ass into the precinct, and send a Narcotics team to this corner. When he glanced at the stoop, he saw that the look on track mark's face had changed. Alex jerked his head at Ray, indicating that Ray should hold off on his phone call. For the moment.

Ray took over pinning the teenager against the wall and cuffed him, while Alex approached the stoop, resting his left foot on the step, his weight hanging on the railing. "Who are these guys?"

Suddenly skittish, the fiends reared back, track marks shaking his thumb towards the door behind him. "Not outside," he growled. Then he got to his feet and labored up the stairs. His ankles were swollen, ballooning grotesquely over his trainers, a condition Alex had seen before in long-term heroin addicts. Both detectives followed, but he pointed a thick finger at Alex. "Just you."

A spike of adrenaline kicked straight down his spine. Moving distrustfully, he climbed the stoop, several steps, and then faltered at the door, afraid. Luring a cop into his apartment, the cop's partner on the street, and then shooting him. The guy would be insane if he did that, another David LaValle, and psychopaths like David LaValle, even amongst the population of murderers that Alex dealt with every day, were uncommon.

In any case, this junkie looked like he would drop dead of a heart attack before he laid a hand on Alex. Ray was outside, and backup a phone or radio call away. This morning, he'd taken a hell of a risk to his life and pulled it off like a damn action hero. He was on a roll. *Trust your gut.*

He caught Ray's eye and nodded. Ray bit down on his lower lip fretfully, but he wouldn't argue in front of the fiends. "All right," Alex said, his stomach light and uneasy, and track marks opened the door, and then Alex shadowed him into the dank entryway of the building.

His pupils dilated. It stank of piss, shit, and sweat. He made out a stained mattress propped upright against the wall, discarded bottle caps, a lighter, a broken syringe under his heel. His skin prickled, beads of sweat rolling down his chest and ribs, and he strained his ears and eyes against the velvety murk. He took shallow, hissing breaths through his teeth, and the stench soured his stomach.

"What's your name?" he asked the witness.

"Mal." The witness gasped in wheezy breaths, as if every organ in his body had suffered the abuse of too much heroin for too long and struggled to sustain basic functions. "Your partner Puerto Rican?"

"Huh-uh," Alex grunted. "Why did you drag me into this shithole?"

"I don't like Ricans. Fucking spics."

Alex released a strident exhalation through his nostrils but let the racism wash over him. If the guy had said something anti-Semitic, he wouldn't react to that, either. You can't. "These white guys, they come to this corner."

"Yeah, Crazy Eight. He call himself that, like he's a real gangster, but his name's Bailey." Mal rocked his bulbous weight from foot to foot.

"And the other one?"

"I seen him with Bailey a couple times. Don't know his name. Anyway, Bailey, he was doin' some work for the crew, you know. 'Till he started keepin' more'n he was sellin', know what I'm sayin'."

Alex scratched the side of his nose. "Yeah."

"So that was it for *that*. Then, him and his pal, the guy in the other picture you showed me, they come here like last month, I dunno, they have a gun, they try to hold up a couple runners on Rocko's crew. Rocko don't take that shit. Roughs 'em up a bit, you know, says they try it again, they dead men..." He trailed off. In an upstairs apartment, something clomped across the floor. Both Alex and Mal listened intently, Alex touching the Glock at his hip.

"So?" Alex prompted.

"Crazy Eight's *always* chasin' more dope. He gotta get money some other way, don't he? Scrap prices fuckin' shit right now. He comes back..."

"With his friend?" Alex flexed the right arm, straightening the elbow out, then curling it up, feeling the pain knotting in the joint. It had stiffened badly.

"Nah, alone. He comes back, I guess like a week before this stick-up job in that bodega on 123rd hit the papers. He was in here, all excited, sayin' he was gonna come into some big money. You sure you ain't sending Narcs here?"

"Not if you tell me the truth. You might have to testify."

"As a CI?" Mal knew the system.

"Yeah."

"If I testify in court, nobody from here better know it was me who snitched."

"We'll protect you if it goes to court."

"Yeah, okay, so he was sayin', when he comes into this cash, he wants me to hook him up with some real good dope. Not this street shit that's been cut to fuck with baking powder or fuck knows. But you know, the good shit."

"Did he say how he was gonna get the money?" Dust and mold clouded inside his lungs. His breathing was getting wheezy.

"No, but I guessed it wasn't gonna be *legal*, if you know what I mean." Mal laughed. "It wasn't like Crazy Eight was gonna get a *job* or nothin'. But he wasn't gonna hold up another dope crew. He don't wanna end up in the river, and he keep fucking with the local crews, well, that's how that shit plays, huh. But he didn't say nothin' else. He's a stupid motherfucker, but he ain't stupid enough to announce to the world that he's gonna hold up a damned store."

"That's it?"

"Yeah, that's it."

"You hook him up with the dope?" Alex squinted, trying to read the witness' face, but his expression was indistinct in the sunless entryway. He visualized an anxious Ray bouncing on his toes, fiddling with his cell phone and the bag of weed.

Mal laughed again, scornfully shaking his head. "I ain't *seen* him since."

"Where would he go?" His head and stomach threatened revolt. But he saw evidence, a lead, so tantalizingly close, yet just beyond his reach. Hearsay from one dope fiend to another about some amorphous hustle to pay for more heroin was worth precisely nothing in court. *Please give me something else, something tangible,* he willed Mal, his brown eyes searching.

"Fuck knows." Mal slouched against the wall, as if the effort of standing on his own two feet rivalled Alex sprinting flat-out for ten blocks.

Alex gulped down a lump of disappointment lodging in his windpipe. He walked on a wire, pressuring a witness to tell him the truth but not pressuring him so much that he started making up crimes or hearsay, just to appease him. Prevaricating witnesses or informants inventing felonies had landed cops in all manner of shit, from the comical to the outright career-ruining. Thinking carefully, he decided on caution and tact over coercion, and he handed Mal his card with his name, email, and office phone.

"Alright, Mal. But if you remember anything else or if Bailey appears or you hear word of him, you get a hold of me. Got it?" Then he backed out the door before he felt any sicker. Out on the street, the turbid city air and the exhaust streaming over I-95 felt comparatively refreshing and cleansing.

They let the teenager go but confiscated his ounce of weed. Alex would have given it back and forgot he ever found it, as he cared more about not doing the paperwork associated with entering an ounce of pot into an evidence room, but Ray found it morally repugnant to let the kid keep it and agreed to do the paperwork.

"What the fuck was that, Lex?" Ray asked once they'd abandoned the corner, their retreat flipping a switch, and Alex sensed the drug crew returning to their posts.

"What the fuck was what?"

"You going into that building. Anything could have happened."

Alex coughed out fumes and debris intermingling in his lungs. "That guy wasn't gonna do shit to me," he said vehemently, because he suspected he was wrong.

"Someone in there coulda had a thing against cops."

"There was no one there," Alex grunted, sucking in a deep breath, forcing more gunk out of his chest. He almost collided with an abandoned fridge and mattress blocking half the sidewalk and had to swing hastily to the side.

Catching his arm, Ray said truculently, "You didn't *know* that. You should have at least waited for backup. We could have called in an RMP."

"And by then, the witness probably woulda changed his mind. It was fine. I know what I'm doing."

"Yeah, I know you do. But Jesus, Alex, one bad call, you could be in a shitload of trouble."

"I wasn't. I made the right call." Alex freed his arm from his partner's grip, rearranging the scarf around his neck, shooting Ray a hard look. They might have the odd 'lover's tiff,' as police partners and married couples do, but behind his brown eyes, the questioned glimmered, *You trust me? You trust my judgment?*

"He say anything useful?" Ray softened his voice.

"Yeah, he told me about all the jaywalking and parking in handicapped spaces that goes on here," Alex cracked, breaking up the tension.

"Alex..."

"He confirmed that Bailey calls himself Crazy Eight and said Bailey and Kitchener tried to hold up a runner for one of the local crews last month. It didn't go so good, and they got their asses kicked by some dealer named Rocko. And then he said that Bailey reappeared a week before the robbery, saying he was gonna come up with cash for heroin, evidently good heroin, that wasn't cut with whatever weird shit they're cutting it with this week."

"Huh," grunted Ray with an optimistic smile. "Your One-Oh-Three friend wasn't useless then."

"Not useless but could be better."

"We know more about these shitbags than we did an hour ago. It's a start."

They were standing in front of their car, parked on 178th, the icy wind blowing, Ray unlocking the car, and Alex's cell phone trilled.

Becky's name lit up the screen.

He stared at it, his hand trembling. Someone kicked him in the ribs. No word from her since the day he had rushed out of her apartment on the call to PO Irvine's murder, and now she was ringing his cell. He had phoned her the following weekend, when she said she would return from her parents', but he had only spoken to her voicemail. When she did not return the call, he disregarded his raw nerves, and with three open cases, he had so much work on anyway that he did not have the time nor the space in his head to worry about it, barring those sudden, dark moments alone in his apartment.

Anxiety rushed at him in a sickening wave. He should not answer personal calls while on the job. But he waved at Ray to wait and pressed the send button.

"Hello?" The word scraped out his throat.

"Hi, Alex," she said.

"What's up?" That sounded appallingly nonchalant.

"I'm sorry, I should have gotten in touch sooner... It's just—"

"I can't really talk," he admitted. "I'm working."

"Are you outside?" she asked.

He supposed she could hear the street noises, traffic and people. "Yes."

"We should talk later then," she said haltingly.

"Yeah," he agreed.

The phone beeped, and he heard nothing. "Becky?" he said, but she had hung up. Baffled, he stared at his phone, vibrating like a live sparrow in his hand. He didn't understand why Becky had called him, or why she didn't call him a week ago, or her abrupt manner on the phone, or indeed, the behavior of women in general. This was why, after the *NYT* reporter, he had stayed the hell away from relationships.

Ray said gently, "Lex, c'mon. We need to head to that meeting with McNally. At least we got something we can tell him."

They climbed into the car, Alex driving, and he wheeled onto Broadway. For about a dozen blocks, they drove in silence. Alex pieced his shattered thoughts back together – relocating his mind to his cases and then to this meeting with McNally, who wanted an update on the Kitchener case and something else, but he hadn't specified what. The prosecutor had kvetched that his boss was jumpy, and he abided by the institutional law of shit rolling downhill; the DA kicked Simon, who in turn kicked the detectives. An armed robbery in broad daylight that led to the deaths of two people, a cop and an innocent civilian, should not happen in Eisenmann and Bloomberg's New York. It wasn't the '90s anymore.

Hesitantly, Ray said, "Look, this is hard to say, but I don't think she's very good for you, or to you."

He didn't answer. Because he knew his partner was damned right.

"You know she and I have mutual friends. I mean, *they* wouldn't date her."

Defensive, he snapped, "I thought you disapproved because you didn't like the fact that she was not quite divorced."

"Well, there is that. But honestly, Alex, and I told you this too… My friends say she's unstable as fuck when it comes to relationships. She's hurt just about everyone she's ever been with. She's nuts. You know, you can't change people. I know you know that."

Alex stretched his arms against the steering wheel, the left elbow smarting, and he waited for the traffic light at 125th. Of course, Ray had warned him but he'd foolishly hoped that this time, Becky's pattern of dysfunction, and his own, could finally be broken, something new, bright, and fresh emerging from the ashes of his long history of catastrophe, but he could see now that Ray had been right from the starting gate. He was who he was, and her too. Feeling his mouth drying out, he squeezed out saliva and swallowed it, but bitter, resigned hopelessness slithered up his throat. He couldn't make relationships work with women who were saner than himself, nor could he make them work with ones who were crazier. A perfect, discouraging catch-22. Anyone who wanted to sleep with him and concomitantly deal with his shit must be crazy, and if they were crazy, they inevitably panicked and ran away.

At 110th, he turned east, passing beneath the lopsided towers of St. John the Divine reaching longingly for the sky, the highest structure in this neighborhood, the Euro-gothic Cathedral built at the end of the nineteenth century by Anglican bishops who thought New York needed a Euro-gothic cathedral and never got around to finishing it, and then whoever eventually completed the second tower had not bothered making it identical to the first. 110th hugged the edge of Central Park, the grey and red brick buildings of Harlem on the left, the park on the right, with its spindly, leafless trees swaying in the breeze, revealing green and brown open grass and slivers of silver lakes.

They turned onto Park Avenue, and traffic thickened as they progressed downtown. Horns and sirens and engines roared outside the car, and Alex gripped the steering wheel tightly, like the Crown Vic might take off on its own if he relaxed his hands.

Breaching their obdurate silence, Ray said, "I'm guessing that witness didn't tell you *what* kind of hustle Bailey was planning."

Cop-talk-as-usual. He could handle that. "No, just that he wasn't gonna hold up any more dope crews."

"Oh, well, that's smart." Ray pulled back his lips in a bemused smile. "Does the witness know where he is?"

"Nope. Said he hasn't seen him since."

Battling stalled lines of cars, drivers cutting across lanes, and suicidal pedestrians, they wove in and out of downtown jams, Alex pounding the horn at anyone moving slower than he wanted, a New York tradition as venerable as bagels and lox. He darted off Fourth onto Houston Street. Then he ran into another jam on Lafayette Street. A cyclist came within a breath of clipping the rearview mirror on Ray's side.

"Fucking lunatic," Ray exclaimed. "Anyway, so if that bum's telling you the truth, Bailey's not been back to buy drugs there."

"I don't think he's buying drugs anywhere. He thought he was gonna get a wad of cash from the store, but he disappears, and Kitchener ends up with all the cash from the robbery. The books from the store said there was only like a grand in the safe, and we found around nine hundred on Kitchener. Bailey, he's a fucking hardcore junkie. That's what Fred told me, and so did the wit on 178th. He's not gonna give up a fucking penny, and he's apparently in debt to a dealer. I don't see him charitably giving Kitchener all the money, then skipping town."

"You think Kitchener's killed him."

Alex bobbed his head as he swung around a corner into the underground garage beneath 100 Centre Street, and then he threw the car sharply into reverse and backed into a space.

Ray played devil's advocate. "Or someone else has. Or Kitchener's beat him up, scared him, taken the money. And Bailey's done one too many stick-ups, screwed one too many dealers in New York, so people know his face. He's got to get the fuck outta dodge, so he goes to Baltimore, DC, wherever. A new start."

"God only knows." He yielded a sigh, air hissing through his lips, and he massaged his aching elbow.

Yes, Bailey could be dead or trying his schtick in Baltimore. Kitchener could have killed him, or someone else did. The pain that had lashed him after Becky's phone call dissolved into a stultifying melancholy, and he eyeballed the downtrodden crowds in Foley Square, this ring of courthouses where criminal and civil tragedy played out. Virtually no one goes into a courthouse – unless they work there – because their lives are going perfectly well. There was so much misery the world, and nothing he could do about anybody's, least of all his own.

Simon had said he would meet them in the square, a smoke-break McNally meeting. As they walked beneath the phallic statue, Alex began talking about putting a tail on Analisa, but his words were lost in the noise of a brass band blaring out a wailing and gratingly cheery tune that would better fit a high school football field. It sent his attention reeling. What the hell? The City Council attempting to give the DA's office and courthouses a festive atmosphere.

Another sound thundered in his ears. His own heartbeat. Spotty white lights spiraled in front of his eyes, obliterating his sight. Rain and blood ran together on a dark street. Panic swept through him like a great wing, and he was gasping for air.

"Alex! Ray! Here!" Simon called out. He had ensconced himself on a bench near the statue.

Spinning around, Alex jumped as if he'd been attacked by a perp. He rolled his eyes wildly at the courthouses and government buildings, momentarily confused until he regained his bearings.

Simon was holding a cigarette between his fingers, and he had a deli sandwich resting on his thigh. "Alex," he repeated.

Alex wanted to get away from the square, from the noise, but he didn't feel like explaining why he didn't want to be here; he didn't know how to explain why he didn't want to be here, or why he was sweating and clammy in spite of the cold, his eyes unfocused, his heart racing.

"Alex, you all right? What's wrong?" Simon cocked his head, cigarette in his mouth.

"Yeah, it's okay, I just need to sit down," Alex distantly heard himself say, and he sank onto the metal bench beside the lawyer. His chest was heaving. The spicy odor of tobacco tickled his nostrils. Simon and Ray were frowning at him with weighted concern, and he floundered for a reason, but his lips and tongue had withered like the city pavement on a scorching summer day.

"Feeling all right?" Simon asked again.

"My arm hurts, and I threw my back out again," Alex responded in a croaky voice, the half-truth suddenly coming to him with ease, inspired. His colleagues were accustomed to him complaining about his back, a chronic ailment for the last two years that at its worst, had him pale, breathless, incapable of staying on his feet. Simon and Ray would buy it.

Simon, reassured in his way, started salivating about the Kitchener case, and Alex woozily lowered his eyelids, not listening. Ray related Mal's inadmissible hearsay that put Bailey and Kitchener together, which wasn't nothing, and he reiterated yesterday's lab results and ATF trace, which weren't helpful.

As Simon ranted, Ray lightly touched Alex's shoulder with reassurance and empathy, hopefully assuming that Alex was upset over

Becky, or injured from the early-morning altercation in his apartment. Those stories were valid, rational. The thing that had overtaken his mind wasn't.

"The other thing I wanted to tell you was that the Court of Appeals reversed the sentence on *People v. David LaValle.*"

That got Alex's attention, as if Simon had fired a pistol in his ear.

"What?" he said.

"Bastards!" Ray exclaimed.

"They reversed the death sentence," Simon repeated. "And declared the statute unconstitutional. If New York is to use capital punishment in any more cases, the legislature will have to enact a new statute. Given that we now have a Democratic legislature and the governor is now a Democrat, I don't see that happening."

"What was the fucking point then," Alex said hoarsely.

"The justices said that the statute's deadlock instructions had a coercive effect on jurors."

That was not what Alex had meant. He didn't give a shit why the Court of Appeals reversed the sentence. If anything, he should be pleased; at least relieved. The Court of Appeals had kindly taken the burden of capital cases off his shoulders. But it upset him. In his feverish brain, the ball set in motion that day by the jury sentencing LaValle to lethal injection rolled into him fighting with Sarah and then ultimately into Zoë dying in the car wreck. Now the Court of Appeals' decision meant there was a nihilistic pointlessness to everything. And that seemed as irrational as panicking in Foley Square.

Simon hit his stride. "Basically, the law said that the decision for a death sentence *or* for life in prison had to be unanimous, and if the jury deadlocked, the sentencing would then fall to the trial court judge. They could sentence the defendant to life, but conceivably with parole eligibility in twenty years. The Court has written that jurors who did not favor the death penalty might ultimately vote for it anyway, out of fear that a dangerous defendant might be let out of prison in twenty years. They deemed that to be an 'unconstitutional risk—' Alex, are you *sure* you're all right?"

Ray was grumbling under his breath about "fucking lawyer's nonsense games."

"Yes," Alex said firmly.

"You look like hell."

"Don't I always?" Alex countered, shielding underneath the wiseass.

"How did you hurt your back again? I thought that was a lot better."

"Well, you should fucking hear what went down in my apartment at about seven am this morning." When they used that voice of concern with you, your own voice had to be especially nonchalant and calm.

"What happened?" asked Simon, his grey eyes like spears.

Alex told the story, something he could elucidate and grasp himself. Otherwise, he had no idea how to explain the strangling white noise and panic, or the shock pulsating through his body when Simon had announced the reversal of the death sentence. Oh, if only he believed the words coming out of his mouth attributing it to Becky or to his neighbor's shitbird boyfriend. That would be simple, but he knew it was bigger than that. It had little to do with either one. He'd seen this shadow before – it dogged him in his first years in rehab, and it infiltrated his mind and body like a virus following his shooting. But he'd never spoken of it, nor did he understand it. It was winging towards him, and he was terrified.

Chapter Thirteen

December 23rd

"Is that when you started feeling more depressed?" asked Gillard.

"What do you mean?" Alex played at a strand of the ace bandage that had unraveled from the back of his hand.

"You think you started to have a tougher time dealing with things around then?"

"I guess so." Grating his back teeth against one another, he dug his fingers into his temples, and he felt his pulse. Her questions were relentless, driving him further and further into places he feared going. Straight after the '87 shooting, a police psychologist had interviewed him, asking how he felt, and he'd assured the psychologist he was good, he was sturdily weathering it, and the psychologist believed him. The department sent the psychologist because they needed to act like they cared about his mental health, and he needed to dishonestly answer the questions, so they would let him back on the streets once his wounds healed. His actual emotions had belied words, but the job demanded that he tough it out.

"You guess so?"

"I think I was – and am – just stressed." He allowed himself a wry smile. "Maybe I have SAD. Is that what they call it? Where you get depressed by bad weather? And I had this relationship end."

"That upset you?"

"It was on the edge of ending for a while." *Since it started,* he thought grimly. "And I'm used to that by now. That's like every relationship I've ever had."

He wrinkled his forehead, annoyed that he had mentioned Becky. The psychiatrist was better than most cops at interrogation, eliciting personal details he had never intended on telling her.

"Do you think it was another thing getting you down and making you feel stressed?"

"Yeah." It hadn't turned him into this strung-out emotional garbage fire, because break-ups never had before, but how could he articulate that without sounding hopelessly defensive or opening his flank to more probing questions? He'd convinced the department psychologist in 1987 that he could withstand trauma and his mental health was rock-solid. He could convince Gillard.

"The LaValle case was one you investigated," said Gillard, more of a statement than a question. "Did you find it difficult, to hear that the sentence was reversed?"

A 1 train rattled along the elevated track, the wheels thrumming against the metal rails, the noise dwindling as the train disappeared downtown. When the subway had gone, he said in a quiet voice, "I don't know. I never got how I felt about the death penalty straight in my head anyway."

His mouth tasted caustic, bitter. Yes, it had been difficult. But not because he was disappointed that LaValle (or anyone else) wouldn't be getting the needle. He nipped at his thumbnail and then noticed Gillard watching, scientifically cataloguing his nervous bad habit.

"You testified at the sentencing hearing," she said.

"So? I was subpoenaed." He dropped his hand to his knee. "You know how it works. I say what the DA tells me to say. That's my job. Doesn't really matter how I feel about it."

"You didn't feel good about it."

"Well, no, I guess I didn't," he admitted.

"But you were upset when McNally mentioned that case on November 10th. The day the Court of Appeals handed down its decision."

"I don't know. It was nothing. I was just stressed. The thing with Becky, that was obviously over. We had three open murder cases that were all driving us nuts 'cause we weren't getting any breaks—"

"Ray said you were upset. He would know. You've worked with him for how long?"

He ran his right hand through his thick, greying hair. "Three years."

"He'll know you well, after three years."

"Sometimes, I don't think I know *him* well," Alex countered.

She wasn't deflected by his wiseass parries. "Did you talk to anyone about it?"

"About what?"

"The reversal of the death sentence, for a start. Why you were feeling so emotional about it."

"Not... no."

"You sure? You didn't have a conversation with Detective Hurley several days after that?"

"Jesus, what are you, Doc? A fucking lawyer? This is like a cross-examination."

Like a good police interrogator or trial lawyer, she knew the answers before she asked the questions. He wondered how on earth she could have known he went to Staten Island. He'd signed out a car with a short note about convening with a precinct detective about a case, which was mostly a lie.

He had indeed been meeting with a precinct detective, but not about a case. The department was half-assedly cracking down on cops using police cars for personal business – something you could flagrantly get away with a few years ago – but people still did. You had to be a bit more underhanded about it. Unless you'd really pissed off your colleagues or your boss, most cops were inclined to look the other way.

"What did you talk to Hurley about?" She remained implacable, brushing aside his querulous reaction.

"Have *you* had a chat with Hurley as well?" Talking about it, to Gillard, to James, to anyone, gave it life and power.

"No, I haven't talked to Detective Hurley," said Gillard. "You worked on your other day off that week. Any particular reason?"

"I needed the overtime hours," he said, which was a lie. "And someone had to do that tail. I got the authorization to do it, I'm the primary, so I figured I'd do it. Had nothing better to do on that RDO." That was completely true.

He caught himself gnawing at his nails again. Why did it matter if he'd worked some overtime hours on an RDO? Every good detective did it when vagaries of an investigation required it. And Alex did it a lot because Ray and Marcus had an aversion to overtime.

Gillard's eyes fell to the file in front of her. He was unnerved, like a suspect in an interrogation who starts thinking you must be psychic. How much did she know? What did that file say? Or more worryingly, what had Ray and Gibson said to her? One or both of them must have uncovered the details of his trip to Staten Island. James had a big mouth.

Chapter Fourteen

November 13th

As soon as the interminable I-278 traffic cleared on the edge of Brooklyn, Alex, driving an unmarked blue Crown Vic, crossed the Verrazano-Narrows Bridge that took him over the channel between Brooklyn and Staten Island. The highway arched across the expanse of flat, grey water, suspended under the great towers by shimmering, delicate cables. Here was the last narrow point, and then the East and Hudson Rivers spilled out into the Atlantic. To his left, he saw the New Jersey coast huddled on the horizon, low flatlands on the edge of the ocean, and to the southeast, a glimpse of the parks, boardwalks, the narrow blocky buildings of Gravesend and Coney Island. To his right, he saw the silvery towers of the Financial District and the Empire State Building's distinctive spire peering out beyond their glistening rooftops, and further along, he glimpsed the smoky factories, warehouses, and marshy docklands of Bayonne.

A huge container ship chugged laboriously towards the city, at the end of its long journey from somewhere on the other side of the Atlantic. You discovered a surprising view of the geography as you drove over the Verrazano-Narrows Bridge. You found that you were indeed very small and insignificant, and New York City very big. You discovered an overpowering feeling of space. You never noticed that when you lived and worked in the myopic canyons of Manhattan. And you witnessed how the urban metropolis of New York City had utterly consumed the landscape, and you knew it had been here long before you were here, and it would be here long after you, and the eight million other people living in the city at this very moment, were gone.

That feeling of vastness and space and existential insignificance vanished as soon as he drove off the bridge onto Staten Island. The landscape changed from the urban maze of skyscrapers and canyons of tenements and townhouses to suburbia: strip malls, condos, detached houses, and green lawns. Many of the houses had been built fast and cheap, rows of soulless, identical cinderblock and plaster structures, but they had lawns and driveways and sheds. Some people liked lawns and space. One could argue that Manhattan's urban canyons were soulless, although Alex wouldn't agree, and he disliked the ticky-tacky houses.

Moreover, you had to pay a toll to get out of Staten Island, not in. But James Hurley, transferred here three – nearly four – years ago under ignominious circumstances, hadn't left. Alex's failure to remember which highway exit he needed in order to get to James' precinct was a reflection of how infrequently he visited. Dammit, how had three years snuck away from him? He kept thinking that by now, the NYPD would have forgotten or stopped caring about the reasons James was launched here in the first place and, if James wanted a transfer back to Manhattan, or the Bronx, or Brooklyn or Queens, or anywhere that wasn't the ass-end of nowhere, he could get it.

He missed the exit, and he wheeled off the highway at the next one. Through a couple traffic lights, and then back on the highway going north, only to discover the exit he wanted was solely southbound, not northbound. "Fuck this place," he said aloud. While he cruised along another five miles of extra highway to the next exit, and then circled over the I-278 on a small overpass and veered around to the southbound side, he couldn't prevent his mind from wandering to the clusterfuck that ended with James stuck here.

It started out as the sort of murder case that didn't interest anyone: one Washington Heights crack dealer shooting another. The case had been a grounder, and without fanfare or trouble, they processed an arrest warrant for a Dominican dealer named Rodrigo Díaz. Díaz had a couple priors for possession and distribution, but no violent felonies (until now), so Alex and James had gone to pick him up with only a handful of uniforms from the Three-Four Precinct for backup. They found the perp loitering in front of a pizza joint near his apartment on Dyckman Street.

He had looked resigned and placid enough as they approached, although he was a big guy, probably 6'4 and surpassing 300lbs. Alex had been saying, "You're under arrest for the murder of Manuel Escobedo," the usual things you say, and had started with *Miranda* as he held out the handcuffs, reaching for him. Díaz didn't say a word. He didn't even look at Alex but remained slouching indolently against the side of the building.

Suddenly, with a single, effortless movement, he punched Alex right below his ribs, dropping him to the ground. Winded, Alex doubled up into a fetal position, groaning, clutching his stomach, in spacey shock at the emptiness in his lungs. His face felt wet. He looked at his hand. It was painted in blood. Then he got scared. He couldn't breathe, and he was bleeding profusely.

One of the Three-Four officers, Sergeant Evelyn Smyth, crouched down beside him. Supporting his back, she helped him sit up. All he heard was her languid Harlem accent, telling him to calm down, to breathe slowly; he had the breath knocked out of him, and he'd smashed his forehead when he fell. "Y'alright. Breath. Y'alright." She kept saying that. He didn't see James or anyone else. Blood streamed out of his head wound like a red waterfall in his eyes. His lungs had collapsed. He held his chest and stomach, convinced he was dying in spite of Smyth's assurances that he wasn't. She was holding him upright. Then his lungs re-inflated, and he got his breath back in time to see Smyth's partner and two other cops hauling James off Díaz, who was also lying on the sidewalk, bleeding and moaning.

James fought against their restraint, snarling and spitting out a stream of invective, somewhere between a trapped raccoon and a Quentin Tarantino movie. "I'll get you, you motherfucking son of a bitch! I'll ram my foot so far it so far up your fucking asshole, like a rat running down a fucking sewer. And then I'll perform a fucking living autopsy on you with that Goddamned baton, and I'll be hanging your nuts on my motherfucking Christmas tree!" The three cops held onto him with grim fortitude until he stopped struggling.

James' pale Irish skin had flushed cherry red, and his blue eyes were crazed and bloodshot. He broke free from his captors and rushed over to Alex. "Aw, Jesus, man. Are you okay?"

"Dunno," Alex wheezed between pained breaths. The bottom of his ribcage burned. He took off his jacket and held it against his head, staunching the blood. Blood was pooling on the pavement, soaking the front of his shirt and his tie. Head wounds bleed a lot, even minor ones. He dared not stand up yet – he had to sit here and breathe for a while.

Half a dozen radio cars and two ambulances screeched to a halt on Dyckman. Gibson and Marty Vasquez sprang out of an unmarked car. Detectives took statements while EMS hoisted a half-conscious Díaz on a stretcher. The ambulance crew thought Alex would need stitches for the cut on his forehead, and they were concerned about the organs in his upper abdomen, but he declined their offer of a lift to the hospital. James and Marty took him. An ER doc stitched up his head, and they scanned his abdomen. The spleen and everything else looked unhurt, but they advised that if he felt sick or in any way not right, he should get himself back to the ER forthwith.

Everything deteriorated from there. When Díaz recovered enough to be released from the hospital, he hired a lawyer and sued the NYPD in federal court for violating his civil rights, claiming that he'd been beaten senseless, *a la* Rodney King. The NYPD issued charges and specifications against James, looking proactive about cleaning their own house. The DA's office convened a grand jury. Jammed up with multiple investigations, James admitted to Alex and to his Detective Endowment Association rep that after Díaz had assaulted Alex, he had lost his mind and kicked the shit out of the man. Even after he'd taken him down, he had kept pounding on him until those officers dragged him away.

"Oh, James, you'd better get a defense lawyer," Alex had said miserably. The DEA rep had looked like he wanted to have a nervous breakdown. Somehow, all 5'7 of James had taken down the hulking perp, surprising as hell given that Díaz, as it turned out, was into bare knuckle fighting. Out of loyalty and love for his partner, James must have seen red. But responding to the assault and neutralizing the perp would have been one thing. Beating the living crap out of him was another. Still, James would have got away with it had Díaz not filed suit, as neither Alex nor the Three-Four cops would have ever breathed a word.

Díaz, however, alleged that the police had attacked without provocation, the biggest fucking lie going. He took to the media, asserting that James had assaulted him when he had done nothing but demand to know why he was being arrested. *Done nothing other than punch me so hard I thought I had a ruptured spleen*, Alex thought bitterly as they hunkered down against the storm. On the heels of other police brutality cases like Amadou Diallo, this was not looking good.

Then there came the endless rounds of depositions and hearings. Alex lost track of how many times he answered the same question: "Your partner and my client were less than fifteen feet away from you, and you didn't see what happened?"

"Well, no," he always said, "I was lying curled up on the sidewalk. I couldn't breathe, and I had blood gushing outta my head." His own medical reports backed his story. No one could argue with the laceration on his forehead, the reports from EMS, or the severe bruising on his upper abdomen.

Although Alex was quickly cleared of any charges and specs, it was apparent that James, on the other hand, had probably used excessive force, even if most cops on the street thought his response perfectly justified. Sergeant Smyth and her partner admitted under oath that James had gone nuts, thrashing Díaz long after he'd incapacitated him. To this day, Alex could not say what happened – he hadn't seen it.

The upshot was that the department settled with Díaz, but he was still charged with first-degree assault and resisting arrest. He pled out on the original murder charge, twenty years for murder two. IAB launched James out of MNHS, transferring him to the 123rd Precinct detective squad. Buried and punished, but he wasn't on modified assignment, and they let him keep his gold shield, a tacit acknowledgment that he'd only fucked up a little.

Afterwards, Alex had spent months worrying that he'd become lackadaisical, afraid that his demons had finally dulled his street sense. Maybe if he had been more alert when he had approached Díaz, the son of a bitch would not have caught him off guard.

"Who knows," Gibson had said in one of the many conversations he had with her. "But these things happen. I mean, if someone weren't violent, you wouldn't be arresting them at all. How many people can throw a punch like that, at that kind of speed and force with no warning? Could you?"

"Not many," he had to agree. "And no, I couldn't. He didn't even look at me. One minute, I was reading *Miranda,* and he was looking at the ground, the next, I was on the ground wondering what the fuck just happened."

"He was an amateur boxer, wasn't he?"

"Hardly amateur. He was involved in a gambling ring: guys bare knuckle fighting each other and taking bets on it."

"And you're beating yourself up because you couldn't avoid a punch from someone who's making money spending every evening beating the shit out of other guys? He knew exactly where to hit you, to knock the wind out of you and take you out immediately."

"Yeah." He placed his palm over his diaphragm.

"I think he would have taken most of us out if he wanted."

She was probably right, but he resolved to be more alert when approaching suspects. He'd been lucky – his injuries had not been more serious – and James had been unlucky, reacting to seeing his partner hurt the way most cops would have reacted, but getting jammed up for it.

That had been almost four years ago. Why was James still here? He had surely served his time, and he'd been acquitted of all charges and specs. But he had a mouth, and he'd probably shot it off to the wrong person during the investigation.

Alex rolled into the One-Two-Three Precinct's parking lot. The officer on security glanced his shield and raised the barrier. Wearily, he climbed out of the car and leaned into its flank, rubbing his cheek and jaw. For thirteen years, himself and James had been like brothers, but now they only exchanged the odd email, and he never came here. He'd been pissed at himself for letting that perp assault him, pissed at James for losing his shit and then losing their partnership. And he'd never resolved his own anxieties nor debriefed with James. The shitshow of multiple agencies investigating the incident had left the detectives no space to deal with their feelings or work it out in their heads and hearts.

Shortly after the department settled the lawsuit, Alex had walked into the MNHS office to find James' cubicle empty, thirteen years unexpectedly erased. Just a desk with an old IBM, and no sign he had ever been there. A young A team detective, who had joined MNHS the previous month, was working in the neighboring cubicle, finishing CompStat reports from his eight-by-four.

"Where's Hurley?" Alex asked.

"Gone," the detective said.

"Where?" asked Alex, appalled.

The detective shrugged. "The One-Two-Three precinct. He came in an hour ago, cleaned out his desk. Said you should probably give it a day and cool off before you phoned him."

Distraught, Alex phoned his partner. "You didn't tell me you'd been launched. I thought you were acquitted. I thought you'd have a CD in your file or... I dunno. No one told me. But Staten Island? Fucking hell. I walk in, and you're... gone."

His voice shaking, James replied, "I'm sorry, Lex. I didn't know until yesterday. It's politics. It's all fucking politics. They said I gotta start a set at the One-Two-Three *today*, and I had less than twenty-four hours to pack up my whole fucking life. The shit rolled downhill, and I got caught in the shit avalanche, and I didn't even know how to tell you, and I couldn't keep my own damned head straight. But at least I'm not pushing papers in pre-arraignment division. I'm still a detective."

Alex felt like crying, but he was an NYPD detective, and he'd better fucking not. Spikey emotions lanced his throat, his chest, his eyes. But he went on his way with death investigations at MNHS, while James went another way, and the lancing pain ebbed to a dull ache that only troubled him when something sparked a memory.

"Can I help you, sir?" asked an officer, tugging back him into the present. Some precincts you could walk in looking like the Taliban and no one would stop you, while others demanded that visiting officers proffer about six forms of ID.

Sniffing in a harsh breath, he flashed tin. "I'm Detective Alex Boswell. Manhattan North Homicide." He clipped his shield to the lapel of his jacket, making it obvious that he was a cop.

Like all precincts, it was noisy and busy: phones ringing, cops shouting, cops running, paperwork flying, keyboards rattling, two straight-shouldered uniforms herding a scruffy and insensibly drunk collar towards the cells, and Alex had to jump out of their path. Then another pair of uniforms hustled a cuffed, tall, black hooker past him. Pausing, she looked straight into his face, licking her lips lasciviously. "A fresh one! I don't recognize *you,* honey."

Before he could respond, one of the uniforms barked, "Shut the fuck up, Rowena!" roughly shoving her forward, and she tittered in amusement.

He imagined that Rowena must be a regular here.

A detective approached him, eyeballing his shield. "Sorry about that. Detective..."

"Boswell," he supplied. "I'm looking for someone in the detective squad. James Hurley."

The cop's face broke into a grin. "Ah. Boswell. You must be James' old partner from Manhattan North Homicide. We've all heard about you."

"Oh, great." Alex felt the blood pouring into his cheeks. That was never what you wanted to hear from someone you didn't know. "I hope only the good ones."

"Of course the good ones! James thinks of the world of you," said the cop, more embarrassingly. "C'mon. I'll take you upstairs."

James Hurley occupied a cubicle near a window, with a view to the harbor and Manhattan. Feral paperwork had overtaken his desk and had begun its infestation of the floor, and case files were stacked like the Leaning Tower of Piza in the cubicle's corner. James had cleared some space around his computer, and he was typing a DD-5. Ever averse to paperwork, he looked bored, chewing at his lip, fingering a paperclip he'd bent out of shape. He didn't see Alex, although he must have heard someone behind him because he said, "What? It'd better be fuckin' good."

"You still have a free-form filing system, I see."

James spun around in the office chair, wearing his smartass grin. "Lex! Holy shit. I never thought you'd actually show up here!"

"Better late than never."

"And you coulda been a fuckin' librarian, right?"

"I have less crap on the floor."

"Bullshit. You had the worst desk in the squad." Hurley punched Alex playfully in the shoulder, not so bad since it distracted Alex from his inner turmoil.

Alex eked out a smile. "I'd thought I'd come over and see if this place had broken you."

"I'm a broken man, Lex," James laughed. "A pale fuckin' withering shadow, like a two-month old corpse. Ain't that right, Maurice?"

And Maurice, a black detective wearing an African-patterned jacket, retorted, "Nah, man, it's just 'cause you're Irish."

223

James smirked at his colleague, and then he asked Alex, "You got anything on the wire? How's the squad? Anything juicy?"

"It's fine. Same as ever, I guess. Different people, same shit."

"Are they fuckin' weird? If they're not weird, MNHS has lost its fuckin' soul."

"They're weird. One of the new guys on the C team has been running over the geese in Prospect Park with his car and inviting people over for barbequed goose."

Chortling, James spun his chair around in a three-sixty. "That's fuckin' nuts. Is there much *left* of a goose after you've run it over?"

"Dunno. I haven't been. I don't think I could stomach a goose that's been eating city garbage."

"Hah, yeah, I'd still go, just to see."

"Yeah, you would." Alex showed his teeth in a rueful smile. "Well, new partner's finally starting to figure it out. Gibson is Gibson. People keep killing each other or themselves, so never a shortage of work."

"Yeah, when I met your new partner a few years ago, I thought he was as wet as a jelly dildo and about as useful."

"Ray's a good cop. He does all right." No one else in the Homicide squad, before or since, had come close James' mastery of invective.

"Hope he's got rid of the chip on his shoulder that was the size of my cock," said James.

"Ray's settling in," Alex assured him. Diverting James from abusing Ray, who didn't really deserve it, he asked, "How's things here?"

"Great, actually. Fuckin' first rate," said James sincerely.

"Really? You're not bored to death of issuing summonses?" Alex's eyes drifted to the window and the skyscrapers arching out of the river like the vertebrae of a giant sea monster, draped with Christmas lights. "At least you have a view."

James laughed again. "Nah, dude. Staten Island's not so bad. You saw the downstairs squad room. There's lots to do, and I even got a house with a lawn and a little garden. I should show you it someday. Managed to even grow some veggies, some tomatoes, carrots, and a cucumber the size of a fuckin' horse penis. Who would imagine, eh? The quiet life does me good. Or else I'd look like you!"

"Like me? You'd better start drinking harder." Grinning, Alex raised a hand, threatening to swat James' head. The banter seemed effortless,

224

like it used to be. There was no clumsiness nor tension. They could pick up their relationship like the Díaz case had never happened. And James seemed in genuinely good spirits. Maybe gardening suited him. Alex tried imagining James outside, digging up carrots, but it was such a bizarre imposition that he had trouble visualizing it.

"Honestly, Lex," James said, picking up his coat. "Do you know what's great about this place?"

"Well, not the theater or the restaurants."

"Would it surprise you to know that Manhattan is not the center of the world?" retorted James.

"Yes," he answered, arching a mocking eyebrow.

"Breaking news, eh? Better phone CNN. But seriously, dude, there are hardly any murders. I spent years in the Street Crime Unit dealing with every cocksucker in uptown Manhattan and then another thirteen years of my life breaking my fuckin' balls in MNHS, which only makes you realize that assholes, psychopaths, and idiots are three fundamental elements making up the universe. Getting out of bed every morning, thinking, I'm going into work to deal with latest shitbird who's killed someone for absolutely no Goddamned reason. Plus, I get to live in a house here, rather than some rat and cockroach infested hole of an apartment above a sex shop in some scummy corner of Manhattan. I know those fuckwits at IAB sent me here as 'punishment,' but it's the best fuckin' thing that ever happened. I don't think I want to go back to it."

"No?" Alex couldn't conceal his surprise, or his pangs of disappointment.

"The pressure gets to you," James explained. "Like… you wanna solve whatever case lands on your desk, make a collar, not fuck it up so badly that the DA can't prosecute, whatever, but with homicide cases, you feel you have to get the cocksucker who killed somebody… or else someone gets away with murder. Fuckin' literally. Hear me?"

"Yeah, I guess so," Alex shoved his hands into the pockets of his jeans.

"You never feel like you've got your nuts shoved into a pressure cooker?"

"I can't say that metaphor has ever come to mind, James."

"Here it's a lot of petty crime, robbery, DV stuff. And drugs. Heroin. Jesus, lots of fuckin' heroin. But at least it's low on murders."

225

"So's Manhattan these days," said Alex. "You want a low murder rate, come back. It fucks with my head, sometimes, actually having *time* to think about a case."

"Yeah, but there's less of you now. How many detectives in the old squad these days?"

"Twelve."

"Jesus. It used to be *thirty,*" exclaimed James. "It's shrunk faster than your penis in a cold bath."

Laughing softly, Alex replied, "But we're not the murder capital of the country anymore."

They started to leave, James introducing Alex to a couple people in the precinct. "This is Alex. He was my old partner from Manhattan North Homicide."

For all he claimed to be happier here, he seemed pleased that he had been a part of MNHS, and that Alex still was. It was no secret that even amongst the NYPD, there was a mystique to homicide cops, as if they had special knowledge of or power over death itself. Alex doubted he had either, but James' colleagues seemed star-struck.

As he opened the door to leave the detective squad room, James said, "Aw, shit. Sorry, Lex. Have to make one phone call. The guy I need to talk to at Social Services is going on vacation tomorrow."

Alex smiled. Typical James: sharp but scattered and discombobulated, like his mind raced ahead of his ability to organize it, and he didn't care. James only gave fucks about those things when his bosses or colleagues made him. Quite unlike Ray, who color-coded his notes with a highlighter after an interview or interrogation and was horrified by Alex's habit of throwing old paperwork into his locker in scrunched up balls.

James cradled the phone against his face, on a charm offensive with someone in Social Services. "It's Detective Hurley at the One-Two-Three. Yeah, the weather has been pretty shit. California, eh? You'll never come back to this hole! Oh, it's about David. Yeah, you heard he got collared again. Yeah, he threatened his ex with a steak knife. Oh, I know, she makes up crap like that all the time, but I'm sure he did it. The evidence is pretty undeniable this time. He shouldn't be hanging out with those guys. Yeah, short of putting locks on his door, you can't stop him. Can he be detained under the Mental Hygiene Law? Dude, I don't know, you'd really have to ask the DA. Yeah, that's it, we need to sit down, have a chat, you know, talk to the DA, see if we can find some way to keep him outta trouble. Yeah, I know. Have a great time in Cali, bye!"

"What was that?" asked Alex.

"A perp we picked up a few weeks ago. He's crazier than a fuckin' barn swallow on crack. Social Services has been dealing with him for a while. He's a sweet guy, really, but he does a lot of drugs and likes to wave a knife in his ex-girlfriend's face when he's high. You know, it's different when the vics are alive. They're more appreciative."

Chapter Fifteen

November 13th

The neighborhood around the One-Two-Three was so torpid and quiet that Alex thought his breathing sounded loud. Most of the shops were closed, blank faces of metal grates and shutters, only the bars open. This wasn't a place to buy a bagel or pizza at midnight, or even at 2000 hours.

A block down the street, James led him into a pub called the Dublin House. James had always found the best way to connect with his Irish roots was to drink Guinness in Irish bars. Like its brethren across the river and everywhere else in the world, this pub's walls were covered in advertisements for Guinness, rusty farm equipment, photographs of peatbogs and villages of white stone houses with thatched roofs, and road signs pointing to places with slightly unpronounceable names requiring a Transatlantic flight to actually get to, like Ballinasloe, Drogheda, and Glencolmcille.

The predominantly white clientele could be heard well above a cluster of musicians playing jigs and reels in the corner. A session. Obviously, James found a bar with a fucking session. Alex should have anticipated that, having spent years following James to every session in Manhattan. This one had three fiddles, two flutes, a concertina, a guitar, and a set of Irish bagpipes. The players sat in a circle, staring at either the floor or one another, thrashing out tunes, oblivious to the punters around them. They pounded their feet against the floor, a relentless thumping cutting through the pub noise.

Out of nowhere, an invisible fist thrust into his belly, and Alex reeled, woozy and nauseated. James asked him if he wanted a drink, but he wordlessly shook his head, and his blood was pooling in his feet.

"You sure?" Usually Alex drank coke or Pepsi.

"Nah, I'm all right. Water's fine." His voice sounded hollow. He heard his pulse in his ears now, racing flat-out to keep time with the breakneck tempo of the tunes. Bright lights lit up his peripheral vision, flickering, the wattage increasing, whirling faster and faster like a manic disco ball in a SoHo night club. Sweat tickled his eyes and drizzled along his back. The gunshot scars on his right side burned and itched. The walls and ceiling of the pub loomed closer, falling in on him. The pain would crush him, his eyes were stinging and hot, and then the concertina player raised his eyes from the floor, the tune screeching to a halt. Several musicians got up for the toilet or the bar. Alex breathed out softly through the gaps in his clenched teeth.

James ordered a pint of Guinness, chatting with the barmaid, whom he obviously knew. Wistfully, Alex eyed the taps and the whiskies, standing to attention in a line on the wall. Oh, if he could, if he didn't have to explain it to AA or himself, he would deal with this – whatever it was – by getting blind drunk. It had worked for the shooting, until it didn't.

James said, "Wanna hear the session?"

Fuck, the last thing he wanted. "I saw a pool table in the room at the back." The pool table in the alcove, he'd noted, was separated from the musicians by a wall and the cacophony of drinkers in the pub.

"Aw, Lex," said James. "You know you'll just kick my ass from here to Nassau County."

Alex forged an artificial smile through his discomfort. "I'll go easy on you."

"Alright. Let's listen to the session for a couple sets, then we can go to the back."

Any sensible, sane explanation for why he did not want to listen to the session eluded him. Just the instinctive recoil in his gut, like someone had asked him to strip naked and jump into the Hudson.

James accosted the session, saying to the piper, "Heya, Richie. How's it going?"

Alex reluctantly followed him and shakily eased himself into a chair behind the musicians.

The piper said, "Hi, James. You playin'?"

"Nah, have a friend over from Manhattan," said James, waving his hand towards Alex.

"Is your friend a cop?" He resettled the pipes on his lap.

"Yeah. He was my old partner when I worked in Manhattan."

229

"When you were working homicides?"

"Yeah."

"Is he a homicide detective?"

"Yeah."

"In Manhattan?"

"No, fuckin' Mars. Yeah, Manhattan."

"Huh, a real Lennie Briscoe." The piper looked at Alex again, captivated. "Does he really work in the 27th Precinct?"

"Hah, that doesn't exist," James cackled with undistinguished relish.

Every civilian in the country must view his job through the lens of *Law and Order*. Alex also tried to laugh at the thought, but he couldn't escape the fear that reality might disappear at any moment.

The other musicians returned from the bar and the bathroom, arranging themselves in their seats, picking up instruments, several of them nodding or muttering greetings to James. A fiddle player made a preliminary twiddle, fingers flicking across the neck of the instrument, a half-forgotten segment of a tune squeaking under his bow. Then he lowered the fiddle and said, "James, do you play that last tune? That reel in D we played at the end of the set."

"No, not a fuckin' clue," said James.

"You should learn it," sniggered the fiddle player. "It's called the 'New Policeman.'"

"Very funny," said James drolly.

"We've been playing it with one called 'Farewell to Old Decency' and called it the James Hurley set."

Then the fiddler squeaked out another twiddle before firing into a tune, which some of the others picked up, and it overwhelmed the whole space in the back of the bar, echoing between the junk-covered walls and the low, heavy ceilings. Mouth half-open, Alex dug his nails into the wooden table. His internal organs were turning into mush. His heart pummeled his sternum in a frenzy. It would stop if it kept beating this hard. How many sessions had James dragged him to in the thirteen years he'd worked at MNHS? Hundreds of the things. Alex had even picked up on the difference between a jig, reel, polka, and strathspey. *So, what the fuck?*

He shut his eyes, biting the inside of his cheek. His breathing sounded loud, labored. He tried to swallow but his mouth was like a desert, his tongue covered with adrenaline, foul-tasting and bitter. It would only last for a few seconds, like in Lincoln Center and Foley Square. He bit his cheek harder, drawing blood, a salty taste in his mouth, and he clung to the pain like a lifeboat, caught amidst huge waves, the Atlantic storms that always slammed into Battery Park, heaving water onto the walkways and roads, and then sucking debris into the ocean.

Precipitously, the storm sheered off, and he was in a pub, listening to an Irish session flying through reels. He ran his tongue against his teeth, pushing his fingers into his cheek, which hurt. It was still bleeding. Cupping his shaking hands over his face, he spit out some blood into a napkin, and then wadded it up. He glanced at James, who, to his immense relief, was paying no attention to him because someone in the session had given him a whistle, and his fingers flicked breezily against it as the squeaky high notes cut through the other instruments.

The set ended, and the musicians chattered, which sounded like surrealist beat poetry from a Greenwich Village hole-in-the-wall open mike. What was the first one? 'The Morning Dew.' Isn't it also called 'The Hare in the Heather?' What about the second? 'Beautiful Gortree.' And the last, does anyone have a name? 'Good Morning to Your Nightcap.'

Alex remembered mornings like that. Exhaling a protracted breath, he got to his feet, and his legs felt shaky, untrustworthy, but he scurried to the bathroom and emptied his bladder. That didn't help him feel better. Whatever this was, he couldn't piss it out. He vigorously scrubbed his face with cold water and rinsed more blood from his mouth. Then he drank a little water from the tap. His heart fluttered, scaring him. Cardiac problems? Was he hallucinating because his heart couldn't pump enough blood to his brain? He took the pulse in his wrist, counting beats. Fast but strong. A drunk guy tripped into the bathroom and peed at the urinals. Feeling faint and troubled, Alex guzzled another mouthful of water and ran out the door.

On his return to the session, James, looking apologetic, handed the whistle back to its owner. "Sorry, Lex. I've been coming here every Monday and playing some tunes with these guys. It's a bastard of a drive for you to come out here, I know. And Jesus, stop chewing on your fingers. They're not Angelina Jolie's pussy, are they?"

231

No matter how weird you felt, you had to enjoy James' way with words, when you could not quite believe that he had just said *that*. A smile came unbidden to Alex's lips, his hand falling to the table. Farewell to old decency indeed.

"But anyway, let's go shoot some stick, eh?" said James.

The musicians took off on another set, and the detectives retreated to the pool table in the alcove, plugging fifty cents into the slot on the side of the table. Balls clunked into the holes, and Alex racked the balls. In the past, pool had reliably lowered his blood pressure, which was how he got good. Thankfully, the walls and the din of voices in the bar drowned out the tunes. Alex only heard the thumping of their feet.

"You see that flute player?" said James.

"What, the grizzled old guy with the beard?" Alex maintained the banter, faking it.

James rolled his eyes. "Oh, yeah. No, the other one. I'd really like to fuck her."

"Best of luck to you. I think I saw a wedding ring on her."

"Did that ever stop you?"

"No, but I'm like those LED warning signs on the highway. Slow down. Accident ahead."

James missed his first shot on the break and then leaned on his cue like a pole on a rush hour subway, a cockeyed grin on his face as he watched Alex knock one ball after another into pockets. "Watch the fuckin' master work," he commented, wiping Guinness foam off his lips. "You beautiful, sexy bitch."

"Huh," grunted Alex, feeling heat touch his cheeks. Then he fired the cue ball against the side of the table, where it banked into the twelve, the twelve bumping the four into a pocket.

"That shit's good," James exclaimed. "I forgot you were a fuckin' shark."

Alex tightened his lips in a wan half-smile. "No, you haven't. The flattery isn't gonna get me to back off."

"A great white. You're pretty hot with your stick and balls."

"That's what she said."

"You got anyone saying that recently?"

"No," Alex lied promptly, annoyed with himself for letting the banter touch on Becky. "You?"

"Yeah, Laura and Shira. They don't *know* about each other. But I'm just keeping my options open, you know."

Alex blew out a mordant breath, and his cue ball glanced off the fourteen, the ten following it into a pocket. "We're in our late forties now. Should we still be 'playing the field?'"

"Fuck yes. Life's too fuckin' short and getting shorter by the day. My mother thinks I should have a wife and about ten kids by now, but fuck that."

"Well, she is Irish."

"And I'm a disappointment. Thank fuck my sister had three kids." Then James took a long drink from his Guinness and looked remarkably serious. "You said you were coming by tonight. I mean, it's fuckin' great to see you, but I'm guessing you had some kind of reason to schlep out here on your RDO. You haven't come over in three years. And not just that there was no one in Manhattan whose ass needed kicking at pool."

"It's true, there wasn't," Alex replied lightly.

"Okay, other than that."

Alex chalked the tip of his cue. "I didn't know if you'd heard. You remember the LaValle case—"

"Jesus. That shitbag. Of course I do."

"Did you know it went to the Court of Appeals?"

"I figured it would. Don't all death penalty cases get appealed?"

"Well, it got appealed and then it got reversed."

James' blue eyes widened. "You mean, they fuckin' let that motherfucker out? He killed a pregnant cop! On *what* grounds! We fuckin' did everything right—"

Alex bent over the table and nudged the eleven ball into a pocket, only for the cue ball to dive in after it. "Ah, fuck. They reversed the sentence, not the conviction. He'll spend the rest of his life in Attica but he's not getting a needle in his arm."

"Oh, right," James said, breathing out in relief and then scratching his free shot. "So?"

"That's it. The sentence was reversed. You worked on the case. I thought you might wanna know." Alex transiently regretted his decision to come here. He didn't know why he thought James would care. James hadn't been interested in whether or not the prosecutors sought the death penalty when they were investigating the case, and he did not seem that interested now. Faintly, Alex heard the fall and rise of the Irish tunes in the other part of the bar. It hurt his head.

"You know why they reversed it?" James asked softly.

"McNally tried explaining it. Something to do with juries being afraid that if they couldn't decide between sentencing a defendant to death or to life without parole, the judge could then give them only twenty years."

James looked confused. "What?"

"I don't know." Alex sighed. "I'm not explaining it very well."

"But it's not anything *we* did?"

"No, fuck-all to do with us, or even the DA. It's evidently something the statute says about jury instructions. Whole damned thing is unconstitutional. McNally says there won't be any more death penalty cases in New York unless the legislature passes a whole new law."

"You seem kind of upset by it," observed James. "I didn't even think you liked the idea of the death penalty."

"I don't. And I'm not."

"Don't feed me bullshit, Alex. I know it's been a while, but I can tell you're not happy. Are you upset by the Appeals Court reversing that sentence? Or something else. What's been going on?"

Averting his eyes, caught out and too numb to speak, Alex played the cue ball off the eight and five balls, duly sinking the thirteen into a corner. He would miss the next one and give James a chance.

But James had stopped watching the table, and he watched Alex, his lower lip in his teeth. Then he said with uncharacteristic deliberation, "You were in that car accident with Zoë Sheehan the same day as that dude's sentencing hearing, weren't you?"

The question stabbed him like a knife to the belly. "Yeah," he mumbled.

"Did you ever talk to anyone about it?"

"What? For Christ's sake, it was over two years ago."

"Is that what's on your mind?"

As if he knew. Uneasy, he rubbed his eyes with the heel of his hand, and a repulsive feeling upset his insides. "I dunno. I guess. In a way. But what's there to say? You know what happened."

"I know you fell off the wagon and ended up getting a lift home with Zoë, who shoulda been picking up McNally from that bar."

"McNally was pretty flipped out," Alex said sadly, recalling McNally leaving the bar with that TV actress. The lawyer had never breathed a word about that, but Alex's mind turned to one time, Simon's face going white when *Law and Order* happened to be on the TV in the MNHS squad room, and there was that redheaded actress, playing a witness. Yeah, Alex had idly wondered, but he didn't have the stomach to ask.

"Simon and Zoë had a thing, didn't they?

"Oh, yeah. He was upset. Went on vacation for three weeks after it happened, climbing mountains somewhere. Scotland, I think he said."

"He's a sleazy bastard, isn't he?" James contemplated. "Always getting his knob polished with ADAs half his age. Talk about playing the field."

"He's the expert," Alex said, hoping to keep James diverted from discussing his troubles. "We should be so lucky."

"How does he do it?" James laughed.

"Dunno. Must be his rugged charm."

"Anyway, you need to talk to someone." James stabbed at the cue ball, and it bounced into a group of four balls, scattering them every which way.

"What? Like a professional?"

"Maybe. Or maybe a friend."

"What's there to say?" Alex put two of those four balls into pockets.

"How do you feel?"

"I feel shit about it. Do we have to do this?"

James rested on his cue, looking at him soberly. "Yeah"

"No fucking point." He pretended to focus intensely on an easy shot, a clear trajectory from his target to the pocket.

"Why not?"

"I don't wanna talk about it. What's past is past."

"You don't look good, Lex."

"Do I ever? I always look annoyed and cynical because I always am. My sunny disposition has been ruined by crap relationships and too much boozing, I've been a New York City homicide cop for too Goddamned long, and my back kills me so much that I'm at the mercy of my physio."

"Yeah, I hear you, but normally you just look irritable. Now you look..."

"How do I look?"

"Hopeless. You look hopeless. And when we were listening to the session, it was like…"

"Like what? What are you trying to say?"

James hesitated, pinching at his upper lip. This wasn't easy for him, either. "Uh, like after the 190th Street shooting. Those episodes you'd have, where you acted like you didn't know where you were."

"Jesus Christ, James. It's nothing like that. It's a fucking session. Maybe I'm dealing with trauma from you dragging my ass to every session in Manhattan." None of it made sense: the session had nothing to do with the car wreck, or the '87 shooting, and his heart was beating fast again, and the cue shook in his hands.

"You look like shit."

"I should cover the grey, then." Putting on a quirky, sarcastic grin, Alex ran his hand through his hair. "I don't remember a damned thing about the car wreck. I was off my fucking face." The cue ball cracked against the two and fifteen balls. A half-truth, or maybe all of the truth. Alex didn't remember the accident, but he hadn't thought himself as blackout-level wasted when he'd left the bar. Yet Zoë leading him to her car remained his last shred of memory, and one of the things about being that drunk was that you never quite remembered how drunk you were.

Like any veteran detective, James possessed a high-tech bullshit Geiger counter. "You seem to be remembering it a little. Well enough to be bothered by it."

"I told you. I don't wanna talk about it. It's all over."

"It doesn't sound that way to me, Lex."

"Nothing will change the fact that Zoë died, or that she probably wouldn't have, at least not then, if I hadn't fucked up."

"It obviously still upsets you."

"I know. Why are we talking about it?" Alex skidded a ball off the side of the table, missing the pocket by a hair.

"Have you thought about talking to POPPA or EIU or some kind of shrink?"

"That's cute," he said laconically, wiping his face with the back of his hand, and then he sagged onto his cue and watched James pointlessly bounce the cue ball off the side of the pool table. "And get stuck on modified assignment for the rest of my life."

"It's confidential," said James.

"Yeah fucking right. You remember the shit I had to deal with when I went into rehab? Nobody thought I should be on the streets. How's it gonna be if they learn I'm in counseling? Rubber gun duty, just like that." He snapped his fingers.

James stepped in, invading Alex's personal space, an attempt to bully his old friend into leveling with him. "Then talk to me. Come on, when I was in the squad you would talk to me. You keep this shit inside, dude, it's not gonna be good."

"There's nothing I need to talk about. It was two years ago."

"You're blaming yourself for it. "

"Yeah, Dr. Hurley. I get that."

"You know it's not really your fault. You know as well as I do that if the driver who hit you hadn't been DOA, he woulda been liable."

Alex cleared his throat, twice. Something tightened around his windpipe. "Yeah, legal liability has nothing to do with how fucked up it is in my head."

"You're hung up on chaos theory," suggested James.

"What? Chaos theory?"

"You made small decisions – fuckin' stupid decisions, but still small – like going into the fuckin' bar, and that kinda ended up in you driving across an intersection at the exact moment some fuckwit in an SUV ran a red light, and you got hurt and Zoë was killed, which is like a big fuckin' deal. Obviously. It's like…" James cheated and poked the four ball with his forefinger, so it rolled a couple inches. "When you break at the start of a game. The tiniest change in the angle or speed of your cue causes the balls to scatter in totally different directions, right?"

"Yeah."

"And to be honest, you have no fuckin' idea – not even you – how the balls are gonna scatter, or how they woulda scattered if you'd hit the cue ball harder or softer or at what angle or whatever. There's no way you could ever know, unless you were psychic. Get it?"

"Yeah, I get it. But what's talking about it gonna fix? I really, really don't want to."

"I don't know," admitted James, looking downcast.

Alex turned away from James, stretching his torso and one leg over the pool table, firing the cue ball into a cluster of three balls, two stripes and a solid. He did it with too much force, the solid, James' ball, rolling into a pocket. Fuck – he never scratched like that. James knew more about his inner demons than most people. It had been James who helped him survive those first months at work in the aftermath of 190th Street, who at once comprehended his trauma and helped him hide it from those who wouldn't. It had been James, along with Marty Vasquez and Bill Ryan, who had been with him the night that a stomach ulcer ruptured after a few drinks. It had been James who had been with him when a doctor told him that he would die if he didn't quit drinking and the cold realization dawned on him: some time ago, he had crossed the line from 'heavy drinker' to 'alcoholic.' Just because you weren't like the homeless guys on the street drinking lighter fluid didn't mean you were much better off.

Looking lost, James fumbled for words, his hand opening and closing expressively around the pool cue.

Alex stared down at the table and absently slid his hand along the green felt. "I guess after it happened, I thought, maybe it would have been better if it had been me, rather than her. But it wasn't. I've had families of murder victims tell me the same thing. Why was it him, why not me? I imagine that's a normal thing to feel."

"Yeah, I think so," said James, taking a long swig from his pint. "What do you say to families when they tell you that?"

"I tell them that the universe is shit. Except I say it more diplomatically than that."

"Did you ever talk about *that* to anyone?"

"I've talked about it to McNally." He picked up the chalk, working it into the cue. "'Cause I felt I should. It was his girlfriend who didn't walk away from that accident."

"Yeah. How'd he take it?"

"He came over to my apartment while I was recovering, to see how I was, if you can believe he has a sympathetic side."

"Who knew he had *that* underneath his crusty-as-a-month-old bagel hard-on personality. Was he?"

"Yeah, of course he was. He blamed himself for it anyway. Not me." McNally remembered nothing from that night, not even phoning Alex, but he'd been wracked with guilt for everything he didn't remember doing.

"Is that what you talked about?" James pressed.

"I dunno, I was in a lot of pain, doped up on Vicodin. High as a fucking kite. Broken ribs hurt like a bitch, and they gave me shitloads of heavy-duty pain meds so I could breathe. And it was the same side as the gunshot wound, so it was worse for me. They said if I wasn't breathing right, there's a risk of infection in the lungs..." He reached for the ribs on his right side, probing the injuries from the shooting. "And I had horrible pain my lower back for weeks – at first it was so bad I couldn't walk more than a few feet – and it's still sore. Every time I lean over to hit a pool ball, I can feel it."

"Your back still hurts after two years? Have you *at least* talked to someone about that?"

He laughed dryly. "Have I ever."

"What does that mean?"

"It's a long fucking story." He stopped talking and tapped the cue ball into the ten, silently watching it roll across the table, his attention drawn to the telltale twinge in his back and the realization that James had cleverly got him talking about the wreck in spite of his efforts to avoid it. His old partner had always been formidable in the interrogation room.

James asked, "What's the story?"

He sunk down on a stool near the pool table, holding the cue between his knees. "You really wanna know?"

"Yeah. I know we don't talk much now, but I always wonder how you are. You'd think in the days of email and cell phones, we could do better."

"You would think," Alex lamented. "You still come across to Manhattan for pipe band practice, don't you?" For all the years Alex had known him, James had been playing the bagpipes in the Emerald Society Pipes and Drums, the NYPD's pipe band.

"Yeah, but you know me. I'm shit at organizing shit and I always end up in a hurry. Look, I'm getting another drink. You sure you don't want anything?"

"I'll have a coke." The inside of his mouth felt like chalk, and the salty taste of blood from biting his cheek lingered on his tongue. His chest was tight, like someone pulling a draw cord around his heart. Looking for any distraction, he occupied himself by reading the Irish road signs and staring at the photographs on the wall. Peat bogs, lonely sea cliffs facing the Atlantic swell, white thatched houses, pubs with names like "O'Brien's" and "Cleary's." And those damned jigs and reels, throbbing through the walls.

When James returned with a drink in each hand, Alex took a welcome sip of the coke and swilled it around in his mouth. "I spent about a year arguing with my insurance company about whether I could get an MRI or not. When I went to the ER, they'd X-rayed my spine to see if it was broken, which it wasn't, and they said I'd just torn muscles and ligaments in my back. Insurance company, because MRIs are fucking expensive and they're cheap, evil bastards, said, well, based on that diagnosis, an MRI is unnecessary and we're not gonna pay for it. I said that after four, five, six months, it still hurt. X-rays evidently don't show a lot of stuff. Or don't show the same things as an MRI. I went back and forth with them for months. My GP said I should have further tests. Insurance company has docs on the payroll who look at your case, on paper and say it's an unnecessary procedure. The system is fucked up. Anyway, they finally caved last year, and I had a scan, which showed that one of the discs in my spine *had* been damaged, but it had kinda healed, and it wasn't worth doing anything, like surgery, at this point. Doc said that they coulda done more at the time. They still could fuse the vertebrae, but the insurance company won't pay for that unless it gets worse, like the disc compressing a nerve, because they think I'm fine getting regular physio to keep everything in line."

"Is that the health insurance you – we – get through the DEA?" asked James.

"Yeah. I mean, they outsource to private companies, but yeah, your union at work. I was thinking about moving to Canada."

"Fucking insurance companies." James scowled, his pale cheeks flushing. "They'll fuck you up the ass with a hacksaw while feeding your own entrails to you and telling you it's all for your own Goddamned good."

"That's about the gist of it."

"Now what?"

"I live with it, which is more than can be said for Zoë," Alex said tonelessly with a grim smile that did not reach his eyes. "You've gotten me to say more than I wanted. Let's leave it, okay?"

James exhaled discontentedly, shifting his gaze away from Alex's distressed, closed-off face and contemplating a road sign to Galway, as if he would like to go there. Then he dug two quarters out of his pocket and plopped them on the table. "After this, another game? See how many times I can humiliate myself?"

Alex downed his coke, salving the sticky dryness in his throat. "Yeah, okay." And then, in a flash of his old sardonic manner, he added, "You're still shit at pool." The striped balls were long gone, the eight ball waiting for him. He played a tidy bank shot and sunk it into a side pocket.

Chapter Sixteen

November 14th

It was Alex's second RDO in the set, but he was working anyway, clocking the overtime hours with a tail of Analisa Santos. He'd volunteered to do it because he would not be taking Becky to a Broadway show or seeing her at all, and while he had considered contacting Sarah, he ultimately decided against it. Fragility had suffused into his soul, a plate with thin cracks spreading across its surface, and if she bitched at him, he feared that he might shatter. The conversation with James had been hard enough. It was also his case, and he wanted to do a lot of the surveillance himself.

Gibson had organized a rota, shared between MNHS and the Two-Eight squad, and the detectives had authorization to keep the witness under surveillance for a week. Everyone prayed that evidence would come out of it: enough for search warrants or wiretap warrants, if nothing else. It was a typical robbery-homicide case, an absolute son of a bitch to break in the absence of Kitchener's confession. There was no connection between the perps and the victims, other than being in the same place at the same time. The perps had been prepared to kill, but probably not planning on it, and, as the ADA had predicted, the paltry eyewitness testimony (and missing witness) had little value.

Trying to be inconspicuous, Alex had signed out the white 1998 Suzuki Esteem the squad kept around for surveillance, instead of a Crown Vic or Taurus. Nothing screamed 'cop' in Washington Heights like a white guy in a Ford Sedan. Some years ago, James Hurley had christened the Suzuki "Mollie," after an ex-girlfriend, whose one redeeming characteristic, James explained, was that she had a big ass. The name stuck. The car looked like a heap: dents in the bumper, the upholstery inside marred with holes and coffee stains, the sun visors attached with duct tape, about five lights illuminated on the dash, and a can of WD-40 in the door pockets because the door latches jammed. The interior reeked, a combination of BO, fried food, and cigarette smoke. No amount of car shampoo nor air freshener would get rid of it.

Even driving Mollie and dressed in faded jeans and a tatty, threadbare fleece, Alex didn't blend into the neighborhood as well as his black and Latino colleagues, but he did his best to maintain a low profile. He parked about four addresses down the street from Analisa's apartment, far enough away for her to not notice the car, but close enough for him to see whether or not she left the building, or anyone entered it. Then it was a matter of waiting and boredom. Most tails were. He nursed a large Styrofoam cup of coffee and ate a chocolate croissant for breakfast, hearing Ray rebuking him. "You know you'd feel a lot better if you didn't eat such shit all the time." Yeah, he probably would. But Ray wasn't here. His only company was the police radio, which he'd tuned to the Three-Three's channel, but he kept it on a low volume. To pass the time and look busy to any passerby who glanced in the car, he fumbled through the *New York Times* crossword while keeping one eye on the front door of Analisa's apartment.

Washington Heights bustled around him: men in suits and women in heels with professionally arranged dreadlocks hustled to work; mothers stood on the stoops with a baby on their hips and a toddler in tow; teenage gangsters in clothes three sizes too big slouched off to school or maybe not; the homeless and the dope fiends, their eyes haunted and faces hollow, wafted hungrily through the crowds. They melted together like snowflakes in a blizzard, minding their own business in the way only New Yorkers knew how in the swirling, fast-paced melee of street life.

Alex's mind roamed as he surveilled the apartment and the people circulating past his car, his thoughts inhabiting a Washington Heights that was recurrent, changing, self-referential, his old maps overlaying current ones. Paths through open-air drug markets on the corners, through dog-leg alleyways and boarded up, derelict apartments; nights sweating in a hot car or a police van on a stakeout at 155th Street or 167th Street or Malcolm X, playing rummy with James and Bill Ryan or Marty Vasquez or Sam Rizzo or Matt Cohen, keeping hold of a jittery CI, who will tell you when your suspect walks in or out of the bar you're watching, while trumpets and saxes duel in a nearby club and drug touts shout out the names of their products, a soundtrack to the eternal night of waiting.

Or charging into a smoky apartment or townhouse, your gun drawn, on the heels of Emergency Services. You wonder if the dealers inside the crackhouse are better armed than you. You hope not, and you rush past the surreal disjunctions – the *Santeria* shrines, the paintings of saints, the candles, the offerings to God, to superstition, worshipped by desperate, semi-conscious addicts, and by the dealers placing little value on life, and you disparagingly say to yourself that if there is a God, he can't possibly give a shit.

Or a call to a DOA in a narrow building with rusty fire escape stairs clinging to it like a peripatetic centipede, hidden in the shadows on an alleyway that you hadn't noticed until then, and neither has anyone else, because the DOA has been there for some time, the smell sending you staggering.

You think you know your way around, but you get lost in a city constantly evolving through your synapses, over bridges, through subway tunnels, along one-way streets, and you are not the person you were years ago, and the streets no longer the same streets, although you keep re-treading old pathways worn into your memory.

Every block told a story. On *that* 157th Street in 1989, Alex and James had been assisting the Three-Four squad with an investigation of a nightclub shooting, a nightclub that was long gone, replaced by apartments and a BBQ joint. But in '89, the sidewalk had pulsed with energy: an open-air drug bazaar, people buying and selling crack and dope in plain sight. The shooting had made the crowd on the street restive and high-strung.

Alex, James, and Detective Vito Indelicata from the Three-Four squad knew who the street players were, and they'd started pulling people out of the club, collaring a couple guys for possessing illegal weapons or drugs but considering them suspects in the homicide, or at least likely to roll on the shooters. The arrests flicked a switch. A frenzied mob banded together and swirled around the detectives. Alex, James, and Vito clumped together, scared, vulnerable. Vito thought he had the neighborhood in hand – he was the ballsiest detective in the NYPD and was convinced he owned these streets – but when he tried getting tough with the hostile mob, no one listened.

Alex called in a ten-eighty-five, police officer in need of assistance. The crowd expanded, growing more fractious, and a hellfire-and-brimstone preacher spurred it on, bellowing: "Remember Michael Stewart! Remember Bernhard Goetz was *acquitted!*" Michael Stewart was a black graffiti artist, picked up by the transit police, who died while in custody. Bernie Goetz was a white commuter who shot four unarmed black youths on the subway and said it was self-defense.

There were no established procedures for this clusterfuck, no advice from the Patrol Guide or *Practical Homicide*. Just fear, and Alex had plenty of that, more fear than Vito, who kept inciting the mob with gruff threats and street talk, and more fear than the pissed off residents of the Heights, who didn't care that they were police. The detectives had their guns drawn, the three of them sweating, standing back to back. The mob wheeled around them like an angry cyclone. Terror squished Alex's insides into liquid, and he radioed in a ten-thirteen, upgrading the eighty-five.

He saw the vicious glint of dark metal – people were armed, probably more than they were. His heart hammered like a coked-up drummer. He was dripping with sweat. He heard sirens, drawing closer, the sweetest sound in the world.

The cavalry arrived: four squad cars and a van full of ESU officers. The uniforms took control of the scene, the show of force dispersing the mob. Only five minutes after the initial eighty-five. The longest five minutes of Alex's life. Back in the MNHS offices, Lieutenant Corcoran had read Alex and James the riot act for going into that club without backup to hand: "You should know better. Especially you, Boswell. Sure, I know Indelicata thinks he knows the neighborhood better than any cop in the department and does reckless things, but I need my men to use their brains. I don't want to be investigating your deaths. Or having a riot on our hands. *Jesus.* That situation needed one spark. Just one. Got it?"

One could agree that Vito Indelicata was an overconfident son of a bitch who had profoundly misjudged that situation, but one could also argue that police resources were badly stretched, and a detective couldn't expect backup every time he went looking for witnesses. "Yes, sir," they said. They didn't argue.

Alex finished breakfast and scribbled a couple answers into his crossword. He gazed broodily at the apartments occupying the real estate that once housed that club. It seemed as if his near miss had happened in a place a thousand miles from here, now only captured in fleeting shadows, a familiar building façade, a bodega blaring the same salsa music on its PA. A shiver coursed down his back as he relived the hate in the eyes of that crowd as they encircled three white cops – himself Jewish, Hurley Irish, Indelicata Italian, but none of that mattered – one spark away, as Corcoran had said, from killing or hurting them, as if two centuries of racism and oppression could have found vindication in that moment.

At 0900 hours, a silver Toyota Prius drove past Alex and parked a couple spaces in front of him. Idly, Alex eyeballed the vehicle. The driver emerged, a black male in his forties, wearing an iron grey suit, carrying a leather briefcase. He walked up the stoop to Analisa's apartment, buzzing the door. A second later, he disappeared into the building. Had drug dealers become environmentally conscious and started driving Priuses, rather than the traditional Mercedes E-Class or Cadillac Escalade with blacked out windows? Probably not.

Alex picked up his radio. "Manhattan North Homicide Unit 929 to Central. Advise to run New York plates YMV-776. K."

"Ten-four," Central replied.

A few minutes later, Central said, "Citywide to MNHS 929, K."

"929 standing by, K," he answered.

"Operations advises that's a ten-nineteen on the vehicle. Plate YMV-776 is silver Toyota Prius, registered to Columbia Properties, 167 East 112th Street, New York City. No outstanding warrants on auto or owner. K."

"Ten-four," acknowledged Alex. The car was registered to a property agent, the one listed as the owners of this building. Presumably she must be meeting her landlord. He chewed on his lower lip and scratched a note with the day, time, a description of the car and its driver. The man exited the apartment at 0920 and drove away in his Prius.

At 0930 hours, Analisa appeared with her son. Alex took his eyes off the crossword. She was carrying boxes under her arm and her son had a red backpack. She helped her son into her rusty Ford Aspire, loaded the boxes into the trunk, and then drove out of her parking space. The Aspire spewed unhealthy dark exhaust. Alex picked up the radio, reporting to Central that the subject was on the move, and then he started Mollie but lingered for a second, allowing Analisa to get some distance ahead of him. He watched her turn right onto Amsterdam. Then he eased Mollie onto the road, making the same right, uptown. Keeping three or four cars between himself and the Ford, he trailed after her. No one would look out for cops driving old Suzuki Esteems, so she paid him no heed. She jerked to a halt at 160th, parking illegally in a loading zone. Traffic and lack of parking space made it impossible for him to do the same, so he had to go right on 160th, around the block, swearing and holding his breath.

When he came around to 160th and Amsterdam again, the egg-shaped Aspire hadn't budged. He released his breath in relief and parked behind a delivery truck, watching. Dominican music blasted out of a greengrocer, and he felt a touch of queasiness. Biting at the inside of his lip in discomfort, he gently pressed his hand into his belly, as if it would stabilize his digestive tract. He watched Analisa re-enter her car, without her kid, and he radioed Central, asking them to identify any schools in the immediate area. He was advised that PS 4 was on 160th.

As he ten-foured that radio transmission, she took off, driving with more determination downtown on St. Nick's, and he shoved the Esteem into gear and followed, always three or four cars behind, the distance they tell you that people tend to not notice a tail.

Central crackled in, asking, "MNHS 929, are you still on the move. K?"

"Yes," he said. "Subject's just made a left turn onto East 116th Street. K."

The light on Madison stopped them. A blue and white 102 bus blocked Alex's view of Analisa. When the light changed, he mashed the clutch down and cajoled Mollie into swinging around the bus, the Suzuki responding in its indolent manner, the engine and gearbox groaning with the effort. *You wouldn't want this piece of shit in a vehicle pursuit*, he thought. The Aspire and its 50-horsepower engine hadn't got far. The little car belched smoke from its exhaust, while only three cabs and a Buick separated them.

Analisa hung another downtown turn on Park Avenue, split in the middle by the Metro North railroad. Occasionally, a train clattered

247

overhead. At East 97th, the train tracks dove underground. You could turn one corner, cross one street, and find yourself in a different city. There were no more shops where you could buy a used cell phone, a chrome bumper for your car, a crucifix, exotic fruit, or exchange gold for cash. On Park Avenue below 96th, you could buy high-end jewelry, a latte or a cappuccino, a pricey business suit, a gown, or advice for avoiding taxes by hiding money in offshore accounts. Alex cruised at an easy thirty, keeping a couple taxis, a Two-Three Precinct radio car, and a BMW between himself and the Aspire.

His thoughts inadvertently slipped back to Staten Island. And with it, the sting of pain and loss. His fingers tightened around the steering wheel. He guided Mollie around three more cabs, barely holding Analisa's little grey car in his sight. Why had James brought up the car wreck, of all things?

He should not have been in a bar, and he would always blame himself for that. Sure, most people in his AA meeting had suffered at least one relapse, and his sponsor had told him that every difficulty he faced would make his spirit more resilient, but his sponsor didn't know about Zoë. His sponsor also believed in a higher power who would cover your back if you had faith, so Alex sometimes took his advice with a lot of salt.

And until yesterday, he hadn't appreciated or admitted to himself the loss in his life that James' transfer to Staten Island represented. He wondered how he had let the past three years slip by. He'd closed himself down and shut off those emotions like blocking a burst pipe, but he hadn't repaired the hole. Cops get transferred all the time. James wasn't dead, so he shouldn't feel so damned sick about it. He wasn't entitled to that. His AA sponsor once told him he should explore his pain, but he preferred to bury it and work himself into the ground. He did both, but underneath his unfazed façade, he missed James dreadfully, and he grieved that their telepathic connection was a once-in-a-lifetime thing. After yesterday, he marveled at had how easily they fell into their old rhythms and repartees, as if their partnership had never ended.

Back on the job, he felt like he had a massive, bleeding gash in his chest, like someone had cut out his coronary artery.

He forced air out through his nostrils, his breath shuddering. Waiting for a red light, he massaged his fingers into the sinews of tendon and muscle around his collarbone and his shoulder. *Stay with the job, dammit.* Where was Analisa going? Trundling along on Park. Disappearing behind an SUV taxi, and then reappearing when the taxi took East 72nd. The light changed, and he urged Mollie onwards, catching up with Analisa just in time to see her wheel onto East 68th.

Ahead of him, the Aspire slowed down, as though searching for an address. Analisa crossed Lexington, then Third, and then stopped beside a white van. She spoke with the driver and slid into a space in front of it. The van driver opened the back doors of the van. Alex was at the other end of the block, too far away to read the plates or the address, at least with his eyes. He made a risky move, driving past them, getting a good look at the van's plates, committing them to memory, before swinging around the block and wrestling the Esteem into a space on the other side of the street. At least parking seemed to be oddly plentiful. Sometimes life hurts and nothing feels right, but sometimes, there is a parking space where you want one in Manhattan. It eased his depressive mood, just a fraction.

He contacted Central. "MNHS Unit 929 to Central. Advise to run NITRO check on 234 East 68th Street and also check New York plates, FGM-774. K."

A NITRO check was the city's computer program that tracked recidivist offenders, mainly for drug collars, and checked buildings for "kites," or drug complaints. It would tell him if there were any outstanding warrants or complaints for anyone in the building. Perhaps more of a useful exercise for a South Bronx project than a building on East 68th, but appearances deceive. You never knew what skeletons might tumble out of closets, even ones in an East 68th Street townhouse bigger than his whole apartment.

"Ten-four," said Central.

He watched Analisa and the van driver carry folding tables out of the van and into the apartment. Once the tables had been cleared, Analisa rearranged the boxes in her trunk before lugging them into the building. Alex, Analisa, and the Transit were parked along a row of narrow townhouses, four stories high, with window boxes, Dutch shutters, and stoops rising towards smartly painted doors with filigreed windows and brass handles. Each townhouse was an individual, white, ruddy stone, bright red brick, grey with white trim and a shingle roof. Analisa was moving her boxes into a white one with elaborately coiled wrought iron handrails and gates guarding the stoop, and over a dozen flower boxes huddling in the window wells like storm-bound refugees.

Central crackled over the radio, "Citywide to MNHS Unit 929. K."

"929, standing by. Go Central," he responded.

"Operations advises that New York plate number FGM-774 is registered to a Ford Transit van, white in color, four doors. Vehicle registered to Stefan Ruiz of 394 Utica, Brooklyn, New York City. Operations advises no record or outstanding warrants on auto or owner at this time. Operations also advises: no NITRO record for any registered tenant or owner listed as resident in 234 East 68th Street at this time. K."

"Ten-four," Alex said, disheartened. Fuck, he'd prayed for a break, although he knew that the chances of Analisa venturing to a drug corner while he followed her around had never been very promising. "929 copies. K."

Foreseeing a soporific and tedious day – like most surveillance ops – he turned off the car and reached for the crossword. He blended in here, although Mollie didn't. *You can't fucking win.* Time dribbled out of shape like clocks in a Dali painting, and he whittled at the crossword and studied people walking in and out of 234, but they looked like Upper East Side Jews, the women in ankle-length skirts, the men in suits and wearing yarmulkes. How many drug dealers wear yarmulkes? The same ones who drive Priuses.

Well, you never know. But it must be a catering job, a Bar Mitzvah. Alex phoned his office and got through to a detective on the C team. He asked her to call Five Boroughs Catering and inquire where Analisa was meant to be working today. If word got back to Analisa that the police were still sniffing around, it might shake her resolve.

His physical discomfort increased to distracting levels while he watched nothing happening at 234. Cramps in his back and legs from sitting in the car too long, his belly empty, his bladder full. An acidic burn corroded his stomach, a persistent incursion. He radioed in a ten-sixty-three, alerting Central that he would be briefly out of service for a meal, and then, with worried glances at the townhouse and at Analisa's Aspire, he climbed out of his car. He prayed she wouldn't leave while he wasn't surveilling her, but his body screamed for a break and a pee. His thighs and his right knee twinged, and he limped away from 234 towards Third Avenue, walking off the stiffness.

He'd already spotted a deli on the corner called the Food Emporium. He used their bathroom before buying more coffee – there was a link, he reflected wryly – along with a sandwich. Roast beef, onions, tomato, to which he added a hefty amount of hot sauce. The short walk loosened the muscles in his legs, but he felt an electric shock in his spine as he crawled back into the car. Cursing the old injury, he worked his left thumb in a circular motion near his kidneys. The pain sunk his mood even further. Here he waited on what should be his day off; a lonely, aging cop with a bad back and an alcohol problem and a kid who didn't talk to him.

It started to sleet, Mollie's windows steaming up with his breath, and he repeatedly rubbed off the condensation with his sleeve in order to keep his eyes on 234 and the Aspire. How long did a fucking Bar Mitzvah take? A while, he knew. His back had completely seized up when Analisa and the van driver reappeared at 1600. They putzed about for fifteen minutes, loading boxes and tables into the two vehicles. Alex let his bad habit win and chewed a suppurating hole in his forefinger. He'd resolved to control this, but like a stressed smoker, the compulsion overpowered him, and he couldn't do much about it. Then, to his unfathomable relief, she drove off. He wiped the blood off his hand, shoved his foot against the clutch, stalled because the Crown Vics were all automatics, and then shifted the Suzuki into second gear.

He had assumed she would drive uptown to pick up her kid, but she didn't. To his surprise, she drove downtown, and then on East 57th, she turned towards the West Side. He sat on her tail, hidden from her notice by the heavy Midtown traffic building towards the rush hour, crossing the breadth of the city to Eleventh, where they went south into Hell's Kitchen. Mollie's windshield wipers squeaked like tortured guinea pigs at each stroke smearing sleet across the glass. A few more city blocks edging past, jerkily stopping, starting, the intersections frequent, 50th, 49th, 48th, Alex, bored and surly and fed up with manually changing gears, counting the numbers as they inched downtown, the traffic thick, backing up from one block to the next, the tail lights of the cars distorting his vision so he had to squint. Amidst the red line of lights bespeckling Eleventh, Analisa's turn signal flashed orange.

Alex parked on the next block, between 44th and 45th, and he watched her exit the car and march into a nightclub called Roxy's. His heartrate spiked. The joint had been owned by the Italian Mafia, some cousin in the Luccheses, back when Alex worked at the Tenth, but that was a long time ago, and he remembered the FBI shutting the place down. It had been called Donatella's in the '80s. Hell's Kitchen had moved up in the world but there were these atavistic places around, memorials of the bad old days sitting shiva amongst trendy bars, restaurants competing for places in the Zagat guide, and unaffordable apartments. His mind shifted into overdrive. Why was she going into a Midtown club after her catering job? Selling drugs? Moonlighting as a stripper?

He contacted Central, urging them to check the club on all the databases: NITRO, for drug complaints; CARS for crime complaints, parole information, warrant cards, and career criminals; SAFEnet and WOLF for any other active or open cases or warrants in this location; and BETA for any firearms permits on the premises.

As he'd guessed, the place was under investigation for narcotics sales, money laundering, and racketeering. Its owner, Sonny Drogo, had kites against him, and Manhattan South Narcotics had eyes on the club. Some things never changed. The place was still a front. Then Alex waited, boredom quickly resuming, and he wriggled his hips and stretched his legs, trying to make himself comfortable. Traffic froze and unfroze with the light at the corner. Sleet splashed against the windshield. Sometimes, he forgot that he still needed to see, letting the condensation build up, a thin barrier of his own breath between himself and the world. The isolation of his day, the fact that his only conversations had been with a dispatcher, seemed more pronounced.

He turned up the police radio, listening for incidents happening here, in his old precinct. Someone called out to an assault. Half a dozen perps taken into custody in a successful 'buy and bust.' A cop on the scene of a suspected robbery. A couple sector cars sent to deal with a family of raccoons who had taken up residence in someone's storm gutter. A typical late afternoon in the city. Plenty of his own troubles lurked in this neighborhood. The brittle, shadow version of himself who had walked out on his wife and daughters for one, the old wounds bleeding into fresh ones.

Half an hour later, Analisa shot out of the club, striding swiftly to her car and peeling away from the curb as though she had just robbed the place. Whatever she had gone in there for, she wasn't happy about it.

Then they both had a lengthy drive to the Heights, where she collected her son from an after-school activity, and at last to 157th. That took more than an hour because a burst water main blocked off Lexington, diverting traffic everywhere else.

By 1800 hours, Alex had completed eight hours of overtime, and his body hated him for it. Two-Eight detectives would take over the surveillance duties tonight. He drove back to the office, and while he was far too tired to write a 'five, he did it anyway, because anyone reading the file ought to know about the club. Lastly, he called the Two-Eight squad and reported the suspect's movements. Keep alert, he advised. She was up to something.

Then he hobbled to the 137th Street subway station and painfully ascended the stairs. The turnstile spat back his Metrocard. Spewing a few choice words, he fed the bloodsucking ticket machine his credit card. The first machine he tried didn't work, but the second one did. Then he punched through the turnstiles. Standing hurt. Leaning against a pillar hurt. Lying face down might not hurt, but you wouldn't do that in a subway station. A 2 train screamed into the tunnel and then its brakes let out a wheezy sigh, and Alex squeezed onto a seat between a woman wearing a headscarf and brightly colored African robes, and a black guy wearing a pinstriped business suit.

Tilting his head back, he closed his eyes. The African lady disembarked at 125th. With the finely-honed craft of a native New Yorker, Alex pretended that the man who took the empty seat next to him wasn't having an earnest conversation with a live, wiggling earthworm he held in his palm. Life on the New York City subway was never boring.

Chapter Seventeen

November 15th

Alex chugged a straight expresso, jump-starting his heart. Eight hours of surveillance should supersede his insomnia, but last night, his seething brain had flicked through images like endless and grotesque TV commercials. Zoë Sheehan walking into the Blackthorn. Officer John Irvine's lifeless eyes, wide open on 123rd street. The rat-tatt-tat report of an assault rifle on 190th Street. It went on, grisly visions and cold fear and the throb of the pulse in his neck against the pillow, and he hadn't muted it nor fast-forwarded to sleep. He hadn't eaten much for breakfast, waking up without anything like an appetite.

Groggily, he reread the 'five he wrote last night. Dry cop-talk, so lost in passive voice that it circled back on itself. Usually his reports were more coherent.

He heard heels tapping across the floor, and then Gibson's head popped over his cubicle wall. "Whaddaya got from yesterday's tail of Analisa?" She hadn't read the 'five.

"A sore back," he answered wearily.

"Anything else?" she asked with a wry smile.

"Dropped her kid off at school, then went to work, a catering job on the Upper East. Before work, she met with someone who I think was her landlord. Central said the car was registered to a letting agent. After the catering job, she went to place that used to be a strip club in Hell's Kitchen that's got some connections with organized crime."

"Whoa. Some?"

"It's been under investigation for years. When I was in the Tenth, a bunch of Mob guys were indicted by the feds. Club was closed for a while, then re-opened with a new owner, supposedly as a legit business. I ran it through CARS, SAFEnet, and NITRO. It's not a legit business. There are active kites at the location."

Gibson touched her lower lip and considered possibilities. "Nice young upstanding mother. Why's she going to a Midtown strip club that's being investigated for drug complaints?"

"She's working there? Meeting someone there? Buying drugs? Looking to unload drugs or money? Fuck knows."

"One of the Two-Eight detectives is on it today. See what they find out."

"If I get the chance, I'll see what I can find out."

"What do you mean?"

He fiddled with his tie, pulling the knot away from his throat. "I had a CI who sometimes worked in that place when I was in the Tenth. If he's not dead or in prison or a federal witness protection program, he's probably still around there."

"Yeah, but you were in the Tenth in the early '80s," Ray commented. "Which I'm sure *feels* like last year to you. What are the chances the informant's still there after more than twenty years?"

"I'm still here, aren't I?" Alex grinned.

"But you're not there."

"He's probably done more crack though," interjected Wheeler.

"I doubt there's a street drug he *hasn't* done," Alex replied. The banter – his responses – felt forced and out of sync.

"You got the number for the local medium," said Wheeler.

"I really want a search warrant for her apartment and her car," Alex said, folding his arms over his stomach, the look on his lined face troubled. Their harassment chafed like salt rubbed in a wound. He must be sleep-deprived and worn down. Normally, he gave as good as he got.

"Going into a strip club ain't illegal," said Gibson. "But it ain't a book club."

He finished the last drops of his expresso and crunched the paper cup in his hand. "Don't know if it's still a strip club or a normal club, but my gut tells me she didn't go in there just to dance."

Gibson nodded considerately, her thumb and forefinger on her chin. "Could be. Guess we'll see if she goes back." She slapped the cubicle wall in a thoughtful way and vanished into her office.

Alex twirled his chair around and opened the Ferrin file to 'fives from the Two-Oh detectives, who had canvassed the apartment, and the ME's report, the lab results, the GSR test, a SAFIS report, and the tox scan.

Those documents had arrived during his two RDOs. Three days ago, Ray had gone to the DA's office in Brooklyn and taken statements from Ferrin's colleagues. Alex had interviewed Ferrin's rabbi at the Lincoln Center Synagogue, the rabbi, disconsolate, telling him Ferrin was much loved by the congregation, a stalwart member of the board, a longtime volunteer at the Hebrew school.

"Did he ever say he had problems with anyone?" Alex had asked.

"He put bad guys in prison," suggested the rabbi. "I'm sure he had problems with a lot of people."

"I mean, anyone closer to him than that."

"No, no."

Alex crossed his legs, brushing dust off his knee, considering the rabbi for a moment and thinking of confidentiality laws, how he could phrase his next question without running afoul of them. "If he had, uh, anything, any troubles, anything bothering him, would he tell you?"

"I would hope so," sighed the rabbi, puffing his cheeks out in a heavy exhalation.

"He has an ex-wife and a son in Westchester. Any problems there?" Alex probed. The ex-wife had been tearful, the twelve-year old son inconsolable, and they had told him that Ferrin was a good father, always paid child support, saw his son as often as he could. And while Alex was tempted to believe them, a detective lives in a world where everyone lies. He always has to doubt. But the ex had an airtight alibi.

"No, he had a good relationship with her," mused the rabbi, his gaze distant. "He saw his son every weekend."

"Did you know he had a gun?" The .22 had been registered to him.

"What? I didn't. But lots of people have guns."

"Was he unhappy or upset about anything?"

"No...What? You think... No, not Sean, he wasn't the suicidal type if that is what you're asking. Sean, he always said, God gave him a purpose. Why would he kill himself? That's meshugge."

Pouring over the file, Alex ran his fingers along his jaw, reflecting on the scene, the ME's assessment of the gunshot wound at the autopsy, his own gut feelings, and he thought, *who the fuck is the type*. A melancholy, lonely detective, perhaps. He was biting the nail of his left ring finger and jerked his hand away from his mouth, stung by the pain of biting too much.

256

The 'fives and witness statements Ray had filed following his visit to the KCDA's office stated that Ferrin worked harder than anyone, and his colleagues had nothing but praise. Like the rabbi, they too had been sure that some pissed off drug dealer had murdered him. Ferrin, a smart and tenacious prosecutor, had a knack for getting into the heart of cartels. *How* remained a mystery, as CCTV tapes from the lobby showed only residents in and out during the twenty-four hours before Ferrin's death. Theoretically, someone could have hidden in the building for three days. They hadn't yet worked through a weeks' worth of CCTV footage or, for that matter, contacted every resident of that building.

Anyway, Ferrin's colleagues had eagerly handed Ray a list of names, Ferrin's most insalubrious defendants. Ray had stapled the list to the 'fives and noted with color-coded highlighter that he'd already made a few calls discounting some of them as potential suspects because they had been incarcerated.

Alex scanned the list, trying to take it as seriously as his partner's careful color-coding denoted, but doubts chewed at his entrails. Whatever the ADAs in Brooklyn believed, he thought it unlikely that Ferrin had been killed by any of these people. No evidence supported it. No substantive evidence at any rate, although you could imagine a conspiracy embroiling the doorman and the security company who ran the CCTV cameras and whoever else you wanted. The CIA. Aliens. The Mafia. Realistically, if someone had busted into the apartment, with its doorman and more locks than Rikers Island, stolen Ferrin's gun (the slug probably came from the .22 – ballistics would confirm), and then put the muzzle against Ferrin's head, the investigation should uncover evidence of a struggle, of forced entry, and there hadn't been any.

With a husky exhalation, Alex picked up the ME's report. The toxicology scan was clean. No alcohol, no drugs. The guy was a clean-living soul. He exercised, shopped at Whole Foods, ate vegan, went to Temple, a fucking Upper West Side archetype.

Before Alex could read any further, his desk phone rang. He picked it up, saying tonelessly, "Manhattan North Homicide. This is Detective Boswell."

"Hi, Alex," said the voice on the other end of the line. "This is Elias Ortega. How are you?"

"Hey," he said. "I'm getting by. What's going on?"

"Just giving you an update on the case, really. It's not very exciting, unfortunately."

"No one's been in touch with me about it," Alex said.

"The name of the perp is Jimmy O'Sullivan. He's been arraigned, charged with assault two, menacing two, menacing a police officer, and criminal possession of a weapon. Gun is registered to his father and he, uh, borrowed it for the day. Had been going out with the vic for about a month. She said that he got really drunk and just went nuts. Anyways, I reckon he's gonna plea out. DA hasn't told me what he's gonna plead guilty to, though. Dunno, they may want to talk to you first. Oh, you managed to break a couple ribs and his collarbone when you took him out. You must have hit him with a hell of a lot of force."

"We went down pretty hard, "Alex said. "I threw all my weight into him, and I'm not light. How's Jess? I haven't seen her in the building."

"She's pretty traumatized. She's gone home to her family. They live in a nice suburb of Boston. If we need her to testify or whatever, she'll come down. Don't think she wants to."

"No," he sighed, tensing his belly muscles. "I'd imagine not."

"Perp sure won't be back. He didn't know you lived upstairs. Well, not you personally, but a cop."

"He out on bail?"

"No. Anyway, that's the update. If there's anything further, I'll let you know."

"Ten-four," said Alex, hanging up the phone, yawning in spite of the expresso hit. Something popped under his right shoulder blade as he stretched it, and he thought of Becky, and her massages that melted the knots in his back and shoulders.

Kneading his own shoulder, he resumed reading the Ferrin file.

Half a sentence later, Ray approached the desk. "Who was on the phone?"

"Sergeant Ortega at the Two-Four," Alex answered. "He's working on that domestic in my building."

"Ah, right," said Ray. "How's that going?"

"He's arraigned on like half a dozen counts. Probably gonna plea out."

"Hope that asshole pleas out to jail time." Then he asked, "Have you gotten a look at that ballistics report on Ferrin?" He scrunched his lips together and glanced down at the ADA's file spread across Alex's desk.

"What? No. We have a ballistics report?" The ballistics lab wasn't famous for its speed. You could wait weeks for a report. He thought they were still waiting.

"Yeah, got it this morning." Ray reached for the file, moving the 'fives and supplemental reports to the side, revealing a ballistics analysis.

Alex cast his eyes over it, but it was full of math and technical language about breech markings and striations.

Ray, who had already read it, explained, "Slug the ME pulled out of his head matches the Smith and Wesson we found at the scene. You know the gunshot was point blank. The GSR swabs also came back positive. You've seen that SAFIS report that says the only prints they found on that gun belong to him. And they found prints on the damned thing in the first place. How often does that ever happen?"

Not often. Guns are notoriously useless for lifting fingerprints – the uneven metallic surface and the fact that people tend to slide them in and out of holsters or their waistband smudges prints so they are unidentifiable. But sometimes – about five percent of the time, a fingerprint expert once told Alex – you find a print on a gun, usually on the trigger, the trigger guard, the slide, or the cartridge.

Picking off a scabby flap of skin from his thumb, Alex reread the SAFIS analysis. Ferrin's prints on the trigger, the cartridge, and another on the barrel, which was unusual. The gun had not been in a holster nor shoved down someone's pants. If you touched the barrel for whatever reason, and then jammed the gun into your holster, that print would be rubbed off.

"We can't find *any* evidence of anyone entering his apartment or even the building around the TOD," Ray added. "I checked everything for up to a week before. Nada. And the neighbors all check out."

"Fuck," Alex exhaled, surprised by his heart sinking into his belly. Had he not informed the ME at the autopsy that he thought the man did it himself? Had he not sensitively suggested it to the rabbi? He wasn't investigating the murder of an officer of the court or chasing every drug dealer in Brooklyn. They could close the file. He should be relieved. But he was strangely depressed and felt the coffee in his stomach fizzling upwards into acid reflux.

"When I talked to his co-workers, they said he was perfectly fine. Why would a perfectly fine man kill himself?" Ray looked off into space somewhere behind Alex's right shoulder, speaking more to himself.

"He'd kill himself if he wasn't perfectly fine."

You eat vegan, have a gym membership, commune with God on a daily basis, and you can't hold back the despair.

You go to work, act somewhat normal, and no one ever suspects a damn thing, not until you stick a gun in your mouth.

Then they all wonder how the hell they could have missed the obvious signs that you weren't perfectly fine.

Two days ago, James had bluntly told him he wasn't perfectly fine. He'd argued otherwise, but what about those dreadful, pouncing seizures of anxiety? What about the anguish laying siege to his brain on a daily basis? And he always had access to a firearm. In the throes of one of those dislocating convulsions, it wouldn't be that hard, would it? He sprang to his feet and hastened to the bathroom for a leak, and then he aggressively washed his hands and face, over and over, as if the water would cleanse his self-destructive soul. Like a mikvah, he thought drearily, but in the bathroom of an NYPD office, which didn't make it renewing or cleansing at all.

Chapter Eighteen

November 24th

Wind numbed his fingers, and the sleet pummeled his cheeks, stinging his eyes. Alex covered his face with his left forearm, and with his other hand, he clawed at the locks on the entryway of his building, and then he shoved his shoulder into the door, which stuck on its hinges for a moment before giving way under his weight.

He trudged up the curving concrete stairs to his apartment, his heavy footsteps echoing in the stairwell. Clumsily, he dropped the keys and then tried again with uncoordinated fingers until he freed the locks and the deadbolt. The apartment was freezing; he could almost see his breath inside. He took off his shoes, draped his socks over the radiator, and then he cranked up the thermostat.

The cold penetrated every bone, and he stripped off his soaking blue woolen dress uniform and sat on his bed in his boxers, relieved to be free of clothes. The uniform felt uncomfortably tight around his belly, a niggling reminder he had gained weight since he last wore it. Dammit.

Like most detectives, he only wore the uniform for NYPD funerals – in this instance, Officer John Irvine's. Despite the apocalyptic weather, hundreds of police officers had packed the vast nave of the Riverside Church, the neo-gothic inter-denominational cathedral towering over the block on Riverside Drive, between West 121st and 120th. They had formed ranks six or seven officers deep on the streets outside. Irvine had received the full pomp and circumstance of an inspector's funeral: the bagpipes, the bugles playing 'Taps' when a department flag was folded and given to his family, heartfelt speeches from top brass about service and sacrifice, and then speeches from Irvine's family, his colleagues and commander. The senior minister of the church had officiated the ceremony.

As the primary detectives, Alex and Ray had an obligation to show their faces, pay their respects. So, Alex had stood in the ranks, freezing his balls off, and five police helicopters buzzed the Morningside Heights rooftops in a lopsided triangle – 'missing man' formation – the bugles played, and six pall-bearers walked the casket through the sea of blue. Amidst the piercing bugle cries, vertigo seized him, his heart fluttering arrhythmically. Blood and rain darkened the street. But then he heard a deafening roar, the helicopters making a second pass. The arteries around his heart seized, and he turned deathly cold. Afterwards, he had gone straight home, while Ray met some guys from his academy class, and they had gone out for a drink. Ray had asked Alex to come along, but Alex didn't feel up for socializing with people he didn't know.

He flicked on the TV and channel surfed, searching for something light and mindless. On the TV, two detectives, a man and a woman, ambled along a street in Midtown, across the way from Madison Square Garden. No self-respecting policewoman Alex knew would wear a top quite *that* low while on the job. He changed the channel.

The next thing was a movie. A man and a woman cowering under a wrecked spaceship while an insect the size of a small Brooklyn apartment block screeched and waved its clawed forelimbs in their direction. The man crawled on his belly into the wreckage of his spaceship, found a rifle, and then blasted the insect to bits.

Alex pressed the button again, the TV jumping to the local Fox news channel, a reporter earnestly warning the city of a "snowpocalypse." Did everything have to be sensationalized, turned into the end of the world? Even the fucking weather?

Then the news flipped to an attractive female reporter standing in front of the picturesque Federal District Courthouse in Foley Square, talking about the Appeals Court decision to overturn the *LaValle* sentence.

The remote shook in his hand. For an instant, he saw himself in that courtroom testifying, and then he was in Central Park, or the Blackthorn, faced with the hurt in Sarah's eyes, or Zoë's. Chilled, like he had a touch of the 'flu, he watched the reporter and a legal eagle in the studio discuss the implications of this decision when it came to trying terrorists. The legal eagle reassured the worried reporter that terrorists could be executed if they were tried and found guilty in the Federal District Court. Alex thought the feds could damn well have them.

He changed the channel to ABC. They were talking about the Iraq war. There was Donald Rumsfeld's ugly mug at a press conference, announcing an increase in troops. Then footage of soldiers running through a dusty bombed-out building and a discussion in the studio about whether or not the Bush administration lied about Iraq having weapons of mass destruction.

It did an about-face, from the sandy Middle East desert to Times Square. A surreal disconnection. They were talking about the trendiest technological toys to buy for the holidays. You couldn't orient yourself to reality from the television, not even from the news. Especially not from the news. It was such a waste of fucking time.

He stood up and shuffled to the kitchen, the floor cold on his bare feet, and he rummaged around the freezer. The wind howled outside, rattling the roof slates. The external fire stairs groaned, as if they might come crashing to the ground at any second. Sleet lashed against the windows. It swarmed like millions of manic fireflies. A siren wailed. Just outside the building, he heard a car revving, someone struggling with tight parallel parking, the last space on the street. A couple voices carried to the window, a loud New Yorker conversation, though the words were indistinct.

He wasn't hungry. Everything in the freezer looked unidentifiable and unappetizing. The cold clung tenaciously to the nineteenth century building, the radiators failing to shake it. He rolled up a dish towel and shoved it against a drafty window in the kitchen, proclaiming (as he did every winter when the wind blew fiercely through the gaps) that he would fix it this time. When he made second grade six years ago, he'd promised himself that he would replace the windows with double-glazing now that his salary had increased, but he hadn't gotten around to that, either.

A knock rattled his door. His breath caught in his throat. His heart skipped. He looked with alarm towards the door. Who the hell would be knocking on his door? Warily, he approached the door and squinted with one eye through the peephole. It was one of the guys who lived downstairs. He breathed out through his thinned lips, sniffing, consciously relaxing his shoulders, and then he opened the door.

The neighbor stood sheepishly on the landing, his brows nervously drawn together, clutching a basket, white-knuckled.

"Hey, what's up?" Alex said.

"Sorry to disturb you, Detective, but—" the guy mumbled, his gaze sliding away from Alex's eye contact.

"It's all right. You can call me Alex," he said, smiling. "I'm not at work."

"Yeah, okay, Alex. Well, really, we just wanted to thank you for what you did for Jess. It was, like, a really bad situation."

Alex gave a half grimace, half smile, the warmth of his neighbor's awkward gratitude touching the cold loneliness in his viscera. "Yeah, it was pretty bad," he agreed, his voice soft and raspy.

"Don't know what would have happened if you hadn't been there. So… we got you this." He indicated the basket. "We'd thought about getting you a bottle of wine, but Sergeant Ortega said you'd prefer chocolate."

"Aw, thanks," Alex said, smiling more earnestly now and silently thanking Ortega for tactfully directing the neighbors towards chocolate instead of booze. "I was just doing my job."

The neighbor quickly nodded like a sparrow pecking and handed him the basket. "You probably saved her life."

"Is she relatively okay?" Alex asked.

"She's still home with her parents. Outside of Boston." He glanced down the stairwell. "We *told* her that jerk was bad news. Wish she'd listened, but I think she was into the fact that he was different than the usual nice, Jewish boys she said her Mom liked. She's got a restraining order, or whatever they call them here—"

"Order of protection," said Alex.

"Yeah, that. Ortega thinks there will be a plea bargain. Jess doesn't want a trial. Think he'll go to jail?"

"I hope so." The ADA should interview him, but an overworked prosecutor might shitcan the case with a quick non-custodial plea. They shouldn't because it involved a firearm, but he didn't have much faith. He would find out which ADA was riding this case and, if they didn't get in touch with him, contact them before they agreed to a deal.

"Me too. Anyway, good night. And, uh, thanks again." The neighbor backed into a nervous retreat.

Alone in his doorway, Alex folded his arms over his chest, listening to the clumping sound of Doc Martins fading down the stairwell. He shut

264

the door and, still barefoot, he realized, drifted into his living room, gripping the basket of chocolate. There was warmth in it, reminding him that he wasn't tied to the wheel of hopeless duty to the dead, but to the living as well. Like James had insinuated, there was something to be said for working cases where the vics were still alive.

With forlorn curiosity, he dug around the basket, hoping chocolate would awaken his appetite. He ate a truffle. His stomach felt cramped and quiet. He didn't feel good, like he was coming down with something. A leaden ache ran through his muscles. He prodded the lymph nodes in his throat, and he found them bulging under his fingers.

Fuck this, he didn't have time for being ill. Two open homicides, a handful of cold cases, court appearances for older cases, and whatever fresh mayhem he could catch at any moment. Glumly, he stretched his legs across the sofa. On the TV, people battled with the giant roaches. He skipped through more channels and lingered on one of those asinine cooking shows where minor celebrities he didn't recognize attempted to make pastry, and whoever made the least disastrous eclair or profiterole won.

His ears suddenly swiveled to the storm as a roaring gust of wind threw the sleet and snow into the window. It shook the whole building, foreboding and powerful. But he knew that this building had been here since 1800-something, surviving every storm for the last two hundred some-odd years. It would survive this one. What a miserable night. Maybe it was the weather getting him down. Without turning off the TV, he lay back down, head resting on his arm, shutting his eyes, breathing softly.

The buzzer screeched, loud and sudden, zapping his heart. He sat bolt upright, eyes narrowed on the hallway and the intercom. What maniac had ventured out in the storm? A hit of adrenaline fired through his nervous system. He jumped to his feet and padded lightfooted into the hallway, swearing as he struck his knee on the doorframe. Shaking, he touched the intercom button, demanding, "Hello?"

Cracking static, and then, "Hi, Alex. It's Becky—"

Becky, shit! The panic leapt inside him. He'd not heard a word from her since that abrupt phone call on 178th and Wadsworth. He didn't want to see her now that he had arrived at beleaguered forbearance. And now she was buzzing his damned door.

The demons of anger and hurt breathed their fire onto him. His blood felt hot, and his pulse galloped. Probable scenarios unfolded in his head: had she come to break it off "officially," as though ignoring him for two weeks wasn't a clear enough message? Had she come to apologize for behaving like the princess of passive-aggressive douchebaggery and tell him that it would be better next time? Beyond the pain, there was a sun-filled field, and they could both go there. If she said that, would he believe it? It was as likely as those soap actors baking a recognizable eclair.

The truth seemed inarguable in that moment: he couldn't do it anymore. Someone might be strong enough to withstand her precipitous implosions, but it wasn't him. He felt like a derelict building battered by the wrecking ball, smoke and masonry falling all around. And the blows kept coming.

"I was in the neighborhood," she said through the crackly intercom. "I thought I'd stop by. Wasn't sure if you'd be home."

"Where else would I be?" He spoke calmly, hiding the feeling that his insides were exploding.

"Dunno, work," she said.

He let her in. He couldn't help it.

When he met her at his apartment door, she stiffly embraced him. But there was little warmth or affection in it. "You been alright?" she asked, glancing about the apartment, her face taught and troubled as if it reminded her of something unpleasant. She lowered herself onto the arm of the sofa, clutching her purse with both hands.

"As good as ever," he lied, turning off the TV, and then joining her on the sofa. Deliberate, experimenting, he sat a couple feet away, twisting his pelvis around so his body half-turned towards her, and she stayed out of his space. "What brings you to this neighborhood?" he asked caustically.

"Shopping."

"Really?" He didn't conceal the sarcasm. One of biggest cities in the world, shops everywhere, the Village, Chelsea, Midtown, SoHo, East Side, never mind parts of the other four boroughs, yet the place she had to do her shopping in terrible weather was the fucking West 80s. He did not believe that for a minute.

"Yes. How's Sarah?" she asked.

"What? All right. As far as I know."

"You could phone her."

"Well," he shrugged, thinking she was the last person on the planet who should be spouting advice about sorting out his difficult relationship with his daughter.

"If you made the effort," she stated, "She might make some effort too. I mean, she needs to see that her Dad cares. It's what all kids want, even when they become adults."

"You think if things between me and Sarah were that straightforward to fix, I wouldn't have done it after all these years?" he blurted out. "And to be honest with you, Becky, I don't even know why you're trying to go there. You *know* it's a shitshow."

"I think you would happier if you and Sarah could fix things between you."

"Yeah, you think?" He shook his head in disgust. As if she'd not inflicted enough pain on him with her behavior alone, she had to attack one of those older, deeper wounds he carried. Letting his anger show, he stood up, hovering anxiously between the window and the sofa. "What the fuck *are* you doing here? You're incommunicado for two weeks, then you drop by on a whim to talk to me about Sarah? I mean, *what* the fuck? I am completely baffled."

She stared at her hands, flinching. He swiveled away, hands clasped over his belly, his face flushing. Emotional outburst wasn't like him.

"I know, I'm sorry, Alex. I didn't mean to bring up Sarah. I shouldn't have done that. I know it's not simple. I had been visiting my son at college, you see, but, well, never mind, I've just been thinking about a lot of things over the past few weeks."

He sucked in a convulsive breath. "A lot of things. Like what?"

"Like us," she wheezed.

"Well, it's obviously not working." There, he said it. The immutable barrier he had careened into when she'd phoned him on 178th and then when she'd buzzed his door had fallen. On the other side of it waited intractable solitude, an empty bed promising insomnia, solitary nights eating take-out in the apartment, and a hole in his heart he could pack with overtime. But the glorious highs and crashing lows of an unstable relationship – probably akin to smoking crack – would melt away.

"Yes." Tears glistened in her eyes. "I have been really awful to you. It's just, I didn't know how to say. I should have told you weeks ago, but I didn't want you to be upset."

"I'm upset now," he said, his usual dry, sardonic manner resuming. "Since that horse has bolted, you might as well shut the barn door."

"I think my husband and I are going to try again to make it work."

Three or four weeks ago, he might have felt like he'd been shot in the guts. Tonight, it didn't surprise him at all. He recalled one of Ray's 'separation does not equal divorce or available' lectures, which he had ignored, dismissing it as Ray flaunting his holier-than-thou Catholic values. That was one of Ray's least endearing habits, but in this instance, Ray had qualified his Catholic prudishness with more salient concerns that Alex should have taken on board: one of Ray's friends had gone out with Becky, and it had imploded when she ran back to the not-ex-husband.

He flopped onto the sofa, drawing his legs up underneath him.

Yet his rationalizations did not salve the pain, a surge of anger and hurt that he should never be content but always be bound to sorrow and loneliness. He wished he still had a bottle of whiskey in the apartment. And that if he did, he would have the sense to not drink most of it in one sitting, but that would make him the sort of person who could keep whiskey in his apartment, which he wasn't.

The fire stairs shrieked and groaned like a dying beast.

"What's that noise?" Becky whispered.

"The fire escape in the wind."

"Oh. Gosh, that's an awful noise. You're not worried about it falling down?"

"I'm not standing underneath it, am I?"

A hint of a grim smile, and then she shook her head, refusing to meet his eyes. "Well, I don't know what else to say. I'd been thinking about it for a while. You know what it's like, when you think, maybe it was the wrong decision that you'd separated."

"No. Divorcing my ex was one of the best decisions I ever made." He regretted what his behavior in the aftermath had done to his daughters, but he never regretted leaving her, because she was vindictive, petty, and awful to him, and she had brought out a part of himself he didn't like very much, either.

"What's that, Alex?" Becky exclaimed, her eyes drifting to the basket of chocolate on the floor.

"It's from the downstairs neighbors." He worked his palm into his forehead. "I helped them out a few weeks ago."

"You mean, it's not—" she began, jealousy infecting her voice.

Affronted, he glared at her, a renewed surge of anger broiling behind his brown eyes. "Jesus Christ. You're telling me you're getting back together with your ex, and you're gonna get pissed off about a thing that you *think* is from someone I've been fucking? Fuck, Becky, I'm not that lucky. If you gotta know, it's 'cause I broke up a domestic, right in the middle of my fucking stairwell."

"I know, I'm sorry. I'm just very confused right now."

"No fucking shit."

"I wish you wouldn't swear at me. I'm not one of your Homicide squad friends."

Unsympathetic, he lowered his lids, his eyes at half-mast, and he dug his fingers into the tight, sore back of his neck.

Becky contorted her body on the sofa arm, so he saw her back. "I had been talking to him, talking about what we could do better. I think there are a lot of things. Oh, Alex, I don't know why I'm telling you this, just trying to explain why, but what I've done to you, it's not really justifiable or fair, is it? I don't know, I just wish I'd handled it all better."

Through his eyelashes, he could see her outline huddled dejectedly on his couch. He kept his eyes half-closed. "No one handles these things well."

"It wasn't the way I planned."

You planned it like the city trying to plan a new building at Ground Zero, he thought, but swallowed the bitter, tasteless sarcasm. He shifted his legs, so his weight rested on the one that wasn't going numb. "You can plan out conversations in your head, but it never goes like you'd think."

"Yes."

"Look, I gotta get up early tomorrow. I'm on the eight-by-four. If you wanna talk more, you have my number." He doubted that she would, and he hoped she wouldn't.

Then he ushered her to the door, where she dithered, fidgeting with her purse. "I'm sorry. I've made a mess of it. A complete screw-up. Will you be okay? I'm sorry we have to leave it this way."

Resting his shoulder against the doorframe, he answered, "I'll live. I always have."

That wasn't reassuring, but then, his masterful art with understatement had always helped him survive. After she had gone into the wind and the dissolving snow and night, he locked the door behind her, the click of the deadbolts resounding with a pitiless finality.

Chapter Nineteen

November 24th

Aching for a human voice to fill the void Becky had left, he turned the TV back on, surfing to the channel with the giant insects, but he didn't pay much attention to it. He tried to arrange his thoughts, but they kept falling through his fingers, and he toyed with the idea of calling Ray, or James, but what would he say to them? Or Sarah, but he did not know where to begin a conversation with her. *Hi, honey, sorry I never call you. My life is still fucked up, but do you want to meet for lunch?*

He and Sarah could only get along in the middle of an international crisis, like 9/11. He remembered the relief on her tear-stained face in the MNHS office when she had been so afraid he'd been incinerated in the Towers, and whenever they allowed him a few hours off work, they had hunkered down together in his apartment, as if she'd known him like a true daughter, not the half-child, half-father that the terrible situation had made of them. Afterwards, he had hoped that they would find some renewed strength in their relationship. But when normal and mundane life picked itself up from the ashes of 9/11, their dysfunction came along with it.

He fell into a mental struggle to work out the time difference between New York and Sydney and, hoping it was not two am in the latter, dialed the international code for Australia and Elana's number. Ellie had never hated his guts nor held his past behavior against him. She'd supported him during rehab, and she'd never ducked his calls. During their last conversation, she had told him about a new computer program that let you talk to anyone in any country in the world for free, so long as they also had the program. He'd been astounded – he could remember when calling someone in Iowa was a big deal – but she insisted that in a few years, everyone would use it to make international calls. At the very least, it would mean that he had to get rid of his crusty old dial-up connection and install broadband in the apartment. Something else he had to do, keeping up with a world changing faster than he could imagine.

The phone rang and rang, before beeping through to voicemail, the voice of Ellie's husband, cheery and Australian, chirping, "G'day! You've reached Gary and Ellie. Leave us a message, and we'll get back to you soon!"

His heart contracted. "Hi, Ellie," he said to the machine, "It's me. Just seeing how you are but obviously you're not in. Phone, or email when you can. Dunno, maybe I'll get better internet here some day and can use that Skype thing you talked about. Alright, bye." It was spring there: the sun shining on white sand beaches, and people weren't depressed all the time, unlike fucking New York City.

The easiest thing would be to go straight to bed with the hope that tomorrow would be brighter. In daylight, nothing ever looked so grim and forsaken as it did on those winter nights when the cold, sleet, and the dark encroached on the city.

But insomnia teased him, a slow, cruel tormentor. The windows rattled incessantly, and the fire escape moaned. Thoughts swirled feverishly, scattered replays of conversations with Becky, of long past conversations with Sarah, of today's funeral, which fused into memories of Bill Ryan's funeral where thousands of cops had packed a Catholic church in the Rockaways. A heavy silence had prevailed. Never had Alex beheld such great, appalling stillness before. Alex and his MNHS colleagues had held one another, crying, overcome with loss and horror and immense grief. None of it felt real. It was a nightmare. They would snap open their eyes, and the World Trade Center would be standing, and Bill would be alive. He had plans to retire later in September. He was going to sail down the coast. But he had run into the World Trade Center.

Both today and in 2001, Alex had stood shoulder to shoulder with hundreds, maybe a thousand, fellow cops in a church, arches and marble columns rearing above his head and entwining in the vaulted ceiling of the cathedral, and golden light smoldering through the triptych of Christ's life, played out in vibrant hues of blues, reds, golds, and greens on the stained glass. Crushed by the crowd in starry dress blues, he listened to a priest reading from Revelations: *for the Lamb which is in the midst of the throne shall feed them and shall lead them unto living fountains of waters; and God shall wipe away all the tears from their eyes,* and between each word, a thousand images and memories came and went, driving through him, forcing passage through the bloody hollows in his chest. Then staid speeches from officials – were they Rudy Giuliani, or Michael Bloomberg, or the Chief of Detectives, or Jo Gibson? Was it Marty Vasquez, Bill's partner, weeping as he spoke and reaching his hands out as if in supplication to God but trapped in that great church, where neither ritual nor incantation could bring their friend back, nor could the speeches about justice and sacrifice answer their grief and fury.

Wind lashed against the windows, a burglar beating its way into the apartment.

Alex was petrified, trapped in his office, but it wasn't his office, and he was running from something, and he couldn't move, and someone pointed a rifle at him. His eyes flew open, and he was on his right side, breathing shallowly, his heartbeat heavy and fast, the memory of the nightmare melting from consciousness, leaving behind icy fear. The clock said 0300. He lay sweating, his lungs emptied of air, paralyzed. The vivid nightmares were back. They had plagued him on and off for years, turning sleep into a hellish acid trip. Like his singular time experimenting with LSD, he would wake up befogged and exhausted. Sleep wasn't restful or reinvigorating. It was spending a night watching horror movies, but you were a character in the damn movies.

He raised his eyes to the clock again. 0430. He curled up on his left side, starving for sleep. Two more hours would be better than nothing. After a short while, he felt himself relaxing, breathing evenly. A sudden shock, and he woke again in sheer terror but couldn't remember what had frightened him. Only adrenaline and his wildly pumping heart remained. The alarm now said 0600. For half an hour, he dozed, flitting uneasily between semi-conscious thought and the sounds of the city stirring, traffic, beeping delivery trucks, voices on the sidewalk.

Tendrils of daylight were reaching through the curtains, and he was trashed, his body aching like he hadn't slept at all. He staggered out of bed and took a shower. For ten or fifteen minutes, he breathed in the steam and stood with his eyes closed, imagining the scalding water washing away all the pain and hurt in the world. Bleary-eyed, he shaved stubble off the blue-tinged shadows furrowing across his cheeks.

Nor did he find his mood improved by the weather, the wind still driving, the snowflakes fat and wet. The city in a gale was a miserable prison of steel and concrete funneling the wind and snow into a fusillade burning your face and eyes. He ran into the shelter of the 86th Street subway and waited for an uptown 1 or 2, wrapping both arms tightly around his chest. He couldn't stop shivering, not even in the warm, muggy station.

Damp, cranky commuters packed into the 1 train. It smelled like urine, perfume, and cologne, fueling Alex's headache. He stood with his elbow hooked around a pole, his back and shoulders aching, feeling dizzy, his balance wavering. A lot of people cleared off at 125th Street, so he fell into the nearest plastic orange seat even though 137th was the next stop.

The four-block walk from 137th to the office got him soaked, freezing his bones and his internal organs. And even though he'd eaten hardly anything last night, he still had no appetite, which worried him. He had been a bit off food for a couple days now. Well, if he had a bug, he would get over it soon.

As he could not function without coffee, he brewed a pot, and then he flopped into his chair and listened to a plaintive voicemail from Tracy Kazparek, Peter's mother, who was upset that no one had been arrested or indicted yet. The DA wanted to indict someone but needed more evidence of criminal negligence. Which might not be this week, or ever. Alex dropped to his knees, unearthing boxes stuffed with paperwork for Kazparek, stored under his desk. There were more under Ray's desk, and a dozen in a closet.

He located the risk assessments for Peter, subpoenaed from the care home, and he scanned through them, taking notes. The risks Peter had been assessed for included harming himself by flinging his body or butting his head into walls, harming others by hitting or biting, hurting himself if allowed anywhere near sharp objects, hot stoves, or traffic, and he was labeled as 'at-risk' on the streets or using public transport on his own.

Not a word about his heart condition.

274

Alex licked his lips as he typed into a 'five, *Nothing in risk assessments concerning risk of cardiac arrest.* Had they been negligent in not assessing that as a risk?

Vacillating over his words, he looked down at the page, as if it might produce an answer. Had there not been some case a few years ago where the police had taken a perp into custody, and they dropped dead of a heart attack? Had those cops been held civilly liable? Criminally? Alex chewed on his thumbnail – he couldn't remember.

In the files for other care home residents, they had found only one other incident where the service user had been restrained and where there had been noticeable injuries after the incident in question. Marie Adams was working on a subpoena for that guy's medical records, but she did not seem positive that she would get it. Anyway, no one else had died, and the ME could not say if the heart condition constituted a significant enough risk, but a cardiologist might. He should find one.

Ray showed up late, which was unlike him, throwing his sopping coat over his chair. He brooded, "It's horrendous out there. Slow traffic on the BQE. You couldn't see a fucking thing through the spray, and the snow is sticking to the roads now. "

"It's wild," Alex agreed. "I think they've cancelled the Staten Island ferry."

"Is there coffee?" Ray asked pleadingly.

"Yeah, I made a pot."

He felt his guts frothing. The coffee was making him feel ill. But foregoing coffee would also make him feel ill, just in a different way. Eyes and lips crumpled with discomfort, he hunched over the computer, his attention roving from paperwork to the window. The spindly naked trees along Broadway bowed to the wind like broken old men, and the elevated subways crawled along slower than usual.

Ray reappeared holding a mug. "You all right? You've got those kind of raccoon eyes."

"Am I that easy to read?"

"You look tired."

"Becky came by last night."

"Oh." Ray sighed gravely. "I see."

"Breaking up with me." Alex rested his forehead in his hands. "As if I hadn't already figured it out."

"That sucks."

"Said she's getting back together with her ex." Alex could see Ray fighting the urge to tactlessly say, *I told you so.* "I guess you called it."

"I'm sorry, man," said Ray. "I know it sucks."

"Yeah."

"If there's anything I can do…"

Yes, get me really drunk. He banished that thought. "It's all right, Ray. I'm pretty much a veteran of dysfunctional relationships."

"Just would have been nice if things had changed for you, you know."

"It was good while it lasted. This thing's a piece of shit." The computer had frozen on the Kazparek 'five. Haplessly, he clicked at icons on the unresponsive screen and rattled a few keys, and then he turned it on and off, taking his time putzing with the power switch in order to evade Ray's anxious stare. Once the machine warmed up, he opened a template file to type up a new DD-5, the last DD-5, for the Ferrin case. Yeah, it would be fucking nice.

Whirring and humming, the document loaded, and then the empty 'five was staring barrenly at him, and he fought an onslaught of queasiness. He inflated his lungs to their capacity, and he typed:

Ballistics and forensics lab findings received on 11/25/04 report that the victim had GSR on his hands and body, and the bullet removed from DOA's head has striations and breech markings consistent with Smith and Wesson .22 registered to DOA (see ballistics report and NIBIN report for further details). Taken with the Medical Examiner's report that cause of death was gunshot wound to head at point-blank range, and analysis of the DOA's apartment by myself and Det. Espinosa alongside CSU technicians, this suggests that there is no evidence of any other individual entering his apartment at or around TOD, which corroborates statements we obtained from neighbors, the apartment doorman, and CCTV evidence. We have concluded manner of death to be suicide, and this investigation will be closed.

He glared at the DD-5. Simple. Cold. That was it; it would disappear forever amidst the thousands of closed case files stored somewhere in the bowels of 1PP. Writing those sparse lines had broken him, yet they seemed empty. A few forensic details and a boundless, desolate space that their investigation would never touch.

Ray asked, "Is that the 'five for the Ferrin case?"

276

"Yeah. It just seems too short."

Ray studied him for a second, scrunching up his features as if he didn't understand.

Alex didn't understand, either. He had written thousands of these. Too short? He'd written ones much more succinct than this. Police reports were meant to be dry and sparse.

Ray came around and read it over his shoulder. "It looks okay to me, Lex. Don't see what the trouble is."

Yes, that is exactly the trouble. He was flustered and upset about a routine piece of paperwork. But he smiled bleakly down at the keyboard and his nostrils flared, and he filed the 'five online with a flick of a button and printed another copy for the case file. Touching a key, a dialogue box telling him it was submitted, gone. Floating on some database deep inside the entrails of the NYPD's computer system. Worrying at the mouse, he squinted into his empty mug as though the coffee grounds dusting the bottom would offer him enlightenment.

"I just didn't sleep very well," he said to Ray.

"I can make another pot of coffee," offered Ray.

Alex moved the mug to the other side of the desk. "I feel like I've had a caffeine overdose at it is." When Ray disappeared behind the cubicle wall, he ingested an antacid.

Chapter Twenty

November 28th

Alex spent Thanksgiving covering the office with a detective called Angel Ramirez. He volunteered almost eagerly, because he had no family, nowhere to go, no one to see. His mother lived in Florida. In the great tradition of old New York Jews, she had migrated down there in 1992, two years after his father died. He rarely saw her, as he could not stand Florida and he could just about stand her, but he always told her that it was because he couldn't get the time off work. Awkward family relationships were intergenerational. Sarah was spending the holiday upstate with her mother. She always did.

Now and then, he had joined Ray and his family for their Thanksgiving dinner, but Ray and his wife were in the midst of some difficulties at the moment. Their eldest daughter, at thirteen, was beginning to question and challenge her strict Catholic upbringing. Alex empathized with the kid, but he would never tell Ray *that*. Rebellious teenagers aside, Anna didn't like her husband's hours, especially the four-by-twelve tours and the suddenness with which he had to work overtime; she liked the fact the job was inherently dangerous, dealing with murderers and murder investigations even less; and his pay as detective third grade, no better than a patrolman, even less than that.

Three years of this: the stress, the hours, and her with three children and no family nearby, as her family lived in San Diego and his lived in San Jose, Puerto Rico. Relationship drama amongst cops was big boat, a fucking aircraft carrier, but it had taken extraordinary effort on Alex's part to coax Ray into admitting he had a problem. Ray thought asking Alex for his opinion about marriage and relationships was like asking a corner drug slinger for advice about investments. Nor did it help anything that Anna was ill. Ray would not say with what: he was circumspect with the details, but Alex knew it from his partner's oblique

278

references to doctor's appointments and his increased reluctance to work overtime.

Ray's reticence stood out. Most homicide detectives had long abandoned any notions of privacy, their own or anyone else's. The job itself dispensed with any normative sense of its existence. Privacy and discretion lost their significance in a world where you watched the ME cutting open naked corpses and you faced the intimacy of their insides; where you examined a scenes where someone had died of autoerotic asphyxiation, their cock erect as a fencepost; or any investigation where you ripped into the bowels of someone's life, splaying open every secret vice and every disaster.

The Homicide squad was intimately aware of the misadventures of one another's lives, no gossip sneaking past unremarked on. They made jokes as one detective crashed his station wagon into the neighbor's fence, or a detective's wife threw him out of the house, or another detective was diagnosed with diabetes, or indeed, alcoholism. Thus, Ray's evasiveness about his personal life caught Alex off guard, but beyond a few half-assed questions, Alex didn't push his luck. He recognized that outside of MNHS, discretion and privacy had resonance. It did, however, reinforce Alex's feelings of not understanding his partner, and of his partner not understanding him.

A little after midday, Alex sent Ramirez home. The office was quiet and monotonous; no precinct detectives calling for their presence at a DOA, no city emergencies requiring homicide detectives. The younger man had family in Brooklyn. He seemed restless, although he wouldn't dare complain.

"Nothing's gonna happen," Alex reassured Ramirez. "If it does, I'll call you."

"You sure? You'll get shit for letting me off," Ramirez said, smiling curiously. "They already saying you losing it."

"'They' can go fuck themselves," Alex answered cuttingly. He couldn't give a shit about office bitching, and he didn't want to let himself fret over why his colleagues thought he was 'losing it.'

After Ramirez left, Alex spent a few hours making phone call rounds to local hospitals, the morgue, Central Booking, the Tombs, searching for Johnny Bailey. Those were the most likely places for him to turn up, and he hadn't turned up at any of them. They had a 'wanted' card out for him, which meant that if anyone arrested him, the computer would flag it, and the arresting officer would know to contact MNHS or Finnane at the Two-Eight squad.

Resting his cheek on his hand, he pressed his knuckles into his teeth and his cheekbones, staring at the city fading into a bluish-grey haze, the sleet and snow silvery sheets oscillating like waves in the backlighting of streetlamps and buildings. Then he called Vito Indelicata's cell, asking him if anyone in the Three-Four squad had any leads on Bailey's whereabouts. Indelicata joyously yelled, "No, I got nothin' for ya, pal." It sounded like he was with his large, chaotic Italian family, Alex hearing shouting and laughter in the background, underscoring how the quiet and lonely the office felt. He quickly got off the phone after establishing that Bailey remained very much in the wind.

Thinking of people in the wind, he phoned the homeless shelter on 135th and Lexington and several contacts in Vice, asking after Flavia Blanca, the missing eyewit who had allegedly ID'd Khalid's van, but she hadn't returned to the shelter, nor had she been collared. The Vice detective told him what he already knew: she was the sort of person to effortlessly disappear, new alias, selling her wares and buying drugs in a new borough, or a new city. Alex buried his face in his palms. Witness looked like a fucking write-off.

His cell phone burbled. His mother. He exposed his teeth in a painful grimace, tempted to let it ring out before he reminded himself that it was Thanksgiving, and he should answer. "Hi, Mom."

"You never answer when I call the apartment, Alex," she said in her typically accusatory way.

"I'm not at home."

"Don't tell me you're at work."

"I'm at work. Someone has to be."

"Why does it have to be you?"

"'Cause I said I'd do it," he answered, his temper fraying like someone taking a knife to the end of a rope.

"You worked Christmas last year," she said sadly.

"We're Jews," he shot back. "What do we care?"

"And Passover," she added. "Did you even celebrate it?"

"I ate some matzah."

"No seder." She sounded disappointed.

"No." He didn't know anyone who would invite him to one.

"And Yom Kippur," she sighed dramatically.

"I can't fast 'cause it makes my ulcers worse. Are you gonna go through the whole Jewish calendar?"

"Well, it would just be nice if you spent the holidays with your daughters, for a change. I mean, I know Ellie's in Sydney, but you could see Sarah. Brooklyn isn't very far away."

His stomach spun in a backflip. Dealing with her also made his ulcers worse. He almost hung up, and then he wanted to yell, *Yeah, it would be a fucking change!* God, she didn't waste time, punching his buttons, the mother of all guilt trips.

She must have heard his breathing get louder because she said, "Oh, honey, I'm sorry. I didn't mean to upset you. It's just, I think of you, all alone up there at your age—"

"For Christ's sake, Mom," he said, his tongue and his temper getting the better of him. "I'm a fucking adult, I can deal."

"Your language! And I'm not saying you can't. I just worry about you." In the shoot-out between her guilt trips and his acerbity, the guilt trips won.

The office phone rang.

"I'm sorry, Mom," he said. "I'm at work, and I have to get the phone. Happy Thanksgiving."

"My neighbor really likes *Law and Order*," she said as if she hadn't heard him. She never heard him. "The one that's named after a car. With the nice lady detective."

She was also losing her mind. "Named after a car?" Alex repeated, puzzled. The office phone screamed for his attention. He had his left thumbnail in his mouth.

"You must know it," his mother insisted. "SUV. I say, 'that's what my son does. He's a New York police detective.' Every time I watch it with her, I think of you, and how you almost never call."

"SVU. And it isn't what I do. I've never been a sex crimes detective," he heard himself correcting, even though he knew that getting into it with her was never wise. *Shut the fuck up, Alex,* he said to himself. The details of what he did at work had never mattered to her.

"You're always so defensive," she complained. "Why do you have to be so defensive?"

281

"I really have to go," he said. "I'll call later."

He heard her mumble something like 'Happy Thanksgiving' and then he snapped the cell phone shut while reaching for the office phone. He silently thanked the person on the other end of the phone for interrupting his conversation with his mother. It was someone wanting to talk to Greenwood about one of her cases. They didn't want to talk to him.

He hung up and laid his forehead on his forearms, eyes closed against his jacket sleeves, until the phone demanded his attention again. He barely got through the weary greeting, "Manhattan North Homicide, this is Detective Boswell."

The caller shouted at him, demanding answers for why someone called Detective Simpson wasn't doing enough on their case and why had the DA dropped it. The caller accused Detective Simpson of accepting bribes to dispose of evidence, and he threatened to complain to the Commissioner himself.

Alex didn't know any Detective Simpsons. He held the phone away from his ear, and when he finally slid in a word, he said placatingly, "There's no Detective Simpson in this office."

"What? This is Manhattan North Narcotics, isn't it?"

"No, it's Manhattan North Homicide."

The caller abruptly hung up.

The afternoon floated along, interrupted by a few more phone calls that didn't have anything to do with him. A fax machine started calling regularly, and he resisted the temptation to have conversations with the series of beeps on the other end of the line. He caught up on DD-5s, OLBS sheets, DARs, and CompStat forms that he'd been putting off, and he made a half-assed attempt to organize his paperwork and clean out his locker, which had accumulated old coffee cups, crumpled balls of paper, wrappers, a few soft drink bottles.

Towards the end of the day, he worked up the courage to phone Sarah. It was Thanksgiving. One of those things a father should do, even though he didn't really have the stomach for it. He dialed her cell and it rang, nearly ringing out, before he heard her say, "Hi, Dad. Happy Thanksgiving."

"Hi, sweetie," he said. "Happy Thanksgiving. How are you?"

"Oh, all right," she sighed, as if she wasn't.

"Is anything up?" he asked.

"No."

"Really?" He was a detective, and he couldn't stop himself.

"Are you going through one of your phases where you decide that you're broadly interested in what goes on in my life?" she said acidly.

What have I done wrong today, he thought miserably, reminded of why he had scruples about calling her. "I'm always interested. I'm just not interested in you being pissed off at me."

"Sorry," she snapped.

"If you don't wanna talk to me, that's fine." As soon as he said it, he regretted it, realizing that he was sounding like his mother with the guilt trips. No hardball like family hardball, this one being batted through the generations. No wonder Ellie had fled the country and lived ten thousand miles away from all of them.

"Sorry," Sarah said again. She took an audible breath. Her voice quivered. "I should have gone to Rick's today. His parents, you know, speak to one another and are normal, sane human beings."

Alex didn't know who Rick was. Her current boyfriend? He dared not ask, further evidence of his disinterest and radio silence. Covering, he quipped, "I can work on becoming saner, but normality might be a step too far," which wasn't much better.

"Yeah, right, Dad."

There was a pregnant pause. Then he said, "Before I forget to ask, can you call your grandmother some time? She would like to hear from you."

"Oh, God, speaking of crazy…"

"I know my Mom is difficult, Sarah," he said with a heavy sigh. "But she misses you."

"*You* hardly speak with her."

He rubbed the bridge of his nose. "I know. She drives me nuts, but I still make the effort. Sometimes."

"I will, I will," she said, slightly exasperated.

"So, it woulda been better at Rick's? You at your mother's?" he asked, desperate for a normal conversation.

"Mom and I have just had a big blow-out. Like usual."

"Sorry to hear that." He wasn't.

"Her current boyfriend…" A pause, as if listening for something, and then, "He's like a massive dick."

"Same as ever, right? She has a type."

"Dad..." she groaned. "You're not funny. Uh, can we talk later? Mom's upset in the other room. I have to go."

"All right. Love you."

Exhaling an audible, pained breath, he resumed burying his face in his forearms. Emotions swelled behind his eyes, and he sniffed a couple times, but then felt dampness on his cheeks. He rubbed his face against his sleeve. He was working through his holiday checklist. Argue with his mother. Argue with Sarah. He ought to call Ray and pick a fight with him, cover all his bases.

The office phone broke into his maudlin reflections. Sniffing again and clearing his nose with a tissue, he picked it up, prepared for it to be the fax machine. *Fuck you, you squealing, beeping motherfucker.* At least he had the sense to say, "Manhattan North Homicide, this is Detective Boswell," before he said what he was thinking, because to his astonishment, it wasn't the fax machine, and the caller was looking for him.

"Detective, my name is Officer Robbie Strachan from the Two-Six," he announced, sounding young, rigid and formal. "I made a drug collar near Riverside Park, and when I brought the perp into the station house, he looked at the 'wanted' pictures on the board and identified someone called Johnny Bailey, who I believe is wanted by you as a perpetrator in a homicide?"

A case can be broken on one phone call, one positive ID, one statement. It's good to be good, homicide detectives said, but better to be lucky. Before he got too excited, he reminded himself that the perp could be trying his hand, lying to Officer Strachan, hoping for a deal, but maybe not. "Did the perp say where he'd seen him?"

"He said he was dead, sir. Underneath where the West Side Highway goes above Riverside Park."

Alex's chest was hurting, like a blunt knife was sawing open his ribcage. He could not face being alone in the office any longer, his life unraveling. And he had a lead to follow. A break in his redball wouldn't solve his personal problems, but he would feel worth his gold shield. Scraping the lingering moisture off his cheeks with the back of his hand, he asked, "You think you can find the place?"

"What? I don't know. Maybe. I have some idea."

"You doing anything now? Let's go."

"Now?" The officer sounded confused.

"Yeah, now."

"It's dark, and it's blowing a gale, Detective. Shouldn't we do it with a CSU team?"

"Never mind that. I'll pick you up at the precinct."

The young cop uttered baffled noises, but he was not far out of the police academy, thoroughly trained in following orders from people of a higher rank. Yeah, the Patrol Guide and *Practical Homicide Investigation* suggested procedures, but fuck it. Why bring in more personnel on a holiday when the lead might be bogus? Alex could chase it himself. If Gibson wanted to issue him a command discipline for it, let her. His knees ached from sitting too long, and he limped to the empty wheel desk and signed out a Crown Vic with a half-assed note about following up a lead and the case number for Kitchener. Before leaving, he fired through his checklist. Keys. Wallet. Cell phone. Shield. Gun. Cuffs.

Bracing himself, he stepped out onto Broadway, the street a torrent of dark and wind. Horizontal sleet lashed against his face and scoured his eyes. He jogged around the back of the building to the car and scraped snow off the windshield, the wind freezing his fingers, and then he drove to the Two-Six Precinct on West 126th Street. Officer Strachan was cowering from the weather underneath the green lights at the front door. When Alex pulled up, the patrolman scurried to the car, stooped against the wind. He was probably the same age as Sarah, mid-twenties, taller than Alex, fair haired, blue eyed, wiry and strong, like he played basketball or rowed.

"Are you sure this is a good idea, Detective?" he asked tentatively.

"It might save time later," Alex replied, ducking the question. He wasn't sure it was a good idea. "Where are we going?"

"I collared my guy around West 122nd. That's his usual beat. If he saw anything, it'll be around there. Under the highway, he said. He'd gone there looking through some garbage for scrap, or for shelter, and he saw him."

Alex picked up 120th Street, crosstown towards Riverside Drive.

"Sucks to be working Thanksgiving," Strachan said, making idle, nervous small talk.

"Yeah," Alex said. "You got family in town?"

"Have a wife and a month-old baby, but my C/O said I had to cover today, so... You?"

"Not really," Alex lied, remembering his days as a young beat cop. Still married, his daughters babies, and when his C/O ordered him to work on a holiday, he should have been unhappy – even though it was a predictable part of the job – but he never was.

"My tour ends at eight. We'll have a late dinner. It's okay. I mean, my wife's family is in town, so it's not like she's alone with the baby."

He parked near Grant's Tomb, a squat, cylindrical structure of neoclassical columns in the middle of a square, a memorial to the casualties of the Civil War. On a clear day, it would be busy with people eating lunch on the steps, jogging, or rambling into the park. Now the war memorial was half-hidden in the sleet, the square desolate, the pinnacles of the churches, apartments, and university buildings amorphous silhouettes shrouded by sheets of snow. The wild and treacherous night battered them as they followed their flashlights through the park. Wind caught in the metal cables, the powerlines, the rails on the highway. Alex heard the cables whistling and groaning. The wind clawed violently at his chest and throat and hair, pelting his face with snow and sleet, numbing his pain and preoccupations, and as he stumbled through foliage and muddy paths, he felt more alive than he had for weeks.

They walked unsteadily on a boggy track down a hill, Strachan, who obviously knew these paths, leading him to a gap in a fence, used by the dealers, junkies, the homeless, and cops when arresting any of the above. Then they found themselves underneath the great ramparts holding up the highway like the buttresses of a cathedral, which Alex supposed it was, but one devoted to the internal combustion engine.

"Detective," said Strachan, waving at four homeless guys cowering under the shelter offered by the highway. A church enshrining the inequalities of the city as well. The men pathetically clutched garbage bags over their legs.

Alex flashed tin and asked if they'd seen any dead bodies around here. They looked at him as though he'd gone mad, which should have been telling. They hadn't seen anything.

"Under the highway?" Alex repeated to Strachan, who nodded forlornly. His hair poked out from underneath his hat in damp tufts. He didn't seem to be sharing the exhilarating feeling of being out in the raw elements, buffeted by something bigger, more powerful, than your own banal worries.

Alex turned downtown, sliding along a faint path underneath the black mass of the highway curving above his head. He was sinking up to his ankles in the muck. His feet ached as freezing mud and water filled his shoes. He aimed his flashlight into the tangible murk, revealing garbage bags, shopping carts, a burnt- out car, seats and engines and tires, rotting wood, enough bottles to fill half the liquor stores in the city, cans, wrappers, crack vials, crack pipes, syringes, condoms. A landfill collecting the city's vices and its social problems. But no bodies. The wind sent plastic bags spinning into space, where they vanished into the blackness of the storm.

Alex approached an embankment, the ground falling away, and he shone his flashlight down the hill, uncertain of the incline. It didn't look that bad. He took a couple shuffling steps onto the slope, and then his right foot slipped out from underneath him, his left following. He crashed onto his side, clawing desperately at the mud, trying to arrest his fall, but he had momentum, and the thin layer of snow covering the grass made a waterslide. A few dizzying seconds, and the fall broke when he landed abruptly in a stream at the bottom of the bank. A storm gutter, or a stream that had flooded from somewhere, carving a new path for itself. The freezing water sunk fangs into his skin as though his clothes weren't there. He lay where he'd fallen, listening to his own breathing, unsure of whether he was going to laugh or cry or both.

Above him, he heard Strachan calling frantically, "Detective! Detective Boswell! Are you all right?" The young cop's flashlight beam shone back and forth, bouncing off the highway ramparts like a manic spotlight.

He sat up and shouted, "Yeah, I'm okay!"

Before getting to his feet he assessed his general physical state. Nothing hurt. Well, nothing hurt that much. His left hip, where he'd landed when he first slipped, felt a little sore, and he noticed an ache in the left shoulder where he'd tweaked it, but neither constituted a medical emergency. Tentatively, he crawled out of the stream and stood, testing his legs. The hip was weight-bearing.

"Do you need me to come down?" called Strachan.

"No, I'll climb back up the hill." He patted his waist to make sure he still had his gun attached, and then he set off the way he had come down. The bank was slick and steep, he had the wrong shoes, and he slithered, slid, and scrabbled through the grassy mud and snow on all fours, sometimes losing his footing, slipping downwards on his knees, thinking he was going to fall right back to the bottom again. Out of breath, he scrambled to the crest of the hill, where Strachan grabbed him by the armpit and elbow, and with surprising strength, as if he was light, hauled him up the rest of the way, and he flopped onto flat ground with the grace of a fish pulled out of the water.

Panting, Alex sat in the mud, fighting to slow his breathing, and Strachan squatted beside him, concerned. Alex felt hot from the exertions, but he sensed his temperature plummeting fast. Everything he wore, down to his boxers, was sopping wet.

Strachan looked at him. "Detective, what are we doing here?"

He met Strachan's apprehensive gaze and considered the question for a moment – what were they doing here, out in this storm, sitting in the snow underneath the highway, or what were they doing here, as cops, as people, existing in a more general sense? Alex didn't have an answer for either.

"This is crazy, sir. We're not gonna find this guy's body tonight. He's been dead for a while, hasn't he? I don't think he's going anywhere. Not on a night like this."

"You're right," Alex said. "Let's get outta here." He shivered, the wind freezing his wet clothes so the cold seeped into his bones, his organs, and he didn't want to explain to Ray or Gibson or the others in the squad how he ended up in a hospital being treated for hypothermia.

Strachan helped him to his feet, and then he found their path, walking at a brisk pace back to the gap in the fence and onto the real paths, gravel firmly underfoot. Thank God the war memorial was vacant. Otherwise, people would wonder why Alex was covered in mud, like a bog monster that had crawled out of the Hudson. More likely, they would not care or notice, since this was New York, and you expected a certain amount of weirdness and inexplicability.

Once in the car, Alex turned up the heating to maximum, silently apologizing to the department for sullying the driver's seat with mud and water. Would he ever get the mud out of this suit? It would have to be

288

dry-cleaned. He drove Strachan back to his precinct, not saying much. Just a few words about Strachan's informant and one of those time-filling conversations you always have with young cops where you ask them how they envision their career trajectory. Joining a specialized unit? Taking a sergeant's exam? Detective Bureau?

"I'd like to make the Bureau," answered Strachan, glancing askance at Alex as though having second thoughts.

After leaving Strachan at the Two-Six, Alex remembered to check his cell phone and found three missed calls from Ray. He listened to Ray's voicemails, which started in intensity from, "You must be on the subway and not getting a signal," to a more strident, "Alex? Are you all right? Can you call me as soon as you can?" His wet clothes clung clammily to his skin, and his breathing shook, uneven and labored. But he called Ray.

"Is everything okay?" Ray asked.

"Yeah, fine," Alex said, clamping his jaw so his teeth wouldn't chatter. Fine being relative: he was soaking wet, numb with cold, upset, but he had some idea of where Bailey might be, and he hadn't broken any bones falling down a hill into a stream.

"You have plans for tonight?" Ray said.

"A shower." It might be the only way he could get warm again.

"I think you should come to mine. I'm sorry I didn't invite you earlier. Anna said I should have. I mean, as you know, things are, uh, difficult, but the girls were asking about you, and Anna would like to see you. So... You're off duty now, aren't you? Why don't you come over?"

His sodden shirt stuck to his ribs as he exhaled, his cold-infused brain forming a shaky image of Ray's little house in Astoria, turkey dinner, a brightly lit kitchen, Anna's homemade pumpkin pie, a fireplace, Ray's three daughters playing board games or rummy. Domesticity, a house with a family, where carpets were fitted, shoes had a proper place, and shirts did not clutter the bottom of cupboards. The life he had blown off two decades ago.

"I will," he answered. "But I'm going home first for a few minutes. I'm serious about that shower. I'm cold and wet and need to change my clothes – I fell in a stream."

"How the hell do you fall into a stream in the middle of New York City?"

He laughed, for the first time all day. "I'll tell you when I see you."

When he arrived at his apartment, he discovered that there were no spaces on West 87th so he parked illegally in a loading zone around the corner on Columbus and stuck the police pass on the dash. Another infraction that could land him with a command discipline, but he was shivering viciously now, and he didn't want to fuck around with parking. Anyway, he planned on holding onto the department car for the night. It was Thanksgiving: no one was going to miss it. He tore off his clothes and jumped into his much-needed shower, dousing himself with hot water. Yet he kept shivering, and he cranked up the shower to scalding. The cold had infiltrated his bones, and he felt an unassailable chill deep inside his guts. But finally, his core temperature crept upwards, and he threw on jeans and a fleece pullover, steeling himself to fight the weather again.

He drove towards the Natural History Museum, its towering columns and domed basilica formidable in the gloomy, pale light. He went around it, whizzing through a dark and deserted Central Park on 79th, then onto FDR and across the Queensboro Bridge.

Snow drove fiercely at the windshield in millions of tiny pixels, like static on the TV. If he didn't know these roads as well as he knew his own hands, he would not have known which way or how sharply they curved. The headlights captured a few road markings, and beyond that, he saw nothing but a barrage of snow and dark. The bridge floated above a black void.

Wind buffeted the Ford. He gripped the steering wheel, pushing back against the angry gusts. Only when he parked in front of Ray's house on 31st Avenue did he breathe easily. His knuckles had gone white and his hands and wrists hurt from holding the wheel in a death grip. He flexed his fingers, loosening them. He hated driving in bad weather.

Inside the semi-detached house, Ray's three daughters bounced into him, like a favorite uncle, and Anna kissed him on the cheek. He took off his shoes and jacket, and as soon as the family rushed into the living room, Ray held him back with a hand on his arm.

"What was that about? Falling in a stream? I assume it wasn't a metaphor. You usually don't speak in tongues."

"I got a lead on the Kitchener case," Alex explained.

"Oh, good. But a stream?"

290

"A patrolman from the Two-Six picked up the 'wanted' card. Told me had a collar who told him he'd seen Bailey in Riverside Park. DOA, allegedly. I went to look. And I slipped and fell in a stream."

Ray's eyes widened with incomprehension. "You went to a park looking for a DOA, by yourself, in this weather, after getting a tip from some shitbird, who probably just saw the composite on *America's Most Wanted* and wanted a deal?"

"Not by myself. I was with the patrolman."

"Jesus, Alex." Ray sighed and spread his fingers over his chin. His angular brows crunched together, and he visibly drew back, as if he'd caught sight of the sinister shadow that had driven his partner into that storm-battered park. "I'm assuming you didn't find him."

"No." Alex dropped the eye contact and studied a stinging scrape on his right hand where he'd torn skin off on that hill. "It was pretty damned dark and wet."

James Hurley would have snatched the double entendre bait, but Ray breathed out forcefully through his nostrils. "Well, yeah. What did you think it was gonna be?"

"Thought I might get lucky," he said. James would have had a field day. "We should go back. Fucking lead might be bullshit, but we gotta check it out."

"Sure. But in daylight, with the K9s."

"Yeah," he agreed, sounding tired.

"Okay. Let's go see everyone. Just don't forget to watch your language around the kids."

"Yeah," Alex repeated softly. Ray thought his kids would be corrupted if they heard the words that weren't permitted on primetime TV.

That evening, he showed the three girls how to win Monopoly, a strategy requiring making any concession, bribes, trades, promises, whatever, to acquire Boardwalk and Park Place, buy hotels on both, and that would clean out anyone unlucky enough to land on it. In the aftermath of avaricious capitalism triumphing yet again, he played Scrabble with Ray's eldest, thirteen-year old Tia, and he realized he was losing because she knew all the arcane two letter words that only existed in the Scrabble dictionary.

As they sat on the floor, the Scrabble board between them, they suddenly found themselves alone, the two younger girls off to play, Ray and Anna in the kitchen. Tia carefully placed the word *quite* on the board and said, "One of the girls at school got in trouble last week."

"Oh," Alex said, playing with a *J* between his thumb and forefinger, thwarted, because he had plans for that *E*.

"She was having sex in one of the equipment lockers of the gym."

He stopped thinking about Scrabble words and looked straight at her, his jaws mashed together. Instinctively, he asked, "How old is she?" The first question that leapt into his mind. Old enough to consent?

"Sixteen. Her boyfriend is too, but he doesn't go to the school."

"Oh," he said again, relaxing his jaw. He imagined the Catholic school having a view on students having sex, but if they were old enough to legally consent, the police department didn't.

Tia studied him, evaluating his reaction. "The nuns said she's going to hell," she finally stated. "Do you think she will?"

Alex chewed the flesh on the inside of his lip, discomfited. What should he say? Were they teaching sex ed at the Catholic school? Did these kids know it worked? Did Ray and Anna explain the whys and wherefores to their daughters? He would not put money on any of that. Still trapping his lip in his teeth, he stared at the board, testing letters. After he prodded *frenzy* into place over a double-word score, pleased he'd played a *Z,* he sucked in a tense breath. "Well, Tia, not everyone believes in hell."

"Do you?" Her gaze had something of Ray in it, when Ray glared at a suspect and wouldn't take any answer but the truth.

He glanced towards the kitchen. "No, I don't."

"Oh. What do you believe in?"

"I dunno." He thought about it. "Jews believe that you have to do good in this life… Just because it's the right thing to do. Not 'cause you'll get something for it after you're dead."

Tia considered this and placed tiles on the board. *Top.* Then she asked, "Why is sex bad?"

God, another question couldn't handle from his partner's thirteen-year old. But her parents and her school wouldn't tell her, not beyond the pronouncement, *don't do it!* She had an intense, uncompromising look on her face. He was an adult who she trusted, who she could confide in, and, as she began to perceive the world in more shades of grey than her school and her parents would like her to see, perhaps one who wouldn't

292

judge her. Because he should have been there for his own kids, because he hadn't been, because he'd been lost in his own head and in a bottle, he would answer her with the honesty she wanted. Cautiously, he said, "You can get sick from it, or pregnant. But it's not always bad. It can be a good thing. Between two people who love each other."

"How do you know?"

"You just have to be careful and safe. And wait 'till you're older and find the right person." *Or you can spend a lifetime having sex with the wrong people*, but that stray thought was far too adult for her.

Just then, Anna called from the kitchen, "Dinner's ready!"

A shadow of alarm crossed Tia's face. She hissed, "Don't tell Daddy I told you!"

Oh, fuck no, he thought. "I promise," he said, putting his hand on his heart. Then they went into the kitchen for dinner, Tia grinning conspiratorially at him.

Over dinner, the house brimmed with light and love, but Alex was a detective, and he could not help but notice the strain lurking below the surface between Ray and Anna. Anna was a little short tempered with the kids, the two older girls impatient with her. Ray kept looking at her, the way he looked at Alex sometimes when he had abiding concerns he couldn't express. At one point in the dinner conversation, Anna said, almost teasing, but more resentful: "You know I won't go to cop parties, Ray. They're not interested in talking to anyone who doesn't carry a gun," and Ray shaking his head with a pained expression and a wearied, "Honey."

While they demolished a pumpkin pie, something almost blew up between Anna and Tia, Tia announcing that she was leaving the table now, her mother sharply rebuking her, saying that it was rude, and Tia, in the sulky tone of all teenagers, spitting, "I don't care!" But she glanced at Alex, as if his presence mattered, and she stayed, sullen but cooperative. Alex wondered if Ray had an ulterior motive for inviting him tonight: his presence dissipated the family tension like an island between the shore and the breakers.

His shoulder hurt – he must have pulled something sliding down the hill, so he asked for painkillers. They directed him to the medicine cabinet, and when he opened the door, he spotted the Prozac alongside the ibuprofen. Anti-depressants. Yes, there was something, but he kept his mouth shut.

They finished the pumpkin pie, and Ray made gin and tonics for himself and Anna, and plain tonics for Alex and the girls. Alex eyed the gin. He could go to a liquor store on his way home tonight. They wouldn't know he was an alcoholic, and they would sell him anything. He quickly interdicted that thought and forged a smile, saying he needed a blast of fresh air to help him digest but in reality, he wanted it to clear his head. He slipped through the sliding glass door, out onto Ray's back deck, and the wind ripped at his clothes and hair, the snow stinging his cheeks, his eyes watering. The tops of the condos slanted in a weird, surrealistic perspective, but nothing seemed bizarre anymore in his distorted surroundings. He heard a noise and twisted his head over his shoulder. Tia had followed him, her only ally in what she must think of as an unfair world. They stood in silence facing the wind, watching snow piling on the windshields of parked cars and trees bending under the force of the gale.

Alex shut his eyes, feeling estranged, and he let the wind have him – let it hammer him with his grief over his failures to be a father to his own kids, his sorrow at his inability to forge a relationship with Sarah out of the wreckage, his regret that she had not been able to confide in him long ago, the way Tia thought she could now. He could trace the paths that led him to their cold war, every wrong turn, every impulsive, mad decision, but he could not gain any more wisdom.

Chapter Twenty-One

December 2nd

A flock of gulls flitted overhead, surfing the breeze, swooping into the grass and searching for tidbits. Snow had congealed into sooty patches around Riverside Park, and the ground underfoot squelched with mud and decayed leaves. The roar of cars on the West Side Highway shook the air, overpowering the hissing of wind through the skeletal trees and the squawking gulls. The park was virtually empty, except for the hardcore joggers, undaunted by the weather, and the police, searching for the body of Johnny Bailey. The joggers would have seen half a dozen RMPs, a van from the K9 unit, and an unmarked Crown Vic stacked near Grant's Tomb. Cops roamed the park, one of whom held a German shepherd, a cadaver dog, on a lead. They searched around trees, bushes, and they excavated the fly-tipped detritus under the concrete ramparts raising the highway over the park and the river.

No one but Ray and Strachan knew that Alex had conducted a preliminary search – of sorts – in the storm. Alex had concealed the evidence, cleaning the mud out of the car himself, on his knees with a brush and a bucket of soapy water. Then he had written a 'five and a DAR explaining that Officer Strachan had contacted him with a possible location for their suspect, and four days later, he organized a search with appropriate personnel.

Alex prodded at a pile of dead leaves and snow with his foot. Blood no longer circulated to his fingers. He could hardly move them. He folded his arms over his chest, shoving his hands into his armpits, searching for warmth. The park was lifeless and dreary, the effervescence it possessed in the wild storm utterly depleted, and he felt awful. His breakfast, a bagel and lox, was having a disagreement with his gut, and it cramped and gurgled. Off by himself searching through underbrush, he pressed his forearm against his belly, as if he could calm the squabbles inside.

"Detectives! Over here!" A uniform calling out. Alex heard the dog barking. The cop, his partner, and the German shepherd were on the top of a steep hill, underneath the ramparts.

He trotted up the hill, breathing hard and trembling. Jesus, was he that out of shape? He'd neglected his regular swims for the past month, but he didn't expect to lose fitness that fast. Then the stench of a decomposing body hit him, and he staggered, his stomach in upheaval, and he almost started retching. It reminded him of working DOAs with a hangover. He grappled with the nausea and doused his sleeve with his mini bottle of aftershave, and then he buried his face in his elbow, inhaling the pungent scent with shallow, gasping breaths.

Fortifying himself, he inched towards the body. The DOA was supine, buried under a pile of garbage bags and a hideously stained mattress with holes and broken springs. Cops were pulling the mattress and garbage bags aside while the dog circled its handler, wagging its tail. Alex opened his mouth to rebuke the officers for removing the fly tip, but his stomach spasmed again, and he felt acid scraping his throat. Fuck it – the integrity of the crime scene didn't matter anymore. He looked at the DOA. White, male, the skin lurid and pasty in death, his body swollen like a balloon, and two holes in his head, caked with long-dried blood. The limbs were twisted into gross, unnatural shapes, broken, like he had fallen from a great height.

"It's definitely Johnny Bailey," said Ray, unfazed, his gaze skimming between the body and a mugshot of Bailey.

"He's not gonna be testifying against anyone," said Alex in a gravelly voice, squatting down beside the body. Bailey had been there for some time, the decay rich and sickening. Ray was staring closely at him. If Alex looked as ill as he felt, he imagined that his face matched the color of the corpse, grey and white. But he had work to do. He breathed in another dose of aftershave and started his routine visual examination of the DOA. His pen quivered in his gloved hand.

He noted deep wounds on the torso and the limbs, the clothes chewed away, but he hazarded that those injuries had been inflicted *post mortem:* rats, crows, city foxes. On the forearms, a network of track marks snaked along the veins. He saw blackened wounds, where flesh had necrotized.

The man had been a hardcore dope fiend. Alex gingerly tugged at the remnants of the shirt, and the rancid stench kicked him in the gut. Oh, shit, he thought, wobbling. He would never hear the end of the teasing if he puked at a crime scene. A veteran homicide detective should have a steel stomach. Impervious to the aftershave, the fetid decay stuck to his nostrils, the back of his throat, and snuck into his digestive tract. He held his breath and made himself think about lividity. Purple-blue discoloration unfurled across the DOA's stomach and forearms. Bailey had died face-down, lying there for at least half an hour, before being dumped here.

"I guess that guy's informant gets a walk," Ray observed. "At least someone gets something out of this."

"Yeah, he'll be pleased. More time on the corners, more coke. And we got a fucking dump job." Unsteadily, Alex picked himself up, and his knees crunched.

"Well, at least we know where he is," said Ray.

CSU officers and Dr. Brown, the assistant ME, surrounded the body like seagulls on a dumpster. NYPD crime scene tape was swiftly erected, and it flapped loosely in the wind. Alex shuffled upwind from the smell, breathing in shallow gasps, and he vacantly watched CSU and the ME process the DOA. He knew that the scene itself wouldn't offer much – the only evidence would be on or in the body itself.

Maybe. Covering his ass, he spent half an hour digging through the bushes and shoving fly-tipped garbage aside, cautious of discarded needles and broken glass. As he nudged at half a burnt-out car, a fresh wave of nausea rippled through him. His legs buckled, and he sat on a tire, panting into his cupped hands, willing his breakfast to stay down.

"Ray, let's go," he groaned. "We're not gonna find anything. There's never anything at a dump spot where the DOA's been for weeks. We don't need to be here."

Puzzled, Ray squinted at him. "You don't wanna canvass this place? Homeless and junkies. Might have seen something."

"The precinct squad can deal." Alex bowed his head, pushing his thumb and forefinger into his temples.

"You feeling all right?"

"Not great, but I'll live if I can get inside. I'm feeling the cold." Yet his hands sweated. Pain in his gut quickened his pulse, and his heartbeat felt like a hammer in his chest. It had to be a virus. At this time of year, things were going around, and getting soaking wet the other night hadn't done his immune system much good.

"What's wrong?"

"My stomach's acting up."

"Another ulcer?"

"No, I don't think so. Doesn't feel like that, and it's in the wrong place." Ulcers hurt, but they didn't make him feel so sick. And the pain was always in the stomach, high in the abdomen, whereas this felt like a knife had lodged in his intestines. With a slight waver, he pitched to his feet, brushing dirt and twigs off his legs, and then picking a rough track through the bushes and debris to the body, where he told Brown and CSU that they were heading back to the office.

"I'll call you when we're going to cut him open," said Brown.

"Yeah." Alex dipped his head, sniffing the aftershave on his sleeve, and he trudged along a path towards the cars at the park entrance.

Ray, trailing after him, asked, "Well, what do you think it is?"

"It's probably just the 'flu or something I ate."

"Want me to drive?"

"Yeah." Alex handed him the car keys.

They wriggled free from the parking space and merged into the tumbling stream of traffic carrying them uptown to their office. Holding his cold hands against the blowers, Alex fixed his eyes on the window, the brick six and seven story buildings of Harlem with their spindly fire escapes. He was getting car sick with the stopping and starting traffic, bracing himself in queasy anticipation every time Ray touched the brakes. The buildings didn't rock as much as the car.

As if assembling his courage, Ray breathed deeply several times and said, "Sorry, Lex, sorry to ask you this... But you haven't been drinking, have you? I mean, with work being stressful at the minute, the thing with Becky..."

Alex shot him a swift, fierce glare. "No," he snapped, bridling at the suggestion.

"Well, it's just... You look..." Ray stumbled over his inability to find the right words and describe how his partner looked. He didn't find them. "I mean, going out, looking for that guy's body in a fucking storm—"

"I was stone cold sober, Ray. I was pissed off because I'd talked to Sarah and my Mom, which usually pisses me off, but I was sober. You saw me after. Did I look drunk?"

"No," Ray admitted quietly. "You were sharp as a tack. It's just that you usually don't do stupid things like that."

"Well." Alex didn't know how to respond, when he usually didn't do stupid things like that. "Sometimes, I do."

"Yeah."

"You believe me?" He said it almost plaintively, and he flicked his eyes towards his partner, wanting to be believed, not knowing how anything would work if Ray started doubting him. It would be another part of his life disassembling.

"I believe you, Lex. I'm just a little worried, you know. You don't seem right."

"I'm under the weather, but I think it's just a stomach bug. And I hate the fucking holidays."

"If you're not holding up, you'll tell me, right?"

Alex nodded, wondering how he would identify the line between 'holding up' and 'not holding up.'

"Promise?" Ray insisted.

"Yeah, I promise." Hell, he felt like he had the mother of all hangovers, lasting for days, but there was something else to it, a heavy presence next to him that he couldn't see, making infinite the distance between him and everything else: his partner, the grey felt interior of the Ford, Harlem, the case

Once they had parked around the back of the office, he cringed at his reflection in the rearview mirror; bruised shadows under his eyes, pale cheeks, sweat shining on his forehead. He thought he looked run-down, yes, hungover even. Tired and ill. Holding up? Not holding up?

In any case, Bailey's body would not improve the DA's day any more than it had theirs. They had all hoped that Bailey would testify against Kitchener. Or, if Bailey had been more of a thug than Kitchener, the latter would testify against him. It didn't matter anymore. But with any luck, the forensic evidence on Bailey's body would incriminate Kitchener in his murder. There would not be many other leads – almost never were with a dump job that had been decomposing for weeks. Two-Six and Two-Eight precinct detectives were canvassing the homeless who resided under the highway, but no one seriously believed that they would find a witness.

Alex curled up in his cubicle and counted his inhalations and exhalations, and then he called Simon. When the prosecutor picked up the phone with, "New York County DA's office, this is Simon McNally," he shuddered at a stagnating wave of nausea and the feeling of glutinous liquid rolling inside his skull.

"It's Alex," he croaked. "We found Bailey."

"Is he in custody?" asked McNally.

"He's dead, Simon," Alex pronounced tiredly.

There was a lengthy pause on the other end of the line while Simon digested that news. Then he said, "The *Huntley* hearing is on for tomorrow."

"Yeah, I know." *Huntley* hearings determined the admissibility, or not, of a pre-trial statement. McNally had warned them that if the judge suppressed Kitchener's statement, the defense would file a motion to dismiss based on insufficient evidence, and they would win it.

"I'm going to phone Chris Leonard now and accept the plea bargain," said Simon. "It's still on the table, but if the indictment is dismissed, we won't even get that. The case is just too damned circumstantial."

Putting his hand on his cheek, Alex said, "He's killed three people, one of them a cop."

"Three? I only know of two—"

"I just told you—"

"Don't tell me anymore," said Simon.

But most cases were circumstantial. They had convicted people on far shakier evidence. "How is it too circumstantial, Simon? He's on video getting outta the van. Van driver is found dead in a warehouse near where they left the vehicle. How is that fucking circumstantial?"

"Judge Maguire usually favors the defense," replied McNally. "And to be honest, the eyewitness testimony placing *that* van at the robbery scene sucks. The only person who actually saw it is the tire thief, who says he has a memory like an archive, but he's got less credibility than Newt Gingrich. He's got perjury convictions. Am I right to assume you haven't found that prostitute Detective Finnane interviewed, the one who ID'd the van?"

"No fucking sign of her. I think she was a figment of Duncan's imagination," Alex said testily.

"Right. And Kitchener had an accomplice, who you now say is dead, who could have killed the van driver—"

"Yeah, but if Kitchener helped him jack the van and rob the store, it's still murder two. Doesn't matter who pulled the fucking trigger." Alex didn't know why he was arguing the law with a lawyer when it was Monday morning quarterbacking anyway. The deal would be done.

"I know, Alex, but Judge Maguire doesn't think we have enough evidence to prove that Kitchener was on 123rd Street when the van was jacked and the store robbed, or that he shot Irvine, or that he was there whenever Khalid was killed. The accomplice could have killed Irvine and the driver on his own, or with another accomplice, who's still in the wind. Or someone else could have killed Khalid and they just borrowed or stole the van and drove it around. Seeing as the accomplice is dead, Kitchener can point to him and say he did it, and that's reasonable doubt. I could amend the complaint to accessory charges for the murder of Khalid, as we *can* prove that the defendant was riding in a vehicle that had been stolen and the driver found dead, but that still leaves us with ten-to-fifteen, same as the plea bargain, only with more hassle. As soon as I'm off the phone with you, I'm taking the plea."

Alex placed the phone on the receiver and jammed the crumpled folds of his shirt back into his trousers, and then cupped his chin on his hands. Prosecutorial poker, he thought, except the ADA was folding, accepting the plea bargain, conceding that the defense attorney had a better hand than he did. If they went to court tomorrow, the judge might suppress the statement, which meant the prosecution would lose everything, or he might not, but McNally had decided to not take that bet. Justice wasn't blind: she was a gambling addict.

Ray said, "What were you arguing with him about? What's happening?"

"He's accepting the plea bargain."

"He's what?" exclaimed Ray, aghast.

Alex felt the sticky sweat on his forehead. "What I said. Kitchener's getting ten-to-fifteen."

"That's crazy. He made a voluntary statement, with his lawyer in the room for Christ's sakes, and we can't use it!"

"McNally thinks the judge'll exclude it." The system effectuated absurdity out of truth, truth out of absurdity, and most of the time, you didn't know the difference.

Ray snarled, "Jesus. He's getting away with manslaughter for felony murder and killing a cop. What did McNally say when you told him Bailey was dead?"

"He said he didn't wanna talk about it."

"What does that mean?"

"How the hell am I supposed to know, Ray? I don't feel well. I'm gonna pop outside for a minute and see if the air helps."

The air outside was frigid and bitter. It had started snowing again. The wind battered the snowflakes together. Soon they were sticking to roads, cars, people, speckling everything in a fine, white dust. The fresh air didn't revive him, and he scampered into the men's room, throwing up. If he got rid of whatever was making him unwell, he should feel better. Coughing, sputtering, he rinsed his mouth out in the sinks. But he still felt sick, and the exquisite abdominal pains persisted.

Then he teetered back into the office and started writing a 'five reporting this morning's activities. He was having difficulty arranging words into sentences. The computer screen devoured his thoughts. After a while, he pushed out a stilted report, but he didn't type a case number into the box. Should it be the same case as the one McNally was about to plea out or a new one? Hesitantly, he opened a blank UF-61, a complaint form that started a fresh case, and then he phoned Simon. The phone rang through to the prosecutor's voicemail. Alex hung up without leaving a message, and while he knew a lot of other prosecutors, he didn't have the heart to chase one down over arcane legal questions.

Half-heartedly, he poked through the papers on his desk. He discovered a month-old Milky Way and two paper coffee cups he should have thrown out weeks ago. If his stomach hadn't been hell-bent on an uprising, he would have eaten the chocolate, but the thought alone made him feel even queasier. Right now, he didn't have a cause or manner of death for Bailey, and if the latter was homicide, he had no idea who did it. Well, he had a pretty good idea, but no evidence. His heart pumped sludge into his brain, and his head spun.

Sluggishly, he wrote a new case number and completed the '61. The office air was stale, smelling sickeningly of cologne and take-out. He needed another dose of fresh air.

As he rose to feet and put his coat on, Ray spun his chair sideways, facing him. "You look like shit. You don't think you ought to call it a day and go home?"

"I'll be all right," Alex answered. He didn't confess that he had already puked and wavered on the cusp of doing it again.

Out on Broadway, he almost collided with Irvine's partner, PO Simmonds, who had been on his way into the MNHS office just as Alex was on his way out. Simmonds' dark cheeks looked gaunt and frail. He clutched his blue hat to his chest in a white-knuckled death grip. Reddened blood vessels burst out of his eyes. Christ, Alex had not even thought about him, so engrossed had he been in his own troubles. Simmonds must know about the plea bargain. With a cop-killing, all NYPD ears would be tuned to the case, and if a cop working in 100 Centre Street or passing through the DA's office or moving a perp through Rikers or the Tombs picked up anything, word of it would fire through the wire like a missile of bad news.

"What happened?" Simmonds' voice broke. "I heard that the DA pled out John's killer. Ten years? Is that justice?"

"I'm sorry." Alex sucked at the air like he couldn't get enough of it. Nonetheless, he noticed that Simmonds wore a uniform, which hung on his body like a rumpled collection of blue sacks. Hadn't they worked in a plainclothes unit? The man must have transferred out of AntiCrime.

"Why did the DA agree to only ten years?" demanded Simmonds.

"There wasn't enough evidence for it to go to trial," said Alex despairingly. Like every time the DA agreed to an absurd plea bargain.

"But he confessed."

"It was probably gonna be excluded."

"Why?"

Alex seethed with self-recrimination. His lips were white and trembling. It had been late, they had been flagging, bone-tired, and they should have read the perp *Miranda*. "These things happen," he said regretfully, in a low, melancholy voice.

"There's gotta be more evidence."

"All very circumstantial," sighed Alex frankly.

303

"The law is so *stupid!* A criminal can confess to two murders and get off with ten years."

"Yes, sometimes."

"How can you just accept this?"

Alex wrapped both arms around his chest, clasping his elbows, and he said with martyred confidence, "What choice do I have? It's the DA who decides on charges."

Simmonds stepped forward impulsively to remonstrate. "You'd just think..." he squeaked out. "That there is something more that could be done."

"Yeah, I wish there was. But sometimes there isn't. Sometimes it's shit. The law, the evidence... And you can't do a fucking thing about it. No one is Sherlock Holmes."

Sweat drizzled down his ribcage, sorely tickling his scars and making him cold. He breathed in, and an uncontrollable swell of nausea winged through him. Oh, not here, he thought, panicked. He muttered an unintelligible, halfhearted excuse to Simmonds about needing to run and do something important. Poor Simmonds! Probably thinking he didn't care at all. Then he rushed into the building, jogging up the stairs and diving into the nearest bathroom, where he collapsed on his knees over a toilet, vomiting until there was nothing more he could bring up. Acid scalded his throat, and he wrapped himself into a ball on the hard tiles.

Between the stress, work, a cop-killing, and Becky, it came as no wonder that his immune system had failed, and he'd come down with a bug. Swearing copiously, he staggered to the sinks, scrubbing his face until a white soapy foam obscured his cheeks and forehead, and then he rinsed and timidly drank some water, clearing the sour taste of acid and puke from his mouth. He wanted to lie down.

But he hobbled listlessly out to the street and stood in the snow on Broadway. Simmonds had gone. Alex brushed snow out of his eyes. He felt feverish, and his whole body hurt like he had a thousand tiny needles perforating his joints and muscles. A few hours ago, he'd been bone-chillingly cold, the kind of cold that makes you wonder if you'll ever experience warmth again. Now he felt like he was wearing a wool coat in the middle of August, and he couldn't steady his breathing.

Chapter Twenty-Two

December 9th

"If the anyone finds my body, cause of death will be drowning in paperwork," stated Ray from where his head poked out from behind a four-foot stack of cardboard boxes. Marie Adams had subpoenaed more records from the Elm Tree Care Home, its corporate overlords, and the Administration for Children's Services. Additionally, she had subpoenaed the financials. Now they had the cardboard Berlin wall in the office.

Alex unfocusedly lifted his eyes from his own fortress of boxes. Since the care home and its parent company had no choice but to comply with the subpoenas, their lawyers had swamped law enforcement in documents. Stalling tactics. Somewhere in this mess, they might find incriminating evidence. They might not. He needed a team of investigators and people who understood finances better than he did. Why was Marie so damned determine to pursue criminal charges? Why not let Peter's parents hammer the care home with lawsuits? Their burden of proof was lower. He scrunched his fist into his eye sockets. Did the prosecutor have an ax to grind? Did she have a disabled friend or relative and she'd made this case personal? Did she think winning a tough case would boost her career?

Whatever her reasons, Alex was bored to tears but a little relieved to have a task that didn't demand moving. It had been a week since they'd discovered Bailey in the park and he'd gotten sick, and he hoped by now the 'flu-like symptoms would have gone, but they persevered, fickle and erratic. A day or two after finding Bailey, he hadn't felt nauseous at all. Then he couldn't eat a damned thing the day after that. Two days ago, he'd felt like his energy levels were rising, but today, he woke up feeling like he'd been beaten up and the nausea had resurfaced. He'd never been a hypochondriac, but both his parents had been terribly neurotic about their health, and it had crept into his synapsis after all. He had spent his life trying to not be his parents and assume every ache, pain, belch, cough, flush, sneeze, bellyache, and twinge signaled his impending demise. Arguably, he'd tipped too far the other way. That was what the doctors who treated his ulcers thought, and so did Ray, for that matter. But he didn't want to live like his father, either, phoning his doctor every week.

Thank God his father died before the digital age. It would have turned him into a nervous wreck. Letting paranoia win, Alex had Googled his symptoms, and the internet, unsurprisingly, produced a terrifying catalogue of maladies. It warned him that every cell in his body was a potential double agent, capable of double-crossing him or conspiring with other cells to kill him. Add some comorbidities, like his father's heart disease and his own alcoholism, and he was astounded that he'd made it as far as age forty-seven without keeling over. And he still didn't know why he felt ill.

The office phone busted into his saturnine meanderings. Shaking those thoughts out of his head like a wet dog, he shoved it under his jaw.

"Have you received the files?" Marie asked.

"Yeah," he replied. "We could build a new World Trade Center with the boxes we got. This is gonna take fucking years to get through. You got any interns you can spare?"

"Have you started going through them? Can you tell me anything?"

"Yeah, we have. But we got bupkes."

"Can you make photocopies of what you've looked at thus far and come down here for a meeting this afternoon? I can look into getting our DIs on it if need be."

Alex didn't want to do either of those things, but he agreed and tiredly dropped the phone on the receiver. Then he repeated the conversation to Ray.

"Do we have the copy budget for that?" Ray asked acerbically.

Picking up the heavy box triggered lightheadedness, the squad room slanting sickeningly sideways. Alex almost squawked out a distressed, "Fuck," but bit his tongue. Reeling, he rested the box on an office chair, recovering his balance, and then he weakly lugged it to the copier. The detectives fed it documents, and it spat out more documents, and they collated those, double checked that every document matched their property log, because Marie would lose her mind if it didn't, and tossed them into another box. They heaved the box into the trunk of a Crown Vic.

"Wanna grab lunch on the way?" Ray asked as he started the car. "How about that deli on 73rd and Amsterdam?"

"Yeah, sure," said Alex in a soft, reluctant tone. He wasn't hungry, but he couldn't turn down an offer to stop at that deli, one of the best on the Upper West.

They merged into a stream of taxis on Amsterdam. Anxiety iced up his veins. It overlayed the Upper West Side, the architectural confusion, the meeting of pinnacles, terracotta, balustrades, and pointed gables of old buildings with the smooth facades, glass and steel, of new ones. His neighborhood didn't feel safe anymore. He couldn't recognize it. People outside the car looked busy, laughing, disappearing into bars and cafés like nothing was wrong, but everything was wrong.

His pulse spurted forward whenever a car buzzed their front bumper or nipped past alongside. He imagined the other cars smashing into the Crown Vic, his willpower alone holding them back. By the time Ray parked near the deli, Alex's breathing was rapid and light, his heart bounding in his ears. He told himself to stop being so stupid. God, if anyone knew that the worst thing could happen at any time, a New York City homicide detective did. Thinking, like a deluded gambler, that you could control those odds was a surefire road to a locked ward at Kirby.

"You want anything?" asked Ray. "Or is your stomach still bothering you?"

"It's not great," he admitted, resting his hand over his belly. "I'd better not push it. Maybe try a smoothie or something."

Ray cast him a worried look and then clambered out of the car. As soon as Ray had safely disappeared through the glass door, Alex hid his face in the dashboard, and tears welled behind his eyes. He was so tired of feeling this way, and he couldn't beat it. He wept for the thing he had lost – his health, his sanity, his cynicism that once kept the voluminous blackness in his head from dissolving him at the center. It had tried taking him after the shooting, and then again when he quit the drink. This time, he had no strength to resist it. He couldn't prevent tears from streaming out of his eyes. Each day, he woke up, hoping that he would feel like himself again, like when you finally get over a cold. But it had infected his brain and metastasized like a cancer.

Maybe he ought to see someone at EIU, the euphemistically named Early Intervention Unit, the NYPD's internal mental health peer advisors, but the thought curdled in his belly. If they diagnosed him with depression, he would be stuck with that for the rest of his life, and everyone knew stories of cops who had been flipped back in the bag, put on some kind of rubber gun duty or modified assignment. He was already stuck with alcoholism, which everyone knew about, and he doubted that he would ever make first grade. Too unstable to join the elite of the elite. Whatever afflicted him, he would have to go it alone.

Reassembling himself, he blinked away the tears and scrubbed his variegated face before Ray returned. A New York City cop shouldn't be crying alone in a car. He was harder than that. He had to be harder than that. Inexplicably, his mind free-wheeled to the people who had been in the World Trade Center above the floors where the planes hit, the ones who jumped out. The cops who responded in that first hour had seen people falling out of those top floors, and that should have told them how bad things were inside. It should have told Bill Ryan that, but he went in anyway.

With the smoke and flames filling their offices, did those people try the stairwells? Or did they gain some power of foresight, the clear-eyed certainty that they would never make it out, and to those on the ground, made what looked like an insane decision? He wondered if he would have had the chutzpah to throw himself out of the 110th floor of the World Trade Center. Then he blew his nose on some Kleenex from his pocket and steadied his breathing, because Ray had emerged from the deli.

He slowly nursed the smoothie. It didn't make his gut feel much worse, a small consolation. He avoided eye contact with his partner, afraid that Ray would notice the incarnadine glaze of tears over his eyes. Distractedly, he sucked on the smoothie and ran his mind through the facts of the Kazparek case and the documents he'd read an hour ago. Those documents had no evidential value. He could barely remember them, and everything seemed tawdry and grotesque. But if he thought about how sick and impotent he felt, or about people in the top floors of the World Trade Center, he might weep again. And Goddammit, he would not do that in front of colleagues.

At the DA's office, they had to wait, as Marie was in court. But they did not wait in peace or for very long. Simon, striding through the corridor, spotted them and sharply changed direction, making a beeline.

"Alex, Ray, it's good you're here. Meeting Marie? I was going to phone you. Just letting you know, I've submitted an affidavit for the Kitchener case—"

"What is it now?" asked Ray sourly.

Ballistics had matched the two slugs in Bailey's head to the Smith and Wesson from Kitchener's backpack, their first break in the case. Just like that, it transformed from a hopeless whodunit into a grounder. The ME said the cause of death was a gunshot wound to the head, and he believed the broken bones to be *post mortem* injuries. Bearing this in mind, Alex envisioned Kitchener shooting Bailey somewhere in the Heights and then panicking at the scheme going awry. He moved the body in Analisa's car and dumped him over the side of the highway. Afterwards, he'd found some trash bags – easy enough as they're always piled somewhere on the street – and the abandoned mattress, and he flung them over guardrails, a hasty attempt to conceal the body.

It might be possible to get a search warrant for that fucking Ford Aspire, although the chances of forensic evidence being in it after all this time were laughable.

Alex and Ray had offered their story to the grand jury. One juror asked how the robbers got from the van, abandoned in Hell's Kitchen, to the Heights, and the detectives proposed the subway, but grudgingly admitted that they hadn't found any actual evidence of that. The juror asked, "Why not? Is there not CCTV in all the subway stations?" Alex explained how the surveillance systems in the subway weren't *that* good; they didn't show the faces of every person who went into the stations nor every inch of the platforms, and a lot of the cameras didn't work. His testimony seemed to satiate the jury, because they indicted Kitchener for second-degree murder.

"Fifth Amendment. Double jeopardy," said Simon.

"What?" said Alex, puzzled.

"It's bullshit. Leonard says we should have joined it to the other murders because they're part of the same criminal transaction, and that

I committed a *Brady* violation by not telling him that you had found the body when I agreed to the plea. It's not even exculpatory! I can't believe he's got a judge to give him a hearing on this shit." The prosecutor sighed, his lower lip jutting out in displeasure. "I don't see how killing a friend on the West Side Highway bears *any* relation whatsoever to robbing a bodega, and the two killings which took place in furtherance of that offense. Different crime. Different elements. The case law is all on point. Well, enough of it is. But we still have to go through with this crap."

Alex raised a bemused eyebrow, but his street-level understanding of double jeopardy synced with Simon's more erudite one.

Ray had a different view and lacked the wisdom to keep it to himself. "It could be part of the same transaction... he killed Bailey the *same day*. We're not prosecuting the murders of Khalid and Irvine as two separate cases, are we? And he took all the proceeds of the robbery."

"In the afternoon," Simon replied. "In a different part of the city. When he wasn't robbing a bodega. Look, if those three victims had been shot in the same place, at the same time, Leonard might have a case. But this is bullshit."

"Will we have to testify?" Alex felt his stomach heaving upwards. He was perspiring heavily under his suit again, his temperature rising.

"Probably, if there's a hearing. Also, the thing I needed to call you about... Eisenmann is having a meeting about the al-Farasi case on Wednesday. He wants you – as the primary MNHS detectives – to be there. The defendants have appealed, and there are some issues my boss and the Appellate ADA want you guys to address."

Christ, another unexploded landmine. Eisenmann, *the* District Attorney for New York County, only involved himself in day-to-day prosecutions when things had potential to combust like a nuclear reactor in meltdown and tarnish his reputation and, more critically, his electoral chances.

"Oh, no, really?" Ray said.

Simultaneously, Alex snapped in an uncharacteristically bad-tempered way, "It's meant to be an RDO. What the fuck does Eisenmann want peons like us for?" A case from two years ago, an explosive redball where everything had gone wrong. It seemed like extraordinarily bad luck that the court was hearing an appeal this week. Even as he wallowed under his current caseload, old ones had to reappear.

"What's the issue with the appeal?" Ray asked flatly.

"Something to do with how you took the accomplice's statement. I have a meeting with the ADA doing the appeal tomorrow, so I'll know more then."

Alex stared at his shoes. "We did it by the fucking book," he said almost inaudibly, tightening the pressure of his arms against his stomach.

"I'm know you did," Simon answered. "But they have the right to appeal and allege whatever bullshit they think they can. My boss wants all our butts covered. He wants to go over some things with you. If it goes back for retrial, God forbid, it will be a media circus. Again."

"Can't believe it," Ray muttered.

"I can." Alex tried to put cynicism back into his voice.

"I'll see you Wednesday," said Simon. "Might be worth having a look at the murder book for that case." With that, he turned and strode in his sauntering gait along the corridor.

Alex sighed, shutting his eyes and slouching against the wall, keeping a tight grip on the pain setting fire to his insides, like arsonists torching one organ at a time. The legal system was unraveling his work. Quite frankly, it often did.

"That double jeopardy thing could bite us in the ass," Ray commented.

"But you gotta agree, the *Brady* stuff is stupid," Alex had no heart for an argument over legal absurdities.

"Yeah, that's true. It's not exculpatory."

"That other case. Jesus." He concentrated on the dappled blackness behind his quivering eyelids. "We *didn't* fuck up taking that guy's statement. We knew we couldn't."

"No, we read him his rights straight off the bat and videoed it."

Marie finally appeared, haggard and disheveled after several hours of hearings. She kvetched about how she wished she that had never left criminal defense, the primary advantage of it being a smaller caseload and more money, and then she said, "You got the records?"

"Yeah, and everything else," Alex complained. "They sent us hundreds of boxes of crap. We'll be working this case for the rest of our lives."

The only personal touches she had in her office, amidst the gilded law books, was a diploma from Smith College in Northampton, Massachusetts and several framed photographs of her German shepherd. She settled in her chair and opened a can of coke and a Hershey bar. "Lunch," she said. Ray arched a disapproving eyebrow, and the prosecutor acted indifferent. "Can I see what you've found so far?"

They handed over the property log and the photocopies, and she flicked through them, contemplatively chewing the Hershey bar. "Procurements. Staff training guidelines. Risk assessments going back to 1995. Anything about restraint in the staff training guidelines?"

"Not yet," Ray said.

"We've got financial records. We've got OSHA certifications. Contracts. We've got state regulatory paperwork."

"Yeah, that's just what we've found so far," Ray explained.

"Go through the training stuff. The risk assessments. Look for any complaints."

"I don't know if there's a criminal case here," Alex ventured.

"Well, neither do I. But I want to find out."

"Why aren't we letting the civil case dig up the skeletons? They'll give each other enough discovery to fill the fucking records room of this office, and then maybe we'll know if there's a felony in there."

He thought she would rip his head off, but she stared out the window, her mouth stuffed with Hershey bar. Snow wheeled around the spires of the Financial District, the towers fading into the blizzard until they were nearly gone.

"The DA has mentioned this case to me," she said after a while. "And Peter's mother has gone to the *Post* and is making noise about the police and the DA's office not caring about the rights of disabled people."

Alex crossed his arms over his stomach. His gut twisted in half. *Fuck the press,* but he didn't say it, thinking, maybe Peter Kazparek would have dropped dead of a cardiac arrest no matter what anybody did or didn't do. Another one of those things you couldn't stop. The ME had told them it was foreseeable but not inevitable, not with luck and the right medications, and she didn't say whether or not the stress of that moment caused it.

Marie considered him, her expression indecipherable. "I'll get one of our forensic accountants to look at the financials. Just forward those straight to my office. The rest of it we will have to pick through and see what we find. All we need is evidence that someone knew of Peter's condition, knew the risks of aggressive restraint techniques, and authorized it anyway because it was cheaper, easier, I don't know." That look came to her eyes, the predatory gleam of an ambitious lawyer eager to prove their mettle with a difficult prosecution.

The one thing they hadn't found: evidence that someone was aware that the risks of 'therapeutic crisis intervention' in Peter's case included death. Alex touched the chapped cuts on lower lip and felt a bulletproof barrier separating him from everyone else. Dealing with people on the other side of the barrier had become intolerably exhausting. Seventeen years in a homicide squad sends you down a lot of holes, ranging from boredom, to repulsion, to terror. It kept the job interesting, and in the past, the high-octane demands of the job had swept him out of the melancholy abyss. But his gaze fell dejectedly on the box, and he wondered where he would find the energy to excavate that archive or do anything at all. Death was irreversible, he thought morosely, and a homicide detective understood that better than anyone. One way or another, they were all going to lose.

Chapter Twenty-Three

December 10th

The meeting with Eisenmann about that clusterfuck of a case from two years ago would be tomorrow. Today, Alex had an RDO, and he should have gone swimming, something relaxing, healthy, and not reading OSHA reports in a stuffy office. But he felt too sickly for physical activity, so instead, he went to Brooklyn. There were no good reasons for him to be in Brooklyn, but here he was, and he disembarked an A train in the subway station at Jay Street. Heaters blasted the tunnels, and he climbed the stairs, greeted by an icy wind off the river.

As far as MNHS cared, Sean Ferrin's case was cleared. With manner of death determined, they closed the file. It did not matter why the poor bastard had shot himself; it only mattered that he – and not someone else – had done so.

But Alex saw the ADA sitting in that luxury high-rise of gleaming smoky glass in the middle of the night, commanding a view of a city where eight million people didn't give a shit about him. It sparkled, stretching out of view, a landscape constructed of points of light, and the sinister, dark rivers, lurking around the glittering islands and peninsulas. Alone, frightened, Ferrin clutched his .22 and stared into the depthless, muffling night-capped city, and it looked so weirdly blank and sprawling that it seemed poisonous.

Alex hadn't told Ray or Gibson or anyone he was here, because he knew they would worry and jam him up with counseling. He had scrambled some eggs for breakfast even though he wasn't hungry, but he ate half of it, only to be sick, and after throwing up, he had sat on the floor of the bathroom with his back against the wall, his knees drawn up, tremors vibrating in his limbs. His stomach and intestines felt like a tangled wire, and he considered seeing a doctor if this didn't get better soon. Dr. Google had told him he was either going to die or be absolutely fine, and he'd stopped his web searches because he didn't want to end up as a paranoid hypochondriac, on top of everything else.

As he crossed Willoughby Street, he passed a violin player, a twenty-something white female, busking underneath a tree the council had decorated with silvery baubles and tinsel. The cascading arpeggios of a Bach concerto fired into his chest like a shotgun. He gouged his nails into his sternum, as if he could rip the pain out. Underneath, he felt ridges, wires from the operation to save his life when he was shot. He staggered into a newspaper box. Brooklyn Heights quaked like a fault opened underneath it, the bustling street, the bright sun, the trendy coffee shops dissolving, and there was only gloom, rain pelting down, pools of blood and water on the street, like pale eyes, barely capturing the glint of the streetlights.

He was blank-minded, in a world of violent, silent lights. Then his hearing returned. Sirens, screaming in the distance. And someone calling to him, "You all right, pal?" No, he thought, the blood was his own, couldn't they see that? The sirens were getting closer. Broken glass crunched under his feet and cut into his hands. "Are you okay?" repeated the voice. And he wanted to say, "Of course not, you douchebag, I'm lying here in a pool of blood," but the sirens and the throb of his own pulse filled his head so he couldn't speak.

A hand on his shoulder yanked him roughly back to Brooklyn Heights. The desolate street of blood and rain melted in the sun, and two uniformed cops were staring at him. He was clinging to a newsrack for the *Metro*. Sweat poured down his chest and back, even though the day was well below freezing. His heart raced like a crack-addict's. The violinist had stopped playing, now kneeling over her case, putting coins into a purse. He blinked in frightened confusion and shook his head like something stung his eyes. For a second, he felt bewildered and didn't know why the buildings looked so unfamiliar. Yes, he was in Brooklyn; he'd come here to talk to people in the DA's office.

"I'm fine. It's all right," he said to the two uniforms. They didn't look like they believed a word he said. "Just need to sit down for a few minutes."

"Are you sure?"

"Yeah." He tried to put on the nonchalant air of reassuring cynicism and world-weariness familiar to anyone who had ever worked with him on a crime scene.

Looking unconvinced, the two cops muttered a vague acknowledgment and continued on their beat. With reluctance, he let go of his newspaper box and walked along Jay Street, shoulders and spine stooped, hands shoved in his coat pockets, searching for a coffee shop. If he could sit and rest, catch his breath, slow his heartbeat, he *would* be all right. This was New York. One could not be far away. Indeed, within minutes, he found a small artisan coffee shop with sheik décor: leather seats, small oblong glass tables, and minimalist modern art on the walls. Whatever – it would do.

The coffee on the menu had indecipherable Italian names, like Americano, expresso, macchiato, driving him to despair. All he wanted was a plain coffee, and he didn't want to work out whatever the fuck the Italians called it. Fuck this trendy thing, giving coffee fancy names.

The barista was looking at him expectantly.

"Whatever you call plain black coffee," he said with as much patience as he could muster.

"Is that an Americano?"

He almost said, *I don't fucking know,* but bit his tongue. "Yes, that's fine," he replied brusquely.

Sipping the coffee, he skimmed the *New York Post*. War on the left. War on the right. Firefights in Fallujah. An invasion of Kabul. Anthrax sent to a precinct. Bomb threats in Times Square. The coffee made him feel a bit sick, but he drank it anyway, grateful he could force fluids and caffeine through his malfunctioning system. Every time the door squeaked, or the expresso machine roared, he flinched. He kneaded his cheeks and eyes. What the hell was wrong? Maybe he *should* get in touch with EIU, but he wouldn't know how to tell their peer-counselors about any of this. Talking to those guys about your feelings became marginally kosher after 9/11, but only if it was about 9/11. Anything else, you man up and deal with yourself.

Yet being hard and cynical about it, like a New York City detective should be, hadn't gotten rid of it. Work hadn't got rid of it. Visiting James hadn't got rid of it. The hardness had eroded, leaving him friable, fragile, bits coming off every day. He finished the coffee with no insights. Just hopelessness and a violent thumping in his chest. He could not even say what *it* was, a part of him, but not a part of him, like his own immune system turning on him and attacking his organs. An image sprang into his mind; his slippery entrails on the ME's scale – lungs, heart, liver, stomach, bowels – bloody and shredded like something had savagely gnawed at them.

Inhaling a pointed breath, he chased the surrealist dread out of his mind, and the cold air suffused in his nostrils.

He plodded along Jay Street to the DA's office, a modern high rise plated with shining windows of opaque glass bequeathing it an artifice of lightness. On entering the building, he flashed tin at the cops on security and asked them where he could find the Narcotics Bureau. They told him, the seventh floor, and waved him around the line at the metal detector. The elevator filled up, and he squashed himself against the back wall. An anvil on his chest, claustrophobia, the threat of another attack. *No, you won't, you fucking bastard*, he told it savagely. Then the elevator stopped, "7" illuminated above the doors. He escaped the crowd and ended up in an open plan office with windows all around.

The nearest ones overlooked the Brooklyn Bridge, with its gothic towers rearing above the river, its cables spanning out from the towers like improbably long, thin fingers. The walk-ups of Brooklyn Heights huddled amongst modern development, glass high rises, pearlescent grey and red stone walk-ups with bay windows and roof gardens, while across the river, the towers of Lower Manhattan rose glittering in the sun, like a city in a fantasy novel. It still looked odd with the World Trade Center gone. Like a person missing a limb. Sometimes, he did a double take, as if he'd expected it be there and was surprised not to see it. The vast fortress of Manhattan's skyscrapers pushed north, dark streets criss-crossing buildings set afire by the sun shimmering off the windows.

Leaving the window, he made his way to the nearest cubicle, which belonged to a paralegal engrossed in typing something on her computer. When he approached her desk, she raised her eyes from her screen without missing a beat on the keyboard. "Can I help you?"

He showed her his shield. "I'm Detective Alex Boswell from Manhattan North Homicide. I'm the primary investigator on Sean Ferrin's case—"

The paralegal spoke in a breathy voice. "Tragic. Jesus, that was so tragic. I don't even know what to say."

"Yes," he agreed gravely. "I was just wanting to talk to…" It occurred to him that he had no idea who he wanted to talk to. He cleared his throat, covering for his hesitation, and then continued, "To anyone who knew him well, who worked closely with him."

"One of your detectives was in here a couple days after he died. A younger, good-looking Latino guy."

He'd forgotten – Ray had questioned Ferrin's colleagues. But as far as Alex remembered, that had been before manner of death had been determined. Smiling through his discomfort, he said self-deprecatingly, "We send out the good-looking ones first and save the dregs for later."

She smiled back, flirtatious. "Oh, I don't know, Detective. I've seen worse."

If he looked as ill as he felt, she hadn't seen much worse.

"What is it you're after?" she asked.

"I'm just following up a few things. Before we close the file. Did you work on a lot of his cases?"

"I worked on some of his cases. Didn't really know him well. Don't know if anyone did."

"What do you mean by that?" Instinctively, Alex flipped open his memo book. Why? What would his shorthand notes tell him anyway?

"He didn't socialize a lot," replied the paralegal. "Never saw him at a work night out or anything. But, well, lots of people have families and all that so you don't see them. He was an Orthodox Jew, and I think they have a thing against drinking." She frowned, perplexed. "Do they? I don't actually know."

"They don't," Alex said pointlessly. "Wine is holy."

"Oh. Are you Jewish?"

"Yeah."

"Well, Sean didn't drink. Like I said, I only worked with him on a few cases and didn't talk much beyond that. Look, you should have a chat with Billy Stevenson." She gestured towards an office in the corner of the room. "He's an ADA. He co-chaired a lot of cases with Sean. I'll introduce you."

They crossed the room, and the paralegal knocked on the door. They received an acknowledgment, the paralegal opening the door, saying to the office's occupant, "This is Detective Boswell. He's from the Manhattan Homicide squad. One of the detectives on Sean's case."

The ADA was a balding black guy, with round glasses and a professorial air, and he indicated that Alex should take the seat. Curiously, he eyeballed Alex over his thick rims, and Alex inwardly recoiled, suddenly fearful that the ADA saw everything: his frangible emotions, the real reason he was here. He crossed his legs and consciously kept his hands on his thighs, so he wouldn't bite his nails. Resisting his bad habit brought an ache to his hands. Witnesses never made him feel this agitated, but then, what was Billy Stevenson a witness to?

"It's all been very, very sad," breathed Stevenson reflectively.

Questions burned Alex's throat. Did you know? Why didn't you stop him? How could you not see that he wanted to blow his brains out? But instead, very professionally, he said, "Your paralegal told me you'd worked with Mr. Ferrin on quite a few cases. Did you know him well?"

"I thought I did," said Stevenson.

There was a weighted pause, and the ADA stared vacantly at the rooftops.

You thought?" Alex prompted.

"I was surprised when your investigation revealed that he had taken his own life. We deal with drug dealers here who don't think anything of getting rid of anyone who gets in their way, and Sean had gotten in the way of a lot of violent people. I thought some defendant, or their family, had taken revenge. You know?"

"We'd thought the same, initially. But there's really not much doubt, the way the evidence is. I..." Alex held his breath until his lungs complained. His tongue was withering. "Did he tell you, or give you any evidence he was unhappy or unwell?"

"That's what confounds me, Detective. He was a quiet guy. He would often be in the office 'till after eight 'o'clock working on a case. But he had plans; he had a great legal mind and was set on becoming a judge in Criminal Term. He was a very meticulous person, very focused on his work and clear about what he wanted to do here and what he wanted to do to become a judge in the next three or four years. He wasn't one of those people who just muddles through life. With all of that ahead of him, I just can't see him planning a suicide."

319

"Sometimes people don't plan. Sometimes it's just an impulse."

"Sean was one of the least impulsive people I've ever known," said the ADA in a sad voice.

"I don't know, it's a different impulse. Not like having a one-night stand or driving 100 miles per hour on the LIE. It's like something breaking…" He trailed off, catching himself talking nonsense and the quizzical look on Stevenson's face. Artfully shifting the subject, he asked, "Did you know Sean had a gun?"

"Oh, yes," Stevenson replied. "He bought it last year."

This Alex knew, as Ferrin had been very by-the-book with his firearms purchase, indelibly inscribing it in the state's records. He had a permit and a premises license for his apartment.

Stevenson continued, "He had been a little worried for his safety, as he was prosecuting the top guys in a cartel with a history of going after law enforcement, and he had already received several threats. The police had their eye on him, but not 24/7. It seemed a sensible thing to do, at the time. Buying the little .22. It never occurred to me that Sean was someone who shouldn't have a gun. If anything, I thought he must be the safest, most levelheaded gun-owner in the city."

That would be a change from most cops, Alex thought wryly. "And he seemed all right recently? 'Safe and levelheaded?'"

Stevenson toyed with a clicky pen. "He was working his butt off. He had a lot on, a big case coming to trial, and one that had come back for retrial. I guess he wasn't very happy about that."

"What do you mean?"

"The defendant had appealed his conviction on procedural grounds – I doubt you care about the legal details of that – and the Court of Appeals sent it back to us for retrial. I guess it's better than having a conviction overturned outright, but Sean was a little upset. He was so meticulous about following the CPL and rules of evidence. No one knew the rules of evidence as well as he did, not even Appellate judges. I think he must have felt a bit insulted by the Appeals Court's decision. Still, these things happen to every prosecutor if you do it for long enough. But… I can't imagine that something like that would send him over the edge."

"If he was already close to the edge…" Alex floated.

"I didn't think he was. But then, he was not the sort of person to talk much to you about his personal life or troubles, if he had any. Even if you worked with him for years, there was a whole side of him that was just... closed off."

"Closed off? In what way?"

"He wasn't an emotional guy. I mean, I knew he went to Temple and was very involved with his synagogue, and he kept fit, went to the gym. I assume you know he has a son in Scarsdale –"

"Yeah," Alex assured him, not wanting the lawyer to think one of Manhattan's most elite detective squads had done a half-assed investigation. "I talked to his ex and his kid."

"Yes, well, he always left the office early on Fridays to go to Scarsdale and see the boy. He had his Bar Mitzvah coming up. He was very excited about that. I can't imagine... That poor child. He must be devastated..." Stevenson lost the train of thought, frowning, touching his chin. "And you know, Sean was very careful of his health."

"We saw the vegan cookbooks in his apartment," agreed Alex.

The ADA smiled sadly. "He used to say that the body was God's Temple, and it should be taken care of. Does that sound like someone who would kill themselves?"

"Who knows," Alex said, grinding his tongue into his back teeth. "I see all sorts in my job."

"Yes, yes, you would. If something was troubling him, he wouldn't say, I guess. He just kept walls up."

"Like he was hiding something?"

"No, more like he wanted to keep his personal life personal. There was us. There was Temple. There was his ex-wife and son. He kept these in separate spheres. There was nothing questionable about it – I don't want you thinking that – it was more like he was a hard guy to get to know." Stevenson paused again.

This time, Alex allowed the silence to cling to every molecule of air they breathed. Phones rang, a fax machine burbled, people chattered amongst the cubicles. Alex scratched at his thigh, keeping his fingers out of his mouth.

Then the ADA reflected, "Well, I suppose in a way, he was hiding something. I guess perfectly healthy, sound people don't kill themselves, do they? I just wished... I'm sorry, Detective, I don't think any of this is helping you. It's all a verbose way of saying, we were completely shocked that he was so troubled."

I wish I fucking knew what would help me, thought Alex. "Then I imagine that you have no idea if he was seeing shrink, or had any kinda history of mental health problems?"

"If he was, no one here knew about it. Did you find anything suggesting that he was?"

Tightening his brows, Alex shook his head. "Nothing." They had searched the apartment for prescriptions, receipts, evidence of Ferrin taking psychopharmaceuticals, but they only found Echinacea and ginseng, which Ray said were meant to boost the immune system and decrease stress, respectively, and a dozen herbal teas. Alex had laughed, teasing his partner for knowing that offhand. *Does that shit even work?*

"He would not make it obvious if he were seeing a psychiatrist. Not even to NYPD detectives."

"Doesn't matter. Even if he was, whatever he said would be confidential anyway." Evidence Ferrin knew he was unwell would make it less unpredictable, inevitable, or at least suggest that Ferrin recognized that he was in trouble, rather than it striking him down out of nowhere, with little warning.

"Yes, there's that," murmured Stevenson. "I'm sorry I can't be of more help to you."

"It's okay. We just wanted more of a sense of closure on the file."

Stevenson's eyes had become distant. "I keep replaying the last few weeks of his life in my head, hoping that I can identify the one thing, the one sign that I missed, but you know, I can't find anything. Maybe you're right, and it was a sudden impulse. Could have just cracked up one night and there was a loaded gun in his apartment. And even if I could find that moment where I knew he was that depressed, it's too late to change it. And sometimes, even if you do know, you can't stop people."

"No, sometimes you can't," Alex murmured in a low voice. As a death investigator, he knew that too well, and he felt utterly adrift and exhausted, his limbs divested of any strength. He still didn't understand why he'd come here. If Ferrin's organs laid out on the ME's exam table could not tell Alex their secrets, then how could a Brooklyn ADA?

"I wish we'd known. Or that someone did."

"Yeah, I guess we can never know," Alex said sorrowfully. "But I don't think I have any further questions. Thank you."

He stood up, and Stevenson did as well, moving towards the door with him. Stevenson pushed his glasses up his nose. "You *are* chasing your own demons, aren't you? It's not *really* the Manhattan DA or your bosses who want closure on this, is it? It's you."

A flutter of panic. Alex instantly jerked his gaze away from the prosecutor and drove his hands into his coat pockets, clenching his fingers into fists. His lower lip turned loose and rubbery. Was he that transparent? He was at a loss for a reply.

"I've been in criminal justice for a long time, longer than everyone else in this office, probably longer than you, and I know people, and I can see that in you."

See what? For a moment, he thought he might deny it. Of course, he was here working the case. But there didn't seem to be any point in lying, and he didn't have the emotional resources anymore. The shrewd lawyer threatened his fragile façade of composed professionalism. Pain flayed his chest, tearing the very life and breath out of his lungs. He knew it wasn't real pain. But it felt real and nearly brought him to his knees.

"Chasing demons, maybe," he rasped. "But I haven't caught any."

Stevenson smiled magnanimously. "For whatever my opinion is worth, Detective, I hope you do a better job of catching them than Sean did. I'm sure there are people who would find it a damned shame if you didn't."

Chapter Twenty-Four

December 23rd

Alex had lost his sense of time. Gillard's questions were relentless, tiring, like his would be if he was interrogating a perp. The walls and the looming grey sky conspired, hemming into a tiny space with nowhere to run. If he had wanted to talk about this shit, he would have referred himself to EIU, but he didn't see the point. Whatever it was, he should man up and handle it. He'd handled the shooting without counseling.

"Are you worried about your health?" she asked.

"What?" His eye sockets felt grimy.

"You're having dizzy spells, abdominal pain, nausea."

"Okay, a bit," he conceded. "You're gonna next tell me I'm imagining it, right? Come on, I probably picked up a bug." Licking his lips, he swallowed with difficulty against a blockage in his throat, and he took a sip of the peppermint tea on the table.

"Not quite. You might be somatizing things to your gut."

"Hah," he grunted. The coffee churning around in his stomach was undeniably real.

"Are you in pain now?" she asked.

"A bit," he admitted.

"Yeah?" She offered another compassionate smile, waiting for more details. Like any smart interrogator, she would sit it out until he relented.

He studied the layers of ace bandage bunched around his hand. "I feel like I have a horrible hangover I can't get rid of."

"I see," she said.

Did she? Alex could not see Theresa Gillard as the sort of person who drank so much that she became cataleptic and woke up feeling like she'd been hit by a semi-truck. He said, "I'm pretty sure I'm not imagining it. Then I'd imagine it better, and we wouldn't be here."

"No, I'm sure you're not. I'm saying the cause might be psychological, rather than *actual* problems with your head or GI tract."

"Psychological? Then it's obviously a problem with my head, all right."

"You know what I mean."

"I went to a doctor," he retorted. "*He* didn't think it was in my head." Then again, he reflected, he hadn't said a word to the doctor about the visions, the panic attacks, the dead weight of despair bringing him to tears.

"What did the doctor say you have?"

"Something called gastroenteritis."

A kind smile touched her mouth. "Inflammation of the intestines. Classic psychosomatic illness."

"What does that even mean?" he said irritably.

Ignoring his shortening temper, she continued, "Your mind, body, they're connected in ways science hasn't even begun to explain. If something is wrong psychologically, you can have physiological responses go wrong. William Styron said, 'It is easy to see how this condition is part of the psyche's apparatus of defense: unwilling to accept its own gathering deterioration, the mind announces to its indwelling consciousness that it is the body with its perhaps correctable defects – not the precious and irreplaceable mind – that is going haywire.'"

"Who the fuck is William Styron?"

"A writer who suffered from major depressive disorder."

That wasn't very reassuring. "But it's not all psychological," he argued.

"You don't think? It's not unusual for you to displace stress to your gut. You have a medical history of recurrent gastric ulcers, don't you?"

"Yeah, but that's 'cause I've fucked myself with the drink."

"But it bothers you more when you're stressed?"

"Yeah," he acknowledged, as though taking a beating on a merciless cross-examination and couldn't muster the initiative to fight it. He wiggled the mug around on the table and then sucked down another mouthful of tea.

She scribbled a few lines on her notepad. "Well, can we go back to your hand? That's what really concerns me."

"Why are you concerned?" he said rancorously. " 'Cause I'm forty-seven years old and still can't use a kitchen knife?"

"Something happened last night, and it wasn't a knife slipping on a bagel."

"Really? Did you go one of the Harlem crystal ball shops and talk to the psychic?" He inwardly cowered, caught in the middle of the downpour, alone on a desolate highway and not even a truck stop in sight to take shelter. All he found were distortions and twisted reflections, where the interview room and the view across Broadway seemed unchanged, exactly as they had been since 1996 – when MNHS moved to this office – but they felt deformed, misshapen by the unendurable impositions of the thing that was eating through his insides.

"Sarcasm isn't going to help you," she advised, her voice empathetic but resolute.

"It's gotten me pretty far."

"You're acting like you're in a lot of pain. You've hardly moved that hand since I've seen you. It must have been a hard bagel."

"Or a sharp knife," he quipped, the panic closing in, and with it, questions, like knives against his throat. The questions he would ask. Why had there been no blood in his kitchen this morning? Only in the bathroom. And why were three towels and a shirt wadded up in the bathtub, soaked in blood? He'd been a homicide detective for long enough to recognize a normal amount of blood for a serious wound, or a minor one for that matter. Those towels and the crime scene in the bathroom looked more like the former. Had he slashed his wrist while slicing a bagel? And what the fuck had happened to the stained glass on the bathroom door? If a witness had told him it fell out because they slammed the door, would he believe them?

She put her elbows on the desk and tilted towards him. "You've been a cop for a long time. You know that's not a minor knife wound."

He was speechless. It was all he could do to not have his face break up and start weeping, so he gazed at the snow floating in front of the window, the people on the street, the tenement buildings with their spidery fire escapes on the other side of the subway tracks. He sunk his teeth into his lower lip, holding it back from trembling.

"Well, okay, for a start, you need to find some kind of closure on the Ferrin case. It's not doing you any good, you know, to keep it open—"

"It's not open."

"In your head, it is."

He touched his forehead with his good hand. "I don't know, I keep thinking…" He stopped. Yes, he could behold Ferrin lost in a black hole of oily, bitter melancholy, driven to such a state of madness that he no longer recognized himself, and then ending his misery with a single gunshot. But he would not say that to Gillard. With forced patience and easy sarcasm, he protested, "We're Homicide. If manner of death is suicide, natural, or accident, if no crime has been committed, we close the damn case."

Gillard wasn't one of the finest forensic psychiatrists in the city for nothing. When he failed to tell her what he kept thinking, she stated, "You feel that you know what Ferrin was thinking, feeling, when he shot himself, because you've felt that way. And it would be that easy, a moment, an impulse, because you always have access to at least one firearm."

His stomach squirmed under a wave of forceful nausea. How could she know? He stared into her impermeable green eyes, wanting to cry, *Yes, yes, you've found out, and I'm afraid of what I might do,* but the words vaporized in his mouth. He yelped, "No, I didn't. Jesus, I can't let myself get personally or emotionally involved in my cases like that."

"You sure?"

"No one can. I mean, I know, I know how to detach myself emotionally from a case. I've had lots of DOAs who were suicides over the years. What do you think?"

"I think you were feeling unwell at this DOA, and when you found out what the manner of death was, you wondered why he did it, and if you might."

Something writhed around his windpipe, and he touched his throat, feeling his pulse pounding. A vigorous shake of his head, and he pushed himself to his feet, excusing himself – saying that he had to use the bathroom. He fled the interview room for the safety of the men's room. The door crashed behind him, shaking the building. Demons, he thought. They were chasing him, but he didn't want to look into their terrible eyes. He looked into his own: they were dull, bloodshot and blank, and there was a little cut below his jaw where he'd caught himself shaving.

Wheeler walked into the bathroom, his sudden entrance making Alex jump with a whinnying gasp, like he'd heard a shot.

"Oh, hey. How's it going? She let you outta there yet?"

"No," Alex admitted, running the hot water tap. "My head's fucked." So was his left hand, and he found it painful and awkward, doing all of life's little tasks with only his right hand. Opening doors, zipping his fly, turning on faucets.

Wheeler joined him at the sinks. "Well, if the shrink doesn't work, you could always hit the booze again. I hear it worked for you for a while."

Forcing a wan smile, Alex replied, "Yeah, my doctor says that would just put me out of my misery."

"Win win," said Wheeler.

Nothing like black Homicide squad humor. Like seven years ago, the other detectives in the squad starting a betting pool over how long they reckoned he would stay on the wagon. Not even behind his back, but in plain view, the bets written on a blackboard someone had propped against a wall, and Alex had to place a bet himself. No one, not even him, put their money beyond a year.

"OCCB and Manhattan South Narcotics got a warrant for that club Analisa Santos went to," Wheeler was saying. "You shook some shit out of a tree. Maybe nothing for Kitchener, or us, but Narc is moving on the club. I heard a Narc detective saying they got word that they're gonna move the product quickly. The investigation into Santos might've spooked them."

"How the hell would they know about that, unless she tipped them off?" Alex hazarded, astonished that his brain was still working like a cop's.

"Well, indeed. As you can imagine, she's getting very popular with OCCB and Narcotics."

"Wiretaps?"

"I hear they're working on it."

"They executing the warrant today?" Alex asked, his voice scratchy. Wheeler was sunny and freakishly good-natured, even when dealing with gruesome crime scenes. Nothing dampened his spirits, a trait which Alex found maddening. If something bothered him, you wouldn't know. If he thought you were weak or crazy, you wouldn't know that, either.

"Ray and Liz went along for shits and giggles. They're already there with the Narc and OCCB guys."

Fuck, he wished he were with Ray and Liz busting into the club. He wiped at the stinging corner of his eye with his sleeve.

Marcus grinned sympathetically. "Aw, you know how Ray gets off. You wouldn't want to be there getting between him and a lap dance."

Letting out a short exhalation through his nostrils, Alex said weakly, "Yeah, no, no one wants that." His mind felt torpid.

"Hey, it'll be cool. In no time, you'll be back to standing over some drug homicide in some scummy back alley filled with vials and syringes, and no forensics, no witnesses…" Marcus crushed a paper towel and put a hand on Alex's shoulder, his face brightening with his weird, sunny optimism.

Alex curled his lips into a bleak smile, making a dubious noise in his throat. Trepidation bubbled in his stomach, and he returned to the interview room where Gillard waited with a disconcertingly sagacious look in her eyes.

As he kicked his chair back from the table, she asked, "What happened at the meeting with Ken Eisenmann?"

God, that meeting! An express train of anxiety slammed into him at the mere thought of it. His gaze fell from hers, and he played at realigning his belt and waistband. The brief conversation with Wheeler had been like catching a passing glimpse of everything he desperately missed; the job, office banter and tasteless humor, homicide investigations – even the shitbag ones – and he ached to be there, not here. Wherever here was.

Chapter Twenty-Five

December 11th

The victim had been fished out of the East River in the middle of February, 2002. She was Iranian, a recent immigrant, a Vassar student, and she had been in the city visiting family. The perps, it turned out, were men who knew her family, engaged in 'payback' for some offense her father had given someone. They had gang raped the victim in a van borrowed from a cousin, and shortly thereafter, she'd jumped off the Queensboro Bridge.

The case reminded everyone why they hated high-profile media circuses, with the certain elements in the press and online expressing outrage over things like the perps being given their *Miranda* rights, being allowed lawyers, wondering why they couldn't just be wire-tapped whenever the police felt like it or held as enemy combatants, which would dispense with due process altogether. It was a maddened feeding frenzy, as rabid as the circus surrounding that mosque near the World Trade Center site. Amidst the chaos, Alex had wondered how the hell he was supposed to run a death investigation with the brass and the media screaming for blood, his or the suspects'.

There were five defendants. One turned state's on his co-defendants and then killed himself before trial; two were deemed to be in the US illegally anyway and deported to Iran; while the last two took a plea bargain: dispositions of second degree kidnapping, second degree aggravated sexual abuse, and third degree conspiracy, adding up to more or less forty years. Simon McNally had wanted to try them for manslaughter one or two, but his bosses yanked on the reins. No court had ever stretched a man one statute far enough to hold a perp responsible for a vic's suicide, and ultimately, McNally had to take what the Penal Law gave him. The perps deserved to be thrown off a bridge, but forty some odd years in prison would have to do.

Anyway, Alex had met the District Attorney himself once since the man took office in 2000. He'd also met his predecessor twice in thirteen years. The first time, that DA had visited Alex in Columbia Pres after the 190th Street shooting, one of a long parade of high-level officials congratulating him on his heroism (for what? Not dying? He hadn't run headlong into trouble like Officer Irvine did) while he was zotzed on morphine and pain. The second time, the DA had sauntered into the MNHS office during the Central Park Jogger investigation but looking for the detectives working that case, not Alex. Usually, impenetrable layers of bureaucracy separated the DA from street cops.

Alex and Ray arrived at One Hogan Place a few minutes late, parking amongst a dozen RMPs underneath 100 Centre Street. Under the weather, Alex huddled pitifully in the passenger seat. This was an RDO. He should be in bed, not here. He'd foregone food since his failed attempt to hold down scrambled eggs, and queasiness and pain gnawed at the edges of his awareness, but not eating saved him from doubling up in agony or vomiting. However, fasting exacerbated his bouts of dizziness and made him feel awfully anemic and fragile. He remembered fasting on Yom Kippur because his ex-wife had insisted on it. He'd felt weak and ill and vowed never to do it again, given a choice. And with nothing in his stomach to keep the acid from attacking the lining, he was drinking water laced with Alka-Selzer, which neutralized it a bit but assaulted his liver with acetaminophen.

After Ray turned off the car, Alex reached for the door handle, but Ray stopped him with a hand on his forearm. "Lex, wait a minute."

He froze and looked at his partner.

Ray played nervously with the car key. "I know, I know I asked you this before, but I really need to know what's going on with you."

"What do you mean?"

"*Are* you drinking? I…" He stumbled over his words, as if they did not fit together the way he had planned. "I mean, if you are, you can tell me, and I promise, I promise that I won't tell anyone, not Gibson, not anyone. What's said in this car stays in this car. And we can just figure it out. But I'm your partner, and I need to know."

"No, no, no, I'm not. I promise, I'm not."

"Then what *is* it?" Ray pleaded. "Please, stop doing this macho, toughing-it-out thing and tell me what's going on."

"I haven't eaten anything since yesterday."

That did not reassure Ray. "What? Why not?"

"Because I get sick if I do," Alex said as matter-of-factly as possible.

"Jesus, have you thought about going to a doctor?"

"I thought it would get better."

"You've been complaining about your stomach for like a *week*. Can you please go see someone?"

"I will. Tomorrow, if it's not better."

Ray looked stressed, and he didn't climb out of the car, as though he wanted to say something else. But he only sat there, twiddling the car keys between his fingers. Alex opened his door. Part of him cried out – he should tell Ray that his screwed up digestive system was only the latest development in generally feeling lousy for the past month or so, but it fizzled out on his dried, bleeding lips.

When they finally joined the meeting, muttering apologies for being late, they found everyone sitting in a circle around a big mahogany table in the DA's meeting room, except for McNally, who was pacing back and forth between Gibson, an ADA from the Appellate Bureau and another ADA from the Sex Crimes Bureau, whose first name was Sheila, but Alex couldn't remember her surname. There was also the assistant chief of Detective Borough Manhattan, Lorenzo Vizzano, and the DA himself.

Simon faced the assorted cops and prosecutors like a jury. "*Strickland v. Washington!*" he spat, disgusted, as if a 1960s Supreme Court case had personally insulted him. "They're saying that they were denied effective counsel, can you believe that?" He paused dramatically. "If those bastards think they can wriggle out of their deals – generous as hell, I might add, since if they dispo'ed at all the top counts of the indictment, they'd be serving fucking life sentences – using *Strickland*, they can't possibly prove that there was a reasonable probability that if it hadn't been for counsel's 'errors,' the case would have come out differently."

The District Attorney regarded Simon. They all regarded Simon. Eisenmann said levelly, "If the Appellate Division were to send this back for retrial, and we don't have, or the judge excludes, the testimony of Muhammed, where are we on the fucked-o-meter?"

"Not a lot," said Sheila, the Sex Crimes ADA.

"Very," countered Simon.

"It was accomplice testimony," said Sheila. "How much weight do you think the jury put on it? We had the forensic evidence from the van—"

"That we could lose as fruit of the fucking tree," growled Simon. "Since if they are able to argue that Muhammed was coerced, the police got that from Muhammed, and Muhammed hung himself in prison, so he isn't here to testify himself now—"

The ringing in his ears grew loud and incessant, overpowering Simon's ranting, and Alex seized his head with both hands, anxious to silence it.

"What coercion?" Ray demanded. "The guy came into the Two-Three voluntarily. He signed the *Miranda* waiver."

Annoyed and protective, Gibson said icily, "Muhammed signed a voluntary statement, same as any witness who comes to us with information about a crime. There is no evidence, none, that anything different happened, and if the defense team is saying otherwise, they're gonna have to start writing some fiction good enough to win the Pulitzer."

Assistant Chief Vizzano weighed in, saying, "There's still a lot of goodwill for the police in this town. It wouldn't look good if the DA's office wasn't backing our best investigators."

"Even with all these wrongful convictions coming to light?" asked the appellate ADA flatly.

Eisenmann looked unimpressed by the Chief's threats. "If that evidence is excluded, it will be on the grounds that NYPD detectives coerced testimony from a witness, who is now dead, and the defense lawyers failed to consider this information and act on it when agreeing to the plea bargain. If I were you, Chief, I wouldn't be sitting in my glass house throwing stones. We're all in this together."

The appellate ADA craned his head towards Alex and Ray. "In all honesty, Detectives, what happened when Muhammed went into the 23rd Precinct? *If* there is anything, anything that could be construed as any kind of misconduct or violation of Mr. Muhammed's rights, even if it really isn't, I need to know so I know what the defense is going to do at the Appellate Division, and I can formulate some kind of argument against it."

"Exactly as the 'fives say," grumbled Ray.

Alex paid attention to his blood speeding fervidly through his arteries, and his head felt flushed and hot. That Brooklyn ADA said Sean Ferrin had a case kicked back to him after an appeal.

"There is nothing that can even be misconstrued?" the prosecutor insisted. "I mean, I am sure you followed your procedures to the letter, but it's how—"

Ray's anger smoked out of his ears. "There's a squad room full of cops in the Two-Three who'll say exactly what we wrote on those 'fives. That defense lawyer's just trying to earn his hundred bucks an hour—"

Pensively, Alex protested, "He came into the precinct, he was obviously a mess, and he told the desk officer he wanted to talk to detectives who were working on the al-Farasi case. They got us, Special Victims, and the precinct squad, and he told us what happened, what they did. That's it."

"What would he have expected from you, or Simon, in exchange for that testimony?" the appellate ADA asked.

"Same as anyone who cooperates. Reduced sentence."

"Moot point anyway," growled McNally, "Given that the witness hung himself in prison."

"The confession is on video," Alex added quietly.

"Yes, we've seen the video," said the appellate ADA. "But what happened *before* you turned on the camera?"

"Nothing. He said he wanted to talk to us, said he'd been involved in the rape and knew the other perps. At that point, we read him his rights and put the video recorder on."

"Can we expect the District Attorney's Office to support the actions of one our top investigative units?" Gibson looked hard at Eisenmann.

The appellate ADA commented, "I have looked up their police department personnel files, seeing if there is anything to worry about. There is a complaint in Detective Boswell's file, from when he worked in the 103rd –"

"Oh, Jesus," Alex groaned. "I was in the One-Oh-Three like twenty years ago. You're digging that shit up? If you bothered reading the file, you'll find IAB cleared me."

"I think by the time people are unearthing unproven complaints from 1985, they're pretty desperate," interjected Gibson.

"Yes, well, Manhattan North Homicide also interrogated several of the boys charged with raping the Central Park Jogger. Now we know those were false confessions… coerced. It's arguable that your squad habitually manipulates confessions –"

Gibson locked her jaw. "Detective Boswell didn't work on that case, and Detective Espinosa wasn't even in the squad at the time, nor was I. That's got nothing to do with them."

"I'm just saying… The defense might bring those up," insisted the ADA.

"Then tell them to fuck off," Alex shot back. Inside, something snapped with a terrible crack. The wires around his sternum burst apart. Oh, he knew he should have had the surgery to remove them! Tears of pain hurled themselves against the back of his eyes.

The appellate ADA spread his hands across the desk. "Detective, could you swear, under oath, that you have never once in your whole career got a suspect to confess falsely?"

Another snap. Alex succumbed to the terrifying feeling of the world rushing backwards. He was dizzy. He couldn't breathe. Nausea flooded his senses. He needed air. There was no up or down or appeals or inter-agency sniping, just progressive decay that would destroy everything. He managed to say, "Excuse me for a minute," and he got to his feet. Blood drained from head like his jugular had become a sluice box. The white and yellow lights enclosed his vision, the room gyrating, blood covering his hands, his knees buckling. And then he fainted dead away.

When Alex came to his senses, he was lying on his left side, sprawled on the floor of a meeting room. The first things that came back to him were the odors – cologne, perfume, cleaning products, paper. After that, sounds – people talking, papers shuffling, phones ringing. Smells and sounds, evidence of life resuming. The voices of his colleagues were far away, and he couldn't quite make them out.

Someone was saying his name. "Alex? Alex? Can you hear me? Alex?"

Reality became more definite. He noticed Ray kneeling beside him, two fingers pressed firmly against his pulsing carotid artery. When Alex met his eyes, he said, "Jesus Christ, Lex. What the fuck? Are you okay?"

It was reassuring, in a way. "Yes," Alex mumbled, "I can hear you."

And McNally squatting down on his other side, fierce hawk-like brows furrowed. "Do you know where you are?"

"The DA's office."

"Can you tell me your birthday?"

He miserably shut his eyes again. "February 12, 1957."

"Do you know who the President is?"

"What?" Alex wished they would go away and leave him some space. And that Ray would get his fingers out of his throat. The President? What kind of *non sequitur* was that?

"The President. Of the US," said McNally, his voice rising in alarm. "Do you know who it is?"

Oh, yeah, that was one of the questions you were supposed to ask when you suspected someone had a brain injury. "John Kerry?" he suggested.

"I hope you're joking, Alex," Simon said in a worried voice.

"I'm waiting for the Supreme Court to tell us," he answered, which should have told them that his mental faculties were functioning. He still had his sense of humor.

"Who is it, really?"

"For fuck's sake, it's George W. Bush."

"He's swearing, like, well, a New York City cop," he heard Sheila say from somewhere behind him. "He's probably okay."

Gibson replaced Ray, who shuffled to the side but kept a hand on Alex's hip, as if scared he would disappear if he lost physical contact with him.

"Can you focus on my eyes, Alex?" said Gibson.

He moaned, "Aw, I haven't had a fucking stroke."

"You did just collapse for no apparent reason," she replied. "We have to check."

A few minutes passed. He sat up, taking a few deep breaths, a sniff or two, rubbed his face with both hands. He clutched his belly, resisting the instinct to curl around the pain electrocuting his bowels. Rather, he laboriously got up and, with as much dignity as he could muster after falling over in the middle of a meeting, he clambered into the chair, his head ringing like he'd been to the firing range without ear protection.

"How are you feeling now?" Gibson asked. The anxiety on her face was plain.

"Better than I was when I was lying on the floor. I guess. But I don't think getting up was a good idea. I think I need to lie down."

"There's a sofa in my office," Simon said, trying his fierce, raptorial best to look spooked.

"Yeah, okay," Alex answered. He cautiously regained his feet, but the earth underneath the DA's office was sliding into the Atlantic.

Simon led him out the door and they took the elevator up to the next floor, Simon saying, "At least we got out of that horrible meeting. That's something!"

Alex affected a humorless smile. "I think it was you doing most of the talking anyway."

"It usually winds up that way," agreed Simon as the elevator doors slid open.

"What's the defense lawyer saying we did? I never got that far."

"They say that they have medical reports for Muhammed – he had been treated for severe bruising and a cut on his head. They're saying the police beat him up and coerced him into confessing *before* you turned the camera on."

"Aw, Christ. He was beat up when he came into the station house, but we sure as fuck didn't do it." Alex remembered the bruises on the perp's face and an angry, infected cut on his forehead, the perp insisting that he had been jumped by a mugger, the same 'mugger' who is responsible for every assault or rape, the stand-up guy for parents, relatives, friends, or enemies. Alex didn't buy the story, and he'd wrangled Muhammed into admitting that his own brothers assaulted him.

"Yeah, I know, his brothers did it," said Simon.

"The ones who've been deported. They're saying that we got Muhammed to lie about his brothers beating the shit out of him?"

"Yes, they're saying he was psychologically fragile, and you railroaded him."

"The fuck we did," sighed Alex in frustration. "You can't cover your ass enough. We got him to sign a *Miranda* waiver and turned on the camera like five minutes after he walked into the station house. What more do they want?"

"Don't worry about it. Defense counsel's got to say *something* to pay off his yacht. And coerced confessions are on everyone's mind since the Central Park Five thing."

They waked into Simon's corner office, with its bookshelves stuffed to the brim with law books, papers scattered everywhere, pictures of mountains and rock climbers, and the squidgy leather sofa in the corner.

"A yacht? Not Legal Aid anymore, then?" said Alex as his knees gave up, and he crumpled onto the couch.

"No, he's got his family paying for some fancy lawyer. But whatever. They're just blowing smoke out of their asses. They have no evidence. They're just wasting the court's time."

Alex curled up on his side, his weight sinking into the squishy leather. He buried his head in a cushion, piecing together the last hour, but everything seemed hazy, disjointed and noxious – the drinking-too-much-the-night-before feeling. The Appellate Bureau prosecutor had mentioned an old complaint in his file and the Central Park Five, he had tried to leave, and then he had been lying on the floor. What if his heart or his liver or his brain or his lungs or his kidneys or something was on its way out? So many organs with the potential to go wrong. His stomach and liver had already tried. Years of bad relationship stability and death investigations should have made him permanently averse to the temptations of 'what if,' but he couldn't help himself. He opened an eye, noticing Simon standing near the desk, fidgeting with a carabiner, opening and shutting the gate. *Click, click, click.*

"Really, what's going on, Alex?" Simon asked. "Do you want anything?"

"I don't know. I feel really fucking queasy. I think I just need to lie here for a little while. What did I do in there?"

"You said something like, 'Excuse me,' and tried to stand up, but your face went white, like the color of this wall, and then you just collapsed. Ray managed to safely get you to the floor, so you didn't hit your head on anything. You were pretty much out for about ten seconds. Not responding to anything. But you were breathing, and you had a heartbeat so we all figured it wasn't as bad as it could be. And you came to within ten or fifteen seconds."

A staccato rap vibrated the door. His heart leapt. Without waiting for an answer, Gibson strode into the room. Alex dug his fingers into the cushion to hide his shaking hands.

"How are you feeling?" she said.

"Like I could run the New York Marathon," he answered, protecting himself with pathetic sarcasm.

Unimpressed, she tugged on the purple silk scarf draped around her neck and sat on the arm of the sofa. "Can you tell me what's going on?"

"I don't know, Lou. There's a 'flu thing going around. I think I've gotten that."

"Ray told me that you haven't been able to eat for a few days."

"Has he?" He imagined that after he and Simon had left Eisenmann's meeting, *he* became the topic of discussion, rather than the Iranians.

"Yes."

"My gut's not been good. I don't know why. I keep hoping it'll sort itself out."

Gibson continued, "And, privately – we left the meeting for a talk – he told me that you sometimes freeze up, like in a panic, and hyperventilate and seem really... 'out of it' was the phrase he used. You did it today, before you passed out. When you got up and tried to leave the meeting, you looked like you didn't know where you were."

He shivered, bluntly reminded of the unnamable thing, the inescapable adrenaline spikes, the acceleration of his heartrate, the panic, feeling like he wasn't where he thought he was, all those sensations which, for the past month, he had been ignoring or blowing off, tuning out like weirdos on the subway, who always get off within a few stops. They hadn't been this bad before. He had weathered it and handled the job in the mayhem of the early '90s.

"I can run you to the ER if you like," offered Simon. "Get checked out."

"I just got lightheaded and fainted. Probably because I'm not eating."

"You should get that seen to."

"I know. I already told Ray I would go tomorrow." He lost his thoughts on a detour, an incident from years and years ago, when he was a rookie, a beat cop in Greenwich Village, and he picked up a call to the DOA. He and his partner, an equally as green Irish guy named Duggan, were the first policemen on the scene.

Someone warned them that it was bad. But they had sat on a couple DOAs before – people dropping dead of natural causes in their apartments or wherever – and they were feeling confident, cocky even, in their ability to handle it. They weren't prepared for what they saw. It was like they had stepped into the old, derelict building on West 11th and been transported from the Village to Vietnam. The victim had been mutilated: blown to pieces, like he had stepped on a land mine. Bits of him everywhere. Blood. Guts. Limbs. He and a friend had been experimenting with making bombs in the basement of their building, and the experiment had either gone perfectly well, or terribly wrong, depending on how you looked at it. The friend was later charged with manslaughter one.

Alex had thought it important that he show his mettle as a cop: look professional, detached, keep it together, meticulously focus on the procedures he'd learned for securing a scene until someone more senior got there. Unfortunately, he stepped over a liver and found the blood exiting his head, his vision blurring, his head spinning and he was down, gasping, holding his head between his knees, and he heard his patrol sergeant, who he always thought was a bit of a prick, laughing about youngsters getting initiated.

"What are you thinking?" asked Simon.

"Nothing. Just an old case."

Gibson had been quietly considering him. "Simon, can you leave us for a minute?"

The prosecutor looked surprised, but he followed orders without protestation, slinking out of his own office.

After he had gone, Gibson said, "I think there's stuff going on inside your head that you don't know what to do with, or how to handle."

"It's the stomach 'flu," he protested feebly. "What do you even mean?" He propped himself on an elbow, his shoulder blades against the back of the sofa.

"I don't think that's what you have. You have no idea what's going on inside of you. But I don't think it's physical."

"What? Does that mean you think I need to see a fucking shrink?"

"Yeah, you're gonna sit down with Theresa Gillard."

"Fuck. Why Gillard?" he asked, unable to tear his gaze away from her irresistible, driving eye contact. Gillard was one of the top forensic psychiatrists in the city, if not the state or country. Surely, you had to be batshit crazy, like under a section 9.27 on a high-security ward at Kirby, to have your head shrunk by her.

"Everyone can see you're struggling. I don't think you can do this alone anymore. I told the Borough Chief and those prosecutors that you had the 'flu, but you know it's more than that."

"I can deal with it on my own terms," he argued listlessly.

She picked up the carabiner from McNally's desk, playing with the gate, like Simon had been doing earlier. "You haven't. Clearly."

"I don't wanna talk to a shrink. I just need to pull my shit together."

Gibson was unmoved. "Look, you have a choice, Alex. You can either talk to Gillard, or I'm going to put you through to medical services. If you talk to Gillard, I will promise you that it will be totally confidential, and nothing will be on record. It will stay between you, me, and her. And Ray, I guess. You know if you see medical services, what happens, what goes on your record, won't necessarily be up to me. Plus, between you, me, and this wall, Gillard is way better than anyone the department employs. There's damned good reasons she's got the name for herself that she does."

"I could go to EIU. They've got peer counselors," muttered Alex, his voice sinking. "You talk to other cops."

"Well," said Gibson. "If it's serious, they'll refer you to a professional."

Gawking in grotesque dismay, he stared straight at her. "You that sure I need a real shrink."

"I think it would be a good idea," she responded, her tone soft yet inarguable.

"What's this gonna cost?" Alex asked acidly. That wasn't much of a choice at all. Speak with Gillard, who would do a living autopsy on him, or speak with one of the department's in-house counselors, some guy with a psychology degree who had done a few training courses on trauma, who could put his whole career in jeopardy if they diagnosed him with depression or whatever. "She must charge more than one hundred bucks an hour."

"I'm calling in a favor. I helped her kid out on a thing a year or so ago," said Gibson firmly. *"Pro bono."*

"You've spoken to her?" he yelped, his blood pressure scooting upwards.

"Yes," she answered simply.

"Then you think I'm going crazy."

"I think you need to talk to someone professional. It's not the same thing."

He bit his thumbnail off, and it bled. "But I'm too fucked up for EIU?"

"She would like to see you."

"Does she?" He closed his eyes, sinking back into the spongy sofa. Gibson must be losing her mind with worry, suggesting that he speak with a psychiatrist who had an MD and a PhD, who had published books and papers in the top psychiatry journals, who had a stint as an editor on the Journal of Forensic Psychology, and who regularly dealt with the city's most intractable psych patients. No, not suggesting, ordering, and she was his commanding officer, so he had to follow her orders.

"You'll do it?" Gibson said.

"Do I really have a choice?" he asked laconically.

"Not really."

Chapter Twenty-Six

December 12th

That night, Alex shivered as though lying naked in the snow. In pain, he breathed shallowly. Sweat poured onto the sheets. Resting on one side hurt, so he flipped over to the other, where he stayed for a while, the pain inside burning hotter. He pressed his palm to his forehead, the skin sizzling like a frying pan.

Through the window, he heard the beeping delivery trucks, heralding morning, and the noises of traffic on West 87th. He stumbled out of bed, listing sideways, and then balancing with a hand on the wall as he shuffled to the bathroom for a piss. Then he limped back to the bed. Normally, he would knock out a low-grade fever with a Tylenol-ibuprofen-Dayquil cocktail and go into work anyway, because sick days were a hassle and the people who administrated NYPD sick pay like the Stasi, but today, he had no chance of keeping those pills down long enough to make any difference.

He had promised Ray and Gibson that he would see a doctor. Besides, if a doctor diagnosed him with a physical illness, it might save him from that conversation with Theresa Gillard. He might have grounds to talk Gibson out of it. Comfortlessly, he steeled his will and crawled out from his sweaty nest of sheets and duvets, where he fumbled with changing out of a tattered t-shirt and track pants and tugged on another old t-shirt, and a hoodie. His legs refused to support his weight, and his heart had dispensed with pumping enough blood to his head. Luckily, the Upper West Side had what must be the highest concentration of hypochondriacs per block in the world, and it was therefore the sort of place where you were never very far from a doctor. He was aiming for the Urgent Care Center on 88th and Broadway. But it might as well be in LA.

It drizzled, a steady, cold rain. He wrapped himself up in all the layers he owned, a scarf, a fleece jacket, his long overcoat. His joints screamed in protest. Every time he inhaled, something stabbed into his stomach. The cold sunk pointy daggers into his bones in spite of all his clothes.

Several of the people waiting to cross Amsterdam dashed across the street between cars, like caribou in a wildlife documentary. He was too tired and ill to follow. Then, the lights changed to the little green man, and he crossed, sloshing through the pools of water rising over the curbs. It soaked into his shoes. The plants were brown and dead, the trees naked and skeletal like victims of a famine. People went about their business, oblivious. A woman in a long, red coat walking five small, wet dogs, like a many-headed hydra. A group of young men with huge silver crosses hanging from their necks and chains dangling from their pockets. A pair of Hasidic Jews with long beards, their top hats and black coats and white shirts strangely untouched by the weather.

The rain beat down heavier, and he couldn't stop shivering as his body failed at regulating its own temperature. As soon as he arrived at the Urgent Care Center, he checked in, and then had to wait alongside everyone else, a collective experience of misery. A fit of paranoia, fed by his Googling, gripped him. What if this was a serious problem? Cancer maybe, or the catastrophic failure of an organ. Something requiring surgery, or something terminal. What was the statistic he had read on the internet? That one in three people will have cancer at some point in their lives. He had visions of all the horrible maladies he'd read about online. The sickening panic bubbled inside him, rising in his throat like bile.

Trying to save himself from steeping in anxiety, he grabbed a *Village Voice* and read the news, an article about a state representative who'd been caught emailing pictures of his genitals to an intern. As he searched fruitlessly for another article that wasn't about political corruption or a war, they called his name.

The doctor, Dr. Feldman, had short, dark curly hair and wiry glasses perched on his nose. While he bobbed his head up and down, his curly hair bouncing, Alex described his symptoms, up to a point. He didn't think feeling upset or panicky had anything to do with his fever or digestive problems, so he said nothing of it.

"Running a fever of 100, huh," observed the doctor after sticking a thermometer in his mouth. "You said you're able to hold down fluids?"

"Yeah."

"Well, that's good. You're slightly dehydrated but still okay. Solid food?"

Alex perched on the edge of the exam table, dizzily clutching the edges. "No."

"How long have you felt this way?"

"Like a week."

"Okay, let's see what's going on. Can you lie down on your back?"

Lying down was easier than sitting up. The doctor prodded his belly, feeling his organs, and that hurt like a bitch, yet he got a bewildering sensation, his mind and his body disconnecting, his mind hovering somewhere around the ceiling, not participating in any of this, the body on the table someone else's.

"All right, we're gonna have a look inside, an ultrasound to start with. There's a lot of soreness and I reckon inflammation in your small intestine. Most likely, you just have an infection, and you'll be fine. But... you may have a blockage and require further tests, possible surgery. Might need more tests after that."

Alex crashed back into his body from wherever he'd been floating. He felt chilled and heard the roar of blood in his ears. "A blockage? Of what?" he asked tonelessly.

"Could be a number of things. Or nothing. We'll have to see." Feldman's face was smooth, the eyes behind the glasses unreadable.

This was like his own capital sentencing hearing. Alex trailed after the doctor down the hall to a different room, this one with an ultrasound machine. He watched Feldman and the sonographer set up the machine and felt ropes in his mind uncoiling, and he was queasy and petrified. The dreamy disconnection didn't come back, and he confronted a rising wall of fear, and he was speechless, staring wide-eyed at the machines until they told him to lie flat. There were so many diseases that might do him in, and he was surprised that he managed to survive in relatively good health for forty-seven years.

"Oy, no wonder you're not feeling well," said Feldman after he'd waited for the sonographer to complete the scan. "No masses. Increased blood flow to the small bowel. Looks like an infection. Nothing else is showing up. It's inflamed and swollen but otherwise normal. I want to wait for the blood tests to be sure and depending on those results and if you don't respond well to antibiotics, we may need to schedule an MRI."

As unpleasant as that sounded, Alex exhaled several strangulated breaths and thought, *Oh, good, an actual medical diagnosis of an actual thing, and it's not in my head.* And not cancer or any other fatal condition, either. Maybe Gibson had been wrong about 'stuff going on inside his head.' Maybe he was depressed in general because his gut had an infection and wasn't working right, and once that healed, the lassitude would lift, and he would feel less downtrodden, reactive, and weird.

The doctor explained that they usually don't treat this aggressively because most patients recover anyway in two or three days, but since Alex hadn't, he prescribed antibiotics and anti-inflammatories. Then he turned Alex's forearm over, swabbing a prominent vein on the wrist with a cotton ball, and Alex flinched at the sting of the needle in his arm, but he'd become inured to needles after 190th Street. Weeks in the hospital feeling like a pin cushion and then years of follow-up appointments and tests will do that. Unmoved, he watched blood fill the syringe.

"What about the fever?" he asked.

"That's just your body fighting the infection. Don't worry, hopefully you'll be feeling a lot better in a few days. That said, if you're not, you need to come back, and we'll make an appointment for an endoscope and some imaging tests. But even later this afternoon, those meds will kick in and you'll be a lot happier. Then you should try eating, see how it goes. You'll feel better if you can get things moving through your system again."

Alex left the Urgent Care Center with his drugs, which he picked up at the CVS on the ground floor, and a list of food he could eat, distressingly bland and healthy and not including pizza, cannolis, candy bars, Chinese or Indian take-out, anything fried, or anything you could buy from a street van. The doctor had warned that his guts would be tender and sore for some time yet, and he had to treat them delicately until they healed. He might be on a diet of sorts for at least two weeks. As he hobbled into the rain, he thought bleakly, *it might be one way to lose weight,* but he would rather carry the twenty extra pounds than put up with this shit.

The walk home felt like a Russian novel. Then the three flights of stairs to his place knocked him senseless, so he had to sit down on the top landing, dizzily huddled against the wall with his forehead on his knees, and then he maladroitly unlocked his door.

His cell phone rang. Ray. He considered not answering, but then he did.

"You took a sick day. Good. Did you go to the doctor?" asked Ray, who would have been a good Jewish mother had he not been born Puerto Rican and male.

"Yeah," Alex answered.

"Did they figure out what's going on?"

"Yeah, they said I got an infection in my gut."

"Is that all?"

"Yes," he said intemperately. It was surely just that; he had meds to fix it, and this whole fucking write-off of a month would soon be over.

"What's the treatment?"

"They got me on anti-inflammatories, antibiotics, and a diet that you'd love."

"How about I stop by your apartment on my way in today," suggested Ray.

"I'll be in bed. But you can if you like."

"Make sure you're still alive," Ray teased.

"Well, I'm hoping I will be, but wishing I wasn't."

"I'll be around at three or so," said Ray.

Alex hung up the phone as his bones and muscles liquefied, and he rolled himself into a ball inside the duvet, sinking into a trance of extreme discomfort. Occasionally, he drifted towards lucidity and consciousness and didn't like it: a world of pain, the fever making him achy, disoriented. He closed his eyes, pulled his knees to his chest, and fell asleep again. Then, the buzzer on his door punched into his sleep like an angry fist, and he stirred, groggy and confused. How many hours had slipped past?

The clock next to the bed stated it was 1505. His fever had broken. His clothes and the bed were sopping in sweat. He didn't want to get up, but he buzzed Ray in, saying, "The door's unlocked," unlocking the door, and then rewrapping himself in the duvet. The sounds of someone stomping up the stairs echoed faintly through the walls, and then the squeak and rattle of Ray opening the door. He had a shopping bag in each hand.

Alex rolled onto his other side and asked Ray if he always did his shopping before a four-by-twelve.

Ray smiled. "Nah, I was gonna make you some soup."

"What?" Alex said.

"When you're up for eating something, it'll be easy on your gut."

Alex rested his head on his forearm. "Aw, Christ. You're not gonna try to put me on your veggie diet, are you?"

"Yes. At least until you're well enough to go back to eating the shit you normally eat." He stepped into the bathroom, and after a minute there, reappeared. "You ever clean this bathroom, Alex?"

"Are you my mother?" he mumbled wearily.

Ray disappeared into the kitchen, and Alex heard him clattering, cursing, hunting for crockery, and the shriek of the kettle boiling. Then Ray re-entered the bedroom with a steaming mug. "Peppermint tea. You should really try to get this into you."

"You are my mother. Has she dropped dead and been reincarnated just to haunt me?"

Ignoring him, Ray placed the tea on the bedside table. "Just drink it. You'll feel better." He disappeared again, and Alex heard him swearing about the state of the kitchen. With tepid reluctance, he picked up the tea. The strong, thorny odor of peppermint poked his nostrils. Did this stuff really heal anything? Fuck it – if Ray had claimed incantation would heal him, he would try that too.

He sipped at the tea and then lay on his side again, waiting for it to make it worse, better, or do nothing at all.

Ray emerged from the kitchen. "Okay, I've made you some soup and eventually found some Tupperware without anything growing in it. It's in the fridge when you're up for it."

"Is this faith healing?"

"Faith?" Ray raised a solicitous eyebrow. "It's science. Though the human body is one of God's most amazing creations. You understand how it works, you can see into the mind of God. There's a lot to be said for understanding what various foods do to your body. How things are digested, absorbed, how your body uses it. Not that a guy who thinks a brownie and a pastrami and mustard sandwich constitute a decent lunch would necessarily *want* to know. How's that tea?"

"It's all right," Alex said.

"I gotta head in to work. Just promise me you'll eat that soup when you can."

"I will," he promised. Dr. Feldman had medicated him, and Ray's vegetable soup might stay down. He should tell his partner the truth, or some of it. As Ray gathered up his coat, Alex added, "Gibson's called in some favor and has got me a *pro bono* appointment with Theresa Gillard. Can you fucking believe it?"

"Good," Ray said.

That wasn't the response he wanted. "What? You think I need to?"

"Yes."

"Even though I've got a diagnosis of an actual thing now?"

"Come on, Alex, you know it's not just that."

"Did she talk to you?"

"Yeah, she did. She's worried, man. If you're not in tomorrow, I'll come by again." With that, he left the apartment. The locks clicked shut behind him.

Alex closed his eyes and plunged into a fitful sleep. Nonsensical images and surreal events ran into themselves in a confusing and horrifying montage that he didn't remember, but the fear stayed with him when he woke up again. It was dark. Lights from the townhouses on the other side of West 87th shone into the bedroom. He was disoriented, jet-lagged, and the bedside clock flashed 1900 hours. Somehow, he'd slept straight through four hours in broad daylight, oblivious to the city passing through its rush hour mania. The pain in his belly simmered on a tolerably low heat. The fever had not returned. He was now sweltering, buried under three duvets while wearing a hoodie and sweatpants. But his muscles and bones still felt like jelly, and his joints hurt like they'd rusted into sharp fragments.

He disentangled himself from the bed and stole into the kitchen, flipping on the light. No wonder Ray had been swearing. It was in an appalling state, worse than he normally allowed it to get, evidence of his steady deterioration. He was no neat freak, but he made an effort to keep it civilized.

A week's worth of dishes had spread from the sink, marching across the counter in an army, invading the neighboring surfaces. Tumbleweeds of dust had gathered in corners. The soup was in a Tupperware inside the fridge, and the rank smell from the fridge warned him that something had died in there.

He shoved the soup into the microwave and fell onto one of his barstools at the counter while the microwave nuked it. He wasn't hungry but he thought so long as his stomach didn't hurt, he should eat something, get his gut moving again, like the doc had said. The microwave beeped, and he glared at it, as if its demands were unreasonable, and then he poured the soup into the bowl and managed to eat about half of it. He would see how that went. The rest he returned to the fridge.

He shuffled back to the bedroom and crawled under the duvets, attentive to the rise and fall of his ribcage against his arm. An achy sense of longing suffused his body and then expanded into the whole room, the unrequited need for someone, not Ray, who would sit beside him, put their arms around him and breathe against his neck. A wave of misery broke over him. Forlornly, he listened to the thrumming of the rain against the window.

His eyes fell upon his cell phone, still and quiet beside the bed. The temptation to call Becky teased him mercilessly, and he writhed onto his other side, facing away from the phone. She was probably with the not-ex-husband now, smiling and laughing, at least until they broke up again, and she would come pleading and apologising back to Alex, and he would tell her to get lost because enough was enough. He shut his eyes, hoping for sleep, the reprieve of unconsciousness, and feeling well enough by 1600 tomorrow to go to work and deal with other people's problems, like death. At work, he couldn't dominate death, but he could make it behave. People might die in crude, ugly, ostentatious ways, but if he could finagle reasons and sometimes arrest someone, it made it more palatable and orderly. He couldn't solve his own problems, but he could solve theirs.

An hour later, he was still awake and worried about everything. For another hour, he listened to rain, fluctuating between a thundering downpour and a pattering drizzle, but when it became apparent that insomnia had won this round, he despondently heaved himself out of bed, changed into the jeans and the hoodie he'd left in a heap on the floor. Once dressed, he clipped his gun and shield to his belt. Lying awake and letting his mind wander would only take him to places where he didn't want to go, so he might as well get the fuck out of bed and go somewhere useful.

It was one thing he wanted to do for the Kitchener case, something he meant to do alone. Fighting against lethargy and aches in his body, he staggered into the rain-soaked, dreary night, and then he limped onto Columbus. The cold rain made him shiver fiercely. When he caught his breath, he hailed a cab. He rarely took cabs. But he had no chance of walking anywhere, much less surviving the subway.

"West 44th and Eleventh," he said to the cabbie. That club from his surveillance. The Two-Eight detectives had an uninteresting and unenlightening tail, but then Marcus had done the next tail, reporting that Analisa had returned the club, only she had spent a long time there, all evening. Marcus had left before Analisa did, with the view that the overtime approval didn't extend to overtime past 0100 hours. Alex thought he would have stayed with the subject anyway, but never mind. Calling in sick today had inadvertently given him a moment of time and space in a city that had very little of either.

"No problem," the cabbie said in a heavy West African accent, and, driving like he was still in Gambia, tore off down Columbus. The lights of the Upper West Side flew past in a blur, and then they were in Midtown, the taxi charging through the traffic like a yellow juggernaut. Within minutes, it slammed to a halt at the corner of West 44th and Eleventh. There was something to be said for the way people from places with minimalist traffic laws and clogged streets, like parts of Africa and India, drove taxis. They got you to your destination quickly, and for them, typical New York traffic was no object.

"Thanks, pal," Alex said, paying the driver, shakily clambering out of the cab. The neighborhood was fragmented, losing one identity, gaining another, gentrification and atrophy, tatty, half-abandoned brick buildings, an open-air parking lot, a storage place, and glass-box high rises with restaurants and bars on their ground floors, springing out of the tangle of scaffolding and warehouses.

He limped across West 44th and followed a totteringly drunk man through a door leading to a dark anteroom with a single forty-watt bulb casting a sallow light and a stone-faced bouncer staring at him. Alex's pupils dilated, taking in the cinderblock walls, the exposed pipes on the ceiling above his head, the heavyset Italian, who gave him a considerate eyefuck, and Alex painfully aware of his gun rubbing his left hip. Not in a mood for taking shit, Alex returned the eyefuck. The bouncer merely grunted at him and asked the young guy behind him for his ID. Alex winced, feeling middle-aged, depressingly too old to be carded.

He pushed his shoulder into another door and found himself in the main bar. The place stank of sweat and alcohol. The floor stuck to his shoes – years of people spitting and spilling drinks. Percussive club music devastated his eardrums, and he couldn't hear his own thoughts. A fulguration of lights leapt and flashed and darted in dazzling rainbows of colors, and Alex felt a migraine kicking off. On the dance floor, a packed, sweat-encased mass of bodies oscillated in time to the throbbing beat. He faltered for a second, fearing he would puke, but he gritted his teeth until the tension in his jaw boosted his headache.

Battling the undulating, dense, howling dam of human flesh, he sidled up to the bar and scanned the bartenders. His old CI wasn't one of them. Alex let out a whistling, defeated exhalation. His mid-section collapsed, and he sank against the bar. What lunacy had possessed him to do this tonight? He should have stayed in bed under three duvets. And what were the chances that after two decades, his CI wasn't dead or in prison and continuing to work in this hole? Slim to fucking none. This plan seemed like madness every way he looked at it. Twenty years ago, the place boasted the cheapest bar on the West Side, a stage where pole dancers sinuously brandished their bodies, and an excellent pool table. Alex would come in and knock back the whisky and beat everyone at pool. The Mob guys hated him but never bothered him. A lonely young detective with sad eyes, hanging around a bar and shooting pool. That had been his cover, a completely honest cover, while Finnegan, his CI, had passed him tidbits of information about Mob ops and drug deals. But the pool table had vanished, and so had the strippers. Nonetheless, his suspect had come here, twice, and the club had flagged on the background checks, so he had to try.

"What do you want?" said a bartender, his voice disappearing in the electronic noise.

"Water," Alex shouted, and as the bartender scooped ice out of a bucket, Alex surreptitiously flashed tin. The bartender's eyes bugged out and then shot around the bar like pinballs. "There somewhere we can talk?" Alex asked in a lower voice. The man's reaction intrigued him.

"You Narcotics?" the bartender asked, squawking the first word and mouthing the second.

Alex shook his head, and then he slid one of his cards across the bar.

The bartender shiftily eyed it as he handed Alex a glass of water, and he mouthed the word, *homicide?* He lips puckered.

Alex nodded and quaffed a mouthful of water. It washed along his warm, scratchy throat.

"Downstairs men's bathroom, five minutes," hissed the bartender. Then he sidestepped along the bar to his next customer.

The classic bathroom meeting. Alex slugged another large gulp of water and then downed the whole pint. People not particularly savvy about clandestine communication did it because they saw it on TV, but it was not covert nor private. It never gave Alex much confidence. But he limped down the stairs and found that this bathroom was more secure than he'd anticipated because it only had one toilet and one urinal and no walls separating them. And the door locked. The drumbeat from the DJ upstairs pulsed through the ceiling like a heartbeat. He dropped the lid on the toilet and woozily slumped down onto it, holding his stomach. The bathroom smelled nebulously of shit and cleaning products, and shreds of toilet paper were scattered around the floor like confetti.

A minute later, he heard a light knock and grunted. The bartender slithered through the door and skittishly locked it. He was twenty-something, mixed-race, wearing a plaid shirt and a flat cap. A veneer of sweat glistened beneath the cap.

"What's your name?" Alex asked.

"Milo Mahmoud," he answered in a croaking voice.

"What did you wanna talk to me about?"

"I know the police have been watching this place." He blurted and looked at Alex importunately. "There've been other detectives in here before you. I know my boss has got hustles going on, I know, and it's gonna go down some day. I know. And I just work here, man. I literally just work here. I can't have a record. I'm just in this job to pay for law school. I can't be caught up in whatever happens. I get a record, you see, they're never letting me into the bar." His chin quivered.

"Your boss is Sonny Drogo?" Alex's guts wound into distracting cramps, and he squirmed and crossed his legs, wondering how to play this. A witness anxious to make a deal and save his own ass came with considerable credibility reservations, but that was both a problem for the future and a problem for the DAs. Alex might also be stumbling into a Narcotics op, and they might not want him in the middle of it. If they had a long-term investigation gathering evidence against the club and its owner, they very much didn't. Still, when all you wanted was reasonable cause for a search warrant, none of that mattered as much, and it could be untangled later.

"Yeah. He owns the joint. I sometimes see him."

"I know. You ever met a guy who worked here called Finnegan?" One last grasp for his old CI.

The witness blankly shook his head. Then he said breathlessly, "I don't know anything about any homicides. I don't. Honestly. Didn't think my boss was into *that*."

He probably was, because drug dealers tended resolve disputes with 9mms rather than angry emails, but Alex smiled placatingly and said, "That's fine. I just wanna know about someone who came into the club the other week."

"Did *they* kill someone?" Mahmoud squeaked.

"She might be a witness," Alex said blandly. "Analisa Santos." When the name rang no bells, he added, "Pretty Puerto Rican lady. Short, with long hair."

"Oh, *her*," exclaimed Mahmoud with a small smile of gratitude. "I saw her last week. She went straight upstairs."

"Upstairs?"

"Yeah. Downstairs it's like a normal nightclub with a bar. But upstairs, rich guys…Or guys who know my boss… it's always guys… They can get like a lap dance or like… whatever… Maybe more. Maybe drugs. I don't know what goes on up there. They don't say. I just work at the bar, you know. But there's definitely *stuff* that goes on up there that I shouldn't know about."

Alex twitched an eyebrow and stiffened his neck. "Can you remember anything else about her?"

354

"Uh… she came in and said she was working here. I thought she was gonna be at the bar, but then she asked me where Drogo was. I thought, she's not working at the bar. He doesn't hire bartenders, cleaners, whatever. I know that much. He's got a manager, and he deals with all that. Drogo only deals with the sketchy shit."

"Gotcha. What did you tell her?"

"I said the boss' office is upstairs, and she went upstairs. Then my shift ended. Haven't seen her since."

"Okay. And you don't know anything else about the 'sketchy shit' up there? Details?"

"No, sorry," the witness groaned, and then he grinned like a gargoyle. "But I can try to find out if it'll keep—"

"No, no," Alex interrupted curtly. "Just keep your head down. Don't start doing any stupid Jack Reacher shit. You don't wanna piss off these people, hear me? You've been helpful. Take my card and call or email me tomorrow. You gotta come into my office and give that statement under oath, okay?" He shoved the card into Mahmoud's hand.

"Under oath? Like in court?" Mahmoud exclaimed in fright and rubbed his hands together, agitated.

"Not in court," Alex corrected. "My office. Just to my boss and another detective or two."

The witness held his grave young face in both hands, whimpering, "But you said under oath. Doesn't that mean testifying?"

"Maybe. Some day. But now you're only talking to us. It's like *first* half of *Law and Order*." Court might happen later, but one step at a time. For a judge to accept a CI's statement as evidence supporting a search warrant, the CI had to give the statement under oath to the investigator and their supervisor.

"Okay, okay." Mahmoud looked relieved. "I'll email and like, find a time. But if this place gets busted, I gotta stay out of trouble."

"I'll take care of it. But you might wanna think about looking for a new bar job."

The witness nodded with revolutionary fervor. "Yes, I know, but this place pays way better… But I should, I know." Then he walked backwards out the door, tapping it shut behind him.

Alex sat mutely in a ponderous melancholy, waiting expectantly for the witness to disappear. He heard the crunch of footsteps recede down the hall, and then he pushed himself to his feet. His blood pressure nosedived, and he staggered headlong into the wall, smashing his knee into the urinal. "Fuck!" he hissed, grappling with reserves of willpower. He held himself upright with the top of the urinal and leaned over, tenderly nursing his sore knee, waiting for his heart to pump blood back into his head.

Once he seemed steadier on his feet, he took a piss – that pint of water had gone through him – and then he drank a few swallows from the sink. It occurred to him that while he still felt like shit, Ray's vegetable soup hadn't precipitated vomiting, and it had been a couple hours. Eyes down, he hobbled up the stairs and threaded through the frothing, steaming crowd and thrashing music, and then he sprawled out into the night where his lungs worked. Lightheaded, freezing, he tightened his overcoat around his sides. He was afraid of fainting, like in the DA's office.

It was still raining. He dizzily clung to a lamppost and stared hard at the traffic on Eleventh, sizing up approaching cabs, but every single one had its roof lights dimmed. It was almost 2100 hours, the time when people go out in Midtown. Impatience and desperation scorched like lava through his body. He was sick. And there were no cabs. Why was there never an available taxi when you needed one? Cabs were plentiful when you didn't. Twenty minutes later, the rain had soaked his clothes, and he shivered so savagely he could barely stand, and he started phoning a private hire cab, but suddenly he saw a taxi cruising down Eleventh with its light on.

He hailed it and unsteadily toppled into the backseat, breathing in the air-freshener-leather-sweat aroma. He told the driver where to go, and his heavy eyelids fell shut. If the cab driver noticed the sweat on his face, he didn't say anything.

Chapter Twenty-Seven

December 14th

"Are you nuts?" Ray exploded. "You could barely stand up, you had a fever, and you went to Midtown by yourself to talk to a fucking informant! You were a *mess* when I dropped by your apartment."

"I took a cab," explained Alex, as if it had been the perfectly rational thing to do. "I didn't have to walk very far." He did not tell them that he had precisely the same thought when he nearly collapsed in the bathroom or felt close to fainting in the middle of Eleventh Avenue.

"You're as bad as my kids," drawled Gibson. "When they're too sick to go to school and then want to go out with their friends that evening. I should give you a command discipline." If you took sick leave, you weren't meant to be running around town, for work or for anything else.

"I was feeling better."

"You need to take care of yourself," she scolded, reminding him of his mother. "You got no color in your face. I should send you home."

"I got probable cause," he entreated. "Santos went into a club with known associations to organized crime. She wanted to talk to the owner. NITRO and SAFEnet tell me it's got kites, and the owner, a guy called Sonny Drogo, has been under investigation by Manhattan South Narcotics. The CI knew that. The skels who ran it when I was in the Tenth are long gone, but same shit, different dealers. I just can't believe she unwittingly let Kitchener use her car. She's got to be tied up in his shit."

"Can you bring this informant of yours here for a sworn statement?" queried Gibson doubtfully.

"Yeah, I think so."

"Is he credible?"

"Ish."

"Ish?" Unconvinced, she dragged the word into two syllables.

"He thinks Narc's gonna bust the club, and he doesn't wanna be charged with anything if they do."

"Right, so he'll tell you whatever you wanna hear if it gets him out of a jam."

Alex contorted his features into a lame and distracted smile. "Yeah."

"And Narc is on board?"

"They will be. It's a cop-killing," Alex surmised unpersuasively.

"Meaning, they have no idea you've been in that club talking to witnesses."

"Yeah."

"Fine," Gibson sighed, her jaw firm with censorious approbation, and she cautioned, "Narc's not gonna be pleased that we're messing with their op, and we haven't told them. But we'll register your CI on a contingency basis. Do you have any evidence that Santos actually *knows* this place is a drug front?"

"No," he admitted, feeling listless and sticky. "It's a guess."

"Well?" she said.

"My CI doesn't think she was talking to Drogo about working behind the bar. Said he doesn't deal with the legit side of things."

"You got anything else?"

Sweat dripped along his skin, and he loosened his belt one hole, horrified by how damp his shirt felt. "Soccer equipment?" he said sarcastically.

"It is a little implausible," Gibson agreed with another long-suffering sigh. "Write up a warrant application, then go home and rest."

"Yes, ma'am."

"Your informant better get his butt here quickly."

"Ten-four."

After that meeting, Alex typed up his affidavit, arranging his evidence: the location of Bailey's body, Analisa's initial sketchy statement, the statement of the bartender, and Analisa's visits to the club (one with organized crime connections and active complaints) as observed by detectives. He officiously listed what he expected – or wanted – to find. *Evidence relating to a homicide or drug paraphernalia.* That would give them permission to lawfully overturn any mattress, cupboard, or hole in the wall where one might hide a murder weapon, or heroin.

Therefore, given that the witness herself stated that Kitchener often stayed in her apartment and his guilty plea for the robbery in case 04-28-114, wherein he stole $1015 from Armando's Groceries on West 123rd Street and Malcolm X Bvld., we believe Santos had a clear interest in the proceeds of said robbery, which constitutes the basis of our probable cause.

The joints in his fingers ached, and his brain felt like a wet sponge. Only half an hour into the eight-by-four, and fatigue pulled him under like a deadly rip tide. *Our view, based on this evidence, is that Santos colluded with Kitchener to murder Bailey, which therefore meant that two perpetrators did not have to split the cash taken from the safe of the bodega.*

He printed the affidavit and ran it through all the background checks, which he'd done when he tailed Analisa, so he already knew she would not show up on any of the federal or state databases. But he had to do it again for the warrant, a redundant exercise in bureaucracy that depleted his reserves. Then he attached it to an email and sent it for McNally's approval. He left it there and followed Gibson's orders to go home and rest. Even without orders, he doubted he could finish this tour with his body aching and broken down.

Four days later, Alex and Ray spent an evening with Finnane and Gribaldi, the Two-Eight detectives, eating Chinese take-out and drawing up a tac plan for their search warrant. They knew from their surveillance that Analisa lived alone with her son, but sometimes her aging mother was there. Neither was likely to hurt anyone. As his colleagues devoured the take-out, Alex restricted himself to plain rice, only a small amount of it, and he looked mournfully at the sautéed mushrooms, beef in black bean sauce, and Szechuan chicken being split amongst the other detectives. All at once, he missed Chinese food, but he felt like he would be sick if he ate it. He'd gone back to work in time to interview the bartender, along with Gibson and Ray, and then submit the warrant application to a judge, who granted it the next day. Loaded up with drugs, he'd expected his body to bounce back to health, but his appetite was virtually non-existent, and he felt flattened under the terrible, sickening sensation that catastrophes were lurking everywhere.

Once a tac plan had been devised and approved by Gibson and the boss in the Two-Eight, they drove up to 157th, two detectives' unmarked cars and four marked ones. Neighbors peered through their windows at the pageant of police cars parking along their street. Braver, or at least nosier, neighbors appeared on their stoops. Alex was reminded of the people who had watched them eleven years ago when they went into that nightclub, but the street had none of the raw, violent energy that had combusted in their faces. Since 9/11, people weren't that pissed off at the police anymore. One guy lounging over the railing of his stoop even wore one of those 'NYPD' baseball caps that had appeared everywhere after 9/11. You wouldn't have imagined that in Washington Heights in the '90s, not in your most outrageous fantasies.

They buzzed Analisa's door and identified themselves.

She said abruptly, "I've answered all your questions."

"We have a search warrant," Alex said to the intercom.

She swore in Spanish.

"You have to let us in," Alex told her.

The buzzer sounded, and they marched in a herd up the stairs and threw open the apartment door. Analisa showered them with an earful of Spanish cursing. An wizened old lady, her mother, sat on a chair in the corner, participating in the rapid-fire Spanish abuse.

A thin man in his thirties with a goatee flung open the bathroom door, leaping into the room, Analisa shouting at him in Spanish, her voice strident and scared. He threw a punch at Alex, who had been standing nearest to the bathroom and not paying as much attention to a closed door as he should have been. He ducked and caught the guy's wrist, spun him around, twisting his arm, hard, behind his back, forcing him to the ground. The guy screeched in pain. Alex felt the gristle tearing and joints popping as he applied torque to the arm, and he grabbed his other arm, yanking it behind his back, and then he slapped on the cuffs. Ray, the Two-Eight detectives, and the uniforms now had their guns out.

"Is there anyone else in here?" Ray demanded, gesturing around the apartment with his gun, outraged by the near-attack on his partner.

"No," said Analisa.

The uniforms were clearing all the rooms anyway, kicking open every door, guns drawn. They didn't want any more surprises. There was a

Spanish exchange between Ray, Analisa, and the guy Alex had cuffed on the floor.

"He's her brother," said Ray.

Alex stood up and hauled the brother to his feet, shoving him up against a wall, frisking him for weapons or drugs, but he didn't have any. He gave the collar to one of the young uniforms: he was long past caring about more arrests on his record, especially for low-grade felonies, like attempted assault on a police officer. Besides, his head was spinning, his lungs paralyzed like he'd taken a blow to the gut. He scrubbed away the sweat beading on his forehead and counted his sobbing, mangled breaths so his colleagues wouldn't notice.

But they weren't paying attention to him anyway. Whether it was sparked by the sight of her son being thrown to the ground and cuffed, or half a dozen cops in the room with their guns out, no one knew, but Analisa's mother started retching for air, clutching at her throat. She didn't speak a word of English. Ray established she had some kind of breathing condition. COPD or something. Then she stopped breathing. Someone called in a ten-fifty-four while Ray and Duncan Finnane crouched on either side of her. Ray was saying calming things in Spanish. Finnane was administering CPR. Analisa was crying. Fucking chaos.

Alex, breathless and blinded by white lights and vertigo, needed to lie or at least sit down but he couldn't, not here, not without making it obvious that he was also unwell, so he shoved his back against the doorframe, fighting his own private war while everyone else dealt with Analisa's mother. An ambulance arrived, EMS with oxygen tanks and breathing apparatuses, and they strapped her onto a stretcher, put a mask over her face, wheeled her out of the room. One of the paramedics assured Analisa that her mother would probably be fine, and Alex hoped so too because the last thing they needed was a fucking lawsuit. A great surge of air poured into lungs. Oh, thank God. He wouldn't be joining Analisa's mother in the bus. His head braked its violent spinning. He bit down hard on the inside of his lip, worried that he wasn't safe to be on the street if he had vertigo spells and wasn't on his toes during a warrant entry. In a few more days, he would feel better. That was what the doc had said, right?

361

Analisa was shouting at Ray in furious Spanish. Lots of swear words. Alex recognized those. Then she could only stand by, helpless, as the police excavated her apartment. She was upset. Her kid kept asking what was going on, and she snapped, in Spanish, for him to be quiet and go to his room. She was panicky, a look of powerlessness Alex recognized. Executing a search warrant in front of a perp – overturning their whole lives – had inspired many a suspect or witness to talk. While everyone foraged around the apartment for the evidence specified in the warrant, Alex kept an eye on her, hopeful this might break her. Moreover, he didn't feel like he would be helpful to the search. His head was so fogged up that he would probably miss ten kilos of heroin if he fell in it.

When her eyes glazed over with the sheen of unrestrainable tears, he approached her, hands in his coat pockets, unthreatening. "There something you wanna talk about?" he asked gently.

"Fuck you, you asshole," she said, proving that she was just as adept at swearing in English as she was in Spanish.

"I think it might be better for us to talk at the precinct."

"Are you arresting me?" she snarled.

"No, we're not," he replied mildly. "You don't have to come with us. But if you have something you wanna say, you know. And it would be better." He held her gaze. He knew that he had to be careful; he could bring her in, but it had to be voluntary, plain to her that she could leave whenever. Otherwise, the courts would consider it custody, and they would have to *Mirandize* her.

She squared her shoulders, acting hostile, but then she sniffled, looking away and mumbling, "Fine. We can talk. But I want to talk to the *Boricua* cop."

"My partner?"

"Yeah, him."

"He'll come to the precinct with us."

She bobbed her head tersely, sort of an agreement.

Alex found Ray in the bedroom with Finnane, gutting a desk. "Whaddaya got?" The bedroom was the size of the Mounted Unit's stables, but neat and orderly. It smelled dulcetly of perfume and scented candles. There were only women's things in it. Makeup, clothes, about thirty pairs of shoes. If Kitchener had stayed here, he either didn't leave anything or Analisa had disposed of it.

"Some letters from her landlord saying she's in arrears," said Ray. "Bank statements dipping into negative numbers. Still looking."

"She's strapped for cash."

"I'll say," drawled Finnane, who was originally from Georgia.

"I got her to agree to come to a precinct for a chat," Alex related. "So long as Ray comes along. But I think we'd better go now before she changes her mind."

"If you've got the synergy with her, you should go. Gribaldi and I will finish up this search," said Finnane.

"Synergy?" said Ray.

Finnane shrugged. "It's a great Scrabble word."

Alex and Ray left the apartment with Analisa and her son, and they shepherded them into the back of the car. They didn't want to take the kid along, but Analisa insisted that with her mother now in the hospital and brother under arrest, thanks to the NYPD, she had no one to watch him, and she wasn't under arrest, was she? For his part, Miguel was thrilled to be riding in a police car. While Analisa stayed somber for the drive to the Three-Three Precinct, Miguel kept asking them to turn on the sirens, put him in cuffs, and could he see their guns. It made his day when they arrived at the precinct and co-opted a detective in the Three-Three squad into babysitting, giving him a tour of the precinct while they interviewed his mother. As they steered Analisa towards the interrogation room, they heard the detective telling Miguel some bullshit story about why the lights at the front of every New York precinct were green.

She'd quashed the vulnerability Alex had seen in the apartment like illegally seized evidence, and she slouched on the metal chair, subdued and glowering. "Fuck this shit," she said belligerently, shoving the table like she wanted to scoot backwards, but the chair was bolted to the floor.

"You want anything?" Alex asked. He was facing her, the memo book on his thigh, out of her view. He breathed in the smell of sweat; hers, his own, he wasn't sure. "Tea? Coffee? There's a nice bodega on the corner, can get a sandwich or something if you like."

"Doesn't matter." She placed her elbows on the table, covering her eyes with her palms.

"We're gonna record this interview, okay? Just standard procedure." Alex popped a tape into the machine on the table and checked that it was ready to go.

"Whatever," she huffed.

Pushing 'record,' Alex spoke to the machine. "This is Manhattan North Homicide Detective Alex Boswell. With me are Detective Raphael Espinosa, also of Manhattan North Homicide, and Analisa Santos, a thirty-four year old Puerto Rican female, from 146 East 157th Street, Washington Heights. We are in Interrogation Room Two at the 33rd Precinct." A slight, reassuring smile at Analisa, then, as if none of this mattered, he blithely pushed the tape recorder to the side, out of her immediate line of sight.

Then he thought about how his life and health had fallen apart over the last month. He thought about how he'd survived for years in a chronic state of falling apart to some degree. That was why he went to weekly AA meetings. Every person in that church basement lived in one of two conditions and often, both at once: just about to fuck up or having just fucked up. With that shared empathy and experience, the rebounds, the relapses, those tinctures of what solitude buys, they understood, and Alex found strength in their solidarity.

And just as he connected with his fellow addicts in an AA meeting, he could connect with many of the people he carted into these rooms. If they found themselves in an NYPD interrogation room, the odds were fairly good that they had fucked up. Plenty were addicts themselves, trapped in never-ending patterns of dysfunctional behavior, a thrall to the demons in their heads. He got them. They were his demons too. And he used that. You use whatever you have at your disposal. He had psychologically hurt himself in interrogations if he thought he could break the perp as well.

Leaning back in his chair, re-crossing his legs, he spoke with sincere pain and desperation, letting his real emotions through. "I know things are hard for you. I know you're hard up right now. Money's tight. Landlord's at your back."

"So?" Her eyes flashed.

"We know you're working a second job," stated Alex. "That sucks."

"What second job?"

"Don't give us this bullshit," said Ray gruffly.

364

Play acting a bit, Alex said, "Lay off, Ray. Analisa, you got a job working nights at that club in Midtown?"

She glanced from one detective to the other before her gaze dropped to the floor and a squeaky noise came from her throat. Then she sniffed and nodded. This was too easy. Alex handed her a box of Kleenex, and she snatched one, blowing her nose and then squashing it in her fist. "Yes. Working at the bar."

"The bar?"

"Yes, the bar."

"Serving drinks?"

"Yes, duh. What do you think people do at bars? I need the money or I'm gonna lose that apartment." She paled slightly, and Alex thought they should revisit that, but not yet.

"The catering job struggling to pay the rent?" he asked. "Those jobs don't pay shit."

"Yeah, pay is shit. Rent's going up," she said shortly, tears glistening in her eyes. "Even in the Heights."

"Everywhere in the city." He was a lucky son of a bitch to own his place on the Upper West, and luckier still to have bought it in the early 1990s, before Manhattan real estate rocketed into the stratosphere. "It's gotten crazy."

"They're driving the working class outta the Heights," she wheezed. "It's gonna be just like the Upper West Side. Who can afford the Upper West Side?"

Well, he thought. "Does this have anything to do with Harold holding up that bodega?"

"He said he was gonna get me the money this month."

Ray, still in 'bad cop' mode, leveled, "A convicted armed robber promised you, what? Seven, eight hundred dollars? You didn't wonder?"

"I didn't think he was gonna rob a store or kill anyone," she wailed, blowing her nose loudly.

"How did you think he was gonna get it then?"

"Get a job. Go to the OTB. I don't know. He said he wasn't doing no more crime. He ain't never killed anyone before."

"Did he give you any of that money when he borrowed your car that morning?" asked Alex, already knowing the answer.

She whimpered and squished the Kleenex against her nose. "I didn't know he had the money. Didn't know what he'd done that morning."

"We found nine hundred fifty bucks on him when we picked him up at Penn Station," Alex told her soberly. "He was trying to skip town with it."

She emitted a strangled sob. "He was just scared. He'd killed the cop. He didn't want no one to die."

Except for the three people he's killed, thought Alex.

"So, he admitted to you that he killed the cop," said Ray.

"No, he didn't say nothing when he came by that morning. You said he did. And the news said he did."

"He was leaving town with the money he said he was gonna give you, and you still want to protect him." Disappointed, Ray shook his head.

"I ain't protecting him, Detective," she said with more strength in her voice. "He said he'd help me with my rent. Didn't say how. He was looking for a job. I didn't want him robbing or killing no one. I'm trying to raise my son right. Don't want him anywhere near this stuff."

"It would have been much easier if you'd told us this from the start," Alex said in a wounded voice, as if she'd hurt him with her dishonesty. Suspects expected cops to be strident and bellicose, like interrogation scenes on TV. They didn't expect them to be vulnerable and a little anxious, the most efficacious weapon in Alex's arsenal for throwing them off-balance.

"Yeah, then you would have been saying I knew something about these murders, and I don't."

Like a sudden, cold wind, the white lights flickered in his peripheral vision. *Fuck you,* he thought, touching the corners of his eyes, brushing his eyelashes with his fingertips. Why were they here, with no rhyme nor reason? This interrogation wasn't stressful or even remotely difficult. His heart fluttered like a sparrow's wings. These episodes were becoming more frequent, more random. That scared the hell out of him.

Ray said, "No, things are better for you when you tell us what's really going on. You telling us the truth now?"

The lights were spreading like an evil vapor, and Alex lowered his eyelids. His heart was hammering in aching terror, and he heard a grating shriek, metal ripped apart, and he saw bodies, flesh and organs and blood in a grisly pink mess on city streets.

Then, pain in his side, Ray's elbow in his ribs. It snapped him back into reality. He glanced at his partner, who must have noticed the look on his face, the color draining.

"Lex, we should call Gibson and McNally, see what they think."

Ray was trying to get him out of the room. He understood Ray's pretense and left under that partial guise of phoning Gibson and McNally, leaving Ray to solicit more information out of Analisa through their shared cultural heritage. The visions had crumbled into nothing, like a nightmare, and the lights and the panic retreated to a nearby perimeter of consciousness, leaving him winded and limp. He phoned his boss and the prosecutor. He also phoned the Two-Eight detective squad and asked how the search had panned out: had they found anything incriminating? Drugs? Weapons? Bloody clothes? Anything at all? They sounded glum; they hadn't. After consultations with Gibson and McNally, they agreed that unless someone in the club grassed her up, or she confessed to helping Kitchener kill Bailey and dump his body, they didn't have enough evidence to arrest her. They could poke around the nightclub and corroborate Santos' story, or the bartender's, but Gibson cautioned that a displeased Narcotics captain had put the kibosh on that. The MNHS investigation had stepped on enough toes, and their cop-killer had been indicted, hadn't he? McNally exhorted that the least the detectives could do was obtain a formal statement from Santos about Kitchener promising to pay off her rent.

Alex started back towards the interrogation room, but then changed course for the precinct's bathroom instead, where he scrubbed the sweat off his face and flushed his eyes with the water. Like a rock to the head, it reminded him of Gibson's orders – a requisite meeting with Theresa Gillard. His healing guts were writhing. The lights, the visions, the panic, his recent illness – this shit could get him committed to a psych ward. They wouldn't let him keep his gun after that. This could be his last case. No one would let a mad homicide detective stay on the streets. His flesh creeped, and he ran his pasty tongue over his lips. He saw himself locked in a ward, so doped up on antipsychotics that he didn't know who he was. When they let him out, he would be pushing papers in Siberia – the moniker of the car impound near La Guardia.

Just let me close this case, he pleaded, as if it was something sentient, and he could reason with it. Then he lingered outside the interrogation room, one hand on his painful chest, feeling sparkling anguish, beyond despair, as if there was something far more invidious and destructive than despair and no word for it. He leaned a shoulder on the one-way, watching Ray working on Analisa, the two switching fluidly between Spanish and English.

In the precinct's squad room, braying noise erupted, a Narcotics squad bringing in a string of freshly apprehended perps. Dope, crack, weed. The perps were taken individually to the bathroom, by female and male detectives, depending on the gender of the perp, and cavity searched. His day could be worse. He could be a narcotics detective, looking up the ass of some skel for a vial of crack or a bag of heroin.

Meanwhile, Analisa sobbed into a snowy pile of tissues. Ray spoke to her in Spanish, his tone mollifying and gentle. She swapped to English, weeping, "I'd never work in that club if I had a choice."

"We heard you were working upstairs," Ray said empathetically. "Where you have to do things to guys… Like sexual things?"

Offended, she recoiled and sprang upright. "Sexual things? *Puta madre.* What the hell are you talking about? I work in the bar. I serve drinks, and I'm exhausted, and I can't be the best mother to my son because I'm sometimes at that place until three in the morning, and then I have to work my other job. But *cosas sexuales? De ninguna manera.*"

Patiently, Ray replied, "We heard you weren't working at the bar."

"You heard wrong," she said bluntly. "I don't know about no upstairs. It's just a nightclub."

"Why that club?" asked Ray, retreating and trying another approach.

"They pay well for a bar job. And the tips are good. Better than minimum wage. Harold's in prison for a long time. Miguel's father is a *pendejo* and he's in prison in California. I can't be on the streets with my son or stuck in a homeless shelter with the alcoholics and junkies. The catering company, they don't even pay for my fuel."

"A lot better?" said Ray.

"*Sí.* Why else would I put myself through that…*mierda?* I hate working in bars. But I can pay my rent and food and give my son a good life." Then they switched back to Spanish.

Alex felt a pang of sympathy for her and moved his hand over his chin as he watched her crying to Ray. Single mother. Shitty low paying job. Yeah, it sucked. But God knows he'd seen desperation and social

368

deprivation a thousand times over in the last twenty-six years, and he wondered if she was lying, or if the bartender had been. Someone was. But that was the first rule of homicide investigation: everyone lies. Yet in that moment, he knew how she must feel, how it must be to look at your whole life and realize you've made an utter SNAFU of it.

Taking a plunging breath like he'd just discovered air, he went back into the room, lowering himself into the chair next to her. Taking over from Ray. Tag-team, back and forth, breaking the suspect down, a battering-ram against the diaphanous barriers of half-truths and flat-out lies.

"I know, it's not an easy situation, not easy at all," he said sincerely. "But you've gotta help us out here. Tell me again, what happened when Harold came to your place that morning."

She asthenically repeated the same story that she had told them when they'd first arrived at her apartment in October. Harold wanted her car to move soccer equipment, two goal posts and some balls. He borrowed it for twenty minutes and then disappeared.

"Did he say he needed your help? He was in a bad situation, injured, wasn't he?"

"Yes, he was hurt in the arm. I told you, he said it was a bar fight." She had a hang-dog look about her, wearied of answering questions.

"A bar fight. With guns. Did you know it was a bullet wound?"

Emphatically, she shook her head. "No. But I'm not surprised. He had lots of friends with guns."

"Did he have one?"

She avoided his eyes and played with the ostentatious rings on her fingers. "I ain't seen no gun."

"You haven't seen a gun," echoed Alex. "But you knew he had one."

"They're easy to get," she said.

"Did he tell you he had one?"

"He wouldn't tell me. He knew I don't wanna know."

"But you did know."

"I thought he might," Analisa conceded, still refusing to meet his gaze. "But I'd never seen it."

"Bailey was a pretty bad guy," Alex said, angling back towards the 'fight,' the bullet wound, now that they agreed that Kitchener had a gun. "You said so yourself."

369

"He was."

"Maybe he and Harold got into a fight, huh? Is that what Harold said? Harold didn't mean to kill him, but sometimes, things get outta hand. Then you thought you'd help him. Right?" The out. He was pretty good at making this shit up too, but he'd spent most of his life listening criminals' stories, the bogus excuses, the terrible misdeeds, the dire luck, and the sociopathic greed and capriciousness.

"He never said who he got in a fight with. Never said he killed anyone."

How far do you push it before your interview crosses the line into interrogation? Or you give a defense lawyer grounds to say you coerced testimony, which they'll allege you did anyway? He pushed a little further. "You knew he wasn't moving soccer equipment around at eight in the morning."

"He said he was."

"You believe that?"

She glared at him. "You say he was moving a body, so he was moving a body. But he didn't tell me nothing. I say, 'just bring the car back in twenty minutes,' so he did."

"You didn't think—"

"I didn't think nothing." Fresh tears speckled her eyes, and she clasped another handful of tissues.

You didn't want to think, he thought.

"You met the owner of the club?" asked Ray.

"What?" she said, perplexed by his *non sequitur*.

"You met the owner, Sonny Drogo. We know you did. We were told you asked to see him."

"Yes, but what does it matter?"

"You know he's not *just* a club owner. Like Harold was *just* moving soccer balls."

"One of my friends works there and says the pay is good. I met the owner and we discussed shifts. My hours have to be weird because of the catering job and my son. That's why I met him."

"Working in the bar?" Alex let the sarcasm drip gently into his voice.

"Yes. I said. In the bar."

"You're unlucky as hell," he commented, letting his voice crack as if that hurt him too. "You don't know your boyfriend's still using; you

370

don't know he's just killed two people and wants your car for some strange reason; you don't know the club you happen to get a job in happens to be under investigation for laundering drug money."

"I guess I am." She turned away from him in distress.

They went around in more circles but always arrived at the same place, like the tourist boat circumnavigating Manhattan. Analisa stuck to her guns with her story, and they had nothing else on her. Then again, Alex reflected, there is a part of everyone, himself included – especially himself – that made no sense, and the city was full of people who never made any sense at all. Maybe she had really believed that Kitchener had reformed. Maybe she didn't want to know that he hadn't. Maybe she went to the club looking to unload Kitchener's drugs or flog a firearm, or maybe she happened to stumble into it because it offered decent pay, a job that covered her rent. Maybe she helped Kitchener shoot Bailey, throw his body over the guardrails of the highway, and gathered the trash bags to throw on top of him, but no one would ever know, the forensic evidence would not say, and neither would she. Like Alex had told PO Simmonds outside of the squad offices, sometimes the evidence wasn't there no matter how much you wished otherwise, and you had to live with that.

"You wanna get outta here?" Alex asked, wearing his own inescapable exhaustion on his sleeve.

"Yes. Or call a lawyer," she said curtly.

"Then we're gonna be here a lot longer. I don't want that. I doubt you do. Write a sworn statement saying Harold promised you the money, then we're done."

"That's it?"

"Yeah."

After Analisa had diffidently signed her statement, Alex and Ray took her and Miguel to Columbia Pres to see her mother. The car ride was quiet and unbearably awkward. Analisa had nothing more to say, so she stewed in her unhappiness in the back seat, while Miguel enthusiastically announced that he wanted to be a cop, to his mother's pointed silence. Alex didn't have anything to say, either. He'd given the case all he had, and he felt hollowed out and drunkenly tired, and something with sharp teeth was chewing on his guts.

Ray helped Analisa and Miguel out of the Ford, and Alex whispered to his partner that his stomach hurt, and he would wait in the car. Ray crinkled his brows, and the muscles bunched in his jaw. But he guided Analisa and Miguel towards the big revolving door, tossing Alex a remonstrating look over his shoulder.

Alex channel surfed on the radio, and the weeping sprang upon him like a mugger. Fuck, what was this? His emotions exploding like he had a pipe bomb in his chest. Through streaming tears, he reminded himself that he hadn't had an attack in the precinct. He'd done his job. He'd proven that he still could. He might not have proven a damned thing with regards to Analisa's guilt in that homicide, but he had proven he could just about function. If he could resist it, he could stay out of the psych ward. That was the worst outcome. Being locked up, attending group therapy meetings, suffering the indignities of invasions of privacy and meds forced down his throat. And his gold shield would be revoked on a permanent basis because a severely depressed detective would not be allowed to carry a firearm. But from work, he suspected he could talk his way out of an involuntary commitment. He knew the New York Mental Hygiene laws were designed for the well-being of lawyers rather than patients, and he could play it. He held that certainty close.

Wiping at the tears with the back of his hand, he prayed that Ray would stay in the hospital for a few more minutes. God help him if his partner saw him like this.

Chapter Twenty-Eight

December 21st

Alex hung back near the door, thumbs hooked on his belt. Prickles of perspiration were turning chilly on his forehead. In front of him, Ray and Vito Indelicata questioned the CEO of the corporation that owned the Elm Tree Care Home. A squadron of four lawyers surrounded the man, like protective fighter planes. The facts of the case slid out of Alex's mind; the reasons they had brought this guy and his lawyers into the 34th Precinct house forgotten in the flak-filled fog of mortar exploding in his brain. At first, he tried to claw his way out, asking the witness a few pointless questions, but it didn't feel right. Overcome with hopelessness and not feeling like himself, he retreated into a bedeviled silence.

His cell phone rang, the noise a discomfiting echo in his bleak tunnel. His hand flipped open the phone before his brain processed it. McNally. He dipped his head and slipped out of the interview room. Squad room dissonance hurt his ears. He put the cell to his ear, his face and eyes pinched with pain.

"I need you and Espinosa down here forthwith," barked McNally.

"We're in the middle of an interview," said Alex. "In the Three-Four," he added, emphasizing their distance from Centre Street.

"Well, if you're in the Three-Four, can't you leave it to the precinct squad?"

"Fuck," Alex complained. Yes, but he didn't like leaving Indelicata a free hand with his cases, or ordinarily he didn't, but the black mortar in his head had knocked the breath out of his lungs, and he said morosely, "What's the problem, Simon?"

"Kitchener case. And we need to talk *this afternoon.*"

"Did you have that hearing for it?"

"Yes, that's why we need to meet now."

"Are you losing the hearing?"

"Not yet. But you need to get your butts here, so we don't."

Alex extracted Ray from the interview room and told him McNally wanted to see them forthwith. A cop-killing took precedence over everything, and Ray was at his wit's end with CEOs and lawyers anyway. "If I hear any more corporate double-speak..." he snarled.

Alex nodded solemnly, as if he agreed and shared Ray's exasperation, but he was hoping fresh air and the drive downtown would clear his head from the blackness laying siege to his psyche. It probably wouldn't. Getting out of the Three-Four seemed wise, though, because Indelicata had mercilessly heckled and berated him for giving up the drink, and Alex dared not give any whiff of fragility around the Three-Four squad.

They bumped along the curving, potholed flanks of the West Side Highway, Alex silent, staring out the window at the Hudson glistening in the sun, thinking, he could lose himself in its cold depths. He felt his body ticking with uncontrollable internal tremors, and a vein in his forearm began palpitating. Ray studied him with one eye and the road with the other, but after he sputtered out a few complaints about CEOs and profiteering at the expense of autistic kids, they both sat in uneasy silence. Neither detective spoke at all on the drive through the heavy, mesmerizing traffic and narrow downtown streets. Alex's sense of desolation worsened as they turned off onto Centre Street. He got out of the car and felt like the only things stirring were himself and a cold wind, the whole square and its courthouses insensate, bereft of everything human except for the post-9/11 military guys standing dolorously beside the columns at 100 Centre Street's south entrance, cradling their rifles.

After the security line at One Hogan Place, people wandered apart in a noiseless eddy of motion and were sucked away into the cloying, grey stillness. Sound itself had detached from reality, the voices discussing a case and a soccer game dissonant, the humming elevator otherworldly. The detectives wandered down the Trial Bureau's hallways, and through a cracked door, Alex saw Marie and a few other ADAs hungrily examining a collection of Scotch that had been part of an asset forfeiture, and he envisioned that some other version of himself, in some other time and place, might have an opinion – jealousy or amusement or that nagging bitch of a doubt that asset forfeiture didn't quite parallel due process – but he only squinted through the half-opened door with indifferent curiosity.

Then they met McNally in his office, rather than outside, which never foretold good news.

Playing with his carabiner, Simon stridently announced, "Judge Maguire is a fuckwit, and there's a chance we might not be able to proceed on double jeopardy grounds."

The ADA's abrasive bellicosity crashed in through Alex's numbing haze, and he blinked and stared at Simon, stupefied. "I thought you said the motion was a load of shit," He sighed languorously, shoving his fingers into his eye sockets, his breath hot against his hands.

"I thought it was, but Judge Maguire is a fucking idiot and he's buying it. Yesterday, at the hearing, Kitchener took the stand and testified that he had promised his girlfriend eight-hundred fifty dollars for her rent, and he thought robbing a bodega early in the morning, before it opened to customers, was a good idea. He talked Bailey into it because he thought Bailey was stupid as fuck, short of cash, and in trouble with some Heights dealers if he didn't get some."

"He's confessing to a murder to get out of being prosecuted for a murder?" asked Ray, astonished.

"Yes."

"It corroborates *her* story," Ray said flatly. "Did you see our latest 'fives? Guards in the Tombs reported that Kitchener received a phone call from Analisa shortly after we interviewed her."

"Yes," Simon brusquely acknowledged, snapping his carabiner a few more times and pinching his own finger in the gate. "He then testified that their takings from the store weren't as much as he hoped. They wouldn't cover Santos' rent if they split it. So, he had to get Bailey's half. After it all got fucked on 123rd and they drove downtown and dumped the van and driver, Kitchener said he convinced Bailey to take the subway to the Heights, saying they'd leave town in Santos' car. But Kitchener said he wasn't actually going to do that, because you can't steal your girlfriend's car, apparently. You can rob a fucking store and kill two fucking people, but it's nice to know where he draws a line." The prosecutor sniffed, bemused. "Once they got the car, Kitchener threatened Bailey with that .38 you found and asked for all the money. That was never gonna end well, because Bailey was planning on paying off a dealer and scoring big on top of that, and he wouldn't give up the other half. Obviously. Not even at gunpoint. Kitchener said that they argued about it, and the gun accidentally went off."

"Twice. Into Bailey's head," Alex murmured, gently massaging his cheekbones. "Classic."

"The judge would say that is an issue of fact for a jury, not an issue of law for this particular hearing," Simon replied. "Anyway, Leonard is asserting that the defense was never given an opportunity to consolidate the three homicides, and we should have, because *Ashe v. Swenson* stops prosecutors from relitigating issues where the facts have been decided in a previous judgment. It's called collateral estoppel. He's saying that prosecuting the defendant for the murder of Bailey, as a separate a case, requires us to relitigate issues from the previous case for which we already had a disposition. Because those facts provide the motive and opportunity for this one. He's also contending that we deliberately concealed and misrepresented your discovery of Bailey's body when I agreed to the plea bargain."

"Well, we kinda did do that," Ray muttered under his breath.

This was one of those times when absurdity challenged reality and won, and Alex was amazed that the criminal justice system worked at all.

Simon directed his attention to neatening his tie. "Leonard's pushing the precedent further than it was meant to go. He is saying they are the same crime, the 'same transaction' as per *Ashe* and another case called *Grady v. Corbin* because it was all in furtherance of the one objective, getting the money. It's so clearly bullshit. There's a case called *Blockburger v. US* which makes it very clear that if the defendant is tried on different facts with different evidence, jeopardy does not attach. But the judge seems like he wants to play along with Leonard's fuckwitted interpretation of *Ashe*."

"What are we doing here?" said Ray indignantly.

"There's a more straightforward way out of the same transaction test," Simon explained with irritable, hyperbolic patience. "One which not even Maguire, no matter how much he hates me or likes reinterpreting case law in bizarre ways, can argue with. I asked for a stay. He gave me one for a day to get it together. That's why I needed you here now." They waited with bated breath to hear what that was. "There is nothing that stops me from proceeding with this case if I can prove that when I agreed to the plea, I didn't know about the murder of Bailey."

"Alex called you and told you he was dead before you pled out the case," Ray pointed out.

"First, the only people who know that are us three. Secondly, all Alex said was that you'd found the body, and you'd only just found him, so you didn't even know how he'd died. I can prosecute if I can show that I reasonably could not have known he murdered Bailey, and that I didn't have the evidence to prosecute him for it when I agreed to the plea bargain."

"Oh, right," said Ray. "You knew it could come to this. You knew it then. That's why you jumped to make this plea bargain. 'Cause if you'd waited, Leonard *could* have moved to join this with the other murders."

Simon smiled, as if delighted that Ray had cottoned on to his strategy. "I knew the law, but honestly, did you have actual evidence that Kitchener murdered Bailey? At that very moment?"

"No, but we guessed that he probably did."

"A guess isn't evidence, Ray. You'll have to testify about the evidence you had... or didn't have. Alex didn't *tell* me Kitchener had murdered Bailey, did he?"

"No," said Alex, blinking and digging out the corners of his eyes.

"I thought it was pretty obvious..." Ray muttered, aggrieved.

McNally shrugged.

"You told Alex to shut up," insisted Ray.

"Did I?" McNally feigned surprise.

"It's not that obvious," Alex said. Harold Kitchener had murdered a cop, and he didn't care about the arcane legal loopholes surrounding who knew what and when they knew it. None of it mattered. "I can testify."

"All right, good." Simon freed his thumb from the carabiner gate. "You're feeling well enough?"

"Yeah." Every artery in his body was throbbing, and he worked his fingers into the tender muscles over his floating ribs. The gunshot wound twitched as he breathed.

Grumpily, they left the DA's office, and Ray freed them from Lower Manhattan's congested streets by swinging around the bottom of the island, an old New Yorker's trick. He said incredulously, "I can't *believe* you're going to perjure yourself for him."

"I'm not," Alex said. "It's not perjury, not really."

" 'Not really' is not what you should be saying under oath."

"Oh, come on, Ray." He gave a lackluster sigh and let his shoulder fall against the doorframe as the Midtown skyline came into view. "'The same transaction?' It clearly isn't."

Ray let out a sibilant breath. "I know *that.* I agree with McNally about that. But he wants us to say that we had no fucking idea about the cause and manner of Bailey's death when we phoned him up, which isn't true. We did."

"It's got that 'reasonable man' criteria. Who the fuck is 'reasonable' anyway?"

"I know what isn't reasonable, Lex."

"You seriously want this bum to do only ten years for killing a cop? I don't want any more pissed off voicemails from the DI at the Five-Two or the PBA, and I don't wanna run into Irvine's partner outside the office again, asking me why we didn't do enough." What was Ray's problem? Alex didn't see it. It was quite reasonable to say what McNally wanted them to say in court tomorrow. Another one of those moments where he found his partner baffling.

"He's only doing ten years for killing a cop anyway. This other one is practically a public service murder."

"Does it matter? Attica looks the same."

"Yeah, but you swear an oath to God when you go up there," Ray answered resolutely. "I'm not going to lie under God's eyes."

"Oh, fucking hell."

"It's about what's right," Ray said.

"Yeah, what's right is putting this skel away for a long time."

"Not at the expense of your higher principles or your soul."

"Well, then it's lucky I haven't got much in the way of either," Alex answered, finding his irreverence at last. Ray failed to see the humor in it, and Alex torqued his hips towards the window as coals ignited in his stomach, and he desperately missed James Hurley, feeling that same purulent, suppurating wound he'd suffered when James first transferred.

James would have likened it to jerking off by rubbing one's dick between the pages of the CPL or some similarly awful metaphor. He would have brought Alex out of his melancholy with prurient, juvenile commentary about everything until Alex, no matter how depressed he felt, had to laugh. Then James would have exclaimed, "Fuck this, Lex! We'll just tell Gibson that the meeting with the DAs took a *really* fuckin' long time!" And he would have veered off the highway, driven to Zabar's, near West 80th, which had gotten popular and trendy, but Alex had been there long enough to know it before it was any of those things. They would have bought bagels or sandwiches and coffee, walked into Central Park, James making him laugh with lewd observations about people they saw in the park, people they knew, or people he'd slept with.

But Ray did not think like James. Alex could see the disquiet in him, the bewilderment and uncertainty. He was a detective, and he knew Alex was flying towards disaster, but he didn't know what to do, not on a day where they drifted apart, mystified by how one another's minds worked. Alex licked his peeling lips. Neither he nor Ray possessed James' carefreeness and vivacity.

Those thoughts of James stoked his misery. And his old partner was giddily bouncing through life on Staten Island while he suffered here. He chewed through the scars on his fingers, ripping a fresh hole in his thumb, and he didn't care about the bleeding. Oh, he needed James' tenacity and boundless energy again, like he had nine years ago when James dragged him out of a bottle. He pawed the seatbelt away from his throat so he could wrench his body towards the window, and he gazed at the Hudson, no longer glinting in the sun, its surface now choppy and grey.

The next morning, they dumped some loose ends with other cases on Wheeler and Greenwood, and they were in court by 1000 hours. Ray radiated disapproval like the Chernobyl of moral indignation. As they bypassed security at 100 Centre Street, Alex growled, "Just remember, he had our backs with his boss and his pal in the Appellate Bureau with the al-Farasi case. We'd better have his."

He did not see it as perjury anyway. Playing fast and loose with the precise truth, sure, but they did that every time they brought someone into an interrogation room and implied that they had more evidence than they actually had. Somehow, that was kosher for Ray, because it didn't invoke the whole God thing. Ray hadn't said much to him on the drive from the office. One of their tiffs. He would get over it.

The case before theirs on the docket was a *Molineux* hearing, and they waited for it to adjourn. Sitting in the gallery, Alex felt jittery and nauseated, bathed in sweat, holding his knees, his heart beating like it did the first time he had testified in court, somewhere in 1978. What case had that been? His first collar. He'd arrested some guy for trespass – really, selling heroin, but trespass was all they had on him. The perp slouching and scowling at the defense table, and a young ADA who was as awkward and brittle at asking questions as Alex was at answering them. The memory snaked from his grasp. There was only his stress and dysphoria, a gnawing pain in his belly, and an ADA rattling on about why he should be allowed to admit the defendant's priors as evidence.

Out of the corner of his eye, Alex saw McNally speaking in low tones to the clerk. Then the prosecutor slid onto the bench behind him, whispering in his ear, "Clerk says I have enough time before this hearing ends to go out for a smoke. Come with me for second, Alex." He was on his feet, his hand on Alex's shoulder.

Alex glanced at Ray, who had a surly look on his face, and when his partner caught his eye, he could only arch an eyebrow and gesture with a flick of his fingers towards Simon and then the door.

He followed Simon out of the courtroom and into the nearest elevator, crowded with lawyers, a couple detectives, clerks in their white shirts. McNally was quivery with anxiety, a deep crevasse in his fierce brow, rocking his weight from foot to foot in the elevator, his hand shoved into his coat pocket, toying with his cigarette pack. The elevator halted at the ground floor, and they squeezed past the security line, and then jogged out of the overheated, fusty courts, straight into the fangs of the winter air.

McNally lit his cigarette while Alex, shivering irrepressibly, wrapped his arms around his belly. Cold leached into his bones. It froze all the tissue in his body. Being ill had done wacky things to his internal thermostat. "What's up, Simon?"

"How are you feeling?" asked Simon, taking a relieved pull from his cigarette. "You look cold."

"Like shit but I'll live," Alex confessed.

"I never asked... What's wrong? You went to a doctor?"

"Yeah, an infection in the small bowel."

The prosecutor's thin lips drew back even further in a pained grimace. "Ugh... I know how that feels. Had something like that after drinking water from a stream in the French Alps that turned out to be the drainage for sewage from a hut. Me and my climbing partner really should have checked where the water was coming from. I always checked water sources after that. Never been so ill in my life. They got you on antibiotics?"

"They did."

"Is it feeling better?"

"A little. But that's not why you got me out here, is it?"

"No." Simon puffed smoke out of his nostrils. "Have you talked to your partner?"

"About this hearing?"

"Yeah."

"He knows what I think," Alex said.

"Is he on board?" Simon took another nervy draw on his cigarette.

"I hope so."

"You hope so? You've been partnered with Ray for more than three years now. You must have some idea of what he is going to do."

Alex smiled cynically. "I lie awake every night praying that I'll be able to understand what Ray does and doesn't do. Having any influence over that would be a divine miracle."

"I don't need the sarcasm, Detective," snapped McNally. "We've got to call him. If we don't, it's going to look fucking weird. I just need to know that he's not going to shoot us in the collective foot if he testifies."

"I trust him with my life. He'd take a bullet for me," Alex said and extracted some Kleenex out of his inside pocket, blowing his nose with trembling, frozen fingers.

"Then I hope he'll bend the truth slightly under oath for you." The prosecutor bit down on his cigarette.

It occurred to Alex that however much Ray's moralizing and health food fanaticism might drive him mad, his partner had never done anything in three years to let him down. He might not be James Hurley; Alex didn't always get Ray, and he had a different connection with him, but a connection of loyalty, trust, and friendship all the same. Well, Ray always talked about having faith, and Alex needed some now.

Simon finished his cigarette and scowled at the stub with its thin tendrils of smoke wafting into the atmosphere. He looked like a man who wanted another, who would stand outside chain smoking all day if he could. "We need to get back. I don't think he gives a shit about me, but I just hope his loyalty to *you* and the job is enough to keep him in line."

"I'll tell him he has my back," said Alex. "That's all I can do."

The *Molineux* hearing was being adjourned, obviously not in the ADA's favor given the disenchantment on the man's features. He whined to Simon, "Now his lawyer's just gonna make him look like a choir boy. He's been arrested for dealing crack five times, for fuck's sake."

The clerk announced the docket number and name of their case. Marie, litigating the hearing because Simon was a witness, rose to her feet, straightening her ponytail and smoothing out the pleats in her suit. Her icy blue eyes shone with clear purpose. She took command of that courtroom, and Chris Leonard looked shrunken and reptilian, with his pusillanimous little eyes and ashen face.

She explained that the People were challenging the defense's motion to dismiss in the case of *People v. Kitchener* on the grounds that the prosecution did not violate collateral estoppel and double jeopardy due to provisions in the law requiring that the second offense be reasonably known to the prosecutor – this one wasn't – and also, that sufficient evidence exist for the second offense to be tried when they prosecuted the first one, which there hadn't been.

She then pointed out that CPL 40.20 explicitly allowed for successive prosecutions when there were different victims and different elements of the crime, and, with a solicitous glare at Leonard, she said, "*Ashe* only collaterally estopps prosecution when the facts of the case are exactly the same, which they are not here. Double jeopardy has *never* been interpreted by any court as an allowance for the accused to conceal all of his criminal activity from prosecutors and then assert double jeopardy should that further criminal activity later be discovered."

Leonard argued that the People should have moved to consolidate the cases, and, when they had agreed to the plea bargain for the murders of Irvine and Khalid, they had withheld the material fact that they had discovered Bailey's body, therefore denying him the opportunity to consolidate the cases and protect his client's Fifth Amendment rights.

Marie called Alex to the stand.

"Good morning, Detective Boswell," she said.

"Good morning."

First, the routine questions. "Would you please tell us your name, rank, and command for the record?"

"Detective Alex Boswell, Detective second grade, Manhattan North Homicide squad. Shield number 8652."

Then she established a foundation, where he answered questions about his general experience and his role in this specific case. The routine dance felt at the limits of his mental and physical capacity.

She said, "Taking you back to Tuesday, the 2nd of December, can you tell us what you were doing that morning?"

"We were searching Riverside Park for the body of Johnny Bailey."

"Why did you suspect that he might be there?"

"I had received a tip from an informant, who said he'd seen a body in the park who resembled a picture of Bailey that was posted in the 26th Precinct."

"What did you find?"

"With the assistance of a cadaver dog from the K9 Unit, we found and identified the body more or less where the informant said. Underneath the highway near Grant's Tomb." He folded his hands on the edge of the witness box. His sweaty palms stuck to the wood.

"At that time, did you have any evidence linking Mr. Kitchener to his death?"

"No."

"Can you say that you knew, at that moment, what manner and cause of death was?"

"No, the ME didn't autopsy him 'till the following day."

"Did you tell Mr. McNally that you had found the body?"

"Yes, of course."

"What did you say?"

"I said we'd found him, and he was dead."

"Did you say anything else?"

"There wasn't anything else to say until the results from the ME and the ballistics lab came back."

"That's it, Detective, thank you." She returned to her seat, and Leonard stood up, taking his place at the lectern, leering at Alex, his bulging crab-apple cheeks puffing outwards with weird gravitas.

"Detective Boswell," he said. "Tell us again how long you've been a homicide detective?"

Alex had answered that on direct, as part of Marie's foundation. "Seventeen years," he reiterated. He tightened his grip on the witness box.

"Seventeen years," echoed Leonard. "Now, in those seventeen years, I take it you've investigated a lot of deaths where violent criminals have murdered their accomplices... Is that true?"

"Sure." Every stop on this subway train was more demoralizing and calamitous than the last. He'd barely survived the direct. How would he survive the cross? "Some."

"And, if you found the body of a man, who was known to be recently associated with someone already convicted of a violent felony, with a bullet in his head, would you not assume the violent associate to be a suspect in the murder?"

"I've been on the job a long time. I've learned not to 'assume' anything."

"But you would treat the violent associate as a potential suspect?"

"If I had reason to."

"Did you have reason to suspect Harold Kitchener of this murder?"

"As much as anyone who had been around the victim shortly before his death."

"Did Mr. McNally?"

"I'm not a mind-reader, Counselor. I have no idea what he suspected."

"But associates or acquaintances, especially ones with convictions for violent crimes, are often the first place you'd look in a death investigation, as it is your experience that they are frequently involved?"

"Starting with people who know the victim is standard operating procedure for any homicide investigation."

"Which meant Harold Kitchener was definitely a suspect?"

"Sure, he was. As I said, same as anyone who knew the victim. But with someone who had a criminal record as long as Bailey's, there's a lot of people who had a beef with him."

"But you knew, and Mr. McNally knew—"

"Objection," voiced Marie. "Detective Boswell can only testify about what he knows, not anyone else."

"He can if he and McNally have discussed the case and McNally was made aware that my client and Mr. Bailey were accomplices."

"Overruled, if defense counsel can establish that this is indeed the case."

"Well, Detective," Leonard said to Alex. "Had you discussed Bailey's involvement in this robbery with Mr. McNally?"

"Yes."

"So, you can say that McNally was aware that my client had been recently associated with Bailey, and they had robbed the bodega together."

"Yes."

"You just told Ms. Adams that you contacted Mr. McNally after you found the body, is that right?"

"I'm sure the court reporter can tell you," quipped Alex.

Leonard was unamused. "Do you normally call a Trial Bureau chief when you go to a DOA?"

"No."

"The fact that you called him means that you must have suspected that my client was involved in his murder, and therefore it was relevant to the case which Mr. McNally was pursuing against my client, right, Detective?"

"It means Bailey wasn't gonna testify against your client. I didn't know how he'd died."

"Did McNally ask you how he died when you called him?"

"No."

"Why not?"

Alex pinched the bridge of his nose, and then placed his shaky hand back on the witness box. He was a cynical, hardboiled detective who had testified in hundreds of cases, not the insane man who had lost control of his reason and cried in police cars. "Why would he? I said we'd found him DOA. He probably hadn't even arrived at the ME's office when I called."

"Now, you also just told Ms. Adams that you made no determination as to manner and cause of death when you found the body, is that right?"

"Yes," Alex answered. "Only the ME can make that determination."

"But you found bullet holes in the victim's head, didn't you?"

"Yes."

"You must have presumed that was probably the cause of death, didn't you?"

"No, I didn't. I don't make any presumptions as to cause of death until the ME tells me." Of course, you often do know perfectly well how someone died when you work the scene – although you can always be surprised – but nothing becomes enmeshed as a fact in your official narrative of a case until the ME says so.

"Are you really saying that when you see a dead body with a bullet in his head, you don't think, 'The bullet has killed this person?'"

"What I think to myself doesn't really matter." Sometimes the system was insane, sometimes it was absurd; usually it was both.

"What did you think to yourself when you saw Mr. Bailey?"

That I was going to throw up. He replied, "I thought that he had a bullet in his head, but I had no idea how, or why, or when it got there. The body had been there for a few weeks."

"But Detective, isn't it true that you suspected that Bailey was in the park several days before you found him?"

"Yes. Suspected."

"Is it true that you were told by Officer Robbie Strachan at the 26th Precinct that someone had seen Bailey's body in the park?"

"Yes," Alex replied, worried that the lawyer knew more than he'd anticipated. Had he talked to Strachan? He hadn't considered it a possibility, but he supposed some of this shit would have been in discovery.

"Isn't it true that you signed out a department car on Thanksgiving Day, the 28th, in order to investigate what you wrote down was a lead in this case?"

Had the command log been part of discovery? How had Leonard gotten a hold of that information? The subway charged forward, swaying violently, and nausea crawled up his esophagus. It had slipped his mind that he had followed procedure and written down ambiguous reasons for taking the car. The command log was not something that he would usually consider a problem, but this one was a bizarre predicament, and he hadn't told the prosecutors about signing out the car. Nor had he informed them of his misadventure in the park underneath the highway.

He didn't flick his eyes towards the prosecutors, the sure sign of being caught out by a question, instead staring honestly at Leonard, replying evenly, "Yes, I went to meet with PO Strachan at the 26th Precinct. He'd arrested the informant. He'd phoned me that day and reported that he had this information."

"You're saying you knew that Bailey was murdered and his rough whereabouts then?"

"No."

"But you thought it likely and organized this search, is that right?"

"I knew some crackhead about be charged with selling cocaine *claimed* he saw a body that he thought looked like a composite sketch he'd seen in the precinct, and he thought it *might* get him outta the drug rap. At the time, I had no idea if a body was actually there, or who it was. It was Thanksgiving Day, and it was dark, and I recall the weather being pretty awful. No one was gonna look for him at that moment." *Other than me,* he thought darkly but kept his poker-face.

"No more questions." The defense attorney drooped down beside his client.

Marie sprang towards the lectern. "Redirect, Your Honor?"

The judge waved her on.

Alex ran his tongue around the inside of his mouth, finding it bone dry.

"Detective, can you please clarify why you suspected that Bailey's body *might* have been in the park?"

"A guy arrested on drug charges told the arresting officer that he had seen Bailey's body, or what he thought was the body. The A/O contacted me. As a result of that tip, we organized a team to search for him in the area, and he was found four days later. Up until we found him, we had no idea if the informant's lead was a good one or not."

"Did you tell Mr. McNally about the informant?"

"No, not until after we found the body and the other case dispositioned."

"Thank you."

Simon took the stand after Alex stood down. The courtroom pitched like a ship in a storm, and he crawled weakly off the witness stand and lurched in an unstable gait into the gallery, tasting copper. As soon as he collapsed into the pew beside Ray, he let his head sink into his cupped hands, full of drunk, drugged despair, and he couldn't hold it up anymore.

He was fuzzily aware of Marie's direct examination of Simon. His ears were working even though his brain had acceded to the foggy blackness.

"Can you describe what transpired when Detective Boswell contacted you two weeks ago, regarding the case *People v. Kitchener*?"

"I received a phone call from him stating that he and his partner, Detective Espinosa, had found the body of Johnny Bailey."

"Did he tell you how he died?"

"No."

"What did you think after he spoke to you?"

"I was hoping Bailey would be a witness in the case against Mr. Kitchener. As he was dead and that was obviously no longer on the table, I accepted the plea bargain."

"At the time, did you have any reason to suspect that Mr. Kitchener had murdered Mr. Bailey?"

"No, that investigation was very much ongoing. I only knew that he was dead. Could have been a heart attack or a drug overdose or anything."

"Thank you. No more questions," said Marie.

Then Alex heard Leonard's voice over the moan of his own breathing.

"Detective Boswell told you that they had found the body of an individual known to be my client's accomplice in the previously-mentioned armed robbery?"

"Yes, he did."

"And you are now telling us that you didn't come to *any* conclusions?"

"I concluded that Bailey wouldn't be testifying against your client."

"You said the detective didn't tell you how he died?"

"No, he didn't."

"Did you ask him?"

"No. He phoned me just after they found the body. He wouldn't have known."

"You didn't think it was relevant to ask what he thought before you agreed to the plea bargain?"

"No. It's not as if the police would have known with any kind of certainty, since they had only discovered the body like an hour or so before they told me."

"'Any kind of certainty.' But they're experienced homicide cops. Detective Boswell just said he's been in Manhattan North Homicide for almost twenty years. Surely, he must have had some idea. You didn't think it important to ask him?"

"Like Detective Boswell said, cause and manner of death have to be established by the Medical Examiner. And the ballistics and forensic evidence linking your client to that murder was not obtained by the lab until a week or so after that."

"They found a bullet, two bullets, in Bailey's head, didn't they?"

"Yes."

"So why didn't you ask him what he thought the cause of death was before you agreed to the plea bargain?"

"What he *thought* doesn't matter. It's still a guess."

"You wouldn't say that the guess of a twenty-year Homicide squad veteran is a pretty educated guess?"

"He's not clairvoyant. The hunches or guesses of a police officer, whether they have two years' or twenty years' experience, doesn't even get you a search warrant."

"When the cops told you he was dead, you didn't assume it was *likely* my client had murdered him?"

"Could've died of anything. Heart attack. Heroin overdose." McNally shrugged innocently.

"A guy who was implicated in an armed robbery, who had violent associates, who was recently in the company of said violent associates… Given Mr. Bailey's history, that's a likely manner of death, isn't it?"

"I suppose. But someone like Bailey would have plenty of violent associates. Not just your client. And he *was* a regular heroin user."

"But his most recent violent associate was my client, was it not?"

"We didn't know that. No one knew approximate time of death until the ME said so. And even then, if someone has been dead for a while, the ME can only give the roughest of estimates. He was found a few weeks after the robbery and murders of Irvine and Khalid. Anything could have happened in that time. As you know, your client wasn't charged with second-degree murder until a week after our plea bargain, after the ME determined Bailey was murdered, and the ballistics lab matched the bullets in the victim's head with the gun the police had found on your client."

"But is it true that Detective Boswell told you, during this phone conversation, that they found Bailey in Riverside Park?"

"Yes, he said that's where he was."

"Were you aware that Officer Robbie Strachan in the 26th Precinct contacted Detective Boswell and told him that he had an informant who had seen Bailey's body in Riverside Park?"

"The detectives told me that after I had already agreed to the deal for your client, and the ME had confirmed the cause of death."

"Were you aware that Detective Boswell went to the 26th Precinct and spoke to Officer Strachan about this when he received the information, four days before the body was found?"

"Again, he told me about it later. I wasn't even in town that day. I was in Chicago."

"You still have cell phones. Why didn't he tell you then? Or the next day?"

"You asked him that. He said it was a tip from an informant with very questionable credibility. It's the job of the police to follow up on that kind of information, not mine, and if it's information that can be used as evidence in a criminal case, then they tell me."

"No more questions," Leonard mumbled, at an impasse.

Marie announced, "The People call Detective Ray Espinosa to the stand."

Ray shot Alex a surprised look. Alex lowered his hands from his face and glared at him, his clear brown eyes chilling and beseeching, a look born of years on the streets together, of secrets shared in squad rooms, police cars, and bars, of the devotion and fidelity between police partners. Somewhere in his pain, he found the strength for willing Ray to not fuck it up.

"You have my back, Ray," he whispered.

Then his gut felt light, and heat flushed through his body, droplets of sweat trickling down his back and his sides. The courtroom teetered precipitously, white and yellow lights wheeling in a dizzy spiral, and he looked down at his belly with a sinking, sick sensation.

As Ray stood up, he gave Alex a squeeze on the shoulder, holding his gaze for a second, his dark brown eyes penetrating and solemn. Alex wished he knew what his partner was thinking.

Chapter Twenty-Nine

December 22nd

"Prior to going into Riverside Park to look for Bailey, did you have any evidence that Mr. Kitchener had murdered him?" Marie asked Ray after she had established a foundation.

"At the time, no," said Ray.

McNally, at the prosecution table in front of Alex, visibly sagged with relief.

"Why did you search for him in Riverside Park?"

"Detective Boswell just told the court that he received a tip suggesting Bailey might be in the park."

"But did you have actual evidence that he was dead?"

"No. We had no idea where he was."

"Did you have any other theories about Mr. Bailey's whereabouts?"

"Yes. We thought it likely he'd gotten a train or bus out of town."

"Why did you suspect that?"

"He'd made a lot of enemies on the drug corners. Owed money to dealers. If he showed his face, he'd be in trouble."

"Did you raise any of your suspicions to Mr. McNally?"

"No, we didn't."

"Who did you discuss it with?"

"Only Detective Boswell and a few other people in the team in MNHS."

Alex rested his right hand on his stomach, but he nibbled at the nails on his left until the blood leached out and smeared across his palm when he balled his fingers into a fist.

"And when was it again that you found direct evidence linking Mr. Kitchener to Mr. Bailey's murder?"

"A week later, when results from ME and the forensics lab came back to us."

"Thank you, Detective. No further questions."

See, he has your back, Alex assured himself, but he wasn't feeling better. This fervid outbreak of anxiety and melancholy had nothing to do with the hearing. His blood was turning into ice. Something was very wrong if everything seemed all right, and he had no reasons for panicking.

Leonard now stood up for his cross-examination. Flapping papers on the lectern, the troll-like defense lawyer cleared his throat. "Did Mr. McNally talk to you and Detective Boswell about this case, or this hearing?"

"Sure," Ray replied, looking ever so helpful. "He said we'd have to testify about how we found Bailey's body and what we knew at the time we found it."

"Did he tell you anything else?"

"No. Just that."

"But isn't it true that you found Mr. Bailey's body near where you had been looking for one of my client's other victims?"

"Nearby, yes. But we were looking around Washington Heights, where your client's girlfriend lived."

"But Riverside Park isn't very far from that, it is?"

"No, I guess it's not."

"And you first looked in that area the day after the robbery, correct?"

"Yes."

"Your partner testified that he received information that Bailey was dead in Riverside Park, four days before he was found. Did you not suspect Bailey was murdered then?"

"My partner was working alone that day. Office cover for Thanksgiving. I wasn't there when he received the lead."

"Did you know that he spoke to the officer who arrested the informant?"

"Yeah, I knew he went to the Two-Six Precinct to meet with the guy."

"What did he tell you?"

"He told me what he just told you. A perpetrator arrested on a narcotics warrant claimed he'd seen an alleged body, who might or might not have been Bailey, under the highway overpass."

Alex stopped breathing. He didn't know what damage it would cause them if Ray divulged that he had gone out to look for the alleged body with Strachan, but it would inflict nasty scrapes to his credibility. The only people who knew about that were Ray and Strachan. Not Gibson, not Strachan's bosses, certainly not the prosecutors.

"Did Detective Boswell do anything to follow up the lead?"

"Of course he did," said Ray.

Thankfully Alex sat in the back of the courtroom, and no one could see how waxen his face had become or how he doubled over, resting his elbow on his thigh and dabbing blood off his fingers with tissues.

"What did he do?"

"As you know, he spoke with Officer Strachan at the Two-Six, and the next day, he briefed myself and Lieutenant Gibson on what the officer had told him, and we then proceeded to organize a search of the park."

Leonard tacked into a different wind. "You found his body, then your partner immediately contacted Mr. McNally, is that right?"

"Immediately?" said Ray, drawing his brows together. "Well, that day. We went back to the office and did some paperwork, and then I think he called Mr. McNally."

"You were there when he spoke to him, right?"

"Yes."

"Detective Boswell testified that you usually don't phone Trial Bureau Chiefs when you are called to a DOA. Would you agree with that?"

"Yes."

"So why did he call McNally that day?"

"Because the *Huntley* hearing was on for the next day, and as we all thought it likely the judge would dismiss the indictment, we'd been hoping Bailey might testify against your client. We figured McNally might like to know he was dead before the hearing."

"Yes," said Leonard, his eyes lighting up. "So he had all the information at hand, right, before agreeing to the plea bargain, or not?"

"Yeah."

"Then why didn't you and Detective Boswell tell Mr. McNally the most important part of it?"

"Which was?"

"That Bailey had been shot, possibly murdered? Wouldn't you think that would have been important to him when making his decision?"

"You'd have to ask Mr. McNally what he thinks is important."

"But you did not think it obvious – that the fact that Bailey was shot was important?"

"Of course it was."

"Why didn't your partner say, 'We found Bailey, and he's been murdered?'"

"That would have been speculation. We didn't know that at the time."

"He had a gunshot wound to his head, didn't he?"

"So? He could have shot himself."

"Oh, come on, Detective. You don't honestly believe that!"

"Objection, he's badgering the witness," interjected Marie.

"Sustained," responded the judge. "Keep it under control, Counselor."

"You didn't really suspect suicide, did you?"

"Or accident," supplied Ray, enjoying the fact that he had the upper hand.

"Accident?" exclaimed Leonard, "Who shoots themselves in the head, twice, by accident?"

"You'd be surprised, Counselor."

At the same time, Marie said, "Objection, relevance."

"Sustained," said Judge Maguire.

"Surely, you inferred that he must have been murdered when you found him?"

"We thought it was a likely possibility. But we weren't gonna draw conclusions 'till we had the ballistics report and, like my partner said, the ME determined cause of death. None of which we had until a few days later."

A brief pause, Leonard flailing at a coherent question, one that would swoop in and save his cross, a Perry Mason finale. But there were no television screenwriters to help him. "But, uh, what did you think Mr. McNally would figure out from your partner telling him that you had found Bailey's body?"

"He would have figured out that Bailey couldn't testify against your client."

Leonard stood in stony silence for a moment.

"Do you have any further questions for this witness?" said Maguire.

The defense lawyer looked about ready to murder someone himself. "No, Your Honor," he answered.

His expression stone-faced, unreadable, Ray stood down and returned to his seat beside Alex in the gallery.

Alex kept his right hand curled into a fist so Ray wouldn't see his bloodied fingers. "That was well done," he whispered. "Could win an Irish dance competition with your footwork."

Ray gave him a grim smile. "I had to back you, didn't I?"

Judge Maguire asked defense counsel if he had any witnesses. Leonard coughed and sputtered, and then replied, "Yes, your Honor. The defense calls Officer Robbie Strachan. I would like to know what he told Detective Boswell."

Alex felt a pang in his chest. He thought his heart had arrested, and he waited for consciousness to evaporate. He was astonished when it didn't.

Court went into a recess while they awaited Strachan's arrival, and Alex, Ray, Simon, and Marie convened in a witness prep room. Simon was agitated, riled into a frothing fit. He hated surprise defense witnesses, even though it sometimes happened, as there was no obligation under New York law for the defense to disclose their witness list.

"What did Strachan say to you? Why the hell is Leonard calling him? Does he know something I don't?" Simon rounded on Alex.

Acid queasily pooled in his stomach and leaked into his gut, and he crossed his arms, tightening the muscles in his forearms over the pain. "He told me a perp said he saw Bailey in the park. That's it." His voice was flat. Who would have thought a little jaunt through Riverside Park in a storm could lead to so much trouble? Ray was eyeballing him perspicaciously. But he didn't know what his partner meant. Be honest or cover it up? His thoughts were disconnected, his feelings as grey as November rain. Would disclosing his trip to the park be the worst thing? Once, he would have known how to handle it, but he couldn't see a damned thing through the blackness and foreboding. The misty anguish seized his throat.

"It doesn't matter," Marie observed. "Bailey was still murdered at a different place and time than the other two victims. Who cares *when* precisely you knew he might be dead."

"No. The officer showed me the place in the park where he'd collared the perp," Alex admitted in a hoarse voice. Part of the truth, giving the prosecutors more wiggle room, but Strachan was the wild card. "Was just near Grant's Tomb. But it was a fucking blizzard. We weren't gonna see anything."

"I doubt there's anything Strachan can say that will really hurt us," Marie proclaimed. "Until Bailey was *actually* found in the park, you had no idea if this cop's informant was full of shit or not."

She must be right – it ought to make very little difference to the outcome of the hearing, but if Strachan told the court about their abortive hunt for the body in the storm, Alex would come out of it looking not only like he'd been disingenuous on the stand, but like he was out of his mind as well. The very thing he'd been frantically burying, paraded in a Trial Part.

When Strachan arrived, Judge Maguire brought court into session. The officer looked nervous, shuffling into the witness box with the rigid, stiff-shouldered gait of a soldier. His flawlessly polished black boots gleamed, and the silver buttons on his uniform flashed, struck by the ceiling lights. His lips were set in a tight grimace, the wretched expression of countless people who hate testifying. Alex caught his eye, although he didn't know what it conveyed. He had never directly asked Strachan to keep his mouth shut, but he'd assumed discretion was understood. This was about putting a cop-killer in prison for a long time. Even a rookie should get that.

The bailiff swore Strachan in, and then Leonard asked him for his name, rank, command, shield number, before wiggling forward on the lectern. "Officer Strachan, on this past Thanksgiving Day, which was the 28th of November, did you call Detective Alex Boswell about a lead in a homicide case?"

"Yes, sir," said Strachan.

"Can you please tell us what that lead was?"

"I arrested a man named R.J. Phillips, for the possession of half a kilo of cocaine, and while I was moving the perpetrator through the 26th Precinct station house, he indicated one of the 'wanted' pictures on the wall, a composite done by a police department sketch artist." He spoke flintily, that overly formal police-speak, an affliction of young cops.

"The picture in question being Johnny Bailey?"

"Yes, sir."

"Then what happened?"

"He said that he had seen Mr. Bailey underneath the West Side Highway in Riverside Park while he had been searching for discarded scrap metal, I believe. He said he was dead. He said that he hoped a deal could be made with the DA, and I replied that this would probably be the case if his statement could be verified. I made contact with the primary detective named on the 'wanted' card, Detective Alex Boswell, and related this information to him."

"What did Detective Boswell do?"

Strachan's blue eyes darted manically around the courtroom. "He came over to the Two-Six station house and I showed him my arrest report and the statement I had taken from my collar regarding what he had seen in the park."

"That same day?"

"Yes, sir."

"Where was the informant at the time?"

"The Tombs. Uh, the Manhattan Detention Center."

"Did Detective Boswell meet with him?"

"Not that day and not to my knowledge."

"What happened after that?"

Alex heard his heart thudding, the sweat steaming inside his shirt and rolling down his chest and stomach like a warm slime, and his eyes caught Strachan's again, a swift but muddling exchange of glances. Alex had no idea what Strachan would say. The man's face was cherry red. He looked uncomfortable. *What's the worst that can happen?* If he testified about the search, Alex would get his ass busted by the prosecutors and his boss for doing something stupid and then not admitting it. His credibility might recover, and it would only pose a problem for the hearing if they *had* found the body. But Gibson didn't need more evidence that he was unstable. The truth about that night looked like a one-way ticket to the wing of a psych ward.

"He wrote down what I said, made a photocopy of the witness statement, and returned to the Homicide offices, I guess."

"Anything else?" pushed Leonard.

"Not that I can think of," replied Strachan, but without confidence. He was a terrible liar.

"Did he follow up with you later?"

"I indicated where I made my arrest, so the search party knew where to go."

"When did you do that?"

"A day or two after, when my sergeant had been contacted by Manhattan North Homicide and asked for more information because they were bringing in the K9s and Crime Scene Unit to follow up on the informant's statement."

"Were you involved in the discovery of Mr. Bailey at all?"

"They found him a few days later. I was not there, as it was my day off."

Leonard wheezed, "No further questions, Your Honor."

"Do the People have any questions for this witness?" inquired Maguire.

"No, Your Honor," said Marie, breezily passing on her right to cross-examine the witness, evincing how little he mattered to her case.

Strachan climbed off the stand, looking askance at Alex, and he scuttled out of the courtroom, his heavy police boots thumping against the floor. Alex afforded him a slight nod. His mouth felt furry and dry, like it was stuffed with cotton balls.

Judge Maguire announced, "Given the timeframe of events, and as no one has presented any evidence that Mr. McNally reasonably knew or could have known that Mr. Kitchener murdered Mr. Bailey when he agreed to a plea bargain for the first offense, he was therefore under no obligation to consolidate the charges, and indeed, CPL 40.20 specifies that offenses such as homicide, with different victims..."

Alex fought to breathe. His heart was going like an African drumming circle. Constricting coils of razor wire speared his internal organs. *Fuck, no,* he thought, but the dizzying white aura paid him no heed, billowing across his vision, the courtroom obscured in the glaring lights. His breathing couldn't keep up with his heart. He dug his fingernails into his spasming chest. The thing he had pinned down like a perp since the start of this hearing had finally broken free.

Ray noticed his distress and whispered, "Lex? What's up?"

"I can't breathe," he gasped.

"Right," said Ray with authority, grabbing his arm, whisking him out of the courtroom and around the corner, down the long hallway to a bench in front of a different, vacant courtroom, where he sat him down.

Alex clasped his belly and then stared at his hands, expecting to see blood. Yes, red smears, tacky and oozing on his fingers. Somewhere, he heard a siren. He lay in the middle of the road underneath a glaring streetlight, soaking wet because the rain would not stop.

Ray said, "You know what they tell us to do in aikido…"

Alex looked at him hopelessly. He had never done fucking aikido in his life. He was soaking wet because he was sweating, not because he was lying in the rain.

"You have to breathe down into your stomach, not your chest. Easy does it. Slow it down. Focus on here, where your ribs come together…You're hyperventilating… that's all. You'll be fine. You just need to make it more regular and it will be okay." Ray kept up the stream of encouraging chatter, sounding a lot like his AA sponsor. But Alex tried to do as he said. The lights were flashing like emergency vehicles. His head was bursting with thousands of dissonant impulses, and he wanted to sob. But then they wheeled off, leaving him in a narrow, mottled corridor in 100 Centre Street, like sixteen floors of other corridors he'd been in millions of times.

"I'm bleeding," he panted, holding out his bloodied hand.

"That's because you bite your fingers," said Ray.

His heart knocked against his ribs like a drop forge. Ray could probably hear it. Elsewhere in the building, they heard the clumping of footsteps, the banging and creaking of doors, the murmuring of muffled voices down hallways, and further, the whooshing, steady hum of traffic.

A small smile touched the corners of Ray's mouth. "You said you'd tell me if you weren't holding up. So, on a scale of holding up and not holding up…"

"Not," Alex answered.

"Do you think it was a panic attack?"

"I don't know. What does that even mean?"

"It means… you just panic, like your life is in danger. Except it's not. Nothing dangerous is happening, except in your head. You know, Anna used to have these kind of panic attacks, and it looked the same as what you did in court there. Kind of. When did Gibson say you're meeting with Gillard?"

"Tomorrow. I don't know what the fuck is wrong." He spoke tremulously. Ray had seen it. The thing was making itself visible to the people around him, and that scared the shit out of him, more than the panic attacks themselves.

"You're ill," Ray said, as if it was simple, like he had a cold. "You need to get better."

"Ill? With what?"

"Dunno. I'm not a psychiatrist. Some kind of anxiety or depression thing. You know you've always been prone to feeling a little depressed anyway. It's obviously something like that, only a lot worse. It's good you're seeing Gillard tomorrow."

"What's a psychiatric diagnosis gonna do, Ray? Other than fuck with the job." He burrowed his fingers into the bones of his eye-sockets, feeling the soft, quivery convulsing of his eyes.

"It's won't fuck with the job. That's the point, isn't it? It won't be on the record. No one outside of the squad is gonna know about it."

"Yeah, you say that, but what's she gonna do?"

"She'll talk to you and try to work through… well, whatever is causing you to feel like this. She might prescribe you something."

"Those drugs, they have horrible side effects, don't they?"

"Probably. For some people. But so does ibuprofen, and you pop that shit like candy."

"Fuck, I need a diagnosis of something like depression like a hole in the head. I got through 190th Street without a mental illness. What the fuck?"

"She might diagnose you with something. To be honest, I'd freakin' diagnose you with something."

"Then how will you trust me on the street?" Alex said a little hysterically.

"Same as I always do. Doesn't matter." Ray patted his shoulder blade.

"It fucking matters. How can a mentally ill detective be reliable?"

"You're the same person you always were. If you got hypertension or something physical, it wouldn't make a difference, would it? You'd just treat it."

"It's not the same thing, and you know it," Alex said mordantly, drawing back from him.

"I know there's a lot of stigma, but fuck that. It doesn't help anybody. You know officer suicide rates are insane. Nobody talks honestly about mental health stuff, but they damn well should. I'm glad Gibson does.

Maybe 'cause she's a woman and not trying to be macho. I don't know. The psychiatrist will help you fix whatever it is, or manage it, and you'll be in a lot better shape than you are right now."

His eyes were painful and watery, but he slid his hands down to his chin and looked despondently at his partner. "How do you even know all this?"

"Did I not tell you? Anna's been diagnosed with an anxiety disorder."

"Being a cop's wife is an anxiety disorder now?" Alex quipped faintly.

Ray afforded him a fleeting smile and for a second, everything seemed normal: Alex wondering if Ray appreciated or was annoyed by the sarcasm. "I guess the worst case is that you might be on limited duty or have to take sick. You've already got a medical diagnosis… I looked it up on Google. It said you should rest, which you haven't. You didn't look it up?"

"I stopped looking up medical shit on the internet. It just tells you the worst possible thing it could be. It's gonna turn me into my father, who was a raging hypochondriac *before* you could freak yourself out on the internet."

"Yeah, but there's useful stuff there too."

"'Cause the web is bound to have better advice than medical professionals. Anyway…" Alex heaved out a woeful sigh, as if he could exorcise something, but when he took a breath again, the blinding pain fractured his head and chest. "Has it worked for Anna?" he whispered.

"She says she's feeling a lot better," Ray answered. "It's made a big difference. I don't think you should be so worried about it. It's not gonna be a big deal. I'm sure…I'm really sure." He stood up and grasped Alex's arm. "We'd better find those prosecutors, Lex."

Suddenly, the fracture blew apart, like when city manhole covers can't take the pressure underneath the streets anymore and blast hundreds of feet into the air. Breathlessly, he said, "Yeah, okay, I'm just going to go into the bathroom for a second." Ray waited outside the men's room, while Alex darted in and locked himself in one of the stalls. Safely hidden, he lolled against the steel panel, face in his hands, wracked by uncontrollable, shuddering sobs. He thought about Sean Ferrin again, wondering what his last moments were like. What dismal pain or distress had driven him to put that .22 to his head and say, to hell with it?

401

Alex reached for the gun at his hip, touching the metal butt, but then he jerked his hand away as if it scalded his fingers, and he cried harder. He couldn't dig himself out of this morass: being physically ill, feeling depressed all the time, the escalating frequency of these anxiety attacks, the cognizance that he could easily end his life in seconds, another damned statistic in those high officer suicide rates. With more determination, he wrapped his fingers around the butt of the Glock, this time yanking it out of its holster. It quivered in his hand. It was cold, shiny and matte black, heavy and vicious. Ferrin must have had balls. Massive fucking balls. He didn't. His hand seemed frozen, immobile. He couldn't move his wrist and turn the gun around so the muzzle pointed at his own head. Years of firearms training and, perhaps, some remaining shred of sanity paralyzed his right arm.

A noise made him startle, the nerves along his spine spasming. The squeaking of the door, the sound of heavy footsteps on the tile floor, and then rustling, followed by the trickle of someone peeing into a urinal. Incredulous, he gawped at his cubicle stall. If hiding in the men's room of the Criminal Courts Building, crying, staring at your gun, wasn't a reason for a 9.27, an involuntary admission, he didn't know what was.

Pallid and shaken, he shoved the gun back into its holster. He snapped a wad of toilet paper out of the dispenser, fervently blowing his nose. Another wad, and he vigorously scrubbed his eyes. Then he threw the paper into the toilet and flushed. He took a few more lung-busting breaths, unlocked the stall, and stumbled to the sinks. His eyes were filmy and bloodshot, the lids swollen. His tie had loosened itself and gone awry. He re-tied the tie and ran the cold tap, splashing his face. The water felt good, cooling the heat and the ache he felt behind his eyes, but it didn't make a damned bit of difference to their messy appearance

Just then, the door creaked again: Ray, who had obviously been worrying, coming into the bathroom. "Lex. You okay?"

Alex gave him a harsh look, tempted to tell him that he'd been in a stall taking a massive shit, but Ray would know he was lying.

"Come on, let's get Simon and Marie," Ray said.

They found Simon and Marie loitering in the hallway in front of the courtroom, both of them bright and jovial, chatting with another stressed-looking ADA who had four case files clenched under his armpit. There was a flurry of activity at the door, witnesses and lawyers arranging themselves for the next cases on the docket.

"You guys disappeared," said Marie blithely as her colleague muttered, "See you later," and shuffled through the door. "Where did you go?"

"Just out for some water," said Ray, covering for him, the way James used to cover for him when he had been too hungover to be a functional human or cop.

"We won," announced Simon, his mood as changeable as New York seasons. He'd gone from incensed to overjoyed. "Motion to dismiss denied. And Kitchener will plea out on second-degree murder, twenty years to run consecutively with the ten he's already doing. Well done."

"Good to hear," said Ray. "Thank God he's doing serious time."

"Want to go out for celebratory drinks and dinner?" Simon asked jubilantly. "I know a nice place on West 43rd where we can get in cheap."

If someone asked Alex how he imagined hell, it would be Midtown on a Friday night in late December. Smiling apologetically, he said, "I'm still getting over this thing and have to be on this shit diet. I don't know if I'm up for it."

"Come on, Alex," urged Simon. "Don't know what's going on, but I'm sure it would cheer you up. It's a good place, and we can grab a drink after."

Temptation caressed him – if he went out with friends, maybe they could enliven him, and he would not feel like a New York embattled with winter, bombarded under driving sleet. On the other hand, these anxiety attacks were like random bombings, and he was still wary of his gut, treating it cautiously. His doctor had told him that it might take a few weeks to recover.

"I think we should go, Lex," said Ray in a soft, encouraging tone. "You don't think getting out for a bit is better than hanging out alone in your apartment?"

"There's a lot to be said for watching bad movies on the TV over a tub of ice cream," Alex joked, but he felt incarcerated in a maximum security prison, shackled on one side of the glass, pretending to people on the other side that he was coping.

"That's my point."

"Oh, well, fine, I'll go," he conceded. If he wanted his health back and his colleagues believing he was sane, he should act as if he was sane, like doing things he would customarily do, and he'd gone out for innumerable celebratory drinks – non-alcoholic these days – with ADAs and detectives.

Chapter Thirty

December 23rd

By now, the sun had set, and city lights studded the overcast evening. Harlem looked grey and cold. In the gloomy winter twilight, the neighborhood had none of its vibrancy, the color and life having fled into apartments and subway tunnels. Alex scrunched a tissue over his nose and eyes, his sinuses afire, and he haltingly sketched out what happened in court yesterday, but he blenched. Because it sounded crazy. Sane, healthy police officers don't have panic attacks in pretrial hearings. The whole episode was incontrovertible evidence of his mishegoss, and his weak attempts to modulate it felt strangled and pathetic, and the psychiatrist would indisputably support an involuntary commitment now. Never mind Ray's endeavor to reassure him. The stigma was real, and if he mistrusted his strength and his competence to handle his own problems, how could his partner or anyone else trust him?

"You see visual auras before an attack?" Gillard asked him calmly.

"What?" said Alex, his tongue dry, and it felt like it didn't belong to him.

"The white lights."

"Oh. Sometimes I see them, and nothing happens."

"You ever had that before now?"

He gazed up at the ceiling, and a vein in his throat palpitated. "Had what?"

"Panic attacks."

"A little, after the shooting. But not like this."

"What did you experience after the shooting?"

Fuck, he had never spoken of this with anyone. James knew, but they had never talked frankly about it. "Like… I would hear gunshots, or see my partner, Eddie, lying on the street."

405

"Would you feel any anxiety?"

"Yeah, my heart would beat faster. But it only ever lasted a few seconds, maybe a minute."

"Did you ever tell anyone about that?"

His lip twitched involuntarily, and he ardently shook his head.

"You never sought counseling?"

He gouged his knuckles against his cheek. "No. Fuck no. It wasn't something you did. If I'd done that, people woulda said, 'Boswell can't handle it.' And I *was* handling it."

"Are you sure about that?"

"Yeah, in a way. I drank more. That's handling it."

"In a manner of speaking," she said with gentle irony. "When did you realize you weren't handling it?"

"I never didn't handle it. I just realized I'd been using booze to deal. I realized that when I quit drinking. And I went to AA. But no one ever said I couldn't do the job."

"No one's saying that now."

"Really?" He furled his lips, and his nostrils flared.

"They're saying you seem to be struggling, but no one thinks you can't do the job."

"No one's gonna *say* that to your face," he said testily. "But it's what they say in the fucking locker rooms."

"I know there's a lot of stigma."

"No shit."

"We have to move past that. Hiding what's going on from yourself, like you've been doing, won't get you well."

"Yeah. Who told you I'm struggling?" He went for his nails, not caring anymore that she took note of his neurotic habits. Little lapses of attention, of inattention, the brother leaping out of the bathroom with a punch, a scary sign that Alex's head wasn't one hundred percent on the job. You don't go into an apartment with a warrant and not check every bathroom and closet. Inattention can be deadly. That mope could have flown out of the bathroom with a knife, a gun. And Ray said he still trusted him. Alex didn't trust himself, so he wondered if Ray had been lying through his teeth.

"Ray. He said he's been worried for a little while."

"Hope IAB never asks him about me," he said with more vexation than he meant.

"It's not about IA," Gillard said, her voice measured. "It's not about the job. It's your health he's worried about because he gives a damn. People do, you know."

He looked at her in surprise. It was the first time he had heard her swear. "What do you think it's about?"

"Post-traumatic stress disorder."

He shot back in his seat, his spine rigid. He felt like someone had fired a gun in his ear. "What? PTSD?"

"Yes."

PTSD was serious, career-ending. He could not have that, not because of a damned car accident or anything else. That was what you got from being in a combat zone or at Ground Zero when the planes hit the Towers. And he hadn't been at Ground Zero, at least not until a couple days later. He'd been shot, for Christ's sakes, and he'd suffered some trauma, some psychic wounds along with his physical injuries. But not full-blown PTSD. "That doesn't sound like something a New York City police detective should have," he stammered. "I had a case last year where this guy was diagnosed with PTSD. I mean, he was a vet, he'd just come back from Afghanistan. He thought he was in Kabul and shot his wife. The DA pled him out as insane. I'm not... Are you sure about this?"

"I'm sure."

"It's the holidays. It's always a lousy time of year for me." He fought to convince her – and himself – that her diagnosis was wrong, because he was an old police detective who had seen everything. This was his nightmare. PTSD looked as devastating as bipolar or schizophrenia or any mental illness that would shackle a cop to modified assignment or disability in seconds. "I get a bit depressed or whatever, or think about going back on the sauce, but I'm an alcoholic. I've got *that* diagnosis. One's more than enough."

"Yes," she replied smoothly. "You don't think it's related?"

"What?" he said histrionically.

"You just told me you handled the shooting by drinking more. It's not uncommon for people suffering PTSD symptoms to self-medicate with drugs and alcohol."

"Oh, for fuck's sake," he cried, faced with realities he'd been entombing in layers of denial for years.

"You have most of the classic symptoms. The irritability, the flashbacks, the loss of appetite, the physiological symptoms you've described to me, the fact you can't remember the accident… But you don't need to look so panicked about it. It's not career-ending. It's manageable."

"'Manageable?'" He cocked a doubtful eyebrow at her. "Motherfucker."

"Yes. With psychotherapy. Or anti-anxiety drugs like Zoloft or Paxil can help control some symptoms."

"Be honest, Doc. Am I a 9.41?" Yesterday, he'd considered eating his gun. Gillard could sign a paper, bring him before a judge, testify that he was suicidal and hallucinating, and then he would be carted to the psych ward.

"You're a risk to yourself. The etiology of PTSD is more along the lines of suicide and self-harm, not so much violence towards others. Not for most people. Look at your hand. It wasn't an accident."

"What do you think it was then?" he spluttered, flustered.

"I don't know, but I think you did something intentionally to stop a flashback. Or you were suicidal, and you tried to cut your radial artery. If a knife had slipped while you were slicing a bagel, I can't imagine it causing enough damage for you to have a bloody bandage halfway up your arm. Did you cut yourself, intentionally cut yourself, with the knife?"

He adjusted his wounded hand so the pain, nauseating and exquisite, scoured through his wrist and forearm, and he almost keeled sideways in a faint. A moan escaped his lips. "I don't know," he gasped.

"You were dissociating," she said.

"What?"

"When you lose your sense of where you are and what you're doing. That's what it's called."

For a moment, he didn't speak, and he licked the cuts on his dried-out lips. Somewhere, a door slammed, and his heart skittered. How did she know about that? It was a clinical sign of PTSD, of course. And every time he'd lost reality after the shooting? Every flashback taking him to

190th Street? Was that PTSD? Sweat saturated his chest and belly, and his hands were shaking.

"Noises make you startle," she observed. "An increased startle response is also a common symptom."

"Yeah. If it's that," he said falteringly. "If it's PTSD, what happens?"

As if it was straightforward, she replied, "We work on managing it. One way to help is working on remembering the details of the accident without flashbacks and the other physiological symptoms. You can't remember it very well—"

"No kidding. I'd had more than a few drinks."

"—Because your brain has suppressed it, to cope."

"I'm sure you'd know—"

"I hear you were playing pool in that bar and winning."

"I'm a high-functioning alcoholic," he said, dismissive. "I can do a lot even when I'm totally fucked."

She took a different tack. "Do you *think* you had so much to drink you blacked out? You would know better than anyone what you can handle."

He blinked rapidly and then grasped his moist forehead with his uninjured hand. Had he? "I had four or five beers, then a couple whiskies."

"You remember what you drank. Is that enough?"

"I was far from sober." Every artery in his body was pulsing like a warning sign, and his breathing came fast, too fast, like yesterday in court.

"Far enough to black out?"

"Dunno. Didn't used to be. But I doubt my liver is what it used to be."

The bar he remembered with perfect clarity. He remembered feeling depressed and upset. He remembered McNally phoning him, drunk as a coot. He remembered walking into the Blackthorn Tavern without giving much thought as to whether or not he should walk into a bar while depressed and upset. He just did it. He remembered the plastered prosecutor encouraging him to drink, and he'd shunted aside his seven years of sobriety. He remembered McNally leaving the bar with the actress. He remembered kicking the asses of those two ADAs at pool. He remembered Zoë Sheehan walking in looking for Simon, wearing jeans and a leather jacket, her hair disheveled. He remembered her offering to drive him home because he was pretty smashed. Everything after that was gone.

"Do you remember being in the hospital later?"

"I wish I didn't. That was one of the worst nights of my life."

"It's only the wreck itself you're struggling to recall."

"The hospital was later. Nothing like ambulance ride to sober you up." Then in a collapsing, plaintive tone, he added, "I'm a New York City homicide detective. You know, I'm trained... I should be handling this better."

"Nobody trains you to be a victim."

"If I were gonna go completely fucking crazy from PTSD after life-threatening situations, you'd think I woulda done that already."

"Yes. You had flashbacks and nightmares from the shooting, Alex. That is PTSD. I get that you don't want to hear that. But it is. You got away with it not becoming debilitating. That time."

He didn't want to entertain the idea that he'd been sick since 1987, and the hard-ass detective who had coped unwaveringly with the shooting wasn't him. "Why would it get worse now? I deal with death all the time. That's what they pay me to do."

"Yes, well it's different when it's someone you know. And in the sort of situation where it was nothing more than chance that it wasn't you."

"No. But it's hardly 9/11, is it? It's pretty damned mundane. People get into car wrecks every day."

"But Zoë died, and you didn't."

Like he had confessed to Hurley, he wondered if it would have been better the other way around. "I'd have expected it if I'd been at Ground Zero. But this?"

Gillard continued, "It's caused by trauma. Doesn't have to be trauma caused by globally significant events. It's how *you* cope with something traumatic that has happened to you. Regardless of what it was or whether it affected a handful of other people or one person died, or none, or three thousand, or you were in the World Trade Center, or Fallujah, or in a car accident on Central Park West. It doesn't really matter because it's about what goes on in *your* head and how you process that event. And if you never really dealt with the '87 shooting, then maybe this was just a time-bomb, waiting for something else to set it off. How badly were you injured in the shooting?"

"Took a slug to the right side of my ribcage. It went through my lung. They removed part of it." He touched his right side, where spasms and nerve pains and aches still bothered him. "My partner was paralyzed."

"Did you talk about it much afterwards?"

"All the fucking time. I had to give a statement. Testify in court. People ask me about the scars."

"There will have been some processing then. Maybe not a lot, and counseling probably would have benefited you—"

"My lieutenant woulda kicked me off the squad," he interrupted gruffly. "It was the '90s. This place was fucking mayhem. You couldn't have a mentally ill detective operating in that clusterfuck."

"Yes. And it's normal for survivors of a traumatic event to experience kind of a closing off of their cognitive and emotional processes."

He wasn't really listening, attentive to his breathing, and he could feel his achy right lung with its missing lower lobe, although he probably couldn't, and it was in his head, because he never felt the lung injury anymore unless he exerted himself hard, like running for ten blocks.

"However, if certain cells in your brain don't fire, you fail to reintegrate the experience into your cognitive processes, and you never experience what neuroscientists call 'fear extinction.' Which is a way of saying, that's how you remember traumatic stuff without all the fear you felt at the time it was actually happening. You processed the shooting enough to talk about it, to remember it without re-experiencing every emotion, but you still had anxiety and flashbacks."

A lead rock sank to the bottom of his stomach. "How do you know I won't have this for the rest of my life?"

"You probably will. It'll be something you always have to work with, to some degree. It's hard for me to say, at this point, what the treatment outcomes will be. But I can say that for most people, we can control the symptoms and bring them down to a manageable level, even though we don't one hundred percent cure the illness."

He felt like he had been diagnosed with something huge, chronic and incurable, like cancer, except no one died from a mental illness unless they killed themselves. It wasn't a disease destroying your body's cells; your mind, maybe, but not your body. But there it was. Some impalpable chemical misfire had gone wrong inside his head. It had misfired seventeen years ago, and the damage had festered until it infected every synapse. He would take medication for the rest of his life, and the illness would always lurk in the shadows of his consciousness, ulcerating inside his mind.

He lifted the mug of tea to his lips, but when he tried to swallow it, his throat didn't work. Coughing, he touched his Adam's apple, feeling it contracting, bouncing.

"Are you okay?" asked Gillard.

"Throat's tight," he said, risking another tiny sip of tea. This one went down.

"Alright, take a deep breath. Tell me what you do remember about last night," Gillard said.

Chapter Thirty-One

December 22nd

The noise and crowds of Midtown blitzed Alex's senses like a Second World War bombing run. Three days before Christmas, and the lights and signs and herds of rabid shoppers were fiercer and vastly more numerous than a normal evening. The huge tree, thirty feet tall, arrayed in flashing, running lights from top to bottom, loomed over Times Square. The materialist monster screamed on the side of every building, at every intersection and street corner, that it was the holidays, demanding joy and cheer and more importantly, voracious acquisition. Goddamned Times Square. Alex hated this place when he was healthy.

The restaurant, an Italian place decorated with quaint photos of Italian villas, fake shrubs, and fountains, was owned by Simon's grateful complainant, a victim in an attempted murder case Simon had successfully prosecuted about six years ago. Simon told them about the case, which involved an affair and a bungled hit-and-run.

Then Marie related a story about a larceny case she had prosecuted, a psychic charged with stealing $15,000, and after the psychic was convicted, she put a curse on Marie's head, saying no man would ever love her. Given how much of a schmuck her last ex had been, she suspected that the psychic defendant might have communed with the supernatural after all.

Ray talked about his days as a beat cop, a call to an apartment where the residents were being held hostage by their cat. Ray had expected the complainant to be a lonely soul wanting attention from the police, but it turned out that there had indeed been a vicious, psychotic cat, which, after half an hour and some line-of-duty cat scratches, Ray and his partner chased out the window.

Alex's attention drifted away, but went nowhere, like an unconscious sailor in a raft, lost at sea. Mistakenly, he had ordered a cheese pizza, but

413

he only picked at it. Ray had given him a look that rivaled those of his ex-wife when she'd thought he made irresponsible decisions. His stomach concurred with Ray, and he could not think of any anecdotes. He could write a novel with his war stories. But when he searched his brain's archive for one, the doors were barred. He chewed on another small slice of pizza, feeling more nauseous with every bite. As Simon shook hands with his grateful victim and didn't pay the bill, Alex closed his eyes and implored his stomach to settle down.

They left the restaurant, Simon leading them straight through the heart of Times Square and turning onto West 41st Street. There was a Highland piper, like James, bare-legged in a kilt in spite of the cold, busking at the corner of 41st and Seventh. A small crowd of onlookers had gathered in a circle around him. He was playing a march James played sometimes. Farewell to somewhere or welcome to somewhere else, like life, impermanence the only damned thing you could expect. The shrill skirling of the pipe chanter against the robust bassy buzz of the drones overpowered the sirens, the horns, the engines. For Alex, the sound was a physical sensation, a stinging, terrible pain like salt pouring into a bloody gash. *What's wrong, what is this,* he asked himself fearfully. How many times had he heard James play, or withstood more than two-dozen pipers in the Emerald Society Pipes and Drums playing on St. Patrick's Day or at a funeral?

His heart pounded so violently he found it difficult to breathe. The very organ that kept him alive, hurting him. The pale lights blasted through his vision. A final attempt to stop it, reaching for his throat with his hand, but something choked him, his windpipe and esophagus closing, his tongue swollen and dry, and a bitter, alkaline taste as he touched it to the roof of his mouth. He went blind and had no idea where he was.

He was a passenger in a car, somewhere on the Upper West Side. An ear-shattering screech ripped the night asunder. Another grinding shriek answered it; metal slamming into metal at forty miles per hour. Alex flew into the dash, the seat belt jamming into his shoulder and gut, saving him from smashing his face, and then the spinning car threw him against the door. A thudding blow to his ribs, knocking the wind out of him, yet no pain.

As unexpectedly as the violence started, it stopped. The only sound he heard was the rain beating against the roof of the car.

Drunk and dazed, he touched his face and he felt something warm and gooey. He smelled coppery blood and tasted it in the back of his throat. He looked at his hand, shocked; it was covered in blood. It felt dead, like it wasn't his hand. Frightened, he touched his face again. Blood gushed out of his nostrils, soaking into his shirt and tie. He'd scraped up his face. Wherever he pressed, his hand picked up new red smudges. Mopping up blood with his sleeve, he staggered out of the car into the pouring rain and limped around its front end.

The bumper had detached from the car, the headlights mashed to jagged pieces, the grill mangled and twisted, the hood misshapen, half-revealing the car's innards in a gaping wound. He felt his way along the Toyota's crumpled flank to the driver's side and peered through the shattered windshield. Zoë's head flopped to the side, and blood was pooling in the seat around her. More blood than anyone can afford to lose. She was dead. DOA. Oh, God. Alex had seen so many dead bodies that even shell-shocked and wounded, he knew it then and there.

For some time, he stood frozen to the spot, mindboggled. Zoë was dead. Why wasn't he dead? The car was totaled, the whole left side squashed, the windshield smashed, glass everywhere, crunching under his feet. The Ford Explorer that hit them had wrapped itself around a lamppost on the curb. And the Toyota had spun three hundred-sixty degrees after the Explorer had t-boned it.

His blood pressure bottomed out. He fell to his knees on the hard, flooded pavement, retching, vomiting beer and whiskey onto the asphalt. His throat hurt like a bloody slash. He heard the caterwaul of sirens, drawing closer. He doubled over on the asphalt. He knew he was in shock, cold and wet, his body's trembling out of control, and hazy lights blotted out his sight. Weakening, he toppled onto his side from his huddled position on his knees. The sirens were coming closer, and he was lying with his shoulder, flank, and hip pressing into puddles and broken glass, his back to the car, marinating pools of blood and vomit like so many victims he'd seen in his career.

"What's wrong with him? What's going on?"

The question came from Simon, and Alex recognized the skyscrapers and streets of Midtown, and Simon and Marie standing a little ahead of him, the crowds swarming past, and Ray at his side, his hand on Alex's elbow. Alex clutched at Ray's arm, as if his partner could keep him here, in Midtown. Not there, not on that rain-soaked, bloody street.

"He's—" Ray began, and then he said, "I'm not sure, but just... go on, find us a seat in the bar. We'll be there, we'll be there in a minute."

"You sure?" Simon held a cigarette between his first and middle fingers. "It's not gonna be like at that meeting? If he were to fall—"

"He won't," answered Ray with confidence Alex wished he shared. "We'll catch up to you. He just needs a minute."

Alex wanted to tell them about the sirens, the dark street, the smashed Toyota, but he couldn't speak, and his feet were pinned to the sidewalk. He heard voices, not Ray's or Simon's or Marie's, but a couple uniforms from the local precinct – he didn't know what precinct – and they were speaking to him.

"Hello? Can you hear me?"

"I'm cold," he complained.

"You'll be okay," the cop said.

Squatting beside him, they eased his head onto something, and they cleared some of the blood from his nostrils, so his breathing came a little easier. Relief colored the cop's face when Alex made eye contact with him. His partner exclaimed, "Oh, shit, he's one of ours, he's a detective, tell them we've got an injured police officer."

How did they know that? Did they find his shield and ID card amidst the wreckage? Police radios hissed and crackled, the cop saying, "We've got a serious ten-fifty-three. One female, white, possibly thirties, DOA. One male, white, early twenties, DOA. One male, white, we have a DOB on him, 2/12/57, he's a ten-fifty-four. In shock but conscious and breathing. Uh, he's also a cop. K."

"Unit, is he likely, K?" said the disembodied voice on the radio.

Likely. Shorthand cop slang for 'likely to die,' asking for a wager on the part of the cop at the scene over whether or not the victim of a traffic accident or assault or anything had a chance of making it that night, that moment.

"No, I don't think he's likely, K," said the cop.

"Ten-four," acknowledged Central. "That bus is on its way. K."

Those three letters, DOA, ones he'd uttered thousands of times, always professional, detached, unemotional, they smoldered hotly into his prostrate mind. Zoë dead. Confirming what he already knew. And the driver of the car that hit them as well.

Panicking, Alex tried to get up, but the cop put a soft hand on his shoulder. "The bus is coming. Best not to move for now. You'll be all right."

Alex shut his eyes again, cold and scared, a whimper rising in his throat as intolerable pain seared through his side and back.

The cop kept talking to him. "You're a detective. What squad?"

"Homicide," he managed to gasp. All they had to do was give Operations his name and shield number, and they would know exactly who he was and where he worked, but the man was probably trying to keep him conscious.

The uniform smiled, as though pleased he could still respond to questions. "Good, good. Which Homicide squad?"

"Manhattan... North," he muttered.

"What grade?"

"Second." Did any of these things matter?

"Second grade. You must be good. Were you on duty tonight?"

"No." If the cop went away, if he lost consciousness, the pain and the cold would go away. He'd never felt so cold in his life. Maybe he was fatally injured after all, cold being the first thing you feel before you die. He was surprised by how little the thought bothered him. That cop should revise his wager to *likely.*

"Stay with me, Detective," said the cop. "EMS will be here in a minute."

He heard more sirens, and then the growling diesel engine of an ambulance, the uniforms gone, replaced by EMS personnel, shouting to one another and to their radios. They were ripping off his bloodied clothes, strapping him onto a stretcher so tightly he couldn't breathe, immobilizing his spine.

"Can you tell us your name?"

"Alex Boswell."

"What's your birthday?"

"February 12, 1957." They knew this. It was on his driver's license and NYPD ID card. Why couldn't they leave him in peace? If he had catastrophic internal injuries, why bother putting him in the bus? He

417

didn't mind death – if only the pain in his lower back and ribs didn't burn so unbearably.

"Where do you work?"

"Manhattan North Homicide." A vibration shook the ambulance, the diesel engine chugging to life, and it lurched backwards and forwards, and then he felt it accelerate, hard, and he heard the scream of its sirens.

"Can you tell what street you live on?"

"West 87th." The straps pinning him down hurt. Everything hurt. The pain in his side made breathing agony.

"Upper West Side?"

"Yes."

"Can you tell us what hurts?"

"Everything." The ambulance thudded over potholes, heedless of the puddles. Every time its suspension juddered, a fresh round of pain shot through his spine.

The EMS guy smiled at him. "Can you be more specific?"

"My back, my right side."

Tears welled in the corners of his eyes. Ray was holding his elbow and bicep, propelling him along, and he staggered and tripped, swerving into Ray's side, looking at his partner in confusion, wondering how Ray knew to find him here, and couldn't he see that he was hurt?

Then, *here* morphed into the glassy corridors of West 41st Street, a Ruby Tuesday on the one corner, Red Lobster on another, flags mounted from buildings, flapping in the breeze, advertising musicals and shows. Teeming hordes of theater-goers, bar-hoppers, and tourists swarmed around them.

"Lex, we're just going into this bar here. You can sit down." Ray was steering him into the bar, towards a booth in the shadows at the back where the prosecutors waited, looking anxious, Simon with a tumbler of Scotch in front of him and Marie with a pint of beer.

God, his head hurt, and his senses reeled, and he felt like he'd woken up with the worst hangover of his life. But his vision had cleared, the auras and rainy intersection slinking furtively away like criminals, and he saw that the inside of the bar was dark, with bare brick walls and dim lights for atmosphere. Heavy wooden beams crossed the low ceilings, and walls were decorated with record sleeves from '60s and '70s rock bands, black and white artsy photographs of New York streets, and famous actors whose faces looked cold and unfamiliar.

He freed himself from Ray's grip on his arm, and Ray said in a worried voice, "Where are you going?"

He gestured towards the men's room. "I'm gonna be sick." At least he could speak again. "Then I'm going home."

Without waiting for a response, he ran into the bathroom and dropped to his knees in a stall. Clutching the toilet as if he might fall through the floor, he threw up everything he'd eaten. His stomach racked him with a dry-heaving fit, and he sputtered acid into the john, and it didn't feel like it would stop.

Pull it together, he entreated. *What if they see this? Not even Ray will trust you to have his back.* The dry-heaving eased off, but his throat burned, scraped raw, and he cleared his clogged sinuses, blowing runny crap out of his nose into handfuls of toilet paper. He was so damned tired of feeling like this. Last week's course of antibiotics had palliated the debilitating abdominal pains, but they hadn't touched the pain throbbing through his whole body or the mental pain throbbing through his mind. They hadn't done anything. That thought almost brought on a fresh spell of tears. Scarcely breathing, he shuddered and stood over the sinks, washing his hands and face and nursing his flooded, sore eyes, and then he straightened his shirt collar and combed his hair with his fingers. When someone else barged into the bathroom, he retreated towards the door and nudged it open. On the other side, he heard the cheerful din of the bar, but he cringed with that appalling sensation of being incarcerated in a supermax prison, the walls and bars and razor wire sequestering him from the entire city. Fuck this. He would get the hell out of here, catch the next subway to the Upper West.

Ray lurked beside the bathroom door, arms braced tightly around his chest, one ankle crossed over the other. "What's going on? What do you want to do?"

"I dunno. I was sick again. I think that pizza was a bit much."

"Yeah, I thought greasy, fatty stuff is not what you should be having just yet," agreed Ray. "But it's not just that, is it? You had another panic attack out there. You stopped near that guy playing the bagpipes. You froze. We tried to get your attention, but you wouldn't answer or move."

"How long?"

"Three or four minutes, maybe."

Alex looked at him in confusion. The nightmare had lasted hours. Three or four minutes?

"Maybe less, maybe two minutes. You were staring into space. Then I kinda got your attention and got you to move."

He didn't want to talk about this. If he got home, he could sleep it off like he used to do when he suffered flashbacks of the shooting and numbed himself with half a bottle of whiskey. "I feel pretty lousy. My guts, I don't think they were up for pizza... I'm gonna head off. Just tell Simon and Marie and whoever else shows up that I wasn't feeling well."

"Are you gonna take a cab? Do you want me to go with you?"

"No. You know it's a straight shot on the 1 or 2. I'll be fine. Just need sleep."

"I'll at least walk you to the subway station," said Ray.

"It's a free country," Alex muttered, too tired to argue.

All three of them decided to walk him to the subway station, and he urged the lawyers not to, but Simon downed his whisky in one gulp, Marie chugged her beer like she was at a college party, and they all left the bar together. The piper was still busking on the corner, cranking through some fast reels. Alex wanted to shout at him to stop, but that would look crazy. West 41st spun like a dreidel, and he teetered into the side of a building, choking, his heart rattling like a pneumatic drill. If there had been anything left in his stomach, he would have been sick again. The meat market of Times Square heaved around them. People spilled from the overrun sidewalks out into the street. Slamming doors reverberated like bombs going off in his head. Lines of cars fought with one another to merge into single file. The ticker with news and stock market prices raced in three giant bands of yellow lights fifty stories above his head. The blinding, awful lights and glaring neon signs threw so much light across the gridded streets that you might think you were out in broad daylight.

The 42nd Street station had running lights zipping around its white tiled entrance, the colored circles of letters and numbers competing for attention with the other neon signs. A torrent of people poured in and out of the station. As Alex started picking his way down the stairs, another wave of dizziness ploughed into him, and he grabbed the handrail for balance.

"You sure you're alright?" asked Marie.

"Yes," he responded, infusing his voice with as much strength as he could.

He survived the remaining stairs without mishap, shoved his Metrocard into the slot like a gambler at the end of a long bender, and he left Ray and the two lawyers nervously milling around the turnstile. But they let him go.

The tunnels reeked of sour exhaust, garbage, and urine. Did those tunnels ever feel so long? Was it ever so busy? After an interminable escalator, he found a vacant seat on the bench beside his platform. He rested his forearms on his knees, gazing soporifically at the puddles of water and debris on the tracks. A rat moseyed around empty cans and plastic shopping bags and crawled over the rails.

The rat darted into a hole, spooked by a screaming and rattling 2 train. Alex waited for the train to vomit its arrivals, and then he boarded. He could not fight off the forbidding drowsy weakness any longer, and he closed his eyes, sliding into a coma as the train ground its way uptown.

When the driver said, "West 86th Street," he forced his eyes open and staggered uncoordinatedly to his feet. The decelerating subway bucked him into the bulkhead. The doors slid open. Then he clung to another endless escalator, and he got out, inhaling fresh air, blinking at the Gristedes and the Italian-style palazzos on West 86th and Broadway, scrabbling to make sense of Manhattan's grid and remember where he lived. East. Then north one block. He'd been more lucid when wasted, barring the times he didn't make it home.

Klutzy and tired, he fumbled with the three locks. Once inside his apartment, he lobbed his winter coat onto the floor and sunk into the couch. Pangs ravaged his lower back and his ribcage, like a rib wanted to pop out of his body, and he swung his legs onto the sofa, lying on his stomach.

He buried his face in a pillow, but his eyes stung, his sight assaulted by a fusillade of blinding light. Panic tore through his body like a bullet. He tasted blood and lay supine in a puddle next to Zoë's crumpled Toyota, shivering in the rain, so cold he must be dying.

But there was no blood in his mouth. There was no rain inside his apartment. He focused on breathing like Ray and his AA sponsor said. He inhaled into his stomach and counted to ten. But the adrenaline screamed through every artery like boiling liquid. He curled into a trembling ball, his whole body awash in sweat. Ray and his AA sponsor were crazy. They didn't understand. How the fuck could he control his breathing with this monster's talons crushing his throat? Frantic, terrified, he leapt off the sofa. He drew his Glock from his holster and placed it on the coffee table.

What if this didn't stop? What if it harangued him for the rest of his life? Was this what schizophrenics lived with? Manic-depressives? Your mind overrun? Losing your ability to distinguish between the real world and nightmares in your head? Could you come down with schizophrenia at age forty-seven?

He couldn't live with this. He would end it if there was no other way out. It would end him anyway. And he saw no exit strategy, no good outcomes. No one could function on the job or anywhere else in this state. Yes, he would blow his brains out. He wept, his body rocking with violent spasms, tears streaming unstoppably down his cheeks. He strained to summon the strength he had known from long years of willingly putting himself in harm's way, of perps aiming loaded guns at his head, of search warrant entries in dark places, and he begged for his life. But the blackness was rising, faster, and he was falling and there was nothing to hold, the only salvation the Glock on the coffee table, and he whimpered, *You will not! You will not!* A torturous, desperate sob rose in his throat, and in a frenzy of unendurable pain and despair, he shoved his hand through the frosted glass window on the bathroom door.

The jangling crash of exploding glass startled him. He stood there shaking, his pulse bounding. His stomach felt as if it had flipped over. The night was calm and cold, like any Upper West Side December night. His apartment looked like he expected it to look. The scruffy light grey carpet. The wooden floors with gaps in the planks. The coat rack with scarves and a few jackets on it. A black and white photo of the Brooklyn Bridge on the wall.

His left arm was damp, and he looked down with an unsettled, sinking sensation. Blood lathered his left wrist and forearm and poured onto the hardwood floor like millions of tiny red worms. He felt nothing. Bizarre. The blood was bright red, smelling of copper, sticky and warm, and it was everywhere.

Seeing it jerked him roughly back to this side of reality. *Holy fuck, I've got an artery.* It spurted, pumped by his heart like water jetting out of burst plumbing.

Then the pain arrived, sharp and hot, and with it, life and a sense of clarity that he hadn't felt in weeks. He rushed into the bathroom, lunging for the nearest towel, his balance failing, and he fell on the floor beside the sink, cracking his knee on the tiles. Woozily lightheaded, he propped his back against the wall and wrapped the towel as tightly as he could around his wrist and clutched it to his chest. Blood soaked through the entire towel. It seeped through his shirt, a wet and sticky slime on his skin. He tossed the towel in the bathtub and snagged another one off the towel rack, yanking it around his throbbing wrist in the makeshift tourniquet.

Blood didn't soak through this one quite so rapidly, but still, within a few minutes, it was sopping. He'd run out of available towels, so he grabbed the bathmat off the floor. By the time that soaked through, the blood was thickening, slowing to a trickle, but the pain had become grievous, blinding. He scrambled to his feet, holding the sink for balance as his head swam, a hazy film encroaching at the edges of his vision. *No, I can't be in shock now*, he told himself. *I have to take care of this.*

He flicked on the cold water tap and held his bloody hand and forearm underneath the faucet. Pain knifed through him, his legs and head weakening into jelly, and he thought, *I'm going to pass out now.* The fear of falling over, of smacking his head on the sink or floor (he'd arrived at DOAs where someone had died of just that), bolstered his will to stay up and conscious. He held the sink for dear life.

After the initial shock, the water somewhat soothed the wounds, and he could see the damage, a laceration across the back of his hand and a second gash, the one that had nicked the artery, on the underside of his wrist, baring twitching, startled muscle fibers. His knuckles were a kaleidoscope of colorful bruises and smaller cuts. He wanted to lie down and forget about it, but viscous arterial blood leaked steadily from the jagged lips of the lacerations.

The bathroom looked like a crime scene, and he'd lost enough blood to feel faint and queasy. But he rummaged around in the cupboard below the sink until he found an old, hardly-used first aid kit and ripped it open, extracting a rolled-up ace bandage. One-handed, he knelt on the floor, wrapping it around his left hand and wrist, pulling it as hard as he dared, until he felt his pulse against the fabric. Not a professional-looking job, but it would do until he found some other way to deal with it tomorrow.

He was chilled and shivery, but he tore off his bloodied hoodie and t-shirt and flung them into the bathtub alongside the towels. As he stared at his bare-chested reflection in the mirror, the pink scars from his old gunshot wounds caught his eye: a fleshy, twisted mass of scar tissue bubbling up from his right side, and a thin, white scar down the middle of his chest. Then he found a clean t-shirt at the bottom of a cupboard, and he swayed deliriously into the living room and kitchen with the intentions of brewing a cup of Ray's peppermint tea. But he only made it as far as the sofa.

He flopped onto the cushions, deathly cold now, shaking unsoundly, and a leaden weight squashed his lungs so he couldn't quite breathe, and he curled up on his side and dragged a blanket over his shoulders. Reality collapsed into a singularity of pain and dizziness. Nothing that had happened made sense anymore, except for the tangibility of blood gushing out of his arm, the feeling of purpose he had knowing he needed to control it. With that thought, he passed out into a fitful sleep.

Chapter Thirty-Two

December 23rd

Alex clasped his perspiring face with his right hand. He sniffed at the aching mass gathering behind his retinas and looked at the psychiatrist, his eyes dull and blind. "It was like I was there again. I wasn't in Midtown or in my apartment. And I couldn't get back to it. I tried and I couldn't."

"Yes, it's okay. That's a flashback and a dissociative episode. Focus on breathing, like from your diaphragm. You'll be all right."

"Oh, God knows," he said. Wetness bedewed his cheek. Quickly he rubbed the tears off. He was certifiable, unhinged, and he choked out, "What's the next step? Hospitalization?"

"At this moment, Alex, put your hands on your stomach," Gillard advised equably. "Breathe into it. When you inhale, you should feel it move out. And when you exhale, it will come in. Gently. Steady. Can you manage that?"

Pain had deadened his left hand, but he pressed his right hand into the spongy paunch on his belly. He felt his stomach inflating and deflating at each breath.

"You will be okay. I did say you injured your hand stopping a flashback."

"Fuck, I thought—" He dragged in a wheezing gasp, like he was on Everest. "I was tougher than that. I have to be."

"It's not like that, Alex. Lots of people suffer from mental health problems. It doesn't suddenly make you incompetent to do your job or mean you're weak or anything like that."

"Then what does it mean?" he asked sarcastically.

"It means the chemicals in your brain are not working right. Sometimes we don't handle trauma very well and need some help. That's all. Believe me, you're hardly the first cop ever to get PTSD. No one wants to talk about it, but it's rampant."

"How do I fix it? *Are* you gonna hospitalize me?"

"That's on the table *if* we can't control it with other methods." She looked so damned earnest. "Our goal right now is for you to focus on managing the flashbacks, should they occur."

"How the fuck do I do that?"

"The breathing exercises we just talked about. Once you start hyperventilating, you're in trouble, your brain isn't getting enough oxygen, so you have to try to keep that from happening. And reminding yourself that it won't last very long—"

"The last one didn't feel like it would stop." He huskily cleared his throat.

"But it did."

"Yeah. When I punched a fucking door."

"There are perhaps less damaging ways to pull yourself out of one," she observed, with a gentle smile. "Something like a noise or a strong physical sensation can help with that. But the most important thing is to remember that they will stop." She scratched at her notepad, and he eyed it disquietly. "You know what happens before they start. You get the visual auras. Your heart starts to pound. When that happens, you need to ground yourself."

"Ground myself?"

"Give yourself some kind of powerful physical sensation to stop the dissociation."

"Like punching a window?"

"Well, not that. The classic ones are holding onto a piece of ice, or sniffing peppermint, which I see you're drinking anyway. Or if there's something else you can see or hear, the traffic, anything. I had a patient once who put a rubberband around his wrist and would snap it if he felt like he was going to dissociate. You need to figure out what works for you. But you understand the kind of thing I mean?"

Blearily, he nodded, but wondered how the hell he could subtly hold an ice cube if he had flashbacks in a courtroom or a subway station, and what about more dangerous occasions, like warrant entries or footchases, where it could get him or someone else killed? Oh, fuck, how could he depend on himself, much less expect his colleagues to depend on him?

The psychiatrist disrupted his train of thought, saying, "You told me you prevented one from happening in the 33rd Precinct. You managed to ground yourself in the present."

"Yeah," he said, his hand over his mouth. "Ray elbowed me in the ribs, and then I went out and did something else."

"That physical sensation stopped you from dissociating. That's the kind of thing I mean."

"It has to hurt to work?"

"Not necessarily. Just anything really noticeable."

He could wear a rubberband on his wrist. No one would notice, and it would cause less damage than breaking a window. He finished off the peppermint tea, which had gone tepid, but it steadied the airy feeling in his gut. "Why the hell did this start now? Because the *LaValle* sentence was reversed?"

Gillard tossed a stray strand of silver hair out of her eyes. "To be honest, I don't know."

"A cop-killing? Becky?"

"You'll probably never know for sure. But once it starts, though, you start responding to environmental cues with flashbacks, jumping at sudden noises, physical illness."

"What environmental cues?" He asked, his voice gravelly under the strain of holding back tears. "They just come whenever. I don't fucking *know* what sets them off."

"It's okay. Can you remember the first time you had an anxiety attack?"

When was the first one? Leaving Becky's TriBeCa apartment. She'd been distant and unhappy, and he'd bolted from the apartment with a bitter taste in his mouth. He'd gone to the subway station at Chambers Street. There had been a busker, and he hadn't thought anything of it. But he remembered that awful guitar player because he'd dissociated, just as he'd done in Lincoln Center, the Staten Island Irish pub, and last night in Times Square. Depressingly, they were getting more severe. He didn't see how they would get better or how simple breathing exercises or a damned rubberband could avert something so cataclysmic and frightening.

"Live music?" He whispered into his hand.

"Mmmmm... Do you think it is?"

"I dunno. It just seems that every time I hear live music, I have an attack. What the fuck has music got to do with it? I was in a car when it happened. There was no music. I can't even remember if Zoë had her radio on."

Gillard smiled hearteningly. "Well, short of having a flashback, is there anything about it that you do remember? Before you were in the ambulance. Anything at all."

It was like trying to piece together the shenanigans of the night before through the treacle of your hangover in the morning, overcome with anxiety that you might have done something irreversibly stupid. He touched an ephemeral fragment of a memory, beyond the blank space.

"I think…" he began slowly. "I think I was in shock, and I was lying on the street. I heard the bus and the RMPs coming. The sirens, I guess. That's the only thing I can remember about it. Lying on my side, semi-conscious on the road, wondering why I wasn't dead, and hearing those sirens."

"Then maybe that's the cue," she said. "The link between what you can consciously remember and what you have suppressed."

"What?" He wrinkled his brows together, at a loss.

"To your brain, music sounds like sirens. And that's the cue that sets off the flashbacks."

"That doesn't make sense. I can hear *actual* sirens and I'm fine. And I had a bad one in court. There was no music. Or sirens."

"Yes, they can be uncued and become more frequent. It can happen when the illness gets worse…"

"Why the fuck is it getting worse?" He panted shallowly through his mouth, and his eyes failed.

"Count to ten when you breathe," she reminded him, and she slapped the table with an open palm.

The noise got his attention like a cold blast. "Easier said than done," he gasped. But he breathed into his lower lungs and counted. His exhalations were tense and uneven.

"I wish I had more answers," Gillard said. "But psychiatry doesn't have all the answers. It's not like other types of medicine, where you can say, this thing causes this disease. Sometimes, we just don't know. We just have to treat what we see."

"Am I gonna have to tell James Hurley I can't watch him in the pipe band anymore? Or spend my life avoiding every street busker in New York?" The creases around his eyes had deepened, and he squinched his sore lips over his front teeth in a fretful, injured frown.

"Maybe for now. But not forever. You'll get better."

She sounded so damned optimistic. He didn't share it. After all, he thought he'd survived the shooting with his psyche intact, but it turned out he hadn't, the damage like a slow-growing cancer. "But you said it's not curable."

"It's not, but you won't be this ill forever." Gillard ripped a page off a notepad. "I am going to prescribe you an SSRI, Paxil, okay, just to help you feel a little bit better now." She handed him the script. "Go get this filled tonight. Trust me, it will take the edge off, and it will mainly help deal with the depression and anxiety, which we need to get a handle on as well. And I want to see you in three days. Can we meet on Friday? The 26th. The day after Christmas."

"Three days?" he yelped, alarmed. Could he survive another disembowelment on Friday?

"Until we both agree that you're a lot less volatile, I think I need to see you more frequently than once per week. You've done that last night." She indicated his left hand, "And you've been suicidal. I'm not going to put you under a 9.27 or anything like that, or recommend you go in as a voluntary admission. If I thought there was a substantial risk of you killing yourself, I would ask that you sign yourself in. I think you're on the edge, but I think you'll be okay. And I'm aware of the upheaval in your life – well, this job – a commitment would cause, so that is our last resort. Our very last. That said, I want to see you on Friday so we can see how things are going, and I'm going to ask Jo to put you on limited duty, maybe for two or three weeks to start with, just to give the meds a chance to work and get the depression under control. You can work in the office, but I don't think it is a good idea for you to be out on the street until you're feeling better. And for some people, SSRIs can have troublesome side-effects, and they may need readjustment, or a different type, so we'll need to monitor that."

"Yeah, Friday then," he muttered weakly.

"Is it okay if we meet in my office next time? You know where it is?"

"Upper East."

"East 94th and Lexington," she said, placing a business card in his palm.

He slid it into his back pocket. "Yeah, okay."

"You will get better," Gillard assured him again. "Goodnight and take care of yourself. I'll see you on Friday." She gathered up her briefcase and furry coat and walked out the door.

Alex loitered in the interview room, feeling like he'd woken up in the middle of his own autopsy. He'd seen his guts spill out on the floor, and he disinterestedly looked at them, too exhausted and beaten to care.

Then he let himself out and found his boss speaking with Gillard. She bid goodbye to the psychiatrist, the two women smiling and hugging like old friends, before Gillard continued on her way.

"How'd it go?" Gibson asked him. "You look tired."

"I didn't cut my hand with a knife," he said dispiritedly. "I broke a window in my apartment. She tell you what she thinks I have?"

"Yeah," said Gibson. "She did."

He scratched at the prickling scars on his side. "Can't fucking believe it. She says I'm gonna be stuck with it forever. And I probably had it before now."

"Yeah, that makes some sense." She squeezed his upper arm, as if she'd known from the outset, and directed her gaze to his left hand.

"You gonna transfer me outta the squad?"

"No. Did you wrap that yourself?"

"Yes..."

"Can we have a look at it?"

"We? Don't you have something better to do?"

"No, I wanted you to finish with Gillard and see where we all were and then figure out what to do about it," she said at the same time Ray appeared from around the corner of a cubicle. Alex was surprised to see him. The eight-by-four had ended an hour ago. God, Ray must be knotted with worry, if he stayed here and didn't race back to his family drama in Astoria. Ray looked doleful, as if all the stress in his life had become too much. His face could have been Alex's yesterday, last week, most of his life.

"Did you know?" he said to Ray.

"Well, I knew you weren't well. I told you that yesterday. I didn't know what it was, though. I can't believe I let you go home last night, the way you were."

"Hindsight is twenty-twenty," said Gibson.

"Did you know Detective Hurley called me a few weeks ago?" Ray babbled. "We met in an Irish pub in Alphabet City. I think it was called Mona's or something. He said: 'I think Alex is way fucked up, and you need to get someone to talk to him about it, like yesterday.' I said I'd keep an eye on you."

"You met him?" Alex said. "To talk about me? Jesus."

"Yeah, he wanted to meet up. He said you'd popped across to Staten Island a couple weeks ago. He comes across like he doesn't give two shits about anything, but he'd fucking throw himself under a train for you."

"Yeah," Alex muttered, heat flushing his face, imagining a worried James calling Ray, demanding that they meet up in person. He knew the pub they had gone to, one of James' regular watering holes when he lived in Manhattan.

"I wish I'd listened to him then and not let it get to this state," Ray said disconsolately.

"Let's see your hand," said Gibson.

Before he knew it, Gibson and Ray had guided him to Greenwood's desk, the nearest one, and with his hand resting on the surface, they unwrapped the ace bandage. There was a jagged gash slicing through the back of his hand, and another grotesque laceration cutting diagonally across the underside of his wrist, the flesh ragged and stringy like hamburger meat, split wide open, exposing thin pale tubes embedded in raw muscle. Small bloodied cuts flecked his fingers and knuckles. His whole hand and forearm had swelled, the limb distended, discolored with splotchy purple bruising.

"Good lord," Ray said, turning pale.

"You didn't do that with a kitchen knife, not unless you stabbed yourself multiple times," said Gibson shortly. It hurt as she gently squeezed his hand and wrist. He felt loopy, looking at the whole anatomy of his hand and wrist laid bare.

"What *did* you do?" Ray asked.

"Put it through that window that was on the bathroom door," he replied, the misery clutching at his throat. "It isn't anymore."

"This needs to be seen to," said Gibson. "Can you move your fingers?"

He tried, but he could only weakly wriggle his pinky and thumb, before the pain became unbearable, and his first finger, middle finger, and ring finger had straightened and would not move at all, no matter how determinedly he tried.

"Okay, Ray, let's get someone to look at his hand tonight," Gibson said to Ray, as if they had decided Alex's fate long before. And Ray nodded his agreement, saying nothing, absorbed in using a clean bandage from the office first-aid kit to swaddle the wounds.

They went out the door together, silently. Snow floated about in a light breeze. A Battery-bound 1 train creaked along the elevated track, its headlights like pale eyes framing the bright red "1".

After the train roared away, Gibson said, "You know Theresa wants you off full duty for a while, which I think is a good idea. I doubt you'll be able to do much given the state of your wrist."

"I know."

"You're going to take a week of medical leave, to start. At least. You will need it for that hand anyway. Then I'm going to put you on limited until you, me, and Theresa can agree that you're well enough."

"Yes, ma'am. But what if I never get well enough?" A large part of him disbelieved that she could keep him in the squad.

"Theresa thinks you will."

"Yeah," he breathed plaintively, aching with doubt.

"Tomorrow will be a better day." She smiled confidently and crimped her saffron yellow scarf around her neck, and then she headed for the parking lot.

Alex stood inertly for a minute or so, cradling his maimed arm against his chest. Pain crippled him. He wanted to believe that tomorrow would be better, but he didn't see how.

Chapter Thirty-Three

December 23rd

Ray turned the key in his mid-90s Civic and held it for several seconds, the car chugging unenthusiastically to life. "I don't know how long this thing is going to keep running," he reflected. "It has like 160,000 miles on it." He drove downtown to St. Luke's, on West 115th and Amsterdam.

Alex breathed rapidly, the panic swelling. Sweat beaded on his face. He felt droplets trickling towards his eyes. What if he ran into cops or medical personnel he knew? That was more than likely in the hospitals north of 59th Street. The thought of his illness getting on the wire suffused him with abject terror. He brought his right hand to his throat, holding his fingers against the warm, throbbing carotid arteries.

"You okay?" Ray asked.

"I've got a fucking mental illness," Alex shot back, more dyspeptically than he'd intended. He winced.

"Hey, it's cool."

"Sorry. I'm jumpy. It's making me... I don't know... Crazy," he said, upset by how his emotions were rocketing from zero to sixty faster than a Ferrari.

"Don't worry about it."

His prison cell of inveterate, hopeless isolation went on lockdown, while outside the car, the streets were lively and untroubled, bustling with people striding through the snow flurries and scurrying across the road with that confident, New York expectation that no one would hit them.

They arrived at the hospital, Ray parking the car illegally because he couldn't be bothered hunting for a space. As he undid his seat belt, Alex gulped, "Hang on a minute, Ray."

Ray looked at him, puzzled.

Squeamishly, as if touching a dead rat, Alex removed his gun from the holster, turning it around so he grasped it by the barrel, and he held it out to Ray, butt first. "I think you'd better hang on to this for a bit." It took effort to swallow. This was the safest thing to do, a confession, an admission that he was mad enough to be suicidal, and that did not seem like one of those things a detective should ever admit to his partner.

But in the heat of those attacks, death itself lost its blank horror, and he would forget that it might indeed matter to his friends and maybe even to him. How thin was the line between being crazy enough to put a gun to your head and sane enough not to? Thinner than he used to think.

Ray's dark brown eyes bugged out of his head, and he nodded uneasily. He gawked at the Glock as if he had never seen one before. "It gets this bad?"

"Yeah, it does."

Unnerved, Ray opened the clip and removed the magazine. There was a desperate silence between them. Then he asked, "Is this the only one you have?"

"The old Ruger I used to carry before they wanted everyone switch to semi-autos is in my apartment, but I don't have ammo for that anymore."

"That's okay?" Ray asked, sounding afraid.

"Yeah," Alex answered.

"You sure?"

"Yeah." He had to explain it, and words no longer moved from his brain to his mouth. "That one's usually loaded. The .38 isn't. I'm not gonna do anything with an unloaded firearm."

"You can get ammunition for it."

"But I'd need to plan for that. It's not planned. It's just an impulsive, spur-of-the-moment thing."

Ray nodded, his eyes flooding with concern. Uncertainty froze his features, and he shoved the gun into his waistband. "Can you give that .38 to me anyway?"

"Fine, but you gotta trust me," Alex begged. "Gillard does. If she didn't, she'd put me under a 9.27."

"It's just… not what I thought," Ray said lamely.

"Like I said, it's just to be safe rather than sorry."

"I would be very sorry," admitted Ray in a saddened voice.

What a thing to saddle your partner with. "Yeah, I know."

"Okay, Lex, we need to go in and get your hand seen to."

They waited in the ER with dozens of grim-faced refugees from the city streets, sitting on grey plastic seats in the institutional sardine can. Only the signs added colors, plastered on every wall, informing anyone who read them that they had to be mindful of STDs, drug addiction, domestic violence, smoking, alcoholism, depression, breast cancer, and Alzheimer's, and there were numbers you could phone for support if you or anyone you knew had any of the above conditions.

The alkaline aromas of antiseptic and sweat corroded Alex's vulnerable nervous system. He didn't know if he was in physical pain or emotional pain; he couldn't tell anymore. His internal thermostat fritzed. The room seemed cold. And he was shaking. He curled his uninjured forearm around his belly, as if he had to stop his guts from slithering out. His psychic energy was throttled back to zero, leaving him with an overwhelming sense of loss and shame. PTSD. He still could not get used to the word or believe that he had such an illness. He broke it down into three horribly malignant calamities: he was sick; he'd been sick since 190th Street; he was going to be sick for the rest of his life. Moreover, he'd always been a bit screwed up, what with the alcoholism and his personality, always with a tendency towards the melancholy. It made sense out of the terror when reality itself dislocated. It explained the toxic listlessness that had been poisoning him for the past month. The catastrophic but apparitional anguish that had been devouring his mind and his body had a name, a disease, something explainable that could (probably) be controlled.

Here's to hope and for wholeness, he thought grimly, touching the script again, that magic strip of paper. And to keeping his gold shield. He hoped the anti-depressants would level him out enough to act as if he was sane. Godammit, they needed to. If he deteriorated from here or tried harder to kill himself, Gibson would have no choice but to transfer him to Siberia.

Making nervous conversation, Ray said, "We've been subpoenaed to testify in front of a grand jury investigating the managers of Kazparek's care home. You gonna be up for that?"

Work. A distant flare across a vast, dark expanse, and Alex's vision felt too clouded to see it, much less care about it, but Ray looked restless and ill at ease.

435

Alex snapped, "I don't fucking know. I don't know how I'll be in five minutes, or tomorrow." With more patience, he added, "I'm seeing Gillard again on Friday, and she's got me on these drugs now."

"Anna's on SSRIs. Like I said the other day, I think they're making a big difference for her. But they don't work immediately. It might take time. Like a few weeks."

"I fucking hope they help me."

"Yeah, me too. The case doesn't seem to be going anywhere. I don't think we have enough to indict."

"Marie's worried about her career," Alex said, pretending he gave a damn and quelling his irritability. "She doesn't wanna drop it. She thinks it'll be bad PR if she does."

"What's she after?" Ray speculated.

"Trial Bureau Chief," said Alex.

"She tell you that?"

"No, but she's got the barracuda ADA look. Whatever. See what the grand jury does. If they don't indict, it won't be Marie's fault, but she looks like she's covering her ass because she convened it."

"You sure about that? You know the cliché about ham sandwiches."

Alex sighed and shifted his hips in the hard chair, angled perfectly for hurting his lower back. He wasn't sure about anything. Whatever Gillard and Gibson believed, he wasn't sure that there would be a light after this tunnel, or that he would still be a death investigator when he got there. Right now, it assuredly did not feel that way.

A nurse emerged from the door in the back of the room, calling Alex's name. He left Ray fidgeting and playing Tetris on his phone, and he went through the door, where she led him down a whitewashed cinder block corridor, and then through another door that brought them into an examination room. Smiling perfunctorily, she asked him to sit on the bed.

She had a chart in her hand. Reading it, she said, "So is this all correct? You're forty-seven, right?"

"Yes," he answered.

"What is it you do?"

"NYPD. I'm a detective."

"Are you on any medication?"

"I've just started on Paxil," he answered, his voice low and stultified. He didn't feel like he should be talking about himself or saying it aloud, his diagnosis a fearful, shameful label.

"For depression?" the nurse asked, unmoved. Half of New York took anti-depressants, so she probably heard that every day.

"Yeah."

"Okay. Anything in your family history? High blood pressure, cancer, like that?"

"My father died of heart disease."

"Okay. And your heart? Blood pressure?"

"Fine, as far as I know."

"Since you're a police officer, I take it your insurance is through the city, right?"

"Technically my union."

She scribbled something on the charts, and he wondered what new skirmishes awaited in his longstanding feud with DEA insurance.

"What have you done to your hand?" She started unwrapping the bandage that Gibson and Ray had put on it.

"I cut it on some glass last night."

"How did you do that?"

"I live in an old apartment," he said evasively. "It was in panes on the bathroom door. Came off."

"Did it bleed a lot?" Her expression was professionally serious as she examined the wounds, probing around with deft, expert fingers. The pain blazed, like a burning match touching an exposed nerve.

"A fair bit," he wheezed. "It stopped though."

"With pressure?"

"Yeah. I made kind of a tourniquet outta towels."

She flexed each finger, gently folding and releasing it. The first finger, middle finger, and ring finger would not bend. "It must have bled a lot. You probably should have gone to the ER last night or this morning. Can you feel this?" She palpated and wiggled different parts of his hand.

"Probably." *Except I was completely out of my fucking mind.* "Yeah, I can feel that. Hurts."

"What did you do all day?"

"Went to work."

Both the nurse's eyebrows jerked upwards, and she reared back, bemused. "In a police station? With your hand like this?"

"An office." He shivered, suddenly chilled. The nurse wasn't behaving in the blasé manner nurses behave when an injury isn't a big deal. "And I just did paperwork."

"Right. Did someone bring you to the hospital today?"

"Yeah, a friend."

"You're going to go down to Orthopedics for surgery," she told him unflappably. "Right now. This is a deep, open wound, and you're at risk of a dangerous infection and permanent damage. You shouldn't have waited so long to take care of this. You'll be here overnight. What's your friend's name? I'll tell him what's going on."

"Surgery?" he croaked in horrified amazement. "Ray Espinosa."

"The surgeon needs to open up your wrist and have a proper look at everything. See these fingers that you can't move? That tells me you've cut tendons. We also need to see your radial artery, and it will probably need repairing."

"How bad is it?" he asked queasily, his face losing color, and he felt his heart sputtering.

"They won't know until they get in there."

She led him to an Orthopedics operating theatre and took his blood pressure, the cuff squashing his upper arm, and then listened to his heart and lungs, the stethoscope cool and metallic against his chest. She squished her lips together, writing something in the chart, before she gave him another look-over that made him feel like he was being cavity searched, and then she scurried out the door.

Alone in the room, he listened to the hollow sounds of footsteps and voices outside. His hand hurt terribly. The ribs on his right side cramped and spasmed as he breathed. Surgery, and more fucking doctors, and he was petrified that he'd permanently injured the hand. His day had taken him from a serious psychiatric disorder to orthopedic surgery, which sounded outlandish, like his vivid nightmares. But no doubt common, since lots of people end up with psychiatric diagnoses after self-harming. He looked down at the wounds. It was like work. Fleetingly, he felt detached, like he was examining a homicide vic. The cuts were ragged on the edges, bright red bubbling flesh inside, stripped muscle fibers and pale, ropey sinews – tendons? Gooey blood trickled onto his arm. Oh, yeah, it was his hand. His stomach clenched, and he averted his eyes.

The orthopedic registrar, a young South Asian lady with glasses perched on her nose and "Dr. Malpurga" on her nametag, swept into the room. Doctors were getting younger and younger, he thought. She must be half his age. Businesslike, she asked him a few questions, his age, his job, and how he'd injured himself, to which he said he had caught his hand in the bathroom door.

Then she inspected his hand and flexed his fingers and arm, like the ER nurse had done. She pursed her lips into a faint grimace at the fingers that stayed straight, and then she poked the tips of all his fingers with a metal rod, asking in her lilting accent, "Can you feel this?"

He nodded.

"We'll just go next door and x-ray it, all right?"

They x-rayed his hand, and after the machine regurgitated the images, the doctor placed the films against the blindingly glowing screens. He stared transfixed at the x-rays, a jigsaw of bluish, pale bones inside his hand and wrist, and small fragments, foreign bodies, hanging around the radius. From work, he knew the x-rays wouldn't show the mess he'd made of his tendons and blood vessels.

"There's glass fragments in those wounds. You could've got a bad infection if you'd left this. You really should have come in last night after you punched the window."

Baffled, he blinked at her, wondering how the hell she'd figured out that he had punched a window. Maybe the Detective Bureau should hire her.

As if she had read his mind, she said, "I work in a big city ER. You don't think I know what it looks like when someone puts their hand through a window?"

"I wasn't drunk. I don't drink." That sounded like a defensive lie a guilty-as-hell suspect might spit out during an interrogation, a pathetic effort to deflect guilt. But the truth seemed unmentionable.

"Did the nurse speak to you about a psychiatric eval?" the doctor queried.

"Oh, Jesus," he blurted, panicking. Then he hastily added, "I'm seeing a psychiatrist."

Seeing his agitation, Malpurga said, "Okay, okay. That's fine. Is he or she aware you've injured yourself?"

"Yeah."

"Do you mind if I speak to them?"

"Fine," he said miserably, writing Gillard's name and her office number on a post-it note. If the alternative was another psych eval, he would almost pay her to speak with Gillard. He couldn't go through that again.

"Oh, Theresa," said Malpurga, smiling supportively. "She's really good."

Everyone in New York seemed to know Gillard. How many patients ended up in the St. Luke's orthopedic unit after slashing open their wrists? A lot, given the registrar was on a first-name basis with the psychiatrist, and he didn't feel consoled by that.

They made him comfortable in an operating theater and then gave him general anesthesia and knocked him out. He woke up thirsty in a private room, drowning in fumes of antiseptic. Ray was there at his bedside, reading a book and wearing jeans and a blue wool pullover, and he was massaging hollowed-out cheekbones with his palms, like he hadn't slept. He bent forward when Alex awoke and said they had sewn his wrist back together, and Gibson knew he'd been in surgery. Alex vomited, and Ray shot to his feet and grabbed the nearest nurse. The nurse didn't seem fazed. Apparently, that was a common reaction to the general anesthetic, and Alex drifted back into a suffocating daze. A hand with sharp fingers shook him awake. He turned his head and opened his eyes to see James Hurley there, looking at him with a peculiar mixture of confusion, vexation, and pity.

"What the fuck did you do to yourself?" asked James.

"Punched out that window on the bathroom door," he said.

"That was pretty fuckin' stupid. Why the fuck would you do that?"

Alex pretended not to hear him and closed his eyes. Someone gave him a sip of water and tiptoed away. He slept and woke up feeling more alert, and he craned his neck towards James, but instead he saw the surgeon and the anesthesiologist leaning over his bed and asking how he was feeling.

"A bit less out of it," he muttered.

"It's taken you a while to recover from the GA," said the anesthesiologist. "Can you sit up?"

Moving with trepidation, afraid of fainting, he eased himself into a sitting position and lowered his eyelids, waiting for the crippling dizziness to knock him flat or to be sick, but both held off for now. He incuriously peered down at his hand. It was swollen, hideously bruised, the superficial cuts puffy and red, but the two gory wounds had transformed into neat lines of sutures, one slashing across the back of his hand, the other crawling along his forearm and stopping a few inches from his elbow. The painkillers were wearing off, and he could feel it again, an aching, brutal pain, like he had shoved it under the wheels of a bus. "My hand hurts."

"The wound on the back of your hand missed the important structures, but you had an extensive volar forearm laceration," the surgeon said. "Your wrist. We had to repair four transected flexor tendons and your radial artery and clean a lot of glass out of the wound. You got very lucky and missed the major nerves. You would have a lot more rehab and potential complications if you'd severed those. We call this type of wound a spaghetti wrist."

"Spaghetti?"

"The exposed tendons look like pasta in a bed of sauce. Can you stand?"

"Oh." The sense of humor of the medical profession was as sick as his own. Gingerly, he swung his legs off the bed and lifted himself to his feet, the doctor and a nurse close by, prepared to support him if he wobbled. But he didn't fall, and he even surmounted the walk to the bathroom and standing for a piss. Then the nurses brought him jello, which he didn't feel like eating, but they said they wouldn't discharge him unless he proved that he could keep food down, so he reluctantly ingested it.

"You have someone who can pick you up?" asked the nurse.

He called Ray on his cell, and his partner promised to be there within the next two hours. Two more hours to recover from the haze of GA. The nurses told him he'd been here for twenty-four hours, and the surgery itself had taken about ninety minutes. His sense of time had been elongated, and he felt like he'd been in this hospital for a long time. After the shooting in 1987, he had spent three weeks as an inpatient, and hospital time was on a strange, alternate plane, so one day felt much like three weeks.

While he waited for Ray, the surgeon reappeared and explained, "You'll be on Codeine and antibiotics for the next week. And I see here that you're not allowed NSAIDs because you were being treated for GI problems. I would normally recommend it for after, but acetaminophen – Tylenol – should be okay on your stomach, so you can try that. Make an appointment for three weeks' time, so I can see how it's healing."

As she spoke, she gently furled his fingers into a slight claw, which hurt, and he moaned.

"Sorry, I know that's sore. You need it to start healing with your fingers relatively bent, or you could lose a lot of mobility." She bandaged his hand and wrist with a rigid cast that prevented any movement and went nearly to his elbow, and then she placed a sling around his shoulder, hiking it up so his hand was level with his chest. "You'll be wearing this cast for a little while. You need complete immobilization for three weeks, for the tendons to start repairing themselves. Keep the sling on as much as possible because holding your hand above your heart will help with swelling. When you take the sling off to stretch or rest your shoulder, try to elevate your hand. You'll start physical therapy after that. After the three weeks. We'll change you to a splint that allows some movement. After six weeks, all being well, we can hopefully remove the splint, but you will need to continue with PT and take it easy for another six weeks and avoid any massive strain to it. I'll refer you to the physio, and you'll get an appointment in three weeks. I'm cautiously optimistic that you'll regain most, if not all, function in your hand and wrist. About 58% of patients with this kind of injury do. But it's important you follow all rehab directives. And not punch out any more windows."

"It'll probably heal?" he asked drearily, unable to digest most of that, but he grasped that he had a long road ahead before he regained full use of his hand. Fuck. He wanted to sob, and he shakily swallowed the scabrous emotions fizzing inside his throat.

"I think so. If you behave with immobilization and physio."

After issuing a few more instructions about showering and wound care, she wished him luck and signed him out of the ward. A New York City hospital is like a processing plant, the next heart attack, stroke, stabbing, shooting, OD, miscarriage, or whatever, waiting their turn. In the waiting room, Alex discovered Ray flipping through one of those magazines with gossip about celebrities you'd never heard of.

"How's the hand?" Ray asked, flinching at the sight of Alex's arm, casted and immobilized in its sling.

"Fucked," Alex groaned despondently. "Gonna be six weeks before I get my arm out of a fucking cast. And three weeks before I'm allowed *any* movement. Then I gotta get physical therapy, and I might lose some function. They don't know. If it heals, it'll be like twelve weeks. God knows when I'll get back to full duty."

Ray's lips writhed into a pained expression. "Aw, Lex, that sucks. But I'm sure it'll be okay. They told me the surgery went pretty well."

"Did Hurley visit me after?"

"Hurley? No, I don't think so."

"I thought I talked to him."

"They said you were hallucinating coming out of GA. I guess that's a thing."

Alex chewed his dried, clotted lower lip forlornly. His hand throbbed with a dull, debilitating pain, and his shoulder was already cramping, protesting the position of his arm in the sling. Simply dressing himself was going to be herculean. Hallucination-James' derision felt deserved. This injury, crazily self-inflicted in that moment of uncontrollable madness, would stick him with limited duty for a couple months. And he could easily suffer residual weakness for the rest of his life. If 58% of patients recovered fully, that meant 42% didn't. Those odds didn't nurture his confidence. But that was a future problem, and there were so many urgent problems to tackle. Living with this damned mental illness or learning how to live with it so he didn't do this again, or God forbid, do something else. Did it have to be a zero-sum game? Perfectly healthy or too crazy to work? His AA sponsor once counseled him to take recovery one step at a time. "That's how you climb the mountain," he'd said, because he spent a lot of time with Tibetan monks in the mountains around Kathmandu, and he liked profound clichés. "Don't stare at a distant summit that never seems to get closer. Focus on the rocky step that's twenty feet away. Then the next one..." Yeah, Alex got the metaphor, and more than once, he'd lived it and come through it – clawing back to health one damned ledge at a time – but he keelhauled himself for succumbing to the sweeping, overpowering paroxysm of agony and panic obliterating his senses. If he'd held back, the panic might have subsided on its own. If he'd controlled himself, but he hadn't been in control.

"You'll have to be on limited until it heals enough," said Ray, announcing the blinding obvious in that tactless way.

Breaking out of his morose thoughts, Alex looked at him reproachfully. "No shit. Let's get outta this damn hospital and get something to eat."

"Are you up for that?"

"I need to get something on my stomach for the antibiotics." He gently depressed the fingers of his right hand into his upper abdomen. "And it feels sore and acidy."

"You eat anything today?"

"Yeah. They gave me jello."

Ray tossed the magazine aside. "That's not really food. Where do you think we should go?"

"I don't care," he answered in a dejected, breathy voice.

"What about that Greek joint on West 107th? Theophilos?"

"Yeah, sounds fine."

"You can get a salad or something light." Ray took the elbow of his good arm, and he had to move off the chair.

Parking in Morningside Heights being a nightmare, they left the car near St. Luke's and walked downtown along Amsterdam, holding their hands close to their bodies for warmth. Urban wind harried the snow into mini-whirlwinds. Snow piled in the gutters and formed slushy puddles on the curbs. Flakes glimmered in swirling clouds, caught high by the city lights, and danced around the masonry and the weighty buttresses and gables of the West Side's flamboyant, garish architecture.

Alex felt an aching chill as the wind tore through his clothes, and he cupped the elbow of his wounded arm with his other hand. They pushed uphill. His shoulders and the collar of his coat were soaked, and his socks turned wet and cold from the crunchy, deceptive slush on the curbs. The taillights of cars melted together into a red speckled stream crawling along Amsterdam. He sniffed in roast chestnuts wafting out of one street van, burgers out of another, and German pastries out of a third, and they wove through the lines forming in front of the vans. A doorman hollered from a hotel. A taxi's brakes squealed. An ambulance, stuck in an intersection, blared its horn and sirens. A drunk guy took a piss on a ginkgo tree in full view of the world. Two women argued loudly in the middle of the sidewalk, and everyone ignored them. A homeless guy sitting below an ATM rattled a paper cup at everyone who walked by. The city seemed so crowded and insane that it was almost unlivable, but you would not want to live anywhere else.

At the corner of 108th and Amsterdam, Alex and Ray neared an a cappella group braving the weather, singing Gospel carols on the front steps of a Baptist church. Driven by a perverse craving for self-inflicted injury, Alex slowed his pace and listened, eyes half-closed, waiting for his heart to race, for the adrenaline to overwhelm his system. He felt Ray's hand between his shoulder blades, pushing him forward, and when he looked doubtingly at his partner, he saw a smile illuminating Ray's dark, severe features.

"Come on, Alex. Let's go."

And they went on, past the singers, into the snowy night.

Printed in Poland
by Amazon Fulfillment
Poland Sp. z o.o., Wrocław